School Daze

Elaine McGeachy

Ringwood Publishing
Glasgow

First published in Great Britain in 2014 by
Ringwood Publishing
7 Kirklee Quadrant, Glasgow G12 0TS
www.ringwoodpublishing.com
e-mail   mail@ringwoodpublishing.com

ISBN 978-1-901514-10-0

British Library Cataloguing-in Publication Data
A catalogue record for this book is available from the British
Library

Typeset in Times New Roman 10
Printed and bound in the UK
by Lonsdale Direct Solutions

About the Author   Elaine McGeachy

Elaine studied, lived and worked in Glasgow for 8 years before moving back to her hometown of Campbeltown in Kintyre where she now resides with her husband, Stuart.

Elaine works as a Principal Teacher at Campbeltown Grammar School and is also a qualified fitness instructor.

Writing is only one of her many passions in life. She loves to run and is the Secretary of her local running club and Race Director of the Mull of Kintyre Half Marathon and 10k.

Publishing her first novel has always been one of her many ambitions and she hopes to continue her writing career in the future.

Acknowledgements

I would like to thank my family, friends, colleagues and the kind people of Kintyre who have always been extremely supportive and encouraging in all of my endeavours.

In particular, I would like to thank my husband Stuart for his patience, understanding and for helping with the housework and providing me with copious cups of tea throughout the writing process! To my close family – Mum, Dad, sister Mairi and brother Graeme for putting up with my stressful outbursts and tantrums which thankfully didn't happen too often. I appreciate you being there for me, no matter what. Gratitude also goes to Laura McCormick, one of my oldest friends, who took the time to read the novel before anyone else and give me honest and candid advice.

To everyone at Ringwood Publishing, especially Sandy and editor Lynsey – thank you for helping me on my way to becoming an author.

Thank you to my pupils, past and present for making teaching such a rewarding career. I must also thank my teachers. You know who you are. Not only did you inspire me into my chosen profession to which I love, you also urged me to continue to write stories. I hope you enjoy this one.

.

Chapter 1

Caitlyn McDonald looked up at the old steel clock on the cluttered wall. Ten minutes to go. Ten long minutes until this boring school lesson finished. But at least it was ten more minutes with *him*. She glanced over at him as he scribbled away furiously in his school jotter, full of concentration. She mentally scolded herself. She looked back at her work and tried to focus but she couldn't help become distracted.

His name was Cameron. He was a Prefect in his last year of Secondary School, S6, and 17 years of age. But Caitlyn thought he could easily pass for 22. Cameron was exceptionally good looking and he knew it. Dark wavy hair. Intense brown eyes. Soft tanned skin... He was also intelligent and very witty which made him incredibly charming, not least with the other school girls. With his tall, strong, muscular physique he was undoubtedly athletic and his top goal scoring reputation for the Hillend High School's football team confirmed this.

The bell rang loudly, jerking her back into the reality of school life. "OK, time's up. Pencils and pens down. Remember class, homework is due in on Friday. Make sure you answer every question!" Caitlyn shouted as the pupils packed up their belongings into their school bags and left her class for the day.

It was the third week back at school after what Caitlyn felt like a miniscule summer holiday, although it was actually 6 weeks, and now it felt like she'd never been away. The jotters to correct were piling up on her desk, and she had practice assessments planned for all of next week which meant constant marking every night. "Urgh, why do I bother?" she muttered under her breath. However, she really knew why. She loved teaching. Not the tedious marking jotters, paperwork or planning lessons, but the rush of passing on the facts and passion of Mathematics and numbers on to others. Equations, calculations and formulae had always fascinated Caitlyn. Her father, also a Maths teacher, had taught her to count to 100 by the age of 2 and she could rhyme off the multiplication times tables by age 7. Caitlyn's Dad was always giving her puzzles and brainteasers to complete and she lapped it up! She could never understand how some of her friends disliked maths. However, she felt good when she helped her peers after seeing some of them struggle with it at school. With her Mum also being a secondary teacher in Biology, both parents had encouraged her to study a broad range of subjects in school. Caitlyn didn't need scolded, she happily worked hard throughout High School, gaining 8 '1' Standard Grades and 7 Highers. She even went on to gain an A in Advanced Higher Maths before moving from their family home in the outskirts of Perth to Glasgow to study statistics at Strathclyde University, much to her father's pride. That being said, she was never deemed a swot by any of her peers. She enjoyed every minute of being a teenager – going shopping or to the cinema with friends and playing hockey for the school girls' team every Saturday. This all sounds very innocent, and mostly it really was, but the girls' hockey team loved to have fun off the pitch as well as on it. They would commiserate a loss or celebrate a win afterwards with a few ciders which sometimes lead

2

to shots of whatever spirit they could get their hands on (usually a blend from their parents' alcohol cupboard), which occasionally got her into trouble when she got caught. Caitlyn was always clever and kept it well hidden, but inevitably there were times when her hangovers could not be masked. She remembered one time when, after winning the Scottish Schools Cup, aged 16, the hockey captain opened a bottle of champagne and gave it to Caitlyn. Exhilarated by the win and under pressure, she nearly drank it all before they hit the dressing room. That didn't stop her continuing to drink nearly a whole bottle of vodka later that day. Needless to say that was one of the occasions she got caught. She can't remember what happened next, but she knows from her friends' recollections that her Dad came to collect her from the local training grounds, bundled her into the car and the next thing Caitlyn knew it was Sunday morning and she was vomiting the most disgusting black bile into a basin at the side of her parent's bed whilst her mother watched on disapprovingly. That wasn't one of her finest moments and her mother still brings that story up even though it was nearly 10 years ago. Luckily, Caitlyn's parents didn't work in the same school she attended or she would've been under constant scrutiny, and she had always worried that other kids may bully her if her parents taught them.

Her enthusiasm for numeracy and maths never waned. It just seemed natural, and expected from her parents, to become a Maths teacher. She had grown up with her parents talking about school, doing their marking at home, discussing school politics and curriculum. Her Mum regularly tutored students at home and they were always really friendly to Caitlyn when they visited. Her Mum would give her old jotters to scribble on and Caitlyn would love to pretend that she was a student in High School even though she was only 8. Once her Dad brought home an old blackboard after he was given a new state of the art 'whiteboard'. Caitlyn adored it, she bought multi-coloured chalk and would write lists and lists of her favourite things, or do her homework all over it pretending she was the teacher with the only students being her dog or her teddy bears.

Caitlyn hadn't really thought of any other career, it was always going to be teaching. Helping children learn and progress in life made her job satisfying to her. She loved working with kids, always trying to make their learning experience different and enjoyable but she was always professional and avoided overly familiar chat with the pupils at all times. Although her thoughts about Cameron were really worrying her. "Oh my God, how did it get to this?" she exclaimed inwardly. She had always *always* thought of them as kids and although she was only a few years older than the elder pupils at 24, she continually maintained a professional distance from them. Nevertheless, she felt that her tender age did help her connect with them a great deal better than some of the older teachers. Never in her wildest dreams had she thought she could ever become attracted to any of them. That was a line that you just did not cross as a teacher. She didn't *really* like him, she attempted to convince herself, trying to force the thought out of her mind. She had heard the odd joking but leering comment in the staffroom before from a few male teachers about 6th year girls, especially after school discos, which repulsed her. She had also heard stories about young male teachers falling in love with S6 girls and having relationships with them. All rumours of course and again it repulsed her but it did make her think. Some of the male teachers were only in their early 20's and some of the girls were 18. They could easily get together once they had left school and it would not be an issue whatsoever. But the thought of a teacher/pupil relationship was just despicable. Taboo. However, these feelings were troubling her more and more, as they were stirring emotions inside her that she thought weren't possible. As much as it pained her to admit it – she enjoyed the butterflies. It made her feel alive! It made her feel like a teenager again!

There's nothing quite like working with teenagers to make you feel ancient even though you're only in your early twenties! She remembered a time during her teacher training when a student innocently asked her what it was like back in her day at school when there were no computers?

Caitlyn had laughed out loud thinking the girl was joking, but sadly she was deadly serious and didn't realise she was causing any offence. "How old exactly does she think I am?" she remembered asking in the staffroom at lunch. "Do I look really old?" The other teachers found this highly amusing and used her as the butt of all age jokes for her entire student placement. After a while it just became second nature to Caitlyn to be thought of as older, the adult, the leader in the classroom and it felt good. Although the kids were aware that she was younger than the ageing grey teachers of the school, they knew she was the boss in the classroom and that gave her great confidence. She had always been nervous about standing up in front of a class of pupils with all attention focused on her, but after a while it just became natural and she developed a great rapport with the kids and they knew not to overstep the mark with her. When the pupils progressed to their senior year, she relaxed a little with them as they were more mature, as long as they did their studies – Caitlyn was very determined on this.

With Caitlyn only out of school herself 5-6 years, she could've potentially been at school at the same time as him. He stood out from the rest of the pupils. Taller. More mature. More masculine. More like a grown-up man and he seemed to hang on to her every word which of course she couldn't help but feel flattered by. He would ask her how she was, and more personal questions like what her hobbies were and what she did at weekends. And although she always made a point of not sharing her personal life with her pupils and brushed it aside, she wanted to make conversation with him! She didn't mind that he was asking these questions, he felt like a friend. But she continued to tread lightly and be cautious, she would never do anything inappropriate. She wanted to ask back and find out details about his life. But she didn't. Instead she always just said "Fine thanks, how are you? Working hard?" and try to turn the subject back to school. It seemed to work every time, but he had a broad smile and that glint in his eye as if he was trying to flirt with her. She always glanced away as if she didn't notice but it nearly always made her blush. She hadn't had much excitement or any attention at home for what felt like months, she thought miserably.

Caitlyn had been living with her boyfriend Peter for over 2 years in a cramped one-bedroom flat in the West End of Glasgow and they had been together for 5 years, school sweethearts at 17. He was the school shinty captain and although they had been in each other's classes throughout Secondary School, it was on the sports field where they developed a relationship. They would regularly see each other after Saturday games, competitions with other schools, and would playfully argue over which was the better sport – hockey or shinty? It soon developed into something more and they had been inseparable since. *'Sex mad and joined at the hip'* their friends used to say about them. It was true, her and Peter couldn't keep their hands off each other, but they also thought of each other as best friends. Although recently she has started to feel like Peter has been a little distant.

They hadn't been intimate in over 3 weeks, which felt like forever compared to the regular daily routine they'd had for years. Even through their most stressful periods whilst studying, the couple always made time for each other. Peter had worked extremely hard, also attending Strathclyde University for 4 years where he studied Civil Engineering and had now earned himself a lucrative graduate job with a large engineering firm after achieving a first class honours degree. Even although during their student years they lived apart in student accommodation, they stayed with each other regularly and socialised with the same group of friends. Caitlyn was truly proud of

7

him and with a decent salary coming in they decided to rent in the heart of Glasgow's prestigious West End where they thoroughly took advantage of its great social scene and enjoyed the lifestyle. For the first 6 months that is. They dined out at restaurants at least 3 times a week, either themselves or with their friends, went to Ashton Lane for cocktails on Friday after work, but then it all seemed to stop. That lifestyle unfortunately was harder to maintain than Caitlyn had thought. Peter was working more and more hours at his job and was always too tired to go out or have sex for that matter! This had been causing endless arguments recently, that is when she had seen him. The arguments were mainly about money or not spending any time with each other. It also annoyed Caitlyn that any time that Peter did have to spare he would rather be watching his 'mighty Rangers' play than be with her. She didn't really get the obsession that some men, including her boyfriend and Dad, had with Scottish Football.

Caitlyn had a permanent contract at Hillend High School and it helped pay the bills, but they depended on Peter's wage to keep them going. Although they liked their flat, it was small, cramped and in need of restoration. They were really paying for the West End location. She hated fighting with Peter and knew they had to curtail their spending and going out if they wanted to afford a better flat, but she thought it was best just to enjoy their location for the time being, they had the rest of their lives to worry about saving and buying property. That was her opinion anyway. For someone as good at mathematics as she was, she was careless with money and wouldn't think to budget. She would rather spend every last penny of her pay packet. Caitlyn didn't see the need to even have a savings account never mind think about a mortgage. Peter was obviously starting to think differently about planning for the future, even surprising her by stopping his season ticket to Ibrox that year to save money, hence the disagreements. The only flirtation Caitlyn was receiving right now was from a 17 year old boy that she was teaching – *how pathetic* she cringed.

Chapter 2

Jamie Roberts was in early at his desk in the staff room by 7.30am, preparing for the long day ahead of teaching English and Drama, something which he was deeply enthusiastic and passionate about. He had loved studying it at school and was encouraged by his own English teachers to further his hobby of imaginative writing, poetry and drama and to continue to study the subject at University. He enjoyed every minute of student life. Not only the fantastic social scene of parties, clubbing and making new friends, but he loved learning more and sharing his passion with other likeminded people on his course. University also gave Jamie the opportunity to be independent, to live away from his family and be himself. Jamie was a young, attractive, outgoing gay man. He was tall and slim, with blonde hair which he styled differently each day and always brought a smile to a room. He had been popular all his life, with lots of friends, both male and female, and was adored by his students. But he didn't feel comfortable anymore at home under the scrutiny of his parents and his older brother, David. Not that they didn't know he was gay, or that they disapproved, but he wanted to experience life without feeling constantly monitored or judged. Jamie's brother David said he knew Jamie was gay since he was 6 years old and asked for a kitchen set and a Barbie for Christmas instead of a Gameboy like some of the other boys his age. Jamie's family were accepting and supportive, but he still needed to get away and discover who he wanted to be. Which he did, and he was always the

years, and there were many other teachers in the department with much more experience than him, his Principal Teacher entrusted him with his own Higher class this year. The results he had been achieving with his other classes had been well above average and he had little discipline problems, issuing only a few detentions and referrals in the past term.

Jamie had been very worried about the behaviour from pupils and their reaction towards him as an openly gay man. He had had his fair share of homophobic abuse in the past, bullying in his own Secondary School and sometimes verbal abuse from complete strangers in the street - occasionally from teenagers. Jamie had always brushed it off to his family and friends as if it didn't bother him but deep down it still hurt.

He was anxious at starting Hillend as it had such a mixed demographic of children. In his first lesson, a group of popular, rowdy S4 boys continued whispering in the back row despite being asked to be quiet, and this panicked Jamie. Trying to be confident, Jamie spoke out to them, "Boys, are you stuck? Please ask me, do not whisper behind my back. Share with the class." This was risky and Jamie knew it. He dreaded what they were going to say. To his relief, one of them replied, "Sorry, Sir, we've just been talking about where you got your blazer. Is it from G-star? It's well tidy!"
Jamie smiled in relief. "Thanks. Now, no more talk. Back to work." He gained respect from them and he needn't have worried. The pupils didn't seem to care about his sexuality and it never became an issue.

One hour after arriving, Jamie walked upstairs to the classroom he shared with the new probationer, a newly qualified teacher who had been placed at the school for their first year, to set up for his first lesson. Jamie was putting the pupils' desks and chairs together into small groups when his door slammed shut and he was aware of someone's presence behind him. "Good morning, Mr Roberts, how are we today?" a booming voice sounded across the classroom. Jamie spun round to see the Head Teacher. A tall, handsome man in an immaculate black pinstripe suit with a bright red satin tie stood in the classroom doorway, looking Jamie up and down. "Erm... fine thanks, Mr Johnstone, just getting prepared for period 1," he stuttered back to the powerful looking man.

"Andrew, Jamie, please call me Andrew," the Head Teacher smiled back. His eyes were relaxed but Jamie was still tense. He was only on a temporary contract and loved working in such a large school in Glasgow. It had gained an excellent reputation over the past 25 years, and in particular over the last 5 years since Andrew Johnstone became the Headmaster. At 33, he was one of the youngest Head Teachers ever appointed in Scotland, but was extremely well respected in his profession by his colleagues and the community. Jamie knew that Mr Johnstone was a married man and had a young family. He regularly appeared in teachers' classrooms observing pupil work and, to the horror of some teachers, monitoring their lessons. However, Jamie realised that this was an essential part of Andrew's job, and normally didn't mind when he popped into his class, but his visits were becoming more frequent which was starting to worry him. *Have I done something wrong?* Jamie panicked. *Has there been a complaint about me?*

"I have S3 first, my new top set class. I'm still trying to break the ice with them as they're very quiet, and I want them to expand their vocabulary, so I'm giving them a group starter task," Jamie started to waffle but Andrew seemed slightly disinterested. "How was your summer break?" he replied. "Did you go anywhere nice on holiday? You have a nice colour."

"Thanks," Jamie blushed, "yeah, Jennifer and I went to Ibiza for a week." They had gone for a week of sunshine, relaxation and some mad nights out which they had done aplenty. Both of them had a great time lazing by the pool or on the beach each day. They came back the day before term started having spent all their savings on mojitos, strawberry daiquiris and shots of tequila. They both achieved their goal of getting a glorious sun tan, which they were showing off at any given opportunity. "Did you and the family go anywhere?" Jamie politely asked, but really he was not interested. Andrew chuckled, "Unfortunately I was in here, at work, most of the time, but we did a wee week in the caravan which was good, apart from the Scottish rain!" He quickly changed the subject back to Jamie, "So you and Jennifer then, an item?" he questioned, still smiling affectionately. "No no, just good friends, I've not got a boyfriend right now," Jamie gave his usual standard reply as so many people ask him this question all the time. He knew the Head Teacher was aware that he was gay so he didn't hesitate to talk about a partner. Andrew's grin grew wider but he never said a word as the bell rang and he simply waved as he walked out as thirty teenagers descended into the room, immediately bombarding Jamie with 101 questions about the new seating plan that he projected onto the whiteboard in front.

"Sir, Sir," they shrilled.

"Why do I need to sit here?" some screamed.

"I am not moving," he heard others mumble.

"I'm not sitting next to *her!*" one shouted.

"Now, get into the new seats allocated to you" Jamie said slowly and clearly.

A little movement but not enough.

"This is the top set class of the year and I have very high expectations," Jamie continued, without raising his voice. A few others moved into position and Jamie scanned the room making sure everyone was in the right place.

"OK, well done everyone. I want you all to get into a routine of sitting in these seats each day, so that we don't waste precious time settling down at the beginning of every lesson. What should we have on our desks?"

The class were now silent, they were a studious lot but he knew there were a few opinionated characters in the mix that he would need to keep an eye out for.

"A pencil?" a girl at the front finally volunteered.

"Yes, a pencil or a pen as well as your jotter that I issued you in June, and your homework diary."

Some of the pupils had done this already, but the majority of the other pupils were now rummaging through their bags.

"Can I borrow a pencil?" a boy at the back asked loudly. Another girl in the middle chimed in, "Can I borrow a pencil too please, Sir?" Jamie sighed, this class was supposed to be the best in the year, but it was only day one and they couldn't even be organised enough to bring a pencil to school! He bit his lip, he didn't want to start the term off on a sour note. He handed out pencils, warning them to return them and ensure they were organised for tomorrow. Within a few minutes everyone was finally ready to start the lesson.

"Right, well done class, we are all now prepared and ready to begin! This year we are going to learn some marvellous things and read some fantastic texts that may influence your entire life!"

Chapter 3

"Please be quiet," said Jennifer Hill in a pleading voice, "please please, just sit down." The wild S4 class rioted around her as she tried to control it. Some groups of girls had huddled together and were pointing and laughing feverishly at their mobile phones, completely oblivious that they were in a school, never mind Jennifer's classroom in the middle of a Geography lesson. Some of the boys were pinging elastic bands at the wall and playing childish games as if in the playground.

What was it I learned at University? I can't remember! What did my Mum always say? Oh yes, take a deep breath and count to 10.
"David and James! Sit at your desks please! Bryony! Abbie! Courtney! Put the phones away or I will confiscate them!" Jennifer continued to shout orders around the class to try and maintain some sort of decorum. "Miss, Miss!" one small boy shouted at her. "Seamus is hitting me!"
"But he's got my bag!" the boy, presumably Seamus, screamed back. "Give me my bag, gayboy!"

Jennifer walked over to the boys, forcing them to concede and stop fighting and hiding each other's belongings. She took a look around her small classroom and at least everyone was now back in their seats. She had tried to split up the most confrontational of kids within the class, but the majority of them barely had the attention span of a goldfish and it exhausted her just with this one class. "Jotters open, class."

"Jotters open, class" she heard a male voice mimicking her accent from the back, but she chose to ignore it rather than draw attention to it since none of the other kids seemed to have reacted.

Jennifer was young, bubbly girl from the Scottish Borders and had always thought about being a teacher, but had looked into many more professions before finally deciding to opt for teaching. Her parents had helped her make the decision and she sometimes wondered on days like this if she made the right one.

Jennifer was taught in a strict Catholic school back in her small community town, but loved it immensely and was quite shocked at the beginning of her teacher training when she had seen how different school could be and how different the behaviour of children could be. This just spurred her on more to do the best she could. She struggled sometimes at teacher placements during training – she found the work very tiring and had been the target of some pupils' attacks against her. Mostly verbal, swearing obscenities but enough to really shake her up. Although this hadn't deterred her yet.

However, lately her motivation for the job had started to fade, especially with this particular class. She was only 5 foot 2 inches with a slight frame and although this hadn't bothered her in the past with other classes, she had started to feel quite intimidated. She had often been mistaken for a pupil by some teachers and even other pupils, especially when she had just started teaching. She was annoyed by it at first but as she continued to gain teaching experience over the past 2 years and with investment in 4 inch heels and a new suit, she rarely had that problem. Until now.

John, the ring leader of the class, who thought he was God's gift to humankind, and unfortunately for Jennifer the girls in school seemed to agree, was causing her no end of grief. He was constantly interrupting her lessons, misbehaving and being insolent towards her, which persuaded the others to do the same, not that they needed much encouragement. He sat at a desk at the back of the class and threw rubbers, pencils or even jotters, whenever her back was turned. Today, he leaned back to swing on his chair and sneered in Jennifer's direction, "Do you want me to take the lesson, Miss?" A few of his friends laughed overly loud at him, trying to gain his approval. It felt like he was personally taunting her but she refused to give him the satisfaction of a reply.

The thumping headache, the leftovers of yesterday's hangover, didn't make this Monday any easier. She had spent the entire weekend creating new resources for a unit of work she had put herself forward for, to her Head of Department. She was a member of the ICT in Education Steering Group within the school and had agreed to develop new material for her classes in which she would evaluate the use of ICT in class. And although by 9pm on Sunday evening she was extremely pleased at the material she was creating, thinking to herself this will really break boundaries of modern teaching, she was also exhausted and in desperate need of Chinese takeaway and wine! One glass of course had lead to the bottle and she was feeling it now. *When will she ever learn? Drinking on a school night is NEVER a good idea!*

She had a low ability set of 32 pupils in her S4 class, 10 of which had learning support needs, 5 needing behaviour support. She should have at least one classroom assistant in with her to help, but they were absent today due to illness and she noticed their lack of attendance terribly. The assistants are such a great asset to teachers especially in classes like this, to help her not only maintain behaviour but to ensure everyone gets attention. She tried again to turn on her projector to encourage them to work together on a learning game on the board. However, her plan of using the interactive whiteboard had now been completely scuppered since it had decided not to play today. The wonders of modern technology! She would need to note that down in her evaluation. ICT can truly help make learning much more interactive and active, but only if it actually works!

She looked round to pick up her 'back up' material that she kept beside her lesson plans but they were gone. "What are you looking for Miss?" the kids started to chime as they noticed her panic. "If it's your fun worksheet quiz thingies then they're not there," John snidely informed her. "And why would that be, John?" she returned smiling as sweetly as she could at him. "'Cause Mr Greig came in at the start and took them, I saw him I did so I did." Jennifer bit her lip. This time not at John, he was probably 100% correct. Tommy Greig, the teacher next door to her room, was making settling into this school harder than it should be. He was 62 and desperate to retire, off 'ill' every second week, only waiting on in School with the aim of a good pension 'package' she suspected. Tommy seemed to have lost any enthusiasm for teaching long ago and definitely didn't want to change with the times. He was still issuing the same worksheets he had done for years, moaning about how the kids weren't as bad in 'his days' and now they were just unruly and rude. He always looked scruffy, never taking pride in his appearance and usually arrived in school wearing creased trousers with a baggy shirt or sometimes even wore jeans. He was always late for lessons, if appearing at all. He'd been known to go out at lunchtime and 'forget' he had a class, so Jennifer sometimes had to cover his classes. No wonder he had a poor relationship with the pupils and his worsening attitude to the profession just made him unbearable – he never planned any lessons or put any enthusiasm into his work anymore. That's why he hated Jennifer so much, she thought. When she started, she was bubbly and energetic with lots of great ideas to make learning more fun for the students. He hated that idea and resented her for it but it didn't stop him using her materials and passing them off as his own any time Mr Johnstone walked by, which made him easy to resent.

"OK class, can we get out our textbooks, we're going to work on the case study on page 98," and before she even got to give further instructions, the fire alarm screeched through the class. There was a collective whoop of delight from the pupils as they realised they didn't need to be in class, before they all darted outside as fast as they could to meet up with their other friends in the playground.

John was the last to leave the classroom but as he disappeared through the door, he turned back to Jennifer and sneered, "I'll take the class tomorrow, Miss, nae bother!" Jennifer could hear his little gang laughing amongst themselves down the corridor.

"Ha! I might just let him do that," she groaned inwardly as she pulled on her jacket to brave the cold for another weekly false alarm.

Chapter 4

Autumn had arrived and it was typical Scotland 4-seasons-in-one-day-weather in September with Caitlyn awaking early to bright sunshine. She took delight in putting on her new grey tailored suit with a trendy purple silk shirt with chiffon sheer sleeves and an oversized pussy-bow. She finished off her outfit with her favourite black patent round-toe stilettos. She didn't usually dress this formally for school unless it was for interviews or parents' evenings. Normally she would wear black trousers, a plain shirt and her flats since she was always rushing about being busy at work and on her feet all day. However, it made her feel good to look nice for a change, she thought to herself.

In true West of Scotland fashion, by the time she made the 20 minute walk to school it had turned to rain, then to hail until she was soaked to the skin and arrived at school looking like a drowned rat, much to the amusement of a group of 3rd year boys who hung about the foyer sniggering as she ran through the school doors. *What a waste of time straightening my hair!* She could still feel the dampness in her clothes by lunchtime. She had waited up until midnight last night planning her lessons for that day and was quietly pleased that 4 of them so far had gone without a hitch, only 1 more to go after lunch.

As she walked into the small bustling staff room, she looked over to her usual spot where she met up with Jamie and Jennifer and some other colleagues that kept her sane with some adult conversation until home time. Although Jamie and Jennifer were her best friends, inside and outside work, she wouldn't dare tell them about her possible 'crush'. They would crucify her, she thought. They wouldn't let her forget it anyway. Caitlyn doubted they'd believe it anyway, as she was always professional and had always winced at the thought of teacher-pupil relations and cringed when some old codger of a teacher made a leering remark about a young girl. *Although, how am I any different?* she scolded herself. She felt so guilty and must have looked so too, as Jennifer and Jamie both looked up at her accusingly. "What have you been up to, missus?" Jamie chided. "Huh?" Caitlyn tried to look nonchalant, "nothing, why?" Jennifer giggled, "You just had your guilty look on, like you look when you eat the last biscuit or, hang on, I know what it is – you forgot lunch didn't you?" she asked smiling. Each of them would take turn on different days to bring lunch in for them. "Oh shit, sorry guys," Caitlyn mumbled, "I'll run down to the canteen, I totally forgot it was my turn." "No worries honey, we love nothing better than a school dinner, especially on Monday when it's Janice's chicken stew," Jamie said sarcastically, but with a hint of laughter. "I'll get us sandwiches then shall I?" not really waiting on a reply as she exited the staff room door and ran down the back stairs to the crowded canteen. *God, Jamie was right,* she mused, *it is chicken stew but it certainly doesn't look delicious.* She muscled her way in to the busy queues as kids battled to get to the front to try to get served, dodging the killer glares, and opted for 3 chicken salad wholemeal sandwiches with soup. She also bought them each a wee iced cupcake that caught her attention, as a way of an apology, before running back upstairs with her goodies balancing on a small red plastic tray. Most of the canteen food in school nowadays was decent compared to her school days, as well as being nutritionally balanced, but she was always glad to see the occasional treat on the menu. Jennifer and Jamie both seemed happy enough with her choice as they dived ravenously into the food as if they hadn't eaten in days.

They all had a good moan about the fire alarm, each trying to outdo each other on the worst time – getting soaked again (Caitlyn), tripping up on a step in front of her giggling class (Jennifer), wasting his only non-contact period of the day (Jamie) or getting abuse from the pupils (Tommy). He never told them this but they overheard it and couldn't help but laugh at it. The three of them loved meeting up at lunchtime if they could. It wasn't always possible with the busy itinerary of school and often got interrupted with detentions, supported study, rehearsals and pupils knocking on the door asking for things, but it was their great opportunity to chat and have a good moan about school in general. They got to socialise outside their departments with other like (and non-like) minded teachers, and speak to adults for a little time of the day which was good after spending so much time with kids. Although most of the teachers enjoyed their jobs and had good relationships with the kids, the staff room was their refuge away from it all and allowed themselves the chance to rant and rave about the days goings on with fellow teachers.

"I'm still a bit hungover. I think I'll stop drinking altogether," Jennifer declared, whispering to the other pair. Jamie burled his eyes and asked, ignoring Jennifer's last comment, "Do you fancy going to that new club in town on Saturday night? I've got free passes from my brother. We could grab some dinner beforehand in the merchant city?" "Sounds great!" said Jennifer and Caitlyn in unison. "Won't you be snuggled up with your live-in lover?" Jamie assumed, looking at Caitlyn. "And I thought you were off the booze?" he signalled to Jennifer. "I'm giving it up until Saturday," she replied defiantly, but Caitlyn remained quiet while she tried to think of an excuse. Peter had already stated that he would be working all weekend so she might as well go out and enjoy herself.

"I am a bit skint," she finally replied. "Oh me too actually," Jennifer said apologetically to Jamie. "Well how about we just meet at mine and I can make you my famous fajitas and share a few bottles of wine? My brother has already put our names on the guest list so we don't need to pay the entry fee," he said encouragingly. It did sound great, all Caitlyn had planned was to watch the TV and wait on Peter to come home. "I'll think about it," Caitlyn eventually said. "Let's decide at the weekend." Jamie seemed happy with her answer, looking quietly confident that their maybe would turn to yes by Friday.

After finishing her cupcake and checking her mail tray quickly, Caitlyn walked along the corridor to the small dark classroom to take detention. Every staff member had to take detention once a month and it was Caitlyn's turn today. Twelve boys attended. All being given detention for a variety of different reasons, such as being caught smoking, truanting, being insolent to a teacher or for forgetting their PE kit consistently. Caitlyn always found it amusing that she was probably given detention for some of these things herself when she was at school, but the pupils were of course oblivious to this. She issued each boy with the school rules, lined paper and a pencil and ordered them to take a seat. She tried to always be strict during detention so that the kids couldn't play up. One of her old mentors at her first teaching school told her the golden rule of keeping order in the classroom is not to smile until Christmas. OK, so she wasn't going to abide by that but he had something there – teachers aren't there to be the kids' friends, they were there to teach. Some of the boys in this detention room certainly needed to be taught manners and discipline so she didn't mind using the golden rule when in there. One of the boys, John the loudmouth, tried to catch the attention of the others and made a silly remark under his breath that Caitlyn couldn't quite hear. "Any talking from any of you and you simply all come back and do detention again tomorrow, up to you," Caitlyn retorted to the class. John, undeterred, rolled his eyes and laughed, swinging back on his chair. "I'll be on detention anyway." Some of the others giggled. "Well I'll just give you detention after school, or maybe you would like extra homework?" Caitlyn replied sternly.

"I wouldn't do it," John cheekily replied.

"Well that is your choice John, you know just as well as anyone that there are consequences for not behaving. Now, you are here for a reason and I am asking you to get on with copying out the school rules. If you can do that without talking then you get away before the bell. If you speak I will add extra time on or give out extra detentions. It is very simple. You choose."

He mumbled something else under his breath and kicked the chair in front of him. Caitlyn had spaced the few pupils that were there around the room and the rest of the boys soon began to ignore John and focused on their school rules, leaving John on his own to eventually pick up his pencil and do the same. She sighed with relief when the bell rang again, signalling for detention to end and period 5 to start. The boys happily dropped their pencils and bolted for the door as she re-organised the detention resources and headed back to her classroom.

As she walked up the busy staircase, she admired some of the pupils' paintings on the wall, proud that the kids from her school had produced such good pieces of work. Her class was already lined up outside her room as she welcomed them and asked them to enter her class and take a seat quietly. She immersed herself into teaching her last lessons which both went well although she had to deal with a few minor behaviour issues. Nothing she couldn't handle, but she was finding it increasingly difficult to enforce that no pupils were using mobile phones in class, especially with the older pupils who used their smartphones to connect to the Internet. or importantly for them, Facebook, Twitter or Instagram. When the final school bell rang for the day and all of the pupils had walked home or boarded their buses, she packed up all of her marking and lesson plans to take home. It was normal for teachers to wait in until after 5pm for meetings, catching up on paperwork and planning lessons, but Caitlyn liked getting away early and doing her work in the peace of her own home. Caitlyn knew she was lucky that her work allowed her to get away early and she could get to the gym before 5pm whilst you didn't need to queue for equipment. Exercise was her escapism and she religiously worked out every day for at least an hour, usually at her local gym. From her hockey days at school she had always enjoyed keeping fit and being active. Although now she had regrettably given up her beloved hockey, apart from occasionally coaching it at Hillend, she loved to run - pounding the streets around Glasgow or on the treadmill if the weather was bad. It helped her release the stress of the day and kept her in excellent shape. Caitlyn had an amazing figure. At 5 foot 6 she had long, shapely, tanned legs and had a tight toned stomach that her friends envied. She had silky blonde hair, a little lighter than she would've liked due to the sun in the summer. However, Caitlyn still complained about her body and always moaned about her bingo wings and fat bum even though she was a perfect size 10.

Although she normally ran 5 miles on the treadmill, she decided to run 6 today to burn off the cupcake from lunch. The sweat was dripping from her forehead when she finished but she felt great. She loved the elated feeling she got from a hard workout, the endorphins released making her feel invincible. It also gave her time to think and sometimes gave her inspiration for lessons. As her mind relaxed whilst running, sometimes ideas would pop into her head and she would furiously write them into the notes section of her ipod. Not today though, she just enjoyed the peace and thought about the week ahead. She concluded her gym session with some weights and stretching before hitting the showers, still feeling upbeat. As she walked out of the leisure centre on her way home, she saw a young couple kissing in the doorway. She smiled in their direction and she remembered how her and Peter used to be like that. *We could be like that again* she thought defiantly, she loved Peter and ached for him to show her attention like that once more.

Caitlyn was back in her flat by 6.30pm and prepared dinner for her and Peter. By 8pm he still wasn't home and Caitlyn's great mood was starting to deteriorate with impatience and hunger. He was usually home by 7.30 at the latest, but recently he had been working longer and longer hours in the office. She gave him a quick phone but it went to voicemail. He would see her missed call, but she still phoned again 20 minutes later when he didn't reply. Again, it went to voicemail. After doing some housework and a little marking, she decided to eat when he still hadn't returned after another hour. Peter finally came through the front door at about 10.30pm, throwing his laptop bag into the cupboard and heating his dinner up in the microwave. "Hi," he shouted to Caitlyn as he poured himself a drink of juice.

She looked up from her marking briefly and bit her lip, careful not to fly into a rage straight away. "Why are you so late? I thought you'd be home at 7ish?" she calmly asked him, looking back at her work.

"Sorry babe, boss asked me to do some overtime again so had to take it. Starving now though, cheers for dinner."

She nodded accepting his thanks as he started to eat his stir fry furiously.

As he shoved the meal into his mouth he was still looking at his mobile phone with his left hand. "Oh sorry, Caitlyn babe, had my phone on silent from being in a meeting, didn't even get a chance to text you I'd be late. Sorry, honey. Do you forgive me?" he said with his boyish grin that reminded Caitlyn how much she still fancied him.

"You want to get an early night if you know what I mean?" she asked him, trying to look seductive, flicking her hair back.

"Yip, definitely," Peter instantly replied, not getting her intention. "I'm flying down to London tomorrow on the 7am flight so need to get some shut eye, will you drive me to airport?"

Caitlyn hesitated, that's not exactly what she had in mind, before replying, "Yeah, OK then. You never told me you were going to London."

"Did I not say? Thought I did, sorry. Boss only asked me late last week, doing some training course thingamajig.... Will be good on my CV." Peter had now abandoned his plate and glass beside the sofa and had started getting ready for bed. By the time Caitlin had finished marking and tidied up, she could already hear Peter snoring.

Chapter 5

Jamie and Jennifer's meeting after school ended up dragging on until after 6pm so they decided to grab take-out food instead of making something. "Do you still get kids playing up to you in class?" Jennifer casually asked whilst they munched into a takeaway pizza.

"What do you mean?" Jamie asked with a mouthful of pepperoni.

"Well, you know. Like making stupid remarks or shouting out in class," Jennifer quizzed, but didn't make eye contact as she asked, trying to play her comments down.

"Aye! Of course! Are you still getting hassle from your S4 class?" Jamie immediately picked up on Jennifer's anxieties. "Oh pet. don't worry, we all get a shitty class from time to time. You've got some horrors in there!"

Jennifer felt a bit relieved, "I do?"

"God yeah, you've got the worst of the year in there, you'd be lucky to keep them quiet for 5 minutes!"

"But you don't have any behaviour problems. I had to send 3 of them out of the class the other day. 2 of them got referred to the boss and I issued over 5 detentions!" she now looked at Jamie.

"Ach that's nothing babe, it's just a bad lot. Tina Jenkins has your class for English and she's always moaning about them, says she'd like to mace the lot of them or drug them with sleeping pills, ha ha! No, well, I suppose I don't have anything like that, but there's always the odd thing that needs dealt with. Plus I'm so lucky with the classes I have, I've been given mostly top sets this year. I hear stories in the staffroom and from some of the others in the department, and they aren't so lucky and they are good teachers! So are you, Jen."

"I don't know... Surely after 3 years' experience I shouldn't have discipline problems."

"You don't! Well, we all get them, plus, kids are bolder nowadays, definitely. God sake, Jen, it's one bad class and it's only the start of term. They try it on with any new teacher they get, especially if they are young. It takes time for them to find the boundaries of a class, don't worry. Just be tough and fair like always, they'll soon realise what a good teacher you are. And just remember what our old tutor said 'don't smile until Christmas.'"

"Do you really do that?"

"Oh of course not. Not literally, but I do try and be stricter with them at the beginning, especially a class with behaviour problems, as it sets the tone of the class. Then once you have taught them the routines for the class you can let down your guard a bit. And you can smile," Jamie beamed at her.

Jennifer forced a smile back. "I know," she sighed, "they're only kids. It's just getting me down. It's so difficult to teach them everything that needs covered in the lesson without having to deal with their stupid outbursts all the time. It's hard enough with the learning support issues in that particular class. I've got to differentiate all my material and carefully prepare practically for each pupil individually. Some of them struggle with just the basics and I'm trying to help them but then the rest of the class plays up.

Don't get me started on writing in sentences or spelling or grammar - it is shocking! I'm trying to make it interesting and fun but they just act up. One of them threw a pencil sharpener at me the other day when my back was turned! Plus, there's also a few Polish kids in that class, so I've got to try and do some translations for them as we go along, at least they are trying hard. And I'm still bloody pissed off with Tommy. He just gets on my goat."

"Don't worry about him, he's just jealous of you. Plus I saw him doing karaoke dressed as a transvestite last week in that tacky new gay bar in town!"

Jennifer's eyes lit up "What?! No way! You never?" she screamed.

"OK, I never, but I thought that mental image might cheer you up."

They both burst into hysterics. It certainly did cheer her up.

Chapter 6

That Saturday night, Caitlyn, Jennifer and Jamie had managed to scoff all of Jamie's famous fajitas in what seemed like minutes. They had also polished off 2 bottles of pink cava and were now a little tipsy. They were all dressed up and they were all wanting to show off their new outfits, including Jamie.

"OK, where to now?" Caitlyn asked. "Shall we go down Ashton Lane before the club?" Ashton Lane was a bustling cobble stoned lane in the West End of Glasgow full of upmarket eateries and bars that the three of them loved to frequent most weekends.

"Oh don't," Jennifer pleaded "I really am so skint. And you know I just can't resist a cocktail if I go there!"

"C'mon one drink then the club," Jamie piped in "I'll buy you a raspberry mojito."

"OK," Jennifer conceded quickly, "but no chips and cheese at the end of the night."

"Deal," Jamie and Caitlyn chimed in unison as they grabbed their coats.

As they walked into the crowded cocktail bar Caitlyn soaked up the atmosphere. She and Jennifer always got a lot of male attention and she loved being able to turn heads as she entered a room. Caitlyn looked stunning, wearing navy skin-tight jeans and navy silk top with 5 inch peep toe matching sandals, showing off her fantastic figure as her blonde hair fell effortless on her shoulders. She was never one for spending too much time on her appearance, but loved to put on her favourite make up brands such as Mac and Benefit at the weekends, highlighting her natural beauty. As she ordered their usual of 3 mojitos at the bar, she could feel someone staring at her from across the room. She looked across and caught his gaze. It was Cameron! He was leaning across the back wall surrounded by a group of young people. He was wearing casual dark jeans with a tight fitting black shirt and he looked gorgeous. He smiled over at Caitlyn. She quickly looked at her feet and pretended not to notice him although her heart was fluttering like a teenager. *How did he get in here? Who was he with? Oh my God, what will he say to his friends?* She turned around to Jennifer and Jamie, "Code 9, we need to abort!"

"What? Oh no, already?" Jennifer asked as she scanned around the room. "Who's here? Tell me it's not that Jemma girl in S4 again?"

"No, I think it's some boys from S6."

"So what then? Why do we have to go? We've seen S6 out before. Just ignore them and they'll ignore us and we'll all pretend we never saw anyone. They'll probably get scared we'll report them for being underage anyway and go."

"Nah, I just don't feel right, Jamie. One of them is in my class. I don't want them reporting on Facebook what I'm doing on a Saturday night!"

"What that you are human and you are in a nice bar having drinks with your friends?"

"You know what I mean."

"OK, well let's just enjoy our mojitos from the other side of the bar and then we'll go to the club."

"OK."

"Where are they?" Jennifer said oblivious to the conversation, she was still looking around, "I don't see them."

"Stop looking!" Caitlyn scorned "I don't want to draw attention to us."

Jennifer rolled her eyes "OK, Mum," she giggled as she finished the last of her drink. "Finished!" she proudly exclaimed.

Caitlyn looked over one last time at Cameron before she left the bar. This time he was deep in conversation to the guy next to him. He didn't even seem to flinch that his teacher had been there and he certainly didn't look out of place. And he looked so good. I am better being kept away from him, Caitlyn thought to herself as they walked round the corner to the new club.

The three of them danced the night away at the nightclub and just after 2 am Caitlyn slipped away early to get home. After a few drinks she was starting to feel really amorous and looking forward to going home to see Peter. The lights were off when she got home so she decided to strip naked in the hall and surprise him in bed. This usually aroused him quickly and lead to some fantastic drunken uninhibited sex. Disappointedly Peter was already asleep but he couldn't have been for long as the football highlights were still on the television. She switched it off and put the bedroom light on very low. She slowly entered the bed and pressed her firm naked body against his. He was sound asleep. She kissed his neck and whispered into his ear as she slid her hand into his boxer shorts trying to wake him up gently. He turned over with his back facing her.

"Fuck Caitlyn, you're cold! Go to sleep!" he murmured.

"Open your eyes," she continued to talk softly as she tried to pull him back towards her and started to kiss his torso leading to his underwear.

"Not tonight," he groaned, "I'm really tired."

"Come on baby… I'm naked. It's Saturday night…. And needing you to satisfy me," she said sensuously as she tugged at his boxers.

"Not tonight!" he snapped. "Fuck sake, Caitlyn, I've been working all day on top of my 50 hours through the week and I'm bloody exhausted. And fucking Rangers lost today. Again! I'm not in the mood. I just want a good night's sleep!" as he pushed her off of him on to the cold mattress.

"Fine!" Caitlyn retorted, hurt by his abrupt outburst. She rolled over onto her side, seething that he didn't want to be with her. *Was I that repulsive?* she thought. He used to want her every day. But now she was lucky if she got a kiss from him when he walked in the door. Their relationship felt as if it wasn't the same and she just didn't know what had changed. She understood he was working hard at his career but that had never stopped him being affectionate before.

Caitlyn soon fell into a drunken restless sleep and awoke to an empty bed. She looked at the clock and it read 10am. "You've got to be kidding me?" she exclaimed. "Peter?" she called out to the flat

41

to no reply. Her memory of him not wanting her last night along with her annoyance of him barely seeing her this week due to work commitments was coming back to her and she was beginning to lose her temper. She called out again to him as she walked through to the kitchen in her dressing robe. He was there, laptop open and working at the stove. Just as she was about to shout at him he turned round and greeted her with a big smile, "Morning gorgeous. I've made you breakfast. I was going to bring it to you in bed." She relaxed a bit and smiled again. "Thanks, babe," she said as she took the plate of scrambled egg from him and he kissed her forehead. He must have just been tired last night, she thought. She started to feel guilty for trying to wake him the previous evening. "Sorry for wakening you when I got in, Pete," Caitlyn said, through mouthfuls of egg, now starting to feel guilty.

"Don't worry about it," he laughed. "We can make up for it this afternoon," he winked. Caitlyn mischievously winked back.

Chapter 7

"What a fantastic weekend!" Jamie exclaimed as he dished out three portions of chicken pesto pasta for each of them in the staffroom for Monday lunch.

"I know," Jennifer pitched in. "We had such a laugh! And don't think we never noticed you sneaking away early Caitlyn for your crazy romps with Perfect Peter."

Jamie laughed, "Yip, we noticed ya wee tart, you! Although you can't speak," he turned back to Jennifer. "Who was that you were kissing at the end of the night?"

"What? Me?!" she said trying to look innocent, but eyes glistening with mischief. "Och it was just a wee kiss. I met him in the taxi queue. Keith I think his name was. Or maybe Kevin. No I think it was definitely Keith. I was only with him for about 20 minutes, he kept me warm in the taxi queue!"

Caitlyn giggled, "You never told me that! What's he like? You get his number? And did you really only kiss?"

They all laughed again.

"Yes, och yes! It was all very innocent really, but he seemed really nice."

"He did seem really nice," Jamie nodded.

"You never spoke to him!" Jennifer accused.

"But he looked hot!" Jamie retaliated and they all laughed again.

"So no steamy sex then?" Caitlyn probed.

"No. Honestly no, but I did give him my mobile number and he's sent a few texts already."

"What? Really?" Jamie exclaimed, "Sex texts?"

"Calm your jets Jamesy boy, nothing yet, just a little text flirting."

"So you've been sexting back?" Caitlyn quizzed, "Spill!"

"Of course, just a few texts. Maybe 10 actually but it's just a bit of fun. I might meet him this Friday... He's an IT Manager and he's 28. He's got his own flat in the New Gorbals. He seems really nice and as Jamie has said, he is hot! I've not had anyone in over a month you know." She sighed, "It's not like I have a man at my beck and call like Caitlyn."

"And you still can't remember if his name is Keith or Kevin?" Caitlyn asked, choosing to ignore Jennifer's last comments on her relationship.

Jennifer giggled again "it's Keith. I'm sure his name is Keith. I was drunk!" she said defensively. "He signs the end of a text with a K and I'm 100% sure it's Keith."

"OK well find out his full name a.s.a.p. so we can Facebook stalk him. There is NO way that you are going on a date with him until we find out more," Caitlyn demanded jokingly.

"Will do, that's my plan tonight anyway!" Jennifer replied "and what about you, Mr? Did you not pull on Saturday night when I left you?"

"Nah, never pulled this week. I met my brother and some of his mates and we ended up in the city centre at some student party. It was a bit of a shithole so I didn't wait long. No talent."

"Aww that's a shame honey," Jennifer said tilting her head to one side, "although we don't feel sorry for you – you pull more than anyone, I think you need a rest!"

"I do not!" Jamie argued back, but he knew it was partly true.

"Maybe there just isn't any men left out there for you, Jamie. Maybe you've conquered Glasgow," Caitlyn joked.

"Very funny. Maybe I'm just not wanting to pull anymore. Maybe I want a serious relationship. Something a bit more significant."

"You?" Caitlyn and Jennifer exchanged glances, "Are you for real?"

"Yeah, why not? I'd like to find Mr Right and settle down just like you!"

"Aye right Jamie. I don't believe you!" Jennifer screeched "You love the life of a single man."

"Ha ha, you're right, I know I do," Jamie openly admitted, "but I also want to have someone to share things with all the time. Like the way you have with Peter," he said in Caitlyn's direction. "I'd like someone to go out for dinner with. To go away on city breaks with. To go to the cinema with…"

"To have sex with every night…" Jennifer cheekily added.

Jamie laughed out loud, "Yes OK, you got me, that too. But honestly, as much as I love my fun, I would love a partner. Maybe I'm getting old!"

"Yeah, I'll agree with you on that Jamie," Caitlyn said, "you're getting old!"

They all laughed again as they hurriedly finished their lunch before the bell rang to remind them to get back to work.

Chapter 8

It was Friday again already and although Caitlyn usually liked to get out of work early she found herself still in her classroom late marking homework. She was determined to clear her desk so that she could enjoy her weekend without any school work. She had got to her last jotter – Cameron's. She had been extremely paranoid at the beginning of the week after spotting him out in the bar on Saturday and was so pleased that he hadn't mentioned anything in class. He continued to be his usual cocky, handsome self and she had found herself getting up slightly earlier to straighten her hair again and wear a little more makeup than usual each day. She had persuaded herself that it was for 'her' but she knew deep down it was to try and impress and look good for Cameron. Or at least not look as old as Jamie thought they were getting. She was even more pleased that it seemed Cameron hadn't mentioned seeing his teachers out to anyone. She didn't know if she could get into trouble for not reporting under agers and didn't want any stories going about either. She couldn't be bothered with idle gossip and her career didn't need it either. Not that she had done anything wrong, but one too many cocktails and she could've easily said or done something she regretted.

She remembered another time when she was on placement whilst a student, she saw two or three sixth year girls out at a nightclub. Unfortunately that was a night Caitlyn was out on a friend's hen night and was a little worse for wear. Never mind that she was wearing stockings and suspenders underneath a clinging nurse's uniform! She had no idea how much the girls had seen or knew but from the whispers the following Monday she knew some form of rumour was circulating. Luckily no-one had mentioned it to her face but she had suspicions that some of the pupils, and teachers, were talking about it, the story being exaggerated with every telling. She was mortified and petrified it would get to management or her tutors, but they soon moved on to someone else to talk about, and they forgot all about it. Nevertheless, it still bothered her even though she actually didn't do anything wrong. She was always cautious about maintaining her reputation, which made her thoughts about Cameron all the more distressing to her.

As she finished correcting his last question she stopped suddenly. She re-read the last sentence.

Did you have a good night Saturday?

Fuck, oh fuck. What do I do? Without hesitating she ripped out the page from the jotter and re-read it again. She picked up her bag and walked downstairs to the Head Teacher's office. "Mr Johnstone?" she called out peering into his room. There was no response. He must have left for the day. She stuffed the page into her bag and walked across the near empty car park to her car. She would speak to him on Monday about it, nothing they could until then anyway. She would tell him the truth and he would give her advice on what to do.

After an hour in the gym she couldn't stop thinking of Cameron's question. As she walked back to her flat she couldn't help but smile to herself about it. He noticed her. Maybe thought she was attractive? Maybe he even fancied her? She wondered and hoped to herself. Yes, she knew it was wrong. Yes, he was her pupil. But he was only asking an innocent question, she consoled herself. Why was she thinking of going to the Head Teacher? It was just a question. She should maybe have a quiet word with him instead. There was no need on making a bigger deal out of it than necessary she , as she started to feel guilty about thinking about Cameron when she had a long-term boyfriend. She had never ever fancied anyone else whilst with Peter, and had vowed she would never be the type of person to cheat. And she still felt that way, but was so annoyed that she let some thoughts about Cameron enter her mind. She would be professional and nip it in the bud first thing on Monday she decided. He was a good looking boy but not worth her career or her relationship.

As she walked into the flat she looked around for signs of Peter being home but there was nothing. She ran a big bubble bath and opened a bottle of white wine and took out two glasses. It was 8pm and she was so glad that the week was over. She phoned Peter's mobile and he answered immediately, "Hey babe, I'm really busy, call you back in a min."

"OK, but just to let you know I'm naked…"

He chuckled briefly, said "Speak to you in a min," then hung up.

She sunk into the hot bath and took a sip of her favourite Pinot Grigio and began to relax. It had been another long week and she had barely seen Peter. He had been on a course in London and since his return had been working late every night. They hadn't had sex all week, but she knew that the weekend was their opportunity to spend some quality time together. She took another sip of the wine as she texted Jennifer. Jennifer was going on her first proper date with Kevin tonight, the guy she had met in the taxi queue. After a few days of sexting they had arranged to meet at TGI Fridays in the City Centre for a date. Jennifer finally found out his real name after he added her as a friend on the social networking site Facebook and it wasn't Keith after all, it was Kevin. Caitlyn and Jamie were right though, he was hot. They had poured over his profile page the evening before looking for information on him, and so far he looked really nice. They gave Jennifer the nod of approval and she happily agreed to meet him. She was the most excited they had seen her in ages.

I hope you are having fun with Keith. LOL. Seriously though please be careful and remember to text me when you are home safe.

After 10 minutes she replied:

Txting you from bathroom of tgis. He is hot! Things going really well so hopefully will be home in bed with KEVIN by end of night. Enjoy your dirty weekend with Perfect Pete x

She smiled as she poured herself another glass from the side of the bath and leaned back into the bubbles.

The phone ringing wakened her abruptly. The water was now cold, her skin pale and wrinkled and her glass bobbing among the bubbles. "Peter?" she asked wearily into the receiver when she eventually picked up, "Where are you? What time is it?"

"Sorry Caitlyn, I'm on way home. It's been manic in the office. It's about 10 I think. Won't be long," and he hung up again.

As she got up and showered she heard Peter come into the flat and enter the kitchen. "Hello?" she called out to him as she grabbed a towel. She quickly changed into a silk chemise that showed off her curvaceous figure.

She heard him pacing about the kitchen opening cupboard doors. "Where's dinner?" he shouted back to her.

"What dinner?" she asked as she walked into the kitchen to meet him.

"Didn't you make any food?" Peter asked, his voice getting louder, "It's 10 o'clock and I'm starving."

"Sorry, Pete," she said softly not realising his bad mood. "I was too busy getting naked!"

"What?" he retorted angrily.

"Sorry I'm just joking, I just went for a bath. Fell asleep, I was really tired. Thought you we phoning me back? I've had a long week, must've needed that wee nap."

"Tired?" Peter interjected. "You are tired? You finish work at 3.30 for fuck sake! I've been working until 10 and I'm starving. You've been lying about in the bath drinking wine and you've not even got anything for the tea!" he accused, his temper rising.

"I'm sorry," Caitlyn apologised "I thought you were phoning back and I just fell asleep. I've not eaten either. Let's get a takeaway?" Peter stormed into the bedroom without replying. This wasn't like him. Caitlyn hated the angry side of Peter although he rarely showed it.

Caitlyn poured another glass of white wine and took out a cold beer from the fridge for Peter. 10 minutes had passed since his strop and as predicted he emerged from the bedroom. "I'm sorry," he said to Caitlyn as he came over to her. "I didn't mean to get on at you. I'm just stressed. And tired. And hungry."

"It's fine," Caitlyn said as she handed him the beer. "I know you're busy with work. Just try not to take it out on me. I am sorry about dinner. Why don't we order pizza?" She had wanted a Chinese but she knew that Italian food was Peter's favourite and wanted to make him happy.

"OK let's get pizza," he grinned, back to his usual self.

Caitlyn smiled back at him and called the pizza place, as they took their normal Friday night spots on the sofa in front of the TV.

Chapter 9

"Congratulations!" chimed an excited group of women huddled round Caroline Masters, a History teacher in Hillend High, in the staffroom on Monday morning, as she revealed that she got engaged to be married at the weekend. There was lots of screeching and *'ooohing'* and *'aahing'* over her big diamond ring, and Caitlyn was more than a little jealous. Caroline was 28, a few years older than Caitlyn and her friends, and she had been going out with Ryan, the IT technician, for just over a year. She used to socialise with Jennifer, Jamie and her much more before she started dating him.

"How did he propose?" "Have you two set a date?" the questions came thick and fast from the throng of gossiping teachers eager to find out the intimate details, and Caroline just beamed back flashing a big toothy pleased-with-herself grin. Caitlyn smiled back and joined in with the celebratory remarks and did feel genuinely happy for her, but couldn't help feel just a little sorry for herself at the same time. She and Peter had been together for over 5 years now and instead of getting closer together and planning for the future it seemed that they were maybe drifting apart, that something just wasn't quite right and she was upset by this. She maybe hadn't quite realised it until now. Caitlyn wanted to get engaged. She wanted to get married and have kids with Peter. Well, eventually that is. Just to know that she is still wanted and appreciated from her boyfriend would suffice at the minute, she mused. It just seemed to her that he loved his work more than her at present.

"Isn't that wonderful news?" Jamie gushed to Caitlyn and Jennifer as they sat down again to have a quick cup of tea.

"Just lovely," Jennifer concurred, "I hope we get invited to the wedding," she enthusiastically added.

"Yip, brilliant news," Caitlyn tried to sound happy and not as envious as she felt.

"It'll be you and Pete next!" Jamie nudged her playfully on the arm.

"Ha!" Caitlyn laughed. "I doubt that."

"Yeah right, Caitlyn, you and Pete will be happily married by the end of next year I bet."

"A summer wedding!" James piped in.

"Get away! Wheest, everyone will start thinking we're engaged or something. And we're not. I don't think Peter has any interest in getting married to me."

"What?" Jennifer exclaimed "Don't be daft, he's head over heels with you, always has been so it's only a matter of time...."

"We'll see, we'll see."

The bell rang to signal the end of break and Caitlyn was glad to get away from the conversation. She wondered if she should tell them that Peter seemed distant and that their sex life wasn't as good as it was before? She doubted they would understand and she didn't want to admit 'defeat'. "Maybe it's just a wee patch that we are going through?" she pondered. I mean, she still loved Peter to bits and she understood that he does have a stressful job that requires him to work long hours. She gulped down the remnants of her tea and walked briskly back to her classroom to prepare for her next lesson.

She made sure to stop by the bathroom to sort her hair and make-up, at least it made her feel better about herself.

Chapter 10

Jamie couldn't help but smile when he looked around at his class, silently working independently and conscientiously. He had set them a difficult task and gave them the responsibility of working unaided without his support. And he was pleased to note that they all were. All 30 pupils in his classroom were either typing up their report on to the few laptops the department had managed to save up to purchase, or writing dutifully onto lined paper. The students had been working in pairs earlier in the week, peer assessing the draft forms of their efforts and they were now putting the finishing touches to the final copy. He walked round the classroom reading excerpts and nodding his head approvingly. At this point Mr Johnstone, the Head Teacher walked into the room casually and caught his eye. He was wearing another stylish suit Jamie quickly noticed. It was a dark grey tailored Armani suit with a pale lilac shirt and purple tie with black patent loafers. Jamie had a good eye for a designer label, although he couldn't afford them much himself and couldn't fail to admire Mr Johnstone, not just for the outstanding job he does with the school in his role as a leader, but also because he looked fantastic!

"Hello," he mouthed mutedly. Some of the pupils lifted their heads to acknowledge the Head Teacher, but it didn't distract them. He too walked around the classroom observing the pupils focusing on their work. Both of the teachers then walked to the front of the room. "Impressive," Mr Johnstone whispered, "you seem to have a very diligent class. Some of the pupils' writing is of a very good standard. And I don't think I've seen Rebecca and June sitting beside each other in a class before without talking!" he added with a smile.

Jamie smiled back. *Thank God he came in on a lesson like today!* he thought.

"So what are your plans for the October break?" Mr Johnstone asked him, changing the subject.

A little taken aback from the personal interest, Jamie hesitated. "Erm. Uh. I'm not really sure," he eventually replied. This was the truth, he had been so busy with work that he hadn't even had time to make plans. Jamie, Caitlyn and Jennifer and some associated friends normally went up to the North of Scotland for the February week and rented a log cabin with a Jacuzzi. They would take up car loads of food and wine and take turns trying to be Nigella for the group for the night. Most of the group would get up early and ski all day, but Jamie usually waited in the cabin and caught up on reading. However, the authority had changed the holiday timetable for the following year meaning they wouldn't get any days off in February, just in service training days so there were a few drunken conversations between friends about doing a mini holiday in October instead. "We normally go up North for a few days in the February break to ski," he started to explain, "but I'm not sure if we're doing that this year, possibly changing it to October break and making it more of a walking/outdoor holiday than skiing. Maybe to Kintyre."

Mr Johnstone looked slightly somewhat disappointed, "We? You and your partner?" he quizzed.

"No, no partner. Just a bunch of my friends."

"Sounds like good fun. I've been up in the Cairngorms a few times and been to beautiful Kintyre many times," Mr Johnstone continued. "Done a few Munros, not skied before - I don't think I could ski to save myself, a bit like Bambi on ice," he joked.

"Me neither to be honest. I tried snowboarding once but I nearly killed a rogue sheep along with myself, so I vowed never to try it again!" Jamie jested.

Mr Johnstone laughed loudly, "You're hilarious!"

Jamie giggled embarrassedly and looked around the room to make sure none of the pupils could overhear. "The You tube video is even more hilarious. Believe me!"

Mr Johnstone looked as if he was going to burst with laughter. "I'd like to see that one!" he exclaimed as he winked at Jamie. At that point one of the girls at the back of the room put her hand up and was trying to get Jamie's attention by waving her hand side to side.

"I better help Gemma," Jamie whispered, "she is such a talented girl and has such a vivid imagination. Such amazing taste in fashion, always one step ahead of the crowd. I mean, come on, those big gold sovereign rings matched with the metallic green chains? Nice."

"So true!" Mr Johnstone said, "I saw that look in Vogue this week and I just knew some of the pupils from this class would have that look down. I better let you get back to the fashion icons of the

57

future. We should be so proud," he replied smiling at Jamie as he left the room.

Jamie walked over to Gemma at the back of the class and he looked round to see if Mr Johnstone was still in the doorway. He wasn't, and Jamie felt himself disappointed. Did he just flirt with him? Surely not, he was just being friendly he reconciled. But I wish he did flirt. He is really cute, Jamie mused.

"What were you and Mr Johnstone talking about?" Gemma pried. "Nothing," Jamie immediately retorted, a little flushed. It wasn't uncommon for Jamie to indulge in a little flirting with a straight man. Especially straight men that had a wife and had excellent taste in clothing. Jamie had had a few 'banter' sessions with straight men that he always felt like it was 4 pints of lager away from a fling. But he definitely wasn't expecting to flirt with the Head Teacher of his school.

"Actually," Jamie spoke to Gemma, "we were just talking about how wonderful you were and how you were writing a masterpiece." "Why thank you, sir. I am indeed writing a magical mystifying masterpiece that you will be talking about for years to come. You will be able to tell all your old friends that a star, moi, was created in your class. I will *try* to remember you although I am not promising anything," Gemma theatrically announced as the girls around her rolled their eyes.

"OK, OK Gemma, thank you very much, I am intrigued to read it but I will leave my diary free at the weekend to give it the attention it most obviously deserves. Now, is there anything wrong or anything I can help you with?"

"No, I'm good. Thanks for asking, Sir."

"But you had your hand up. Weren't you looking for help just a minute ago?"

"No, I was just wanting to ask what you were talking about," Gemma cunningly grinned.

"You really are nosey aren't you? Ha ha, well none of your business, missy!"

Chapter 11

Jennifer was at the doorway to her small classroom as her second year class were being dismissed. It had been a more difficult lesson than hoped, plotting rainfall on line graphs and she had found herself become frustrated and stressed. She thought the class would get through 2 of the tasks she had planned that lesson but had barely made a dent on the first part of task 1.

She had booked laptops for some of the less able pupils to use so that they could type some of the tasks up, but it took time to prepare it in digital format and was harder to explain to the kids as they were using spreadsheets instead of drawing out like the others. She hadn't taught this class before and although she had read up on them in their notes, she didn't realise how some of them really demanded her attention all of the time. One pupil didn't know how to use a ruler properly and a few of them said they didn't understand graphs at all. She found herself having to do a quick revision lesson on what graphs and charts were and how to interpret them before she could continue to talk about rainfall in different climates, the whole point to her lesson.

As she said goodbye to her second years, she stood in the corridor to ensure good order and a few of her fourth year class were starting to line up in the corridor. Where are they all? she thought, as only 3 of her class were assembling a few minutes later. They must be late from PE or something, she surmised, so she ran quickly back in to her classroom to comment on her last class's lesson plan and record the work issued in her diary. Jennifer always liked to keep accurate records of what happened in every class so that she could read them over at home and help prepare more fully for the next lesson. It also helped if she wrote down her thoughts immediately after a class before she forgot them. She was at her desk for around 30 seconds when she heard a piercing noise from above her head. It was the fire alarm. Again. It bellowed loudly in her room and as she ran to the corridor she could hear it around the school as her class, who now all appeared to be present, whooped with delight and started to pile down the stairs to the front door.

Jennifer joined them along with all the other pupils and teachers as they filed down to the meeting point in the miserable Scottish weather. As she got down the stairs she saw Mr Johnstone standing with her class. "Oh no," she muttered as she walked over just in time to hear Mr Johnstone roar at John, her annoyingly arrogant pupil to get to his office.

"Miss Hill, could you please meet us up there once you have taken your class register?" he turned to her. "Yes," she stuttered, "of course Mr Johnstone," as she grabbed her register. Her class were surprisingly quiet as she shouted out their names. She could feel the other staff members glare at her as she turned to walk up the stairs to the Head Teacher's room. Of course Jennifer's luck was that Tommy Greig just had to be standing there with his well-behaved class and seemed to be smirking at her. Just typical! She thought.

As she arrived into the small waiting room she could hear Mr Johnstone speaking to John but she couldn't understand what was being discussed. She tried to lean against the doorframe to overhear but the floor creaked so she felt obliged to knock. "Come in, Miss Hill," Mr Johnstone shouted. Jennifer's palms were sweaty. She felt as if she were back at school again, waiting for her punishment. Mr Johnstone was sitting behind his desk on a large black leather chair with John sitting on one of the chairs in front of him. "John has something to say to you, Miss Hill. Don't you, John?" Mr Johnstone said looking straight at him but John looked at the floor.

"Don't you, John" Mr Johnstone repeated a little louder and John's head straightened.

"Sorry, Miss Hill," John uttered in a quiet soft voice, eyes looking at the floor. She had never heard him speak so softly like that before. It almost made her feel sorry for him. Jennifer must have looked confused as Mr Johnstone started to explain.

"Miss Hill, John is apologising because he was smoking outside your classroom and set the fire alarm off." He directed his gaze back at John. "I will be phoning his parents directly after this conversation to inform them of the situation and although, John, I know you'll be hoping for an exclusion to get some time off school with Jeremy Kyle, you will be reporting to Miss Hill tomorrow morning as usual. In addition, you will also be attending lunchtime detention for the next two weeks. Do you understand?"

"Yes," he solemnly replied not making eye contact with either teacher in the room.

"Now go and sit in the waiting room," Mr Johnstone instructed pointing at the door and John followed his orders.

"Did you see him smoking?" the Head Teacher asked her quietly as he shut the door.

"No!" Jennifer exclaimed, "they were late for class and I ran in to the room quickly and then the alarm went off," she started to ramble.

"Hey," Mr Johnstone said softly, "it's OK. Don't get so stressed, boys will be boys, these things happen. It wasn't your fault. He's just looking for attention."

"I know."

"I better let you get back to your class. I can see it's mixed bag of characters all right." He smiled jovially at her.

"Yes. Yes, it certainly is," she agreed as she walked out of the room, passed John and back to her classroom.

The rest of Jennifer's Geography lesson on cloud formations, that usually seemed to bore the rest of the students, went by without incident. In fact, without the distraction of John, the pupils worked pretty hard and got through much more of the syllabus than expected. It was the first time that she didn't need to hand out punishment exercises with that class. A reasonable success!

Chapter 12

It was the end of the week and Caitlyn was at her desk even later than usual. Because she was finding it difficult to put some pupils' progress onto paper. Including Cameron's report. *What do I write?* she pondered. What about that he was incredibly handsome, charming and that his teacher may be attracted to him? OK maybe not, that probably wouldn't go down well. She settled for something far more appropriate and meaningful to his work. She had tried not to think about him this week. Well, she tried, but it was hard to disregard her feelings for him as he continued to act in his normal charismatic self-assured way and even came across as mildly flirtatious. She refused to entertain him and maintained her cool professional outlook throughout. She thought about him more each day and was starting to hope that he would be absent so she wouldn't need to see him. However, he did seem extremely enthusiastic about her lessons which just made her like him even more. 10 reports to go, she reminded herself.

Half an hour passed and she had barely written another word. She stared at the computer screen for inspiration but found herself re-reading today's emails instead. Caitlyn was shattered, it had been a long week and she had been getting up earlier and earlier as Peter was going to work before 7am each morning or not arriving home before 10pm as he was trying to complete an important project. She was in desperate need of adult conversation as she hadn't even had time to catch up with Jamie and Jennifer at lunch today. It was 7pm before she knew it and most of the other teachers had long gone and the cleaners were trying to encourage the rest of the staff to hurry up and leave the building.

Caitlyn managed to write one more student report using the power of copy and paste, carefully making sure she had he's and she's and pupil names in the right places before her phone beeped. A message from Jamie – *Tell me u r not still in skl?*

Nope she lied

The gym?

Went this morning

Of course u did. Why aren't u in pub with me and Jen?

Sorry babe, quiet night in tonight, I'm knackered x

Get a grip and get down here now. If Peter's out you should be out ☺x

What? Peter's out? Caitlyn thought, getting angrier by the second. Peter has been working late for god knows how long, doesn't have the energy to kiss me on the cheek but has got plenty time to go to the pub on a Friday teatime? Who is he with? Caitlyn's mind wandered.

I'll be there in 15. Order me a large vino! X. She quickly replied to Jamie's text, slammed her diary closed and shut down her computer for the weekend. As she combed through her glossy hair she speed dialled Peter's phone with one hand. No answer. Rang again. Still no answer. She phoned his work number and it went straight to voicemail. Him ignoring her just made Caitlyn all the more angry.

Caitlyn spotted Jamie and Jennifer instantly as she arrived into the usual post-work pub in the city centre 20 minutes later after a short cab ride. They were sitting on tall stools at the corner of the bar, carefully positioned so they could nosey at who was entering and leaving. The bar was heaving with people in suits and work clothes starting to get livelier as they rid themselves of the stresses of the working week. She made her way over to her friends and even with little make up and work clothes on, she caught a few admiring glances. As she squeezed up on to the free bar stool she tried to look happy as she took a gulp of the Chardonnay Jennifer handed her.

"Whoa! Slow down there missy, it's not even happy hour yet!"

Caitlyn shot Jennifer a look, "I'm just thirsty. In need of a drink, it's been a long week."

"Tell me about it! At least you weren't pulled up to Mr Johnstone's office!"

"What?" Jamie and Caitlyn choked in unison, "What did you do?"

"It's fine," Jennifer smirked, "I was just a naughty girl!"

"Lucky you. I wouldn't mind getting punished in his office!" Jamie giggled as he shouted at the barman for another bottle of wine for them to share.

"Ha ha, no seriously?" Caitlyn said, momentarily forgetting her earlier irritation with Peter. "Everything OK?"

"Yeah, no it's fine. It was just one of my pupils, you know the one, that John boy, it was him that set the fire alarm off. Stupid boy smoking or something. Outside my room! Mr Johnstone made him apologise to me. Although I did think for a minute I was in trouble. Phew!" She took the last swig of her drink and filled up all of their glasses.

"He's a pest so he is," Caitlyn admitted.

"No he's not! I really like him. He's been so friendly to me over the past few weeks, he's really personable," Jamie said defensively as the girls burst into fits of giggles.

"I'm glad you like John that much," Jennifer said, "but he's the bane of my life at the minute."

"Oh whoops. I thought you meant Andrew."

"Oooooh Andrew is it?" Caitlyn exclaimed, "I think Jamie has a little school crush of his own. It'll be you setting the fire alarm off next so you can get punished!"

"I do not! Shut up!"

Caitlyn and Jennifer laughed again and clinked glasses.

Out of the corner of her eye Caitlyn could make out the back of Peter. "Is Peter here?" she asked trying to be nonchalant.

"Aye, he's over there with his snotty work folk. He never saw us though," Jamie nodded in the direction of the back of the bar.

Caitlyn felt hurt and angry. *Why didn't he answer his phone? He was more than capable of coming to the pub!* She was desperate to go over to him and demand answers but she didn't want to start an argument in public. He's had a hard time at work over the last few weeks, he deserves a rest too, she reminded herself. After 15 minutes of deliberating and reapplying her lipgloss, Caitlyn decided to casually walk over to Peter, trying not to act as agitated as she felt. But as she walked over, she scanned the table of guys for him but couldn't find him. Where was he?

"Is Peter here?" she said with a weary smile to one of the men in suits.

"Oh, eh, no, I think he left," he replied, not realising who she was and didn't seem interested.

"Erm, OK. Thanks," Caitlyn said and returned back to her friends.
"How were Peter and his yuppy friends?" Jamie cajoled.

"He wasn't there, think he's went home."

"Ach boring! Does that mean you are leaving?"

"Oh no, I'll wait for a bit," Caitlyn said smiling but really actually wanting to head home to see Peter.

"Well let's order another bottle of vino then?" Jennifer said, eyes twinkling.

"Great suggestion, my dear!"

Jennifer, Jamie and Caitlyn enjoyed the next hour consuming another large bottle of wine as well as slagging of the school, staff, pupils and parents as much as possible before the conversation came full circle and they were declaring their love for the profession, colleagues and students within a few hours. They decided to head home for tea. Or to be more exact, Caitlyn was heading home for tea whereas Jamie was going to meet someone at a new gay bar in the Merchant City and Jennifer had agreed to meet Caroline Masters and some others from work to celebrate her *wonderful* engagement to the best fiancé ever. Caitlyn couldn't think of anything worse to do with her Friday night than fake fawn all over Caroline and her cronies.

68

She had to admit she was the teeniest tiniest bit jealous of her. OK, maybe a lot jealous. It would be nice to have a lovely sparkly diamond on her ring finger - something that would show the rest of the world that someone wanted you and no-one else for ever and ever. Caitlyn felt a little drunk with the wine and was starting to daydream excitedly about getting Peter to bed at home. And since Peter would finally be coming home tonight early, most probably relaxed from a few beers, she might as well treat him to some other fun too by dressing up? As she waited for the train to arrive she stared at her phone and remembered how she tried to phone Peter earlier and he still hadn't returned her call. She phoned him again and it rang out. She decided to text him instead, he probably didn't want to answer the phone in a busy pub.

Hey babe, that's me just about home, going to make you something extra special for dinner… hope you are home and relaxed! Xxx.

As she approached the main door it lay in darkness, Peter wasn't home yet. This bought her some time! Caitlyn was like a tornado running around the flat as she entered, carrying out all the housework chores and preparing dinner so that there would be no distractions when Peter got home and allowed themselves a long lie in the morning.

Caitlyn lit her favourite scented candles and changed into some sexy white lace underwear she had bought for herself in the January sale as she waited on the pasta to cook. She had some killer 6 inch leopard print stilettos (or hooker shoes as Jennifer and Jamie liked to call them) she would slip on just before Peter arrived that she thought would complete the look. She giggled mischievously to herself as she stirred in the homemade tomato and chilli sauce into the spaghetti, not caring that she was in her underwear in front of the kitchen window. She looked at her watch, 8.30pm and still no reply from Peter. She poured 2 glasses of red wine and took a large gulp out of one before resting them on the dining table beside the cutlery she had neatly laid. After about 15 minutes of pottering about the kitchen and staring at her mobile phone she picked up her wine and made herself comfy on the couch. Peter would be home in a minute so she might as well conserve her energy.

Caitlyn woke up at midnight on her couch to the flat in darkness. "Peter?" she called out to no answer. She looked down at her phone that she still was grasping in her right hand. A text! She opened it up quickly, rubbing her eyes to waken up. Disappointedly it was Jennifer.

Caroline's fiancée is sooo not hot but the best man is! Woo for me! Peter seems to know them, find out info for me! Xxxx.

"Peter?" she called out again into the dark. She got up slowly and walked into the bedroom to find him there, fully clothed lying face down on top of the bed sheets. She could smell beer on his clothes and his breath. "Why didn't you wake me? Where were you?" she probed. "Sorry babe, I was working really late and you looked so tired when I came in. I thought it was best just to leave you get your rest." Caitlyn was slightly tipsy from the wine but she instantly sobered up. He was lying to her. He was lying through his teeth – she had seen him with her own eyes!

70

"Weren't you at the pub?"

"No. I was at work. I told you!"

"Not at the city centre pub near your work?"

He flinched a little and turned his head towards her.

"Well, aye, actually I went for one or two after work. Boss was paying. Sorry Miss, am I not allowed to do that?"

She grimaced, she hated when he referred to her as a teacher like that.

"Yes, you are. You know you are, but I phoned you and texted you but didn't get a reply." She said limply "I even made you a special dinner and got dressed up into my fancy lingerie that I *thought* you liked."

Without turning round he drunkenly grabbed one of her breasts as if to check what she was wearing. "Oh aye, so you are," a muffled voice said.

"Forget it," she snapped furiously, slapping his hand away from her. He didn't even move.

Caitlyn jumped up from the bed, riled with anger. She stomped into the bathroom and furiously washed her face and brushed her teeth as silent tears rolled down her red cheeks. She looked back at herself in the mirror. *What is wrong with me?* she asked out loud. *Am I that repulsive? That my own boyfriend doesn't want to come to see me? To be with me? To have sex with me? No wine or chocolate from now on and work twice as hard at the gym.* She vowed this to her tear stricken reflection.

She ripped off her underwear and pulled on her dressing gown and headed back to the couch. She was too cross and irate to even try and share a bed with Peter tonight.

Chapter 13

Jamie walked confidently up to the door of the bar after leaving Caitlyn and Jennifer. He had so many contacts in social circles, he was well known and the bouncers greeted him cheerfully as he walked in on his own and checked in his jacket. The bar had recently opened and was categorised as most by a 'gay bar' but it wasn't. More like just gay friendly and well, relaxed. He scanned the room and quickly noticed some of his friends who simultaneously spotted him and began waving at him eagerly. As he strode over to them a familiar figure caught his eye. It looked like Andrew. Jamie did a double take and sure enough Mr Johnstone, the Head Teacher of his school, was standing sipping a Corona beer next to a table full of people who looked like they were enjoying themselves. He couldn't mistake that tall frame and the impeccable clothes. *What's he doing here?* he asked himself. *I better stay respectable and cut out the tequilas tonight.*

He glanced over once again in disbelief just to be certain it was him and at that moment Andrew looked up and caught his gaze. 'Hi,' he mouthed and waved over at Andrew.

Jamie nodded his head in acknowledgement and turned back to his friends. "Who's that?" one of the girls shrieked looking over Jamie's shoulder. "He is hot!"

"Just a colleague" Jamie confirmed 'A married, heterosexual colleague!"

"Oh well, that's a shame for you" another girl, Claire, piped in. "My gaydar picked him out earlier as a potential boyfriend for you! I think you are in need of some long term love!"

"Thanks honey," he directed at Claire. "But he's taken. Why would I want to settle down anyway when I can be out partying with you guys?"

The girls laughed and clinked their cocktail glasses in agreement as Jamie walked up to the trendy dimly lit bar and ordered himself a vodka and coke.

"Can I buy you that?" Andrew's deep voice from behind was unmistakable.

"Oh hi, urm hello," Jamie spluttered slightly awkwardly, "no I'm OK thanks, I'm actually only having one and heading home anyway," he lied trying to act mature.

"Are you sure? I was just buying a round," he indicated to the tray of drinks he was carrying back to the group of people that were at the table beside him.

"No, honestly, you're fine thanks. Thanks very much for offering."

"OK then, nice to see you," and he turned away.

Jamie tried to peek at the type of people that were in his company. Straight? Gay? Married? Young? Old? Quite a mixture of people Jamie concluded. I thought he would be at home tucked up in his bed by now. Beside his wife. After having a big family dinner. Jamie didn't even think for a moment that Andrew might go out to pubs with his friends at the weekend. He thought of his boss probably like the way the students thought of their teachers. Most of them didn't realise that teachers were humans and had their own social life outside of school, that their life didn't revolve round school all of the time. Although Jamie never suspected that Andrew would ever be in a bar that some thought was gay! How liberal! Here he was thinking he was as straight laced and career focused as they came! I wonder what Jennifer and Caitlyn will say when I tell them? Jamie had to admit though, Andrew did look hot. Really hot. Too hot for a straight, married man!

Chapter 14

"Pleased to meet you too," Jennifer said coyly to Caroline's best man, Stuart. She was being introduced to some of Caroline's closest friends and family that were out to celebrate her and Ryan's engagement. Ryan was quite handsome in the traditional sense but she would never admit that to Caitlyn, who Jennifer could tell was extremely jealous of Caroline, especially now that she was engaged to be married. Although she could freely admit that Stuart, who was tall, tanned and had gorgeous, black, curly hair, was exceptionally sexy with his designer stubble, even without her beer goggles on she was sure. She was even more pleased to overhear that he said he was single. Hoorah! She nipped into the ladies to quickly redo her make up and on her return to Stuart's side, she found Peter in deep conversation with Caroline and Ryan. As she flirted outrageously with Stuart and drank copious amounts of free sparkling wine, she tried to get a little closer to Peter to hear what they were talking feverishly about, but got completely distracted as Stuart started to stroke her thigh underneath the table.

"Shall we get out of here?" he whispered as he ran his hand underneath her skirt.

Jennifer's face flushed scarlet as her eyes darted about the room to make sure no-one was looking, as Stuart's hand rose further and further up her leg to just outside her panties. She didn't stop him, nor did she want him to stop and he started to nuzzle into her neck as his hand stroked the outside of her knickers.

"Yes. Let's get out of here," she eventually replied as she turned to kiss him fully on the lips. She felt as if she was melting into him as his strong arms pulled her close for a few seconds before releasing.

He smiled and slowly picked up his jacket, and Jennifer observed that he was aroused which made her feel faint with anticipation. She grabbed her stuff and he took her by the hand out onto the main street. It was drizzly with rain and although not too cold he wrapped his long dark jacket around her tiny frame anyway to keep her dry. As he did so his hands caressed her body slowly and they couldn't resist kissing passionately like teenagers on the high street. He started to walk away and she followed him to a nearby backstreet where he pushed her against the building wall and kissed her hard whilst pulling up her skirt, parting her legs.

The wine had made her lose her inhibitions and she was lost completely in the moment as she undid his trousers as they embraced fervently. Jennifer entirely forgot that she they were outside where anyone could catch them as he thrust inside her and she groaned in pleasure. His masculine hands expertly ran up her body and touched her breasts underneath her top as she pulled him closer and closer passionately until he climaxed. They giggled awkwardly as they began to re-dress, and just at that point a door opened from a nearby close and elderly couple walked out on to the lane. Jennifer and Stuart looked at each other and couldn't help but laugh as they buttoned up their clothing to the ignorance of the couple. "Do you want to go somewhere quiet?" Stuart asked as he stroked Jennifer's hair.

"I think you were supposed to ask that first," Jennifer replied as they both chuckled again.

"Yeah maybe!" he agreed smiling.

"I need to get home anyway. I have an early start in the morning," Jennifer said, "but we could maybe meet up again?" she quickly added after seeing Stuart's dejected facial expression. She usually liked to try and let the men make the first move about arranging another date, but she felt such a strong connection with him she really wanted to get to know him as well as get some more of what she just received!

"Definitely," he said, "this was quite the first meeting".

She took out her phone from her bag and he took it from her. "Here, I'll put my number in for you. So you can contact me again soon. It really was nice to meet you, Jennifer," he said, eyes twinkling with mischief, as he flagged over a black cab that was passing at the top of the street. As the taxi stopped he opened the door for her and handed back her mobile. Before Jennifer had a chance to say anything else, Stuart pulled her close and kissed her softly on the lips and helped her climb into the cab. He closed the door behind her and it pulled away from the curb, she could see his silhouette standing as the taxi disappeared along the road.

"Where to?" The cab driver grunted at her in a strong Glaswegian accent through the plastic pane of glass.

She sat alone in the back of the cab feeling astonished at what just happened yet euphoric also. She looked at her phone zealously and found his entry. Profile name - Sexy Stu. Along with his number.

She laughed out loud. Sexy Stu all right! She felt herself blush at just the thought of their sexual encounter. She had never done anything like that in her life!

"Where to Miss?" the driver repeated agitatedly.

"Oh sorry, Kent Road please," and the driver swiftly jumped into the next car lane to take her home.

Chapter 15

Caitlyn awoke on her cold leather sofa once again to a silent apartment. The sunlight was starting to emanate through the curtains and she stood up, last night's argument with Peter reappearing into her brain. She walked through into their shared bedroom, intent on patching things up. A good night's sleep had softened her mood. Make-up sex is always better than drunken sex, she reminded herself. She found him in roughly the same spread-eagled position as the evening before and leant over to give him a gentle nudge.

"Hmmf," he snorted without moving.

"Morning," she instigated, trying to sound upbeat but not enough for him to think he was completely off the hook.

"Hmmf," he repeated, again not moving.

"Are you getting up?" she asked, trying not to sound as irritated as she felt.

Caitlyn considered putting on the sexy underwear again, maybe that would entice him…

"What's the time?" he muttered into the pillow.

"Ten past nine," she replied as she looked down at her silver watch. She started to stroke his bare arm and let her hand travel down his back. She started to kiss the nape of his neck slowly as her hand slid into his boxer shorts.

"Stop it!" he ordered. "Sorry babe but I'm shattered. I'm so hungover and I need to wash. I also need to go into work later." His voice trailed off and Caitlyn jumped up from the bed and gathered up her gym gear. *Why bother? Why bother even trying?* she thought inwardly. Caitlyn left him sleeping as she slammed the door behind her and jogged to the gym. She ran hard on the treadmill, running faster and longer than she had in months, clocking up 8 miles in just over an hour. She couldn't stop thinking about Peter and it annoyed her so much that he probably won't be thinking about her, or even think that there was anything wrong. The sweat was pouring off her but pumped with adrenaline she wanted to continue, and attended a spin cycling class afterwards. Usually she made conversation with the other gym goers but she was focused and determined to work as hard as possible. It felt exhilarating. Her legs felt like jelly when she eventually came off the bike 45 minutes later.

That was so hard! she heard others exclaim as they walked back to the shower room. She had to admit that that was one of the hardest workouts she had done in a while but she felt elated, the endorphins were propelling through her system and she had completely relieved herself of stress. *What a stupid argument?* she thought to herself. *Was he not allowed to be tired? Was he not allowed to go to the pub when he wanted? He can't be horny all of the time,* she reasoned to herself. She took the complimentary fluffy white towel the gym provided and leisurely strolled into the sauna to relax before hitting the showers to go home. She entered the flat much more pleasantly than she had left and called out to Peter as she dropped her gym bag on the hall floor. The house remained quiet and as she walked around, she concluded sulkily that Peter must have gone to work. She noticed there were two unread messages on her phone and opened them enthusiastically and expectantly of a soppy apologetic text from Peter to only disappointedly find messages from Jennifer and Jamie. She gathered from their jovial messages that they both seemed to have a great night the evening before and were dying to spill their stories at lunch and shopping in the city today. She knew she should feel good for them, and she did, but their happiness just made her more jealous and depressed. But what the hell, she might as well go for lunch instead of moping about the flat waiting on Peter all day!

Jennifer, Caitlyn and Jamie met in a little Italian themed café in Princes Square Shopping Centre in the city centre of Glasgow. It was quite a pricey and exclusive eatery, but Jamie managed to book them a table online on a inexpensive pre-theatre lunch. As they scanned over the delicious menu, they began to exchange stories from last night's antics, but Caitlyn remained unusually quiet and repressed. Jennifer relayed her 'exhilarating sexual encounter' with the lovely and lustrous Stuart and told them all the intimate details, that were probably a little too graphic for them to digest before any wine, but they listened enthralled anyway and Caitlyn couldn't help seething with jealousy. Caitlyn vowed never to show her bitterness though, as Jennifer and Jamie expected her sex life to be just as good as it had been in the past, all of the time. As far as they were concerned, Caitlyn and Peter were still having wonderful sex every night. She didn't want to admit defeat and tell the truth. *How wrong could they be?* she thought miserably.

"So, how many times have you texted Sexy Stu already then?" Jamie jokily probed Jennifer.

"None!" She exclaimed, "Honestly! I normally text guys immediately but I want to do this right... Although I really really want to! He was lovely!"

"He sounded a bit rough to me," Jamie chuckled.

"Well he was, I suppose. But I like it like that! Well I've only just realised I like that. Love that!" she giggled back, "and where did you get to?" she asked Jamie.

"I went to that new bar/nightclub place in the Merchant City. It was really good. I met up with Georgie, one of my old Uni pals and some of her crew. And you'll never guess who I spotted?" Jamie hesitated. He was about to announce his gossip about seeing Andrew there but he was suddenly compelled to change his story as if to protect him. *Maybe he wouldn't want anyone to know he was there? I'm sure he doesn't want his staff gossiping about him going out on Friday nights attending 'gay' bars?*

"Well, who did you see then?" the girls chimed simultaneously.

"Erm. Shell Suit Bob!" he lied, making up the first possible person that came into his head.

"Who?' Jennifer shrieked, 'That circus guy from the Simpsons?"

"You saw a cartoon character?" Jennifer continued. "Were you on LSD or magic mushrooms again?"

"No, no," Jamie corrected, "Shell Suit Bob. From River City. You know, the Scottish soap on the BBC."

"Ohh," the girls giggled together, "exciting."

83

"Is he good looking?" Caitlyn enquired.

"And more importantly, did you pull this Shell Suit Boaby?" Jennifer asked and then burst into hysterics.

"No!" Jamie replied, laughing heartedly, "Definitely not! I'm looking for love nowadays anyway, not just a one night stand."

"Aye right Mr, since when?" Jennifer asked screwing up her face. "You're not saying much," Jamie accused at Caitlyn, quickly changing the subject.

"Just a bit tired."

"Hot, steamy night for you as well was it?" Jennifer piped in.

"Something like that," she trailed off.

"So how does your Pete know Caroline and Ryan, and of course Sexy Stu?" Jennifer asked Caitlyn intently.

"Hmm?" Caitlyn looked up confused.

"They were talking for ages last night. Not sure on what though. Get him to put a good word in for me with Stuart," she pleaded.

"I don't think you need any good words, I think your actions have spoken volumes!" Jamie interjected.

"And was Peter not with Caroline today?" Jennifer asked Caitlyn.

"What? No. Why?" Caitlyn sharply replied.

Jamie and Jennifer exchanged brief looks.

"Oh no, nothing. I just thought I had seen Peter chatting to her just before you came in, I thought maybe Peter gave you a lift into town or something. I must have got it mixed up," Jennifer explained, "although it probably wasn't him," she added and this made Caitlyn look a bit more relieved.

Although Caitlyn couldn't help but panic inside. *Was he in town with Caroline or a girl instead of work? Was he lying to her?*

Caitlyn tried to hide her annoyance as she explained to them that it definitely could not be Peter as he was working today, as per usual.

"Everything OK in paradise?" Jamie asked thoughtfully.

"Yeah it's good, all good," she replied although she started to doubt her trust in Peter.

Where r u? she texted Peter when she excused herself from the table and went to the bathroom.

Sorry babe, at work, will be back at 6, – sorry for last night, just stressed x

At work my arse! she thought angrily. *Don't be silly Caitlyn,* she spoke to herself. *It obviously wasn't him. Even Jennifer said she only caught a glimpse of him and it must've been someone else.* She tried to put these thoughts to the back of her mind so she could enjoy the rest of her day with her friends.

After an afternoon of browsing the shops without buying anything, Caitlyn took the Underground home slightly after 6pm. Peter was in the kitchen as she arrived in the door and she could smell the aroma of her favourite curry dishes.

"How was work?" Caitlyn asked indignantly.

"Boring as per," he answered, looking up to kiss her on the top of her forehead.

"What did you do for lunch?" she further enquired, studying his face for guilt.

"I forgot to make a sandwich so had to nip into the Princes Square. Ended up getting a burger – whoops! There goes my healthy living. Don't worry, I only got a 99p special, I'm still watching the pennies."

"That's OK. It's fine" she replied, relieved he had admitted being in shopping centre. *It obviously was him then. He must have just been in for lunch when the guys had spotted him. I wonder why Jennifer thought that he was with Caroline? He doesn't even know her that well. Maybe they bumped into each other? Caroline was always in there,* she thought reassuring herself and dismissing any silly nagging doubts. She didn't want to sound like a bunny boiler by prodding him any further.

"Now, let's enjoy our dinner," he declared as he served up the food, "along with some white wine?"
"Of course, yes please," she smiled as they sat down to enjoy their meal, gladly forgetting their earlier arguments.

Chapter 16

The next week at work was flying by at an alarming rate and Caitlyn was struggling to complete all of the tasks that she had put down on her to-do-list. She hated not fulfilling each task by the end of the week as it left her stressed. She also loathed having to take work home for the weekend but with her job it was inevitable. It usually just played on her mind and she could never fully relax. The stresses and workload just seemed to be getting even worse with the development of the new curriculum, there just appeared to be endless tasks to do.

Caitlyn was teaching her senior class for the last period of the week, and after some teacher-led learning activities at the beginning of the lesson on the SMARTboard, they were all assigned questions to do independently. In the meantime she was calling out each pupil to come out to the front of the class to individually discuss their end of unit assessment performance with her.

"Miss?" one of the tall geeky looking 6th year boys called out, hand flailing above his head.

"Yes, Andy?" Caitlyn asked, expecting him to ask for help.

"Can I go to the toilet?" he said pleadingly.

"No Andy, it's only 20 minutes until it's home time, you can go then". She tried to be strict to reinforce the school rule that pupils should only go to the toilets at intervals or in-between classes. She knew herself that kids would just take advantage if they were allowed out in classes as they would just use it to waste time or to

87

get up to something they weren't supposed to. However, he did look genuine in this case, he was now squirming in his seat.

"But Miss, I really do need." He pointed to his empty mineral water bottle on his desk. "I did go at lunchtime, honest."

Caitlyn looked at her clock. "Focus on your work, Andy, if you're still desperate in 5 minutes, I'll think about letting you go. Now back to your work." She felt a little mean about doing this, but she wanted to make sure that her students knew what the rules were and knew not to step over the line.

As she read out the names she was growing more and more nervous as she worked her way through the register as she knew Cameron's name was getting closer. Her heart started to flutter like a little excited teenager. She hadn't felt like this in such a long time. She reminisced to her school days when she would be besotted with a boy, daydreaming about them, being lost for words around them, smiling at the thought of them. God, that's what she felt like now isn't it? No! *Focus!* she instructed herself as she advised the less than conscientious student beside her to attend the supported study sessions that were on offer. This suggestion wasn't met by as much enthusiasm as was desired but it was no surprise. Caitlyn sighed as the girl slowly walked back to her desk, noisily dropping her textbook back down. It was Cameron next. She stared at his name on the list and took a large sip of water before calling out his name. She seemed to linger on his name and looked around the class to see if a student noticed. She half expected them to mock her or recognise that she seemed to be acting differently. Cameron stood up and walked confidently towards her and she tried to look away disinterested as he relaxed into the chair beside her.

Could anyone else feel this tension? She didn't think so. Did the other pupils notice her crimson complexion? She hoped to God they didn't!

She tried not to make eye contact as she launched into a summary of his progress, analysing his excellent score of his Advanced Higher test, but she could feel his dark piercing eyes gazing into her, looking for eye contact. Although Caitlyn was a modest girl, she knew she looked good and couldn't help but be flattered by his admiring stares. She relented and looked directly back at him to ask his opinion. "How do you feel you performed in the test?" she asked, ignoring his flirty gaze.

"Good, I think?" he replied smiling, "Thanks, Miss."

"Did you study?" she said focused on the spreadsheet rather than his face.

"Of course, Miss." He was always courteous and polite when he spoke to her. He seemed so mature and gave respect to his teachers. Just one of those pupils who seemed to be popular not only with his peers but with just about everyone.

Caitlyn was now relieved that she never reported to the Head Teacher about meeting Cameron out in the pub or his little note. He had never mentioned it again so she thought it was best just sweeping it under the carpet and moving on. So far, so good and they both had been talking like any other teacher-pupil relationship, but she felt their eyes and their chemistry was something different. *Maybe he didn't even notice?*

"This is a print out of your progress report so far," she said, and as she reached over to pass it to him their skin touched ever so briefly and she felt her skin tingle like an electric shock. *Did he feel that?* She looked over and his Cheshire cat smile stared back as if in reply to her thoughts. *Yes.* She attempted to make her facial expression nonchalant and ignore it.

"Do I need Supported Study, Miss?" Cameron asked.

She laughed and again guiltily looked around the room to ensure none of the other pupils where aware of her silly flirtation. The other pupils were carefully engrossed in their studies.

"Everyone benefits from extra study," she eventually replied honestly.

"I know. Yes, well I plan on coming."

"Good," she tried to look less elated than she felt. "The time could be useful in doing some past papers in preparation for the final exam. You are one of the only pupils sitting the Advanced Higher so it would give you extra time focusing on the added value unit the others don't have."

"Yes, I'm looking forward to it," he replied.

"Good," she repeated. The one syllable answer was all she could muster and she busied herself with the paperwork on her desk as Cameron excused himself back to his desk.

Don't look at him! She instructed herself. *Do not make eye contact!*

But she couldn't obey and couldn't resist looking at him to see if he was looking back.

"Miss, Miss!" Andy asked again, louder this time, now nearly off of his chair. "I really need to go to the bathroom, I think my testicles might explode!"

The class burst into laughter and turned round to him.

"Off you go Andy, I don't want any accidents in my classroom," Caitlyn said pointing towards the door as he jumped away from his desk, scurrying towards the door, "and I take it you don't take human biology?" she asked after him as he disappeared down the hall. Some of the class giggled or rolled their eyes before settling back to their questions.

She took another deep breath and called out the next name on the pupil register and tried her hardest to put Cameron to the back of her mind. *What is wrong with me?* she asked herself. She felt so guilty for even having these thoughts. *What would Peter think if he found out? Or her work, she would be fired! God, what would her friends think?*

It's nothing! she reassured herself. Nothing was ever going to come of it, so what was the harm? She had never ever thought about another man before, even her fantasies had been completely faithful to her loyal boyfriend. Until now! *What am I playing at?* she scolded herself. *I am going to put Cameron completely out of my mind and focus on my work and my wonderful boyfriend this weekend,* she concluded. Yes, although the couple were a bit strapped for cash at the moment and maybe couldn't dine out, she could plan a romantic weekend in the flat for them. She would listen to his advice and try to be more careful with money. She would buy in his favourite beer, cook him lasagne and just take time out just to relax with each other. They could have a nice big romantic bubble bath with candles like they used to. He had been working so hard recently she had barely seen him or had a proper full conversation with him in weeks that didn't just consist of what was for dinner and whose turn it was to clean up. Maybe they would lie in bed all the next day, only getting up occasionally to get food and drinks for each other. She reminisced how they used to do that regularly and the more she thought about it, the more excited Caitlyn got. Maybe this weekend wouldn't be so boring after all.

Chapter 17

Jennifer was pleased with the progress of her lower school classes. They had progressed a lot since the beginning of term and their behaviour had improved drastically since enforcing stricter routines with them. The majority of them seemed to be enjoying her lessons too and liking more input from ICT. She had hoped to pilot the use of ipads with this class but it was on hold due to budget constraints at the moment. However, she was surprised at the lack of IT skills with some of the younger ones, she had thought they'd all be computer literate from using them from an early age, but it seemed the only things they really knew how to use properly were online games, Facebook and instant chat rooms. She had booked out one of the computer labs for them to complete a presentation and it took much longer than she had hoped which was stressing her out a little. She couldn't believe how noisy a class of 32 pupils could be and how tricky getting them all logged in at once was.

"It's not coming on!" one yelled. She didn't know how to turn on the 'on' button.

"It doesn't work!" another screamed louder. He didn't know how to log on.

"Mine doesn't let me log in," the first pupil shouted again. This time, he didn't spell his name right.

"The internet doesn't work!" another complained. They didn't need to use the internet so they shouldn't have been accessing it anyway, she replied.

"My computer doesn't have Powerpoint," another shouted huffily. After stopping the lesson to go over to assist, she found it immediately and pointed it out to him as she had already done on the board and the other kids around him laughed and joked, "doh", at him for not finding it straight away. "Now, now," she said to them, "be nice." Although she felt like doing that to him too, she had shown on the board what menu to find it twice, he obviously wasn't paying attention.

Two out of the class had forgotten their passwords and she didn't have the power to reinstate them so she had to let them just work in a pair but before long they were causing mischief so she ordered them to sit at the desks in the middle to read which they weren't best pleased about. Maybe that would help them remember their passwords the next time though. 'Miraculously' one of them managed to remember it immediately at that point, but she never allowed them access to the computer.

It was near the end of the lesson that she was really pulling her hair out. One of the boys lashed out and slapped one of the girls in the face. She couldn't believe it. She kept them both behind at the interval to speak to them and deal with the matter, referring it straight to their Guidance Teachers and Senior Management.

"Why did you do that, Steven? Are you OK Rachel?" she asked both of them when she had them on their own.

To her surprise Rachel laughed, "I'm fine Miss. Just a misunderstanding."

"What? What happened?"

94

"Sorry, Miss. I thought she said something else."

"You should never hit anyone, Steven. And never a girl!"

"I know Miss, I'm sorry. It was just a reaction. I didn't mean to take it out on you, Rachel, sorry."

Jennifer faced Steven head on to speak to him, allowing him to lip read as he was partly deaf, "Thank you for apologising Steven but I'm still going to have to refer this. Do you understand?"

"Do you need to Miss? I'm sorry! I'm just getting annoyed with this new hearing aid I'm wearing. I'm pissed off!" he started to rant to her but she let him air his views. "I'm sorry, Miss but I've got this new system I'm supposed to wear and the teachers are supposed to wear this microphone thing but it's just giving me migraines. I can't hear properly with it and the teachers keep forgetting they have them on and talk to someone else. Sorry, again. I'm sorry, Rachel."

"It's fine, Steve, you hit like a wee lassie anyway!" she giggled. Steven laughed with her too, "Why thanks. I would've hit you harder if you were a guy."

"Enough!"

"Sorry," they both said.

"I'm sorry to hear that, Steven, but that doesn't mean you can lash out at anyone. Physical violence is never the answer. Where is your new hearing aid? I've never used it?"

"I stopped using it after period 1 today when Mrs Jamieson shouted at wee DJ so hard it made it squeal so much in my ear that the whole class could hear!"

"Aw Stephen, you should have said! Right well, Steven, you better go to Mr Johnstone's room now, he's expecting you. You can explain what you said to me and I'll give him a little phone."

Steven looked at the floor and sighed "OK. Fine." and walked out the room.

"What happened Rachel, are you OK?"

She laughed "I just said to him, I've just realised that we're in all each other's classes this year."

Caitlyn looked confused, "And? He hit you?"

"Yip. He turned to me and said "I don't wear glasses!" and she laughed.

Jennifer couldn't help but laugh too. "Oh, poor Steven. Just a misunderstanding then? He must get so frustrated."

"Yes."

"Although that doesn't give him a right to hit you."

"I know that but it's fine. It was nothing, it was just a playful thing. I've had worse!"

Jennifer raised her eyebrows.

"You know what I mean!"

"OK, as long as you are OK?"

"Yip"

"OK, off you go. See you tomorrow."

"See ya, Miss!"

Jennifer was attending her fortnightly departmental meeting after a hectic 6 period day and she reluctantly took the nearest available chair which happened to be next to Tommy who didn't even look up to acknowledge her presence. To her annoyance, he politely and pleasantly welcomed the rest of their mixed Social Science faculty colleagues as they eventually all took their seats and busied themselves with reading over agendas, minutes and documents for today's meeting. As a kind gesture, Jennifer offered to refill everyone's coffee as the meeting got underway and everyone accepted apart from Tommy. This was strange, she thought, as he drinks gallons of it every day. Have I done something to offend him?

As the meeting progressed, the topic of behaviour issues in classes came up and a discussion on school rules and sanctions began. They exchanged different methods that worked such as moving disruptive pupil seats, issuing formal warnings as well as detentions, incorporating more group and interactive work to engage the students, planning out detailed lessons, merit systems and rewards for good behaviour once a week. Jennifer honestly admitted to the group that although she employed most of these techniques too, she was still having difficulty with one of her classes.

In particular with problematic and obtuse John who had been really insolent to her all week and was refusing to fulfil some of her instructions including completing homework. His impertinent behaviour was escalating and was really affecting her now as well as majorly disrupting her lessons, although she tried to play it down to everyone else. Her colleagues sympathised with her and reassured her that they all get them from time to time and offered horror stories of badly behaved students that they had dealt with. One teacher gave

97

Jennifer praise on how well she handled her class and comforted her with telling her of some of the horrible disruptions that had happened to her before, including a pupil jumping out of a 2nd floor window breaking his leg, and another threatening her with a knife. This did, in fact, make her a little relieved that she didn't have that to contend with, but it was a little bit worrying of what may come in the future!

Tommy, who had not joined in on the conversation so far, laughed a little before saying to Jennifer in a condescending tone, "It all comes with experience, young Jennifer." He looked around the table for approving glances before continuing, "I can see you are struggling to control your classes but I am only next door if you need some help. I've not had a problem with pupils' behaviour before, but I can imagine it is distressing for you. I'm sure if you work at it, it will improve. Bring back the belt I say," he chuckled.

Jennifer looked at him in disbelief. Had he just said that? He knows I only have 'trouble' with one class, one pupil in fact not any others. And the reason he doesn't have any behavioural issues as he just lets his pupils do what they want in his lessons and never issues any homework! And he has never EVER offered her any help in the past. Jennifer was speechless. She looked around the table but to her dismay the other staff members were nodding in agreement to him and Liz, the Head of Department, thanked him for his suggestions.

She continued to remind all the teachers that if a pupil continued to disobey classroom rules, then they were to be issued with detentions or referred to her to deal with. Liz was always supportive but on this occasion, Jennifer got the feeling that she was talking only to her and that she thought that she wasn't coping with her workload. At this point, Jennifer just wanted to cry.

At least she had another date with Stuart tonight to make her feel better. She had been on quite a few dates and they were now talking regularly on the phone with each other. She had wanted to look him up on Facebook, to look at photos and past messages, but unfortunately he had said he wasn't really an online type of person. Maybe it was because he was a little older. He had invited her out to a small secluded restaurant on the outskirts of Glasgow for dinner. She had never heard of it and she had suggested just meeting at his or somewhere closer to home since it was a school night, but he insisted so she didn't want to refuse. Either way, she knew from the saucy text messages that she was receiving that she was going to get some action with him again tonight, so she didn't care where the starter was going to be!

Chapter 18

It was Friday lunchtime and the staffroom was busy with teachers collecting mail from their pigeon holes, filing away paperwork before the 3.30pm deadline whilst munching down their lunch, and exchanging rants about this morning's classes along with friendly stories about their plans for the weekend ahead. Caitlyn, Jennifer and Jamie were at their usual table, joined, unusually, by Caroline. Caitlyn thought that this was because she just wanted to rub it in that she was engaged and to show off her big, platinum set diamond ring.

"Oh I just had the most wonderful weekend last week," Caroline gushed, "it was just so hectic! I cannot wait to get home and just have a quiet weekend with my fiancé! Ryan is cooking one of his delectable specials tonight!"

"Don't you have him well trained?" Jamie guffawed.

"I know!" she heartily chortled, "What are all of you up to?" she enquired, more interested than she had been in months.

"Quiet one too," Caitlyn replied as she daydreamed about what she needed to pick up from Asda on her way home for her romantic weekend in her and Peter's love-nest. *Haagen Daz Icecream and whipped cream!* She thought as inspiration struck, a smile creeping on to her lips as she imagined what her and Peter could get up to.

"Oh, are you not going out with the gang while Peter is away?" Caroline asked her.

"Sorry?" Caitlyn asked back bemused.

"I thought you'd be out clubbing or something keeping yourself occupied while Peter was away with work. He's such a hard working guy Peter, isn't he? He was telling me last weekend he works over 50 hours per week!"

"Yeah," Caitlyn said back, through gritted teeth. She didn't want to admit to Caroline firstly, that she had no idea that Peter was working away at the weekend and secondly, that he hadn't even mentioned that he was speaking to her last weekend! She was raging! Why was she the last one to know!

Caitlyn's anger was boiling under her cool exterior but she thought Jennifer and Jamie picked up on it.

"Aren't we going out in the West End for cocktails Saturday night?" Jennifer cheerfully asked.

"Yes we are," Jamie replied smiling looking over to Caitlyn for agreement.

"Yes we are then, of course, cocktails AND dancing Saturday night," Caitlyn said, still boiling with fury at Peter. She had now decided that she was going to go out with her friends and have a good time regardless of Peter. However, she wasn't going to reveal to them that Peter had been discussing his plans with Caroline but failed to inform his live-in girlfriend of his weekend plans!

"Great! That's settled then." Jamie said flashing a big smile at the group.

"What's settled?" a loud confident male voice questioned. It was Andrew.

They all looked up at him awkwardly, unsure of how to act in front of their boss. It was unusual for him to eat in the staff room with the other teachers. It was unusual for him to be in the staff room during lunchtimes at all. He was usually on patrol in the common areas of the school, disciplining pupils from his office or dealing with the regular emergencies that occurred in a busy, populated school. The rest of the staffroom seemed to quieten down, people speaking in more hushed tones, groups of people dispersing. Andrew didn't make people feel intimidated the way other Head Teachers had done in the past and in other schools and always came across as friendly and approachable. Nonetheless, a high proportion of the staff couldn't relax with their manager in earshot. In addition, although Andrew was well respected by most, there were many of the older generation of teachers who couldn't help but resent him because of his success especially at such a young age.

"Just the watering hole these three are going to be frequenting tomorrow night," Caroline piped in, like a little girl ratting on a naughty friend.

"Ah, very good," Andrew replied smiling "and where is the lucky location? Are you going back to *Couture*?" he directed at Jamie.
"No. No, I don't think so. I think we're heading out the West End. Probably Ashton Lane for cocktails," Jamie said as he tried not to blush. The girls stared at him as if to demand answers but he never expanded.

"I really liked it in Couture," Andrew continued, "heading out again myself tomorrow, probably will end up there again. It's handy as it's close to the train station, will be aiming to get the last train home."

"That's just when the party will be getting started!" Caitlyn jokily said, and Caroline shot her a look as if to say 'too far – that's the boss' but Caitlyn ignored it.

Andrew let out a genuine hearty contagious laugh that made the rest of them giggle. "Yes, you are probably right. I'm sure I'll be ready to go home by midnight though! Have a good time, guys," he said, as he turned his back to answer the loud mobile phone that was ringing in his hand whilst walking towards the door with a wave of his hand. Jamie let his eyes linger on him as he disappeared out the room.

The girls' were almost falling off of their seats staring at Jamie with curiosity.

"Well?" Jennifer shrilled, "Spill!"

"What?" Jamie coolly replied.

"You never mentioned you met Mr HT, your boss, in Couture on Saturday night?" Caitlyn exclaimed.

"Hang on. Isn't that a gay club?" Caroline piped in.

"I forgot," Jamie lied.

"What? Aye right, you can remember Shell Suit Bob but not your own boss?" Caitlyn asked.

"I barely saw him. I just bumped into him at the bar. And no, just because I was there doesn't mean it was a gay bar, Caroline."

"Who was he there with?" Jennifer asked intrigued.

"I don't know, just a bunch of his friends I think."

"He has friends?" Caitlyn jokily asked.

"I hope you were behaving!?" Jennifer added.

"Of course! He is only in his early thirties for Christ sake," Jamie said defensively. "He is human and allowed to go out once in a while!"

"We know that Jamie," Jennifer said, "it's just still weird the thought of him out in the places we go. Especially if he sees us in our full party mode! I always think of him as much older than he really is just because of his position."

"I know, me too," Caitlyn agreed. "I could've never imagined seeing my old Head Teacher from school out in a cool place like Couture! Thank God!"

"He is pretty trendy actually, Mr Johnston," Caroline commented "and quite hot," she added quietly to ensure no-one else in the staffroom could overhear.

The group burst into fits of giggles. "Caroline!" Jennifer pretended to scold, "You're an engaged woman!"

"That doesn't mean I can't look!"

The end of lunch bell rung out interrupting their conversation and the teachers frantically packed up their stuff.

"Right, get your glad rags on, meeting at 6pm tomorrow night – you know where to be!" Jamie shouted at the girls as they filtered down the corridor to get back to their classrooms for the last 2 lessons of the day, careful not to announce to pupils and staff that they were heading out on the town to party, that would give them all something to talk about!

104

Chapter 19

Caitlyn had felt so lonely and agitated that weekend. She was looking forward to her night out with Jamie and Jennifer but couldn't help being annoyed at Peter. She had phoned him directly after work yesterday and tried to keep calm but she couldn't help getting angry with him. "I'm so sorry, honey," he had apologised, "I am sure I told you. This project is really important for my job. If I can get this work complete in London, the sooner this project can be wrapped up and we can have our weekends free again."

She forgave him, it wasn't his fault, he had been trying so hard with his career and knew that these business trips were just part and parcel of moving up the career ladder. That didn't excuse her feelings of disappointment that she was missing a romantic weekend to which she had been looking forward. Her thoughts started to drift to Cameron. She couldn't help wondering if he would be out tonight. Would she bump into him again in the same bar? She felt excited at the thought that he might be there. She knew she wouldn't do anything with him or probably even talk to him, but it didn't hurt to have a bit of eye candy in the pub now and again. She also knew that Cameron admired her and it would be good to be appreciated a little bit.

Caitlyn spent nearly 3 hours in the gym on Saturday morning. Her friends never came with her to the gym but she didn't mind. She loved the time on her own to spend time with her thoughts while she worked up a sweat. The usual suspects were there, she recognised many of them. The big muscle men that hovered over the free weights, spotting for each other and grunting occasionally, swigging from their protein shakes. The older ladies, now retired and looking for a hobby. Then there was the perfect posers, the lithe girls and guys, who had the tight designer gym gear, perfect tans and haircuts but never broke a sweat, dancing round the exercise machines catching glimpses of themselves in the full-length mirrors pretending to themselves and others that they were working out.

Then there were the 'proper' gym goers. She liked to think that she would put herself into this category. The ones that went there to work hard, pushing their bodies to the limits, engrossed in their workouts usually dripping with sweat. Not a pretty sight most of the time she had to admit but Caitlyn loved it. She felt elated when the last track of the body combat class finished as she stretched off. She weighed herself for the first time in months in the changing room afterwards and was surprised but pleased to notice that she had lost half a stone. She was over the moon! She hadn't been this slim since she was about 18!

She had been for her monthly wax earlier on in the week which consisted of an eyebrow, leg and Brazilian bikini wax and her skin felt so much more supple and smooth than it had been in the past. Her tan from her holiday had started to fade so she topped it up nicely with St Tropez and she felt quite happy with her body as she stared at her reflection. She actually felt quite confident getting naked in the changing room whereas before she would hide herself under her towel, not wanting to bare an inch of skin. At 5 foot 6, even although Caitlyn had always been sporty and slim, she had always felt a bit self-conscious about her figure. But as she slipped into her size 10 skinny jeans she realised they were now far too big for her. She had a skip in her step as she walked home to prepare for her night out.

Chapter 20

Jamie and Jennifer were lounging about in the shared living room of their city centre pad, with a music channel on the LCD TV blaring the latest chart hits. They were sitting on opposite sofas with laptops perched on their laps, both of them still in their pyjamas even though it was 2pm in the afternoon. Breakfast and lunch leftover plates were scattered around them along with their work bags filled to the brim with jotters for marking, discarded long ago in favour of Facebook and gossip forums.

"Did you see Tommy's holiday snaps on his profile?" Jamie quizzed Jennifer jokily without looking away from the screen.

"Who?" she replied as dedicated to her own laptop as him.

"Your classroom neighbour and loving friend" he replied sarcastically.

Jennifer peered over her screen to catch Jamie's eyes. "Are you serious?" she asked, "He is on Facebook?"

"What, you're not his friend?"

"Erm, like NO! I'm not his friend in reality why would I add him on Facebook. Why did you add him?" Jennifer asked quite defensively.

"I haven't, calm down Jenny. I'm just Facebook stalking. I want to find out if he is as evil as you make out."

Jennifer shot him a glance as she typed in Tommy's name in Facebook. She too was interested in finding out what he was really like.

"Oh my God!"

"You found him then."

"He IS on Facebook AND he is worse than I first thought. Even his profile picture makes me cringe!" Jennifer exclaimed "I can't look at him anymore, I just want to punch him!"

"Is he that bad?"

"Yes he is that bad, Jamie! You don't have to work with him directly. I've tried to be nice to him, to warm to him, to let him share my resources, I've given him countless lesson plans that he sneers at, I've set up assessments for him and even have taken his detention duty 3 times this week without even moaning to him and I get nothing in return except for snidey comments at our Departmental Meetings. He is so arrogant, bigoted and sexist it's unreal!"

"He is just jealous of you, Jen. Bite your lip, he'll soon leave you alone. In fact, he'll soon be an OAP – he'll probably get one of those early retirement packages to get rid of him. He has lost any enthusiasm for the job if he ever had any, and it shows."

"I know. It's just hard to live with every day, especially as I think my Head of Department thinks the sun shines out of his arse and I think Mr Johnstone thinks so too."

"Nah, everyone knows what he is like, Jen. C'mon he's the guy who writes one word comments on the report cards, is continually late, refuses to take part in any extra-curricular activities and is out the door at 3.30pm everyday even if there is a compulsory meeting on – he's transparent. Don't worry about him. I mean, look, he's being really classy wearing a football top AND wearing socks and sandals in this picture!" Jamie pointed at one of Tommy's holiday photographs that he had uploaded and laughed out loud. It looked to Jennifer like he was on holiday somewhere in Spain and right enough was wearing a Rangers FC replica football top along with cut-off pale denim jeans made into homemade shorts, white socks and black sandals with the obligatory pint of beer in one hand and a half smoked cigarette in the other. She had to laugh, as he did look funny, it was strange to see him outwith his crumpled shirts and stale chinos.

She flicked through the rest of the photos quickly, scanning them for any signs of family or friends that would make her empathise with him more, make him out to be more human. Although secretly she was really hoping to discover something sinister so she could justify her hatred for him and expose him to the rest of the world.

"Oh my God," Jamie exclaimed. "Did you see that he has his religion down as Protestant and proud?"

"Doesn't surprise me now after seeing some of these photos of him and his prize possession of a Union Jack!" She knew he was an avid Rangers supporter from the comments he had made in work, and the banter he had with some of the other guys, but didn't realise he was such a staunch follower.

"It's all ego talk from him. He's harmless," she continued. She knew sectarianism was a part of living in Glasgow and understood most people said things they really didn't mean or even understand. However, she also knew there were some in the city that take football rivalry far too seriously and religion just gets mixed up

110

in it for no good reason. She really hoped that although she really disliked Tommy, that any animosity they had between them didn't start because of her Catholic background. She was the only non-Protestant teacher in her department but never thought that it was an issue. She had never contemplated that before, but that seed of thought was now implanted in her brain and she couldn't help ponder it for the rest of the day.

Chapter 21

Caitlyn strode into the West End bar full of confidence to meet up with her friends later that evening. Her black lace dress clung to her every curve and she knew she looked good. She was aware of admiring glances from those around her and she loved every second as she joined Jennifer and Jamie, who were already perched at the bar with a jug of freshly made Cosmopolitan.

"You look amazing!" Jennifer gushed, as Caitlyn took a bar stool beside them.

"Ditto. Gorgeous!" Jamie added, as he looked her up and down whilst filling her glass.

"Thank you. You both too," she retorted truthfully.

Jennifer was wearing a long-sleeved navy chiffon tunic dress with matching dark blue patent platform heels. Her hair had been beautifully curled to look naturally effortless whilst her soft makeup had been applied perfectly dewy. Jamie sported a casual black suit, grey shirt with a silver scarf expertly knotted around his neck instead of his usual formal tie. They all looked completely different to how they normally compare Monday to Friday at school. The pupils would barely recognise them if they saw them like this, Caitlyn thought. However, Caitlyn couldn't help hoping that Cameron would be out and would see her looking so good.

The friends continued to gossip as two jugs of cocktails were demolished and they moved on to bottles of Pinot Grigio. Jamie and Jennifer couldn't wait to tell Caitlyn all about finding Tommy Greig on Facebook and wasted no time in recalling all the details that they had uncovered. Jamie didn't want to mention that he had also looked up Andrew Johnstone. He couldn't help it but he had started to feel a slight crush towards him over the past few weeks. No, he scolded himself. Not a crush, just admiration. Curiosity. He hadn't found him on Facebook unfortunately, but did find some of his friends that had posted happy photos of him at various nights out, friendly get-togethers as well as some family outings. He was surreptitiously disappointed that Andrew had looked so content in the pictures. Jamie had found himself thinking about Andrew more often and covertly wishing that he wasn't married. And if only he was gay too of course! That would be nice, he dreamed. Maybe he was still in the closet and pined for a relationship with a man, with me? Jamie wished. He knew it was an absurd thought but Andrew had been paying him more and more attention over the past few months.

Jamie had never 'liked' a straight man before, well not since he was in Secondary School himself and fancied his Music instructor, but he put that down to a silly boy crush. This felt different. It felt more grown up. It felt like the feelings were possibly mutual. Like Andrew felt the same way, as if he was homosexual too. Nothing had really been said about feelings or relationships between them, but every time they were together now Jamie's feelings intensified. He prayed that Andrew would be out in Glasgow tonight, to bump into him, even just to have a conversation with him. He was eager to find out more about this handsome career man. Could he be bisexual? Does he really have feelings for me too? As he looked around the crowded bar Jamie didn't take a second look at the any of the other men, they didn't seem to compare to the stature of Andrew. They were no longer on his radar.

The moment had come that Caitlyn was privately waiting for. Cameron was out. The three tipsy friends had moved on to a nearby club and she spotted him immediately from across the dance floor. She was pleased to see that he wasn't with anyone she recognised, at least not pupils and they looked a lot older than 18. She could feel his eyes on her as she danced and she pretended that she hadn't noticed him. Caitlyn tried to ignore him completely as she knew it could end in disaster. "Psst," Jennifer whispered loudly in her ear, "ain't that that Cammy boy from your senior class over there?"

Caitlyn tried to act surprised as she turned round slowly to where Jennifer was indicating. "Don't look!" she squealed, "We don't want any pupils seeing us and spoiling the night."

"OK, OK."

"Well, is it him?"

"Yeah, think so," Caitlyn replied casually, turning her attention back to her two friends and trying to look disinterested.

"It is," Jamie concluded. "I used to have him in S4. Nice boy. Manners too which is refreshing in a young footballer."

"Quite hot actually," Jennifer drunkenly added.

"Jennifer!" Caitlyn reprimanded as Jamie roared with laughter but she couldn't help smile either.

"Sorry, but he is. For a pupil I mean. He looks much older than the rest. Oh don't worry I wouldn't do anything, he's a student for God's sake! Plus, he's 18," she added with a sly grin.

"Yeah and how do you know that?" Caitlyn asked intrigued, giggling. She felt guilty but relieved that at least Jennifer acknowledged his charms.

"The big *Happy 18th* badge he is wearing kind of gave it away!"

"Don't be daft," Caitlyn said to Jennifer, "I remember you telling me that you did that when you were only 15 just so you could get in to the local bar? It always worked a treat with the bouncers you said...."

"Oh yeah," Jennifer said as she and Jamie giggled at the memory, "but he is 18 I think, I remember his guidance teacher saying years ago that he was older than the rest for some reason."

"I heard he's got a trial with Rangers," Jamie continued. "I heard some of the guys at work talking about it. He's seemingly already been picked for the Under 18's Scotland squad."

Caitlyn couldn't help be impressed. It made him sound even more intriguing.

"Maybe he's here with his rich sexy footballer friends?" Jennifer excitedly looking around the bar at the smartly dressed men nearby but didn't move to approach any of them.

"Hmmm, what about sexy Stu?" Caitlyn enquired.

Jennifer smiled coyly.

"Wow, you must like him or you would've pounced on one of them by now!" Jamie joked.

"Shut up, my loved up friend!" she jokingly chastised Caitlyn. "Just because you already have the man of your dreams. Footballers are nice eye candy. And yes you are right, I normally would've liked to flirt with one of them, but I'm keeping myself for Stuart."

The three giggled.

"Aww, Stuart is it now? Must be serious! Sounds like love." Caitlyn said winking. "And less of the loved up crap, I can *look* too you know!"

"Better just looking anyway," Jamie concluded. "I know it's a cliché, but those footballer types are normally arrogant, big headed and thick as shit."

"Mostly I bet," Caitlyn agreed, "but I bet they have great bodies underneath those pristine suits," as she glanced over in Cameron's general direction again, smiling.

"Never mind them, let's dance!" Jamie shouted changing the subject as one of their favourite old pop tunes came on. He was soon forgotten about after another drink and they danced all night to the music blasting from the sound system.

It was around 3 am when they queued up at the back of the nightclub to collect their coats. Caitlyn wiped away the beads of sweat on her brow and she and Jamie laughed heartily at their new rosy complexion in the mirrors. They had partied all night and they had both drunk much more than they had intended to but were in good spirits. "Where is Jennifer?" Caitlyn asked as she tried to brush some of the frizz out of her hair.

"I don't know actually. I haven't seen her in a while. I presumed she was at the loo. Let's have a party?!"

The pair walked down the corridor to the ladies lavatory as Caitlyn popped in to shout on Jen but to no avail. "Yay, a party!" Caitlyn's eyes gleamed but her words were drunkenly slurred. "Check your phone though," she instructed as she remembered Jennifer wasn't with them.

Surely she's not away home with Cameron? Caitlyn irrationally thought as she searched the room for Cameron's presence. No Cameron. No Jennifer.

"Wait a minute" Jamie said smiling "I've got a text from her, the little floozy! Check your phone"

Sorry guys to ditch you but Sexy Stu has some business for us to attend to, have fun! Ps Jamie please take me home some Irn Bru, take your time though ;-)

"Looks like our party plans are ruined then" Caitlyn grumbled jealously as she tripped over the steps to leave the club.

"Aye, looks like we're ditched." Jamie retorted "Ach, no worries - c'mon let's go and get a kebab and some Irn Bru. Better than a party or a man any day!"

Chapter 22

It was Sunday morning and Caitlyn awoke to her empty bed, feeling worse for wear after her big night out. Her head pounded and her throat felt as dry as the Sahara desert. She lifted her head slightly to see her clothes scattered across the room along with an empty kebab box. At least she managed to get undressed and hadn't lost her handbag, she thought hearteningly. However, she was disappointed to find she hadn't managed to take off her make up by the black evidence on her pillow. She now completely regretted having those tequila slammers after midnight. Whoops. And the Jager bomb shots, she remembered. Double whoops. She rolled over trying to escape the painful sunlight from the window. It also felt worse because she knew she was going to waste the entire Sunday because she felt so awful and would spend the whole day in bed eating junk food, drinking Irn Bru and reliving every detail of the previous evening on the phone to Jennifer and Jamie, gripped by the 'fear'.

She could barely remember a thing from the evening before. Although she remembered Cameron was there. She knew she had consumed far too much alcohol. She inwardly groaned as she tried hard to painstakingly remember. The vague memories started to come back to her in flashbacks along with waves of nausea as she deliberated and toyed with herself panicking on what she did.

"You didn't do anything wrong" Jamie said on speaker phone as she heard him type into his laptop. "I'm feeling fine. I don't think you can handle your drink as well anymore. I'm disappointed in you," he said jokingly.

"Urgh…" was all that she could muster down the phone.

"We had a great night" Jamie rattled on "I'm putting the photos on Facebook now."

Caitlyn didn't reply as she was scared that if she opened her mouth she may just be sick right there and then. She didn't even want to move a muscle and couldn't care less at this point if she made it to the bathroom or not!

"Get some salt and vinegar crisps down you, love, and you'll be grand!"

"We weren't even that drunk," Caitlyn could hear Jennifer piping in to the conversation from the background. "We've been a lot worse!"

"We never fell or spoke to anyone we shouldn't have?" Caitlyn asked quietly.

"God no, we were very well behaved, we just danced. Like who? We did do a lot of dancing. And drinking, obviously! Honestly."

Caitlyn started to feel better then remembered Cameron like a jolt.

"What about that pupil that was there? Cameron?"

"What about him? We saw him when we entered the club but didn't see him again. Don't worry! You didn't do anything silly in front of him, stop panicking! If he did see you, all he can say is that he saw you in a club, looking hot, drinking and dancing with your friends. Oh the scandal…" Jamie said sarcastically.

Caitlyn reflected on this and tried to rationalise her thoughts. Of course there was nothing wrong with going out, she was just pleased she didn't try to talk to him or do anything silly in front of him.

"But that is a different story for our Jen!" Jamie declared loudly for her to overhear.

"Go on" Caitlyn replied, now forgetting her anxiety.

"Well, I arrived home around 3.30am. The good friend that I am, I took my time to give her space and picked us up essentials from the 24 hour supermarket. But after two hours, two hours..." he repeated extra loud for emphasis, "they were still going at it when I came home!"

"Lucky them," Caitlyn whispered under her breath.

"Not even in her bedroom, the tramp!" Jamie affectionately teased Jennifer and Caitlyn could hear her happily laughing in the background.

"Where were they then?" Caitlyn asked curiously, "the living room?"

"Nope."

"Where then?"

"The hall!"

"The hall?"

Jennifer snatched the telephone from Jamie to justify herself. "Yes the hall! And Caitlyn, it was magnificent! We couldn't wait to get to the bedroom. He is just so passionate, the sex was amazing! We actually started in the back of the taxi but the cab driver went mental at us and threw us out down the street!"

Jamie snatched the phone back, "Right that's enough of the details, you slag, we get it. Amazing sex, can't keep your hands off each other, blah blah blah. I am jealous."

Caitlyn had to admit that she was too. She missed the times when her and Peter used to rip each other's clothes off in the heat of the moment, not being able to contain themselves. Sex was all her and Peter thought about, talked about and did! When they would have it next... Where they would have it... What they would do... What positions they would be in... All of their wonderful fantasies and role plays. And now, she hated to admit, it had seemed to fizzle out. Stale. Stagnant, even. Peter was always away with work and when he was here he never seemed to want sex with her. He was never excited to see her anymore, and barely touched or kissed her. They were both busy with work and just seemed to argue about tidying up or spending too much money. She couldn't help feel frustrated and lonely. She hung up the phone and spent the rest of the day being miserable and watching soap omnibuses on her bedroom TV, ignoring Jamie and Jennifer's Facebook messages about new photos from last night, she couldn't bear the thought of looking at them.

By 4pm and after a few power naps and countless bottles of fizzy water, Caitlyn was beginning to feel a little better and forced herself to get up and go for a shower. She knew Peter would be arriving home soon and wanted to look good for him. At least respectable. He hadn't phoned, which was unusual, but she was hopeful that meant that he was on his way home. The shower instantly revived her and she knew she was recovering when she heard her belly rumble looking for food. She decided to ignore the cries for food, she had surely had enough last night with all that pizza and kebabs at the end of the night, and she wanted to keep her stomach flat for Peter.

She chose plain white cotton underwear that she knew Peter loved before slipping on a casual tunic dress. She would normally get back into her pyjamas if she had no plans but she was sure that Peter would phone to ask for a lift back from the airport and was determined to look as sexy as possible. She was intent on subtly reigniting the passion between herself and Peter, and attracting him back to bed.

After a lot of pacing around the flat and more water consumption due to her 'drooth', Peter eventually entered the flat around 8pm, dropping his bags to the floor with a sigh.

"Hey, traveller," She called to him from the living room. "How are you?"

He walked into the kitchen and she could hear doors getting opened and closed.

"Knackered!" he shouted back, "and starving. What's for dinner?"

"Whatever you want," Caitlyn replied and stood up to meet him in the kitchen. "Did you get the bus in?"

"No, got a lift," he replied as he rifled through the fridge.

"Who from?" She moved closer to try and lean in for a kiss but he was focused now on the freezer.

"Just someone from work. Was on the same flight as me. What a stressful weekend, I am so tired. Did you not make dinner?"

"No, thought you'd be home earlier and you never called. I thought we could maybe go out like we used to? Maybe go to that Thai place on the corner? Or we could get a takeaway from that brilliant Indian like we used to get? The one with the awesome spiced onions and vegetable pakora?"

Peter looked at her like she was crazy. "It's extortionate there! I've been working all weekend and desperate just to get home," he exclaimed. "What have you been doing all day?" he said accusingly.

"Nothing much, sorry, I know I should've made dinner but I'm feeling awful."

"Were you out last night again?" he said, facing her directly for the first time since arriving home.

"Yeah. I went out with Jen and Jamie," she whispered, the feeling of guilt washing over her.

"Caitlyn," he scolded, "I bet you spent a fortune on cocktails. I thought we were trying to save money for a new place?"

"Sorry," she said sheepishly. "I know, I was just bored and lonely. I didn't spend that much," she lied as she put her arms around his waist and she could feel his body soften.

"It's OK," he said, starting to smile as kissed her on the forehead gently, "We all need our treats, I'm glad you weren't in on your own."

"I'll make you something now," Caitlyn continued as she pulled out of his embrace. "What do you want?"

"Anything quick, whatever you want."

"Stir fry? Chicken Kievs? Pizza? Super noodles?" she laughed as he made faces at her suggestions.

"How about we just get a carry out?"

"What happened to saving money?"

"As I said, we need to treat ourselves now and again. Let's get that Indian."

"Really?" Caitlyn asked warily, "Are you sure?"

"Sure. I'll go and shower, you go and pick it up."

"OK, deal."

Caitlyn contentedly walked down the road to the nearby restaurant to pick up their regular takeaway order of mixed vegetable pakora, spiced onions, lamb dopiaza curry with pilau rice and a peshwari naan. It had been months since they had done this together and she was now really looking forward to their cosy evening in. This would definitely cure her hangover, she thought. She quickly dived into the supermarket and bought some more juice and a chocolate fudge cake for dessert too. Why not spoil him, he's been working hard all weekend and all I've been doing is going to the gym and out clubbing with my friends!

After their indulgent meal, Peter and Caitlyn sat on the couch watching TV. Caitlyn nudged Peter delicately with her foot and ran it up his leg but he didn't flinch. As she leaned over to him to undo his top button she realised he was fast asleep. There goes their night of passion. Undeterred she continued to unbutton his shirt, pressing her body against his. He continued to sleep. She was disappointed as she was in need of loving from him. However, she realised how tired he must be and nudged him gently to wake up to move into bed.

He walked like a zombie into their bedroom as he dove under the covers fully clothed. She talked to him gently making him aware that she was getting naked in front of him but he didn't stir. "I'm naked," she purred as she stroked his face softly. Still no movement. She conceded, tired herself, and cuddled herself into Peter's warm body. She would try again in the morning.

Chapter 23

After speaking to Caitlyn on the phone, Jamie and Jennifer spent yet another afternoon lounging in their flat, only venturing out briefly to buy the Sunday papers, bacon butties and Danish pastries from the local bakery. The school work that they took home kept getting put off for yet another hour. As they quickly consumed their brunch, they surfed the internet again and gossiped about last night's antics.

"What a night," Jennifer gushed.

"Yeah, yeah, I've heard it all before," Jamie replied rolling his eyes.

"I know. But this time Jamie, I think I really like him. I mean, really like him."

"Serious?" Jamie looked up from the screen.

"Seriously. I can't stop thinking about him and we've hardly seen each other that much."

"Why isn't he here anyway?"

"He couldn't stay over. Had work early in the morning or something. Gutted."

"Well you certainly made the most of your time together by the looks of things," Jamie playfully said throwing a cushion at her.

"Yes, we did," she replied and smiled back mischievously.

"Has he messaged you yet?"

"Yes. Only 10 times but I would blush if I told you the contents…"

Jamie groaned over dramatically and threw the last remaining cushion on the sofa at Jennifer who caught it as she stood up to leave the room.

Jamie was more interested in finding out what Andrew had been doing last night. He daydreamed and wondered if he had been out last night. Jamie couldn't help but be disappointed that he wasn't out in the West End like he thought he would be. He envisaged bumping into him again and striking up an intelligent and stimulating conversation maybe about Education or the current economic climate. Maybe his knowledge of literature would impress him. Jamie fantasised about flirting with him and Andrew asking him to share a few drinks with him. He searched through his Facebook friends again online in the hope that one of them would post another photo or status update about Andrew but again, no luck. He knew he was being irrational and he would be mortified if anyone knew he was doing this, but he simply couldn't help it. He just could not get him out of his head.

Chapter 24

Caitlyn's classroom seemed excruciatingly bright to her on Monday morning and the kids seemed abnormally loud. The remnants of yesterday's hangover were determined to stay with her for yet another day. She arrived an hour early to prepare her lessons as her good intentions of working on the Sunday did not go to plan and unfortunately the bag of marking she took home to do came back untouched. Another thing she would need to try and catch up on today she thought grumpily.

She grimaced as the school bell shrilled in her ears signalling interval and she ushered her class into the corridor and they scurried away to the canteen. A few of them started to run as they panicked they weren't going to get to the front of the queue, but she didn't have the energy to shout at them or instruct them to walk like she would normally. Instead she was looking forward to a few minutes peace to check her emails and grab a quick cup of green tea. She wasn't a caffeine addict and did enjoy a good cup of coffee or tea but tried to be good during the day with her diet. She normally just drank water but she was in need of a warm cup of tea and put a little bit of honey in it to sweeten it up.

"What are you doing here?" Jane Watson said to her as she stirred her tea.

"What do you mean? It's break time," Caitlyn replied, confused.

"It's your interval detention duty, remember?"

"Shit!" Caitlyn had completely forgotten it was her turn once again.

She abandoned her tea and hurriedly power walked down the hall to the classroom a few of the departments shared for detention duty. She opened the door quickly and let the small queue of boys in to the room and signalled to them to take a seat at the desks. Caitlyn always had good behaviour in her lessons and had worked hard to achieve respect from the children. However, detention duty could sometimes be another kettle of fish. It was always the troublesome pupils that were there, and there altogether as a group. If one of them started misbehaving it was quite common for all of them to join in en masse. She kept herself composed and tried to come across as strict but fair nonetheless. The last thing she needed this morning was dealing with any incidents. At least it wasn't lunchtime detention she thought, she only needed to take them for 10 minutes and it would be back to work. Although, I've missed my only break today, she thought miserably to herself.

As she took the teacher's desk at the front of the room, she looked up to find none other than Cameron standing before her.

"Hello Cameron," she uttered trying to keep her poise, "what can I do for you? I presume you aren't here for detention?"

The other pupils on detention looked up, pleased of the distraction. "Get on with your work," she ordered them calmly and their heads looked back to the pages on their desks.

"No," he laughed, "of course not, Miss McDonald. I'm here to speak to you."

The fear in the pit of her stomach grew and her mouth went dry. She couldn't speak. Oh no, what did she do on Saturday, she thought as *the fear* gripped hold of her again. An eternity seemed to pass before he spoke again.

"I was wondering if you could write me a reference for University?"

"A reference?" she choked, aware that she looked flustered.

"Yes. I am really enjoying your lessons, it's one of the only classes I still find interesting and challenging. I'm applying through the University and College application scheme to do Accountancy. I think it would be beneficial if I had a subject related referee."

Caitlyn almost felt deflated. No mention of doing or saying anything on Saturday night. Not even an acknowledgement that he seen her, but was there a glint in his eye? Maybe he was just playing it down. She could still feel some kind of nervous tension between them.

"That is brilliant, Cameron, well done. It is good to hear that you are taking your education further, and I must say you have a real flair for maths – and finance in particular." Caitlyn tried to hold it together and could feel the knots of anxiety in her stomach. Her pulse was racing just being near him. He looked gorgeous. He was tall and ever so masculine, with a little groomed hair growth on his face. She could smell his aftershave that had sultry undertones and she couldn't help being attracted to it. However, she knew she had to distance herself and be professional. "Nevertheless, Cameron, I'm afraid I can't write a reference for you. You can take some of my wordings from reports that I have given you but unfortunately all

130

references need to come directly from your support teacher. Sorry, it's the school's rules."

He looked genuinely sad by her reply but he was mature enough to understand her decision. "That is OK, Miss. I realised that that might've been the case. I'll speak to Mr Hassan my Support Guidance teacher then, he may come and discuss it with you about anything relating to the subject."

"Yes of course, tell him if he needs anything subject specific to talk to me."

She stared at him, longing to strike up a conversation about anything to keep him there for longer as she could tell he was about to leave, but she bit her lip. She wanted to find out more about him. She wanted to know more about his future plans. She was curious.

Despite biting her lip she heard herself ask him, "How are getting on with your footballing career? I heard you're an exceptionally talented striker." In fact she hadn't heard much more than what Jamie had told her and was unaware of how he was getting on, but she continued, "Are you not taking football any further?"

His eyes smiled back at her as if thanking her for taking notice. "I'm doing pretty well thank you" he modestly conceded. "I'm training with the team at Ibrox Stadium most days but not really getting a game at the moment and I'm not confident on it being my full time vocation for the future. And neither is my mum, she is keen that I stick in at school," he concluded maturely.

The slightest mention of his mother was like a lightning bolt reminder to her of his tender age and instantly brought her back to the reality of the situation.

"In fact Miss, I'm trying to keep up my general fitness too as I'm in the local running club at your gym. I'm hoping to get into the athletics and football team at University, if I don't get kept on with the Gers."

He knows what gym I'm at? Has he seen me there? All horrible and sweaty? Oh no!

"Well done, Cameron, that is a great achievement. I'm sure you'll get a game soon. And that is very responsible of you to think about alternative career paths. I think you'd enjoy a Higher Education course in Maths and I think you will make an excellent Accountant," she stated truthfully and avoided getting into a dialogue about the gym.

"Thanks, Miss. See you in class."

And with that he turned again and walked out. Her eyes followed him as he walked away through the main door down the corridor and she tried to ignore her iniquitous feelings for him and concentrate on her work. She looked up again to catch the gaze of one of the students doing detention and hoped that they hadn't picked up on her feelings, which she thought looked obvious by her childlike crush behaviour. The boy stared back, scowling at her before returning to his lines reluctantly.

Chapter 25

Jennifer was calling out the register of her class near the end of the lesson to gather in the weekly homework exercise. She kept the same homework collection day of Friday each week to give the pupils routine. It also gave her time over the weekend to mark all of the jotters to return to the kids at the next lesson on Monday afternoon. The majority of the students handed in their jotters complicitly and she found that the standard of their work was improving as she took time to write detailed comments and feedback in each notebook. Jennifer also requested that each pupil got their homework jotter signed by their parents each week. She felt that this was a good way of reporting back to the parents on the pupil's progress and also made the pupils take it more seriously. Although there had been a few occasions where she knew the homework was getting completed by the parents! That had been a bit of a dubious and awkward situation but it resolved itself within time when they realised it wasn't helping their child develop within the subject at all.

There was also one pupil that persistently refused to complete homework on time, John. There were many who forgot or she had problems with on a few occasions about getting it in on time, but John was blatantly refusing to do any exercise outwith class. He barely did any in class. He was one of the last names on the register and she calmly asked for him to come out to her desk but as predicted he replied cockily that he hadn't done his homework task. She didn't want to cause a scene in front of the whole class and wanted to speak to him privately while the rest of the class were carrying on with their group work. She was conscious of not causing any extra aggravation between them as she had had to discipline him already during the course of the lesson. His poor behaviour had been relatively minor compared to some of his previous stunts like standing on the tables, calling out names or throwing objects around the classroom. But his late-coming, chewing gum and shouting out in class over her instructions was enough to disrupt the lesson and cause Jennifer to re-evaluate her teaching methodology. She'd had to postpone her plans for using the laptops individually as she had spent more time chastising John and recapping points to the rest of the class. He had distracted a lot of the other students with his talking over.

However, she had settled the situation, and she was pleased that she had handled it well enough without provoking him further. John seemed disappointed in this outcome especially as the rest of the class were now working pretty well in their small groups, unmindful of John and seemed to be grasping the topic with only a few random questions occasionally from the groups. She had wandered around the class a few times before settling at her desk to collect in the homework.

"Do you have your homework John?" she repeated quietly but self-assuredly.

"I already told ye!" he roared loudly trying to gain an audience and he burled his eyes, "Naw, I've naw done it."

"Why have you not done it, John?"

"'Cause I've just naw!"

"Did you know it was to be done for today? Did you find it difficult?" she pressed. She didn't think it was, as she always handed out differentiated work to different pupils appropriate to their needs and regularly tested them to ensure that they were at the correct levels.

He glared at her looking appalled, "I'm naw fricking stupid, you know! I just couldnae be bothered with it, ye ken? The Old Firm game was on last night."
"You had all week to do it," she replied firmly. "Now pass me over your homework diary."

He slowly swaggered back to his desk, leisurely took out his bag and rifled through his bag until he pulled out his homework diary that was badly tattered and torn. He returned casually to her desk but she didn't scold him, instead she let him take his time. She was careful not to exacerbate the situation further.
He threw the diary down on to her desk. Again, trying to cause a scene, she thought.

"Do not throw things at me, John," she said controlling the situation, "open it to this week." A few seconds went by and he eventually conceded and picked up the diary and opened it to this week. Sure enough the entry for her homework exercise was there.
"The entry is in the diary," she confirmed to him. "Do you use your diary?"

He shrugged his shoulders huffily and avoided her eye contact. At that point she saw Tommy walking confidently into her classroom. He sauntered over to one of the groups of pupils but she couldn't overhear what he spoke to them, but they burst into hysterics which caused the rest of the class to look round and become louder and a little rowdy as they enquired to what the joke was. She bit her lip with anger. She had just got the class settled, she didn't need another teacher to disturb them from their work. She had had a hard enough job with John and other pupils never mind an adult. Jennifer now witnessed Tommy walking around the class engaging in non-educational chat with her pupils further distracting them from their tasks. She could overhear general football banter going on with some of the groups and Tommy. She inwardly groaned, she would probably now have re-teach this topic on the next lesson.

"I'm going to have to give you a referral to your guidance teacher, John." She continued ignoring Tommy's presence. "This is the third time that your homework has not been completed on time and you know that those are my rules. Your guidance teacher may want to talk to you and you will get a letter home to your parents."

"What? Do you need to?" John pleaded now facing back to Jennifer.

"Yes. As I said, that is my rule and you should know that by now, you've been here long enough."

"Fine then, I don't care. I'm still not doing it," he muttered under his breath.

"Pardon?"

"Nathin'."

Jennifer wrote a small note in his homework diary to his parents to record the non-completion of homework and he walked back to his desk, bumping into the other pupils' desks trying to interrupt their work. Jennifer observed this but as none of the students responded to John's disruptive behaviour she let it lie. However, she was even more livid with Tommy when he immediately turned his attention to John. Again, she was determined not to show Tommy that he was getting to her and attempted not to listen into their conversation but it was hard not to. He obviously had seen that John had not been behaving and that Jennifer had disciplined him, it was plain to see to anyone! He knew that she had issues with John but here Tommy was in her classroom talking away to him as if he was his best buddy! She couldn't help but hear snippets of their friendly chat, "Alright Sir, how's it going?"

"Not bad John, how are you lad? Are you going to the Rangers game at the weekend?"

"Sure am, Sir. Are you? Are you going for a wee swally first?"

Jennifer couldn't help stare at them, speechless, awaiting Tommy's reply.

He laughed heartily "Aye, of course, wouldnae be a Saturday without a pint, a pie and the fitba!"

They both laughed together like old friends, as did some of the other pupils sitting nearby.

That is not appropriate! Jennifer thought. This behaviour made her so angry. Jennifer was raging! The students were definitely not concentrating on their work now!

"Right guys," Jennifer said loudly, "let's get the desks back to normal and we'll finish up with a summary quiz."

"Exciting stuff," Tommy whispered to the few boys in his vicinity sarcastically, but loud enough for Jennifer to hear. Tommy walked towards the door, he still had not engaged in any direct discussion as the kids started packing up and moving desks and as he left the room he turned and winked at her.

Did he just do that?! Argh! I wish he would just retire!

She was glad when that period was over and her Higher class came in. She was rushed off her feet for the whole class with the senior students, going from one pupil to the other helping them with their individual projects but it was far less stressful than dealing with the challenges John presented. She was especially glad that Tommy didn't make another appearance. When the class was over she spent 2 hours at her desk correcting work, redrafting and planning for the following day as the cleaner scrubbed, dusted and hoovered around her. She hadn't even started writing the report cards for her second year pupils, all 80 of them that were due in next week and she kept putting them off to deal with other things. She also had been asked by her PT to create some new interactive Powerpoint presentations for the new National courses that were being introduced to replace the Standard Grade courses and it was taking her longer than anticipated and was starting to stress her out.

She allowed herself to daydream about Stuart to give her mind a little break. She had a wonderful time with him at the weekend and they had been phoning and texting all week. She was hoping to go on a proper date with him this Saturday but he was acting a little coy about it. She also knew she wouldn't be able to relax until she could get some of her workload cleared, so she decided to cancel her hair appointment to make a head-start on the reports. Jennifer couldn't wait for the upcoming October holidays to get away from the stress of school for a little while. 10 more days to go, there was always a countdown to the next holiday.

Chapter 26

Jamie found himself walking by Andrew's office more than usual over the week, hoping to bump into him. He wore his favourite work suits each day and made a special effort to straighten his hair and wear his best aftershave. Each time Andrew had been in his classroom this week he seemed to have failed to notice, unfortunately. Jamie reflected on his weekend with his friends. He had a great night out and enjoyed it but he never pulled. In fact, he had a realisation that he didn't want to pull. Normally Jamie would go out at the weekend with the intention of going home with a tall, dark and handsome stranger and usually did. However, he never even tried, he couldn't even be bothered. The only person he could think about was Andrew, even at School.

Jamie had always been meticulous in his lesson planning and was keen to try new initiatives and Andrew seemed impressed as he continued to stop by his classroom at least a few times per week.

"Does Mr Johnstone evaluate any of your lessons?" Jamie queried the girls at their lunch break in the staffroom near the end of the week.

"Nope, not really" Caitlyn replied.

"Not very often" Jennifer responded. "My PT does though, feels like it's all the time. Like being back at Jordanhill College".

"Yeah it's like crits all over again, you can never be at ease," Caitlyn chimed in, "but they have to do it, part of their job."

"I know they do it more to us young and less experienced staff," Jennifer continued, "but I wish they would do it to the older experienced staff too, as I think some of them have got worse rather than better as time has gone by. Tommy, for example, he doesn't do much teaching from what I gather, steals all my ideas and I bet his lessons are boring as hell. All he does is get them to copy down from the board and never gives them any proper work. Maybe if they observed his lessons then they would realise just how bad a teacher he is."

The others nodded in agreement.

"Maybe we should also get the chance to observe experienced teachers and Senior Management classes too?" Caitlyn offered, "that's only fair. If they are so good, cough cough, then surely we should share good practice – lead by example."

"Exactly!" Jennifer exclaimed, "although I know a few of the Senior Management Team would not be keen on that idea, especially as they haven't taught in a classroom for years!"

Jamie felt pleased. He had stopped listening to the girls' conversation about lesson evaluations after their first response. So Andrew doesn't observe everyone's classes. Well not as often as he does with his lessons. Maybe he likes me? Maybe he likes my company? Maybe he's even attracted to me?

He walked into the school office after his lunch, attending to some of the administration work that he needed to complete, hoping that Andrew would be around. He looked at the wall board to see if Andrew was on playground duty or not. He couldn't see his name.

He peered over the hall and could see that his door was lying open. That usually meant that he was in his room. He tried to be spontaneous and think of something clever to walk in and ask him about but as he approached the entrance Andrew walked out and bumped right into him face on.

"Sorry," Andrew exclaimed harshly but as he recognised Jamie his face softened, "sorry, Jamie. Are you looking for me?"
Jamie racked his brain but he couldn't think.

"I...I" he stuttered, "was just going to ask you about funding for a school trip next year," Jamie eventually said.
Andrew chuckled, "Not much funding for anything at the moment, Jamie. What are you looking to plan?"
"Just another trip to Edinburgh to see a West End show."

Jamie had organised a few successful school outings on previous years and these were well received by pupils. The teachers loved the trips too, and it was usually fantastic for the pupils and teachers to bond outside of school. He always felt that it was so beneficial for the pupils to experience extra-curricular activities and excursions as well as the day to day teaching in the school. However, he hadn't expected to be bringing up the topic of the trip to Andrew just yet, but that's all he could think on when put on the spot and he was desperate to talk to him.

"I see that the Lion King production is coming to the Playhouse".
"Yes, yes. Sounds good, Jamie. Got to be in school holidays though, but I doubt we'll have any type of funding for class cover. I've not really got time to chat about it at the moment."

Jamie's heart sank.

"But why don't you collate some of the details together and we can discuss at interval or lunch one day next week?"

Jamie's face brightened "Yes of course, Mr Johnstone, I'll do that. I've got some literature from the company I've used before and I've already looked into some prices."

"OK then. And remember, it's Andrew."

Jamie turned and walked away back to his classroom to prepare for the next two classes, beaming from ear to ear.

Chapter 27

It was 10pm on the Thursday evening and Caitlyn had her laptop in the living room, attempting to complete some of the reports that were due in, but failing miserably. She kept notes on all of her pupils on a spreadsheet and used these for a basis to report on their progress, but tonight she was struggling to string two words together. Peter was doing overtime in the office and she was feeling lonely. She had already run her 5 miles down to the SECC and back, completed all the house chores and made dinner. However, Peter's lay untouched in the microwave. She found herself thinking about Cameron and, distracted by the thought of what he might be doing, logged on to Facebook. She kept her profile private and didn't frequent the social networking site half as often as Jennifer or Jamie, but liked keeping in touch with her other close friends and relatives. She browsed all of the updated statuses on the home page and scrolled down to look at the photos added by her friends from the weekend. She was always wary about pupils and parents seeing any of her information or photos online, so was careful to scrutinize each picture to ensure they didn't give the wrong impression, even though she knew all of her friends' pages were private. She hesitated slightly before making her next move, but knew deep down that this was always her intention by logging on. She typed in Cameron's name into the search box at the top of the page and waited impatiently on the results to show up.

She looked over her shoulder guiltily in case Peter was to enter. She wondered how she would explain looking at a young boy's profile page. The teacher element of her was pleased that she discovered that his page was for friends only as she always advised her pupils to do this to protect themselves, but she was also dissatisfied that she couldn't snoop a little to find out a bit more about his personal life. Caitlyn knew it was definitely his page from the handsome snapshot of him as his profile picture. It looked like it was an action shot of him scoring a goal in a game. God, he looked good. He looked her age, she thought, he didn't look young at all.

She scanned the rest of the information available, disappointed there weren't more photos. Nevertheless, she did read on to see that he reported his interests as clubbing, cinema-going, football and fitness. There was no mention of his age but what really caught her eye was that he was listed as single. What happened to the lovely Megan? She smiled at the thought of him breaking it off with his girlfriend. It made her feel less guilty thinking about Cameron with him being a single man and not attached. At that moment she could hear a car engine outside her flat and she immediately logged out and shut over her laptop. It must be Peter. She peered down at the street below and could see a dark car double parked. He must have got a lift home from someone. Caitlyn put away her laptop, heated up the dinner in the microwave for Peter and turned up the TV. She poured him a glass of orange juice, put the kettle on and settled on the couch. 5 minutes passed and Peter still hadn't come upstairs. She got up and looked out the window again. The car was still there and

145

the passenger door now was open. Maybe it's not him? She phoned his mobile, but it rang out. She then saw him emerge from the car and walk towards the close door.

"Hey babe," he called out as he entered the flat and locked the door behind him.

"Hey. How was work?"

"Long and tiring!"

He entered the kitchen and Caitlyn walked towards him to greet him with a kiss but he seemed oblivious as he headed straight for the beeping microwave, brushing past her as if she was invisible.

"Starving," he said through biting into his chicken and throwing his briefcase and jacket on to the kitchen table, "cheers."

"No problem," she said as she affectionately stroked his hair as she walked up to him again. "Did you get a lift home?"

He took a while to reply as he munched into his food. "No just got a taxi, it was just me working late in the office". For some reason she wasn't compelled to argue with him even although she knew he was blatantly lying. She had seen him get out of the car and it was definitely not a taxi. Why would he lie? She had never not trusted him before, but she was beginning to doubt him. "Do you have to work late so often?"

"I've told you already, Caitlyn," Peter snapped suddenly angry. "I'm doing this for us and it won't be for long!"

"OK OK, I know. But surely we can get by with the money we have?"

"We can, but why struggle, Caitlyn? We're in this shitty flat, OK it's in a good location but we've used up all our money on rent now and we can't afford to go out all the time like we used to. We're not students anymore either – we need to pay our Council Tax and we have loads more bills. Don't you want a nice big flat and maybe a car?

"Yes, of course. But I thought we were doing fine?"

"Caitlyn! For all that you are good with numbers, you really are bloody awful with money! Haven't you seen our bank balance?"

"Yes, we're only £150 overdrawn this month."

"Overdrawn. Yes, overdrawn – that is NOT good. We also have a credit card bill in for over £500. We're both now starting to pay back our student loans – that's over £400 a month between us! And, we also still need to repay your parents for that loan for the rent deposit."

"They don't want that back."

"I WANT to pay it back. I want us to have a bigger, nicer place to live and still money to do the things we want to do."

They both sat in silence as Peter finished his dinner and Caitlyn poured them both a cup of tea.

"Let's take our tea through to the living room?" Peter asked, his voice back to his normal friendly self.

"With some Tunnocks wafers?" Caitlyn added.

Peter smiled, "Yes, awesome, a Tunnocks wafer and a beer is exactly what I need."

"I know what else you need," Caitlyn replied playfully as she patted him on the bum as he stood up.

Peter laughed softly, "I know what you're after babe and you are right, I am in need of some of *that* too. Let's just get me a little rest first on the couch and then we can have an early night if you know what I mean?"

Caitlyn's eyes lit up and she forgot all about school, Cameron and the mysterious car driver as she snuggled up to her boyfriend on the couch to watch TV.

Caitlyn awoke early in the morning to find Peter already left for work. She remembered her disappointment of the evening before. Yet another night without any sex. Peter had fallen asleep on the couch and her attempts at awakening him had been fruitless. She had switched off the lights and left him in darkness as she went to bed in a mood. He did eventually come in to bed with her as she felt his warm embrace of his bare arms around her in the middle of the night. If she was madder with him she might have pushed him off but she missed his cuddles in bed. But it was now morning and he was away to work, his second home, and it was playing on Caitlyn's mind.

Caitlyn got up slowly and walked to the bathroom, picking up Peter's discarded clothes from yesterday from the floor to put into the washing. She looked at her reflection and wasn't best pleased with the dishevelled and pasty image staring back. Not a good look. She couldn't even blame being up all night having sex as the problem. She only wished she had that problem! Thank God it was Friday and it was only one week until holidays she thought.

However, the only drawback of going on holiday is that she wouldn't see Cameron at all. Well not at school... Maybe he would be at the gym? Oh god, I actually hope not, I look awful when I work out! She brushed her teeth as she wandered around her flat, tidying away Peter's plates from last night and pouring a small bowl of bran flakes for breakfast. She left her toothbrush back into the bathroom and noticed that Peter's wasn't in its usual space beside hers. She gritted her newly brushed teeth together. Working away? Not this weekend surely? She ran back to the bedroom in a rage and flung open the cupboard door. The overnight suitcase was missing.

"Damn!" she shouted out loud slamming the door shut. She took a deep breath and tried to think rationally but she was just so god damn angry! Caitlyn picked up her mobile and called Peter. No answer. She called again. And again. He didn't pick up. She texted Jamie and Jennifer simultaneously.

'Cocktails after work? I'm in need of a jug to myself! C x'

She didn't expect an instant reply from them as they weren't the best in the mornings so she jumped in the shower and began her weekly ritual of exfoliation, hair removal and fake tan application. She played the radio loudly as she carefully picked out a new outfit to wear to work and straightened her sleek blonde hair and affixed a pearl clasp onto her side braid. Caitlyn used a little of her 'weekend' makeup to finish her look and she let herself smile again as she took a final look at herself in the mirror before grabbing her pale pink handbag to walk to work for the day at 7.45am.

"Fuck him," she said under her breath, "I'm going to go out tonight and enjoy myself without him. I'm getting sick of this."

As she collected her paperwork from her pigeon hole in the staffroom just before first period, she bumped into Jennifer and Jamie as they bounced into the room giggling at a private joke.

"Hey, Caitlyn!"

"Hey, guys."

"You OK?" Jennifer enquired, "Long week?"

"Yeah, something like that," she retorted not making eye contact afraid that they may pick up on her unhappiness.

"Sorry we never replied to your text, we were running late. We also had a wee stop off at Starbucks for our Friday treat!" Jamie cheekily said as him and Jennifer exchanged guilty glances. "And sorry I can't go out tonight. My parents are coming through for a visit and we've still not even tidied up. They always get on at me for still living like a student so I'm determined to get it looking ship shape before they arrive. I think they are going to treat me to dinner to that Italian restaurant by Jamie Oliver on George Square."

"Very posh," Caitlyn replied turning hopefully to Jennifer for a more promising response.

"I'm sorry too honey. I'm getting my nails done after work and I've already agreed to meet Diane, my old University friend to go round to hers for dinner. Then I'm heading to meet Stuart, I hope."

Caitlyn couldn't hide her disappointment, "No worries."

"I'm sure Di wouldn't mind if you came along?" Jennifer added sensing Caitlyn's displeasure.

"Don't you and Peter normally go out for dinner on a Friday? Where's he off to?" Jamie asked.

"Yeah we used to," Caitlyn said, "but he's working a lot lately and he's away again this weekend. And thanks for the offer Jen, but I'll leave you two to catch up with each other."

"OK," Jen accepted, "and anyway I'm hoping to meet Stuart afterwards. I did invite him for dinner first too, but he was keen just to meet for a quiet drink afterwards. I might ask my beautician to do my waxing too, just in case!"

The three friends all smiled knowingly.

"Ach well," Jamie continued, "I bet you're in need of a quiet night on your own, get caught up with your sleep without that Petey of yours pestering you in bed."

Jennifer and Jamie giggled and Caitlyn joined in with a bit of a fake laugh, not wanting to admit to her problems. She felt so lonely. She always felt jealous of Jennifer and Jamie's relationship. She knew they sometimes argued, which was understandable for being best friends living and working together, but their quarrels never lasted long. They both were so close and Caitlyn couldn't help feeling left out on occasions. Although, it never usually bothered her that much until now as she normally had Peter all of the time.

Jennifer and Jamie were always banging on about how they were jealous of her having such a fantastic boyfriend as Peter and she normally meekly smiled in agreement. But now, she felt on her own.

Peter was never around at the moment, always putting his precious work first and it was really getting her down.

*Oh well, s*he thought, *I'll just get all of my reports finished.* It wasn't the outcome she hoped for for her Friday night, but was now looking forward to getting the day over. She normally loved Fridays. Everyone was always happier on a Friday and the mood in the staffroom was always upbeat, especially the week before the October holiday.

Caitlyn still hadn't had a reply from Peter by lunchtime. She was sitting in the staffroom eating her sandwich with her eyes glued to her phone. She had now phoned him 8 times and left two voicemails. A bit excessive maybe, she thought, but she was really annoyed and a little concerned. She didn't even know where he was going. He used to be so good at returning her calls and used to text her everyday even just to say good morning if he left early. But recently, he was barely speaking to her on a daily basis and now not even returning her calls or texts. She tried to forget him as she listened in to the staffroom Friday banter as her colleagues discussed where they were going on holiday next week.

"Are you and Peter going anywhere nice?" one of the older languages teachers asked politely in Caitlyn's direction.

"Erm no, nothing planned as yet."

"It's just nice to get a break from here though isn't it?"

"Yes" Caitlyn agreed.

"We're going to France again" the woman continued "David and I have been going there for 20 years and we just absolutely love it."

The woman rattled on about her husband, their family and some of their fun filled holiday tales.

Caitlyn nodded and tried to sound interested but her head was elsewhere and she actually couldn't help feeling a pang of envy at the woman. Jetting off with her husband of many years to a little retreat in the south of France. Sounded amazing. She wondered if Peter even knew she was off on holiday next week. They did normally go away a few days and enjoyed the planning process of their trips, picking out the destinations and boutique hotels they were going to stay in. Although this year Peter didn't manage to take any weeks off while she was on her summer holidays, even though she pestered him every week about flying off to some beautiful Greek island like Crete or Kefalonia. Peter hadn't entertained her or seemed to be as enthusiastic as he once was about their holidays together and told her to think more like Butlins!

Caitlyn scoured the internet in search of cheap deals for them, even ones closer to home but there was nothing that seemed to make Peter happy. It would've needed to be ridiculously cheap for him to agree and she couldn't find anything within his tight budget. She would love even to explore more of Scotland with Peter, maybe go somewhere for a long weekend away. A smile crept on her face at the thought. A luxurious log cabin with a big rustic log fire, maybe with a hot tub on the veranda in the beautiful Scottish countryside. Somewhere near the sea where there are lots of rocky beaches or national parks. That would be so romantic she thought! I could book us up a few nights as a surprise? Her friends had discussed a

153

trip away but nothing had materialised as yet. She knew they didn't have much in savings and although they wanted to budget to get out a new flat but she felt their relationship was in need of some TLC. That's exactly what her and Peter needed. She returned to her classroom 10 minutes before the end of the lunch break now with a smile on her face.

It wasn't until after her gym session that she finally got a reply from Peter. He had left her an apologetic voicemail explaining that he had to go to a conference in Manchester with work but will be back on Sunday afternoon. She messaged him back –

It's fine babe, I just miss you. I wish you didn't need to work so much. I'll make us a big Sunday lunch xxx

He replied instantly this time. *I miss you too. All this extra work won't be forever babe. This overtime will give us money to get a new pad! Can't wait for Sunday. Love you lots x*

That's it, she decided, I will book us a romantic getaway. That will get them back on track.

Chapter 28

Jennifer was locking up her classroom at the end of a hectic day. It was after 6pm and she still had plenty of paperwork to do, but the October holidays began after tomorrow and she had already started to be in vacation mood, she couldn't bear looking at one more jotter tonight. Tommy Greig, the teacher next door, was most definitely away, she couldn't remember a day that he arrived before 8.45am or away after 3.30pm. He regularly left school throughout the day if he didn't have a class and was frequently off 'sick' but would be spotted in the local pub laughing and joking with the regulars that same day. This made Jennifer and other teachers angry, not only were they coping with their own heavy workloads but they had the burden of having to cover someone else's classes too because they 'couldn't be bothered'. That's what it felt like to them anyway.

Jennifer also had to bite her lip as Tommy would get his students to pack up early on a lesson before lunch and allow them away 10 minutes early before the bell so he could get away sharper. Her pupils used to always moan to her that Mr Greig was better and nicer than her. All of these things infuriated her! She wanted to report him to the Head of Department but he always had an excuse for everything. Jennifer was positive that her Head of Department knew some of the tricks that Tommy would pull but it was never discussed, he was just Tommy. And he would hopefully be retiring soon. She remembered a time that Tommy went absolutely crazy at a young girl for forgetting a pen. Jennifer and her class could hear him shouting from her room. She thought that something incredibly serious must be happening and went to check it out. The little girl sat at her desk, too scared to speak, in floods of tears. To try and 'teach the girl a lesson', Tommy gave her a lunch detention. She sat in his room all lunch whilst Tommy had forgotten all about it and went away to the local greasy spoon café blissfully unaware that the girl was sitting in his classroom. Jennifer had found her near the end of lunchtime and let the poor traumatised girl away. She never mentioned it to the boss, just him, but again he shrugged it off like nothing. He was lucky the girl or her parents didn't complain!

As she walked along the empty hall Jennifer could see that many of her other colleagues were still busying away in their classrooms, furiously cramming to try to get their work complete before the holidays. As she turned around after hanging up her keyset and signing out, she bumped into John.

"Hey John" she greeted him.

"Hi Miss" he politely replied which shocked her a little.

She smiled warmly at him and he smiled back. "What keeps you here so late, John?"

"Football training."

This was peculiar, he was acting like a nice human being, she mused. "I didn't know you played football?"

"I like all sport, Miss" he replied courteously, still smiling at her. "I'm not in the school team or anything but I like playing fives with the boys."

156

It felt like a major breakthrough in her relationship with him. Maybe he wasn't that bad? On his own, she felt like she's actually broken down some boundaries. This was the most he has ever talked to her.

"That's great, John. I'm not bad at football either believe it or not, used to play for my school team."

John laughed, "Yeah?"

"We never won anything mind you, but I enjoyed it."

"What position did you play, Miss?"

This time Jennifer giggled, "Any position that was needed on the day!"

John joined her laugh. "I'm a defender. Well if I got in the school team, I'd like to be put in the defence."

"Do you want to get in the team?"

He shrugged, "Yeah, maybe. Maybe next year when I'm in S4. It's all the older lads innit?"

"True. I'm sure if you worked hard at it you could get in the team next year."

"Thanks, Miss. Anyway, I better go, my Mum is coming to collect me."

"OK. Bye, John."

Did that just happen? Maybe he was a nice boy after all?

Chapter 29

Jamie had been busy researching the school musical excursion to Edinburgh and wanted to get the pitch to Andrew perfect. Not just because it needed to be seamless for the planning so that the details could go out to pupils and parents, but he wanted Andrew to be impressed. He sat nervously in his waiting room, clutching brochures and sample itineraries under his arm. He sorted his new pristine purple striped tie against the matching lilac shirt that he pressed twice this morning. He had woken up an hour earlier than usual to prepare the information about the trip and make sure he looked the best he could on a school day without looking like he was heading out clubbing. He wanted to look professional and mature.

Jamie looked around the room at the various cabinets sporting trophies, certificates and photographs. He was proud to be associated with the school and its achievements. It was obvious that Andrew was too. Posters and news articles about the school were posted on every last crevice of the wall and Jamie knew that Andrew put those up personally. It wasn't uncommon for Andrew to be in his office before 7am or after 8pm at night and he knew there wouldn't be a day in the October holidays that he wouldn't come into work even at least for an hour checking in on things. Jamie felt that they were more alike than Andrew would like to admit, and he couldn't help thinking about him. All weekend he had been searching the internet like a lovesick teenager looking at any press clippings or articles that he had been involved in. He searched for his friends on Facebook for a glimpse of a photograph. He found countless photographs of Andrew and his family. They looked so happy, a normal young family. But were they really happy? Is he really secretly gay? Jamie knew that he was gay all of his life but he had plenty of friends who were either closeted or ones that honestly thought they were straight until the right person came along. Plenty of gay men are part of a heterosexual relationship and like it, even think they are in love until they find the man of their dreams and they have to confront their feelings. Elton John was married once wasn't he? Maybe Andrew is just realising he isn't meant to be with a woman. Or maybe he has always known he was gay but trapped in a family with strong Catholic values, maybe pushed into a career path in the public eye... Jamie's mind really was wandering.

A young girl and her mother walked out of Andrew's room. The girl looked glum and tearstained while her mother looked angry. Jamie felt quite defensive towards Andrew, he hoped that the mother hadn't given him too much grief. He had seen and heard what some parents could be like. Even when some pupils' behaviour had been atrocious with fighting, drug taking, swearing and abusive to teachers in school, the parents could be just as bad. On occasions where there had been evidence of misbehaviour or CCTV footage of damage to school property, their kids could do no wrong in their eyes and the parents could be just as disrespectful or even physically abusive when trying to fight their corner. It wasn't completely unusual for a parent to be escorted off the premises by the Janitor, sometimes even the police.

"I will see you both next week," Andrew sternly instructed the woman and her daughter. The young weepy girl looked at the floor but her mother turned to face Andrew and made direct eye contact. "Thank you very much, Mr Johnstone. I appreciate you bringing Amy's behaviour to my attention, I will deal with her at home." She twisted around now focusing her gaze at her daughter who was still intensely staring at her flat black fake leather pumps. "Look at me, Amy," she raised her voice and the girl slowly raised her head to meet her mum's gaze. "What do you say to Mr Johnstone?"

"Sorry," the girl squeaked and her mum's eyebrows lifted higher and Amy knew to speak up, "Sorry, Mr Johnstone". The mother's sombre face softened a little as she ushered her daughter Amy out of the door. "Sorry and thanks again, Mr Johnstone, sorry for taking up your time."

"That is fine, Mrs Donnelly, I'm glad you could come in to see me. Thank you for apologising Amy. I look forward to seeing you back in school next Monday morning fully prepared for School."
Amy nodded as she left the room, "Yes, Sir."

Andrew had a way with people, Jamie thought. He was kind but he was also strong. Some thought of him as a strict and demanding teacher, a powerful uncompromising school leader and although he had a reputation as that amongst the hoi polloi, colleagues knew that he was also fair and understanding. He always put people first. Jamie knew, as well as many others who knew him well, that Andrew would do anything to help his pupils and his staff. He worked so hard for the school, always above and beyond what is expected as a Head Teacher. This made him more irresistible to Jamie.

Andrew's expression changed almost instantly seeing Jamie as he cheerfully welcomed him into his room, "Would you like a coffee, Jamie?"

Normally Jamie wouldn't eat or drink anything during the school day apart from a quick cup of tea at morning interval and his lunch, but he decided to accept as it might give him more time with Andrew. "Yes please, I'd love one." Jamie half expected Andrew's secretary to run in with coffees but to Jamie's surprise he turned a kettle on in the far corner of the room and busied himself preparing two instant coffees for them both.

"What was that about?" Jamie didn't want to be nosey but he couldn't help himself.

Andrew smiled, "Och nothing, all sorted." Oh yes, Jamie thought, confidential too – ever the professional. If it was anything for other teachers to be concerned about Andrew would ensure that the information was sent out in a Memo as soon as it was possible, but if it wasn't necessary then he would keep the details restricted. Another part of his charm.

"Don't you get fed up with dealing with difficult situations? Pupils and parents?"

"Not at all. It can be challenging all right, I won't deny that," Andrew replied calmly as he stirred the two mugs, "it's part and parcel of the job. Do you take sugar?"

Modest too, Jamie thought. "No thanks, no sugar for me, just milk."

"You sweet enough?" Andrew winked as he handed Jamie the mug.

Jamie couldn't help but blush. Was he flirting? He grabbed tightly on to cup of coffee and took a big swig. Too big as it went down the wrong way and he started to choke. How embarrassing, he groaned inwardly, as it felt like a comedy sketch going in slow motion as he splattered hot coffee out of his mouth over his face and down his shirt.

"God, are you OK?" Andrew came to his side genuinely concerned, patting the top of Jamie's back as if to dislodge a clog in Jamie's throat.

Tears rolled down Jamie's cheeks and he waved Andrew away. "Yes, yes," he finally managed to compose himself to say, "I'm absolutely fine, just went down the wrong way."

"Is my coffee that bad?" Andrew asked, laughing heartily now that it was clear that Jamie was OK, and he pointed to the seat in front of him for Jamie to sit down.

Jamie giggled nervously as he sat down and tried to wipe away the stain on his clothes. "The coffee is lovely, thanks".

"So, you were thinking of a school excursion to Edinburgh for next year?"

"Yes," Jamie replied trying to sound confident. He had every reason to be confident as he was excellent at organising trips and activities. He had only been teaching for a few years but he was already known as the expert in organising activities and events for the school. So far he had successfully arranged watersport trips, theme park days out, fundraising events and dances for the pupils

162

and the Parent's Teacher Association. He loved doing this as it was so fulfilling seeing the kids out with the school setting, enjoying themselves and growing as young adults. Jamie was a firm believer that children didn't just learn from the classroom and that their life experiences in extra-curricular activities were just as important.

He was pleased that the senior management team of this school fully supported him in this belief and it really made the school a much more enjoyable place. It certainly helped any discipline problems and lead for the school to have a strong ethos. But this little strange attraction to Andrew was making him unusually uneasy and a little insecure in his ability. Well at least when he was under pressure in his room. He felt like a pupil being reprimanded rather than a co-worker.

Jamie knew he had looked into all the particulars of the proposed excursion in every detail. He had spent many evenings at home on his computer, planning it all out, looking at alternatives, proposed dates and costs, numbers, spoken to other schools that had used the same company and had already sounded it out with some of the other teachers who regularly assisted such trips including Caitlyn and Jennifer who all seemed keen. He had also summarised all the facts onto a brief A4 sheet of paper which he handed to Andrew.

Andrew read over the document thoroughly, scanning it again for the second time before looking back up at Jamie. "It looks fantastic Jamie. Any space for a Head Teacher?"
Jamie sighed with relief and a large smile crept upon his face. "Sure!"

Andrew laughed, "If only. I doubt you lot would want me cramping your style anyway. The kids certainly wouldn't!"

But I'd love it, he thought secretly.

"What other teachers are planned to go?"

"Just myself, Jim Dyce also from my department as well as Jennifer Hill from Geography and Caitlyn McDonald from Maths. We can take up to 40 kids and the bus quote is really reasonable. Although we could easily come back that same night, I've looked into staying so that we could do some sightseeing too with a travel company – Edinburgh Castle, the Dungeons etc. My friend from St Ninian's has been there three times with a school party and swears by their exceptional standards- the kids will love it!" Jamie gushed, barely stopping for a breath.

"Sounds as if you have it pretty well planned. What about dates and costs?"

"I spoke to the agent last night and if we went on the last day of term we could get £10 per person discount."

"Ah, I see," Andrew said, "so this is why you have to come and get the seal of approval from me personally. You want to do it during term time?"

Jamie stared at Andrew expectantly, searching his face for clues of joviality or flirtation, but he was uncertain of his expression and was now hesitant like a little school boy before progressing with his presentation. "It's only actually leaving at lunchtime on the last day so we can catch the early evening show. If we need to leave the day after it is OK, I'm just trying to keep the costs down for the kids as I want to give everyone the opportunity of going. I can get it a bit cheaper if I went with another travel company, but they don't get as good reviews as this one and I'd rather pay a little more for ease of mind and quality."

"Very true, Jamie, I agree with you." Andrew smiled as he handed back the brochures, "And no bother, of course you all can leave on the last day. We normally have fun activities all day that day anyway... for the kids that actually turn up that is!"

Jamie smiled back. "Thank you. That's fantastic, I'll get to work putting a notice in the newsletter and arrange a meeting for anyone that is interested. You're more than welcome to come with us if you want? You definitely wouldn't be cramping anyone's style! As long as you are happy with singing along with all the Lion King songs and letting the pupils see you as a human being?"

"Ha! Yeah I'm sure they'd love that, they'll see my weaknesses and find out my secret shame of being a terrible singer!"

"So you are human?" Jamie joked trying not to sound too flirty as they shared a laugh.

"Yip, last time I checked although I don't think the kids ever realise that I am. We are. We do normal things and have a family outwith school and believe it or not we actually were their age at some point too. Not even that long ago as well!"

"I know, I met two of the girls when I was in the supermarket over the summer holidays and they just stood and stared as if I was a creature of the night. Yes, I do live outside school and yes I do need to eat food to survive like other ordinary human beings!" Jamie said with a hint of sarcasm and full of expression.

Andrew was now in hysterics, holding his stomach with laughter. "Oh so true! You make me laugh."

Jamie could feel his cheeks redden again with delight from the praise from Andrew.

"What about funding?" Andrew continued, back to business.

"Well I've looked into a few grants that we could possibly get that could keep the overall costs down, and I've already spoken to the Finance Manager about funding and she has agreed it in principle."

"Brilliant. It sounds like a great addition to the school calendar Jamie, well done for putting all of this together. I'm sure the kids will love it."

"Thank you," Jamie said sincerely. "I'm certain they will love it. It will be memories for them to keep forever."

"Absolutely."

The room went silent and Jamie jumped out of his seat before any awkward silences.

"Right then" Jamie said as he returned the mug to the table "I better get going and get organised for my next class."

"OK then. Send the paperwork my way for the trip and I'll get it signed off for you as soon as you need it."

"Thank you, Mr Johnstone," and Jamie turned on his heels out of the Head Teacher's office. He could almost pinch himself he was bursting with happiness. Did he really have a crush on his boss, the Head Teacher of his school?

Chapter 30

Caitlyn felt elated when the school bell rang as it signified the start of the October break. It had only been 9 weeks since the summer break but it felt like an eternity, it had been a tiring term. The pupils gushed out into the corridors and within 5 minutes you couldn't hear any of their voices, they had disappeared into their own outside lives once more. She peeked out of her blinds to find that the staff car park was quickly emptying too. No-one liked being behind late when the holidays were starting and since it was only a week's holiday many of them were making mad dashes to airports around the UK to jet off for a quick getaway to the sun.

I don't blame them Caitlyn thought to herself, I'd love to be flying away somewhere exotic with Peter. However, she wasn't too disappointed as she was in high spirits about the upcoming week. She had secretly booked a 3 night stay at a luxurious self-catering cottage in Machrihanish in Kintyre, for her and Peter and couldn't contain her excitement! Her parents used to take her to Campbeltown in Kintyre during the summer holidays when she was a child. It was a remote country town approximately 150 miles and a 3 hour drive from the central belt of Scotland - but it was worth the long journey. It had the most fabulous untouched countryside, white sandy beaches and beautiful fresh clean air. Some of her most prominent and favourite memories of her childhood were of the area and she couldn't wait to take Peter.

She had regularly told him all about it and they had countless times talked about going there together but for one reason or another, it just hadn't happened yet. Caitlyn had researched the trip online and had chosen a newly built cottage overlooking Machrihanish beach that looked perfect for what she had in mind – wood burning stove, hot tub and access to a local Spa. Caitlyn had a few days to herself to get herself organised before Peter's annual leave began and she could land the surprise on him. Daydreams of Cameron had been long gone in the past few days as her romantic getaway had consumed her thoughts. She reminisced about some of the magnificent hikes that she had completed with her father in the secluded Kintyre Way around the rocky shorelines and the sandcastles she built with her mum and brother on Westport beach. Caitlyn also knew that Peter would love the opportunity to play on the Championship Golf Courses that the area boasted. Although a round of golf wasn't her ideal choice of activity, she knew the scenery and walk would be enjoyable and relaxing. She remembered that her Dad, despite whatever score he had achieved, had always returned from his Machrihanish golf rounds with a smile on his face. However, her Mum had always joked that it was because of the extra hour he spent at the 19th hole that did that!

Caitlyn had went into work at 7am everyday that week to give her enough time to complete most of her school work before the holidays and give her plenty of time for the important preparation – beautician appointments as she wanted to wax *every* part of her body, fake tan, nails and hair as well as go to the shops to pick up

168

some sexy lingerie for Peter to appreciate! She would also go to the supermarket to pick up some of their favourite luxury groceries and fizzy wine so she could make them some lovely homemade meals whilst they were there. She loved cooking, especially when she could make someone, namely Peter, happy with the end result.

"Woo hoo, it's holiday time!" Jamie and Jennifer shouted into her classroom breaking her train of thought.

"Hey," she turned greeting them with a big smile, "happy holidays!"

"Look at you," Jennifer exclaimed, "clear desk already."

"And logged off!" Jamie added.

"Yip, I'm good tonight, can't wait to get out of here. I've got some marking and reports to do tomorrow but I'm confident I can get it all done before I go away."

"I'm so jealous!" Jennifer squealed. "It will be so romantic, it sounds amazing!"

Caitlyn beamed back, "Yeah, it sure does, it's going to be awesome! Just don't let the cat out the bag if you speak to Peter remember, it's my little surprise."

"Of course," Jennifer replied mimicking zipping her mouth up, "we are excellent secret keepers."

Jamie and Jennifer exchanged quick glances before looking away. "I can't believe we're not getting to go after us talking it over ages ago. We'll need to go back to Campbeltown later in the year for a wee night out. And knowing you two, you won't even take advantage of the wonderful countryside and spend all your time doing you know what in the hot tub!" Jamie said jokily.

"Not at all actually," Caitlyn said mocking being offended as she picked up her two large bags and put them on to her shoulder, "we plan to do it outside too!"

The three burst out laughing as they turned out the lights and Caitlyn double checked that the laptops were all turned off at the sockets.

"Heading for a drink?"

The three turned round to see Andrew Johnstone, the Head Teacher, walking up the corridor to meet them.

Jamie was the first to answer "Yeah, think we're heading into the city centre just for a few tea-timers. Do you fancy joining us, Andrew?"

The girls exchanged glances.

"Not tonight I'm afraid," Andrew said as he passed them by, "I'm just doing my rounds quickly then I'm taking the family camping again for a long weekend. Hoping to get out of here before 5 if I can. Promised them one last trip before the nights got too dark."

"Sounds good, enjoy," Jamie said trying to look pleased and not let his disappointment shine through.

"We will, thanks. You guys have fun at the pub and have a good holiday. You all deserve it after working so hard the last few months."

"Thanks, you too," they replied as he disappeared back down the stair well.

"Oooh, check you out," Jennifer exclaimed indicating to Jamie. "Do you want to join us, *Andrew? Ha ha!*"

"What?" Jamie said defensively, "I was just being polite. He's just a colleague after all."

"He's our boss!" Caitlyn added "I couldn't relax with him being there."

"Yes, you could," Jamie continued, "you seemed to be pretty relaxed at last year's Christmas party and he was there?"

"Ha ha, very funny, that was different. There were about 100 staff members there for a start, he probably didn't even notice me, it was hardly like we were in direct company."

"No, I'm sure he didn't notice you dancing on the table at the end of the night, hauling poor George Paleman from my department up by the tie to dance along with you to Britney Spears…" Jennifer said barely stifling her laughter.

"OK, OK whatever. I just mean it's hard to let your guard down when you've got your boss there."

"No, I know," Jennifer agreed, "but he does seem really decent and he's pretty young, not that much older than us really."

"Exactly," Jamie concluded.

"But he's away to be with his wife and family. That's nice, he seems such a dedicated man. To his job, the school and to his family. It's good to see that there are men out there like that."

The girls nodded in agreement.

"Yeah he does seem like a great man," Jamie admitted truthfully, but he hated the thought of him being such a family man. He was jealous, in fact. "So we heading into the city for a little cocktail or two before Jennifer here meets up with her beau?"

171

"You meeting up with sexy Stuart again?" Caitlyn asked. "Are you going for dinner?"

"Yes and yes. He's taking me to some fancy restaurant out in the countryside again. I don't know why he insists on going so far out but it does give us privacy. I'll need a few glasses of vino to loosen me up though, I still get tongue tied trying to speak to him. It's easier when we do less talking!"

"And you certainly have being doing enough of the other stuff," Jamie said nudging her and winking at Caitlyn. "They can't keep their hands off each other this pair, at it like fucking rabbits, it is so bloody ignorant when you're in the next room."

"Jealous much?" Caitlyn asked him smiling.

"Completely and utterly!"

"Me too!" Caitlyn exclaimed.

"Pah! What have you two got to be jealous at, it's normally me on my lonesome with Jamie off with some stud muffin whenever wherever even when we're just out for a coffee and you, Caitlyn, come on, you live with Peter. I bet you need a break from all that loving!" she accused playfully as she nudged them both back with her elbows as they exited the school.

Caitlyn thought about telling them about Peter's lack of intimacy at the moment and his devotion to his work all of the time and not her, but she felt embarrassed, she liked to uphold the image of them being the perfect couple so she stayed quiet.

"This is a real quiet streak for me," Jamie said, "I'm not sure what's wrong, this must have been my longest time ever without a man."

"Is that been a week then?" Caitlyn said sarcastically rolling her eyes.

"Two days?" Jennifer jibed.

"Ha ha, very funny. It's been..." he screwed up his eyes, mentally tallying up the days, "6 weeks since I was with someone. 6 weeks since Callum Jacobs."

"Wow, that is a long time" Jennifer admitted, "for you anyway. It's not like you."

"That must be some sort of record for you – what's up?" Caitlyn light heartedly joked.

"Nothing's up, I'm just not that bothered about picking up guys at the moment," he mused. "No-one special has really caught my attention." He knew this was a lie and hoped that the girls wouldn't pick up on it. Jamie was good at acting but for some reason he was a terrible liar and the girls could normally spot a fib a mile away. He couldn't stop thinking about Andrew. He didn't want to be with anyone else. However, Jamie certainly didn't want to tell that to his friends.

"Fair enough Jamie babes, I doubt your cold streak will last for long," Caitlyn said patting him on the head teasingly. "I'll walk you pair to the underground. Are you meeting the others from work?"

"Where are you going? Aren't you coming for a quick drink to celebrate the holidays?" Jennifer quizzed.

173

"Nah, I'm knackered and I'm skint after paying for the holiday. Peter really wants us to save more so that we can get a better flat. Plus, I really need to get on with some housework, I've been putting it off until the holidays and my flat needs gutted."

"Oh come on, just one?" Jennifer whined, "Please!"

"Pretty please, it's happy hour," Jamie cajoled.

"OK OK but just the one," she conceded. She supposed it would beat waiting in the house until late for Peter to return from work and she had already done her workout for the day before work. She had had a sneaking suspicion that she would allow herself to be persuaded to go the pub, every last end of term day always ended up with a few alcoholic beverages of some sort.

Jennifer and Jamie high-fived in front of her, "Lead the way then teachers of tomorrow, upstanding members of the community!"

Chapter 31

Caitlyn wasn't exactly true to her word and ended up staying for 3 drinks and was feeling quite merry as she walked up the steps of the underground back onto the high street. She had lots to do at home in preparation for the surprise for Peter so that he didn't have any excuses not to go. She was glad she kept her own bank account so that she could pay for the trip in secret. As she arrived up to their flat she looked up expectantly, hoping that Peter would already be at home cooking up a masterpiece for them to devour. But alas, their home was in darkness. She busied herself with tidying, cleaning and hoovering with the music blaring for over an hour. Still no Peter and her mood was starting to dissipate. She poured herself a large glass of white wine as she started to make dinner in the kitchen for them both. Her stomach was rumbling already but she wanted to hold off and wait to have her meal with Peter. Another hour passed and so did another glass of chardonnay. She shouldn't be lonely like this as part of a couple, she thought.

Caitlyn hooked up her laptop onto the breakfast bar in the kitchen and logged on to Facebook to pass some time and started to flick through some of her friends photos that had been uploaded. She saw a familiar face in one of them, Cameron? Her heart skipped a beat and she couldn't help letting a little smile creep on her face whilst staring at his picture. He really was so handsome. *Whose friend was he?* she wondered. She discovered that he was friends with her younger sister's boyfriend and played in his Sunday league football team. She felt pangs of guilt but she also didn't want to stop looking. Although she couldn't get on to his page direct, with access to her sister's page she could get into albums of photos he was tagged in. He didn't look like a pupil at all. There were a myriad of photos of him with his friends, older friends, out pubbing and clubbing as well as numerous photos of him playing football and shinty. He must socialise with people from his team that are older she decided. She also recognised some of the gang from her gym. I wonder if he's been at the gym while I've been all sweaty and horrible, engrossed in my workout? I hope not!

Looking over her shoulder, guilt ridden, she clicked away from the photos onto Peter's profile page. She hadn't been on his page in ages and noticed he had quite a few new friends added, women friends. Caitlyn wasn't the jealous type, especially as her and Peter were so close, but she couldn't help feeling a little envious as she seen some playful banter between him and some other girls which obviously were work colleagues. He doesn't have time for playful banter with her anymore, in fact he doesn't make much of an effort at all, he used to message or email her every day. She had been determined to keep the mood light between them and not phone him but it was now after 9.30pm and it was getting beyond a joke. He knew that it was the last day of term today and that she would've been home earlier than usual and hadn't even bothered to be in touch. His mobile rang out to voicemail.

With a little alcohol in her system she had the confidence to dial his office number. She thought it too was just about to go to voicemail also when someone picked up. "Peter?"

"Hello? Erm no, it's Stacey," the girl's voice said back to her. "Peter has just left."

"Oh, OK, thanks," Caitlyn said awkwardly and put down the receiver. He must be on the Underground. I wonder if it was one of the blonde bimbos that were his new Facebook friends who had answered? She navigated to Peter's new friends' pages to see if she could find out more about them. Pages were private but she did see some photos. No Stacey. But they did seem young and pretty. Damn. Do I have something to worry about? One picture did catch her eye though – a status update and picture about 'Jemma's new car'.

It looked suspiciously very much like that car that Peter had got a lift home from a few weeks ago, when he had assured her he had got a taxi. Surely not? Peter wasn't like that. He had nothing to hide. But surely if he got an innocent lift home from someone from his work he would admit it? Why would he lie? She slapped her head and chastised herself out loud, don't be daft, too much time on your hands and too much wine is making your mind wander and play games! Peter is working really hard at the moment and she should be proud of him and his efforts. He would never do anything to damage our relationship, she reassured herself. He's probably going to walk in the door any minute now and sweep her off her feet and into bed, she hoped. Her heart always used to melt at even the thought of Peter but now she had this nagging feeling at the back of her mind that something wasn't quite right. She poured another glass of wine and meandered through to her bedroom to sort her hair and makeup before Peter returned. She better make sure she looked the best she can, she might be competing with sexier, younger colleagues for Peter's affection! Although, deep down she didn't really believe it.

She returned to the kitchen and started to heat up their meal as he walked in the door.

"You're home!"

"Sorry babe, I tried to ring you earlier, it's been an awful day. Is dinner not ready?"

"Yes, yes, it's just coming."

She walked forward to him looking for a kiss but he pushed back to peer into the oven. "What is it? Shepherd's pie? I hate that, jeazso Caitlyn, I'm starving!"

"You love shepherd's pie!"

"I did when I was 18, I'm sick of it now though. I was hoping for a Thai curry or something nice."

"Sorry babe, I thought you would like this. I never knew you were sick of it." Caitlyn was now getting angry as well as disappointed. She opened up the oven and slammed the casserole dish onto the worktop.

"Take it easy, you'll mark the worktop," Peter snapped.

"Give me a break! If you had been in touch all day or replied to any of my messages, you might have given me an indication of what you wanted for dinner! Maybe if you weren't so bloody late all the time we could make something together or go out the way we used to do!" Caitlyn shouted back, her patience finally gone. She spooned out two big portions of the shepherd's pie. Normally she took pride in the appearance of the meal, now she just slapped it down on to the plate, not making it look particularly appetising but she didn't care.

Peter walked out of the room into the hall, slamming the kitchen door behind him. She heard the TV getting switched on and then heard him rummaging about in the bedroom. She took a deep breath and continued to dish out the dinner on to plates. She had a look in the fridge to see if there was anything quick she could make alternatively for Peter. Nothing. As she slammed the fridge door shut her eyes caught sight of the photo magnet of her and Peter at Alton Towers, in hysterics on the log flume. Her temper started to ease and she started to feel bad. He was probably just in a bad mood from working so long and she didn't want to have an argument over something so silly. She took a beer out the fridge and opened it for him, taking it through to the sitting room for him. He came in the door at her back and put his arms around her and pulled her close.

"I'm sorry babe, I'm sorry for being so snappy. And I'm sorry for working all these hours. Work is just pretty full on at the moment and it's getting to me. I promise you it isn't for long and it will benefit us both, all this overtime, I promise. I just want to save money for our future. Do you forgive me?" She turned round to face him, still holding him around his waist. He stroked her hair, pulling her long side fringe away from her face. "You look sexy," he said softly. Caitlyn smiled back at him, her eyes meeting his. "Of course I forgive you, Petey. I just miss you, I was lonely!"

He laughed and then kissed her on her forehead. "I'm sorry, Caitlyn," he repeated. "I love you so much. I will make it up to you."

"Will you now?" she said as she playfully squeezed his bum.

"Ha! I know what you are after!" he said teasingly as he ran his hands up her back, "but first we must eat! And the shepherd's pie is fine, I just had thought of something else. You must be starving too if you've waited on me?"

"God yeah, I'm ravenous! I thought you'd be home hours ago." She pulled away as she went to the kitchen to retrieve the meals. They got comfy on the sofa and munched into their dinners as they enjoyed each other's company.

"That was actually pretty delicious," Peter finally admitted as he put his empty plate on to the floor.

"Oh was it now was it, Mr? I thought you didn't like shepherd's pie?" she said jokily.

"Well, it must be the way you make it as I did enjoy it, honest!"

"Good, I'm glad."

Caitlyn picked up the empty plates and took them through to the kitchen to wash up.

"Put the kettle on!" she heard Peter shout through to her.

Orders, orders, she said under her breath. I've had a bloody full day of work too, she thought. Although, she didn't want to complain, she was just happy that Peter was home. She loved quiet nights in

180

She stood up now, tears streaming down her face. "Well what I was thinking was that it would be nice for us to get away somewhere nice and spend some time together as a fucking couple since we barely see each other these days! You used to always talk about us going to Kintyre together and spend a romantic week away and now all you want to do is spend all your time at your fucking work! For all I know, you're fucking some whore at your office," she added in hastily, instantly regretting it coming out of her mouth.

"Oh, get over yourself, Caitlyn! You know that is not true!" he roared. "You know I'd love to go away with you but it's just not possible at the moment and we just don't have the money. I'm working really hard getting us more money. I want us to get a better house, a home for the future. It wasn't for squandering on a few days gallivanting! I've even cancelled my season ticket for God's sake!"

She couldn't believe her ears, he wasn't even backing down or in the least bit apologetic or even thinking about trying to get out of work. "Don't you want to come?"

"No I don't, Caitlyn. I need to be at work next week and that is final. You'll just need to phone them and cancel, you have to get the money back. We can't afford these silly trips for fuck sake!"

"It's not a silly trip! I bought it as a nice surprise for you. It was for us!"

"Well you shouldn't have!"

"Fine! I'll know the next time not to fucking bother!"

"I can't be bothered with you when you're like this, I'll sleep on the couch."

"Brilliant, you do that then, I'll have a better time on my own anyway! Yeah, great way to start the holidays!" she roared as she stomped into the bedroom, slamming the door hard behind her. She jumped into bed without taking off her clothes or taking off her makeup. She knew her mascara would tear stain the pillows as she cried herself to sleep, but she was beyond caring.

Chapter 32

Jennifer was really tipsy when she left Jamie and many of the other half-cut teachers at the city centre bar. She reapplied her makeup one more time before heading off to meet her new man, Stuart. She was giddy with excitement and she hadn't felt like this for some time. She knew that there was a strong possibility of this relationship going somewhere. Nevertheless, it was taking off much differently than her previous dates. They were taking it pretty slow, slower than other relationships she had had previously, maybe it was because they were a bit more mature? Stuart was a bit older and he had his own house but he'd never invited her over. Normally, a few weeks into dating they would be seeing each other a little more midweek by now and maybe even staying over a few nights through the week at each other's houses, but Stuart seemed a little guarded. She had asked him about going to the cinema or going for coffee before but he always had other plans. They hadn't had any proper dates allowing them to talk and she was really looking forward to tonight as it would give them both some time to really get to know one another. She had so many questions to ask!

However, it certainly hasn't stopped their sex lives developing, that she was extremely satisfied with! That's all they seemed to do. He had stayed over a few times at her flat after nights out but always left before morning and never waited beyond midnight on a week night. She wasn't bothered though and she thought it was maybe best to take things leisurely and not rush into anything serious. She was really happy, happier than she had been in a long time and she wanted it to continue.

Stuart already was seated at the restaurant's bar when she entered the small dark eatery. He sat tall on the bar stool, holding a glass of Springbank malt whisky on ice. He was wearing a smart crisp grey suit with a charcoal shirt underneath, slightly unbuttoned with no tie. Her heart skipped a beat, she had butterflies. He was gorgeous. Even although Glasgow hadn't seen much sunshine in the last few weeks, he still had a nice golden tan to his face from his golfing sessions, not orange or fake looking like some, but natural and attractive. His hair was dark and curly but he had shaved and it really suited him, he looked really sophisticated. She wondered how old he was. She knew he was definitely a few years older than her but they had never discussed personal details. He smiled broadly and kissed her on the cheek to welcome her. "Wow, you look amazing." He looked around the bar briefly before turning back to her.

"Thank you," she acknowledged sheepishly, "you look pretty good yourself. I've never seen you clean shaven before," she said jokily, seductively smiling and stroking his arm.
He laughed heartily and put his arm around her to pull her close, "Have a feel."

She giggled like a teenager as she slowly stroked his face with the back of her hand sending shivers up her spine, "Hmmm super soft".
"Now what would the beautiful lady like to drink this evening? Or are you just wanting to get out of here?" he whispered into her ear

186

whilst running one of his hands underneath her top to the small of her back.

She was falling under his spell, but she was determined that tonight they would do some talking. "You know I would love to get out of here," she said playfully, "but I've been looking forward to this and I am kind of hungry…"

"Aww… I'm disappointed… I wanted you to take me home," he pretended to sulk and guided her hand down towards his crotch where he was obviously starting to get aroused. He glanced around the bar again, obviously looking to see if anyone had seen their little encounter she thought.

She smiled naughtily and pulled her hand away, she couldn't help herself. "OK, you've done it again, let's get out of here."

He smiled widely and took the last sip of his drink.

"But on one condition," Jennifer continued.

"Yes, Miss?" he asked flirtily.

"That we go your place for a change. Jamie will be back soon and I've not seen your swanky pad."

He looked annoyed for a second before replying quickly, "Sorry gorgeous, not tonight. I'm getting work done on the flat and it's a mess. I'm sure Jamie won't mind, he won't see us anyway as I'm sure we won't be out of that bedroom of yours!"

"Aw OK, well let's get some food quickly then," she replied disappointed.

"OK, deal. Next time, I promise," Stuart added quickly, seeing her saddened expression.

"OK, next time then."

He saluted to her as if promising it to her, "I just can't keep my hands off of you! Let's get some quick food, get a cab and get to bed!"

"Sounds like a plan!"

Chapter 33

Jamie stared at his reflection in his mirror for what probably was the twentieth time that morning, double checking his dark denim jeans were perfectly ironed and his shirt pressed. He had been on a shopping spree and bought lots of new trendy designer clothes and couldn't wait to wear them all. It had cost him an arm and a leg but he didn't care and it made him feel good. Jennifer was away meeting her new 'fuck buddy' Stuart and Caitlyn had phoned in tears after a fall out with Peter. He knew that they'd be absolutely fine, it wasn't like Caitlyn and Peter to fall out, it was probably the silliest of arguments over nothing, but he thought he would do his duty as a good friend and arrive with wine in tow – it was the school holidays after all.

He must admit that the trip to Caitlyn's flat in the West End of the city also sneakily gave him the opportunity to drive by Andrew's house as he and his *adoring* family stayed nearby to Caitlyn. He had hoped he would maybe catch a glimpse of him, maybe even bump into him in the local supermarket where he would be buying Caitlyn some cheer me up food and drink? He was excited at the possibility and knew he sounded vaguely (alright very) stalker-ish but he felt an attraction between them. He scolded himself for sounding so immature and needy, but a little drive past wouldn't harm anyone and he was certain that Andrew would see it as innocent. He just wanted a chance to see him or even a little conversation with him would make him so happy! Jamie had found himself thinking more and more about Andrew. Non-stop. His mind would just wander and his imagination was running wild. He would dream about meeting up with Andrew. In his dreams, Andrew would break down, finally admitting that he loved Jamie, had such strong feelings for him and had been living a lie with his family and he'd only just realised that he was gay when he fell in love with Jamie. God, he really was fantasising but he couldn't stop himself!

All the teachers knew where their boss, Andrew Johnstone, stayed and they had seen pictures of the lovely Victorian Townhouse that he shared with his successful solicitor wife and 2 adorable children. From the outside, they looked ever like the perfect family. Jamie was extremely jealous and hoped that everything wasn't as rosy in real life behind closed doors.

It was a beautiful sunny day in Glasgow but the temperature was starting to drop as it grew into the autumn-winter time. Jamie always loved the West End at this time of year, with all the lovely trees that discarded their tawny crisp leaves on the wide pathways and park areas. He drove through the Clyde tunnel and turned left into one of the affluent areas of the city passing by stunning detached mansions and perfectly manicured lawns, all partnered by BMWs, Audis or Mercedes in the driveways. He really should've turned right to go towards Caitlyn's but he wanted to take the long route.

He slowed down as he approached the corner of Andrew's home, trying to appear discreet but looking desperately at each window to catch a glimpse of him. His car was in the driveway but there didn't seem to be much action, he couldn't see any lights or any sign of his wife or children. Disappointed he sped up a little and drove to the end of the street to turn to get to Caitlyn's. He was nearly there when despite knowing that he seemed a bit crazy he decided to turn back and have one more drive past Andrew's house. He cringed at his behaviour and was embarrassed at the thought of admitting what he was doing to anyone, but he just wanted to take the chance to see him, even if it was just from afar. He drove one again slowly down Andrew's street, this time coming from the opposite direction. He attempted to keep focused on the road whilst keeping a sly eye to the side, watching for any movement from his house. A flutter of the blinds? Oh no, what if Andrew saw him driving past twice? This thought suddenly sobered up Jamie's thought process and he drove faster to get to Caitlyn's in the hope that Andrew didn't witness his stalker-like behaviour.

It took him over 20 minutes to find a parking space near Caitlyn's flat making his temper rise and rise and with the disappointment of not seeing Andrew at all he was starting to really look forward to the wine that he brought over for Caitlyn. He was also thinking about sharing his sordid infatuation secret with her. No, he reminded himself, it's just a silly crush and no one should know, Caitlyn wouldn't understand and would persuade him to drop it. And he didn't want to forget about it, even if the feelings weren't mutual, he was enjoying his little fixation and he didn't want to give up on it just yet. "I'm here," Jamie announced as he rang the buzzer and walked up the stairs as Caitlyn let him into the tenement block.

"Are you OK?" Jamie exclaimed, quite taken aback by Caitlyn's state. He wasn't expecting her to be quite so distressed and he felt a little guilty for not coming over immediately. "What's wrong?"

"Oh Jamie," she sighed and burst into tears. This wasn't like Caitlyn, even with more upsetting situations she rarely showed much emotion and was always strong, she was never one for confiding in too much detail unless it was something really serious.

It was obvious that she already had had a few drinks and her face was red and patchy from crying and her mascara had stained her cheeks. However, Jamie still thought silently that she still managed to look beautiful, she just always had a charm about her.

"Here, here, honey," he said softly as he pulled her towards her into a friendly embrace, letting her tear stained face into his chest, "tell me all about it."

After a few minutes of bubbling and sniffling into a tissue, Caitlyn started to talk a little to Jamie, although she was still reserved as ever, picking and choosing what she informed him. "Oh, he's just working so much at the moment Jamie, like all the time and I never see him! For all I know he's having a bloody affair with some slut at work!"

Jamie kept quiet and let Caitlyn do all the talking, just nodding his head and stroking her hair.

"I wanted to treat him, treat us so that we could have some quality time together," she started to speak faster and faster, "as I wanted to make time for us and we'd always planned to go to Kintyre together,

192

I thought he would be so pleased with the surprise but he was just not interested whatsoever. He won't go, his work comes first!"

This was the first time Caitlyn had said some of these feelings out loud and was careful not to reveal too much of her unhappy feelings at the moment.

"Don't be daft, everyone knows how much Peter loves you! He's just been working a lot of overtime recently for you both. You said yourself that you were wanting to save to get a bigger place. In his line of work, you've got to put in the long hours to progress. It's just been a silly argument I'm sure. Come on honey, let's get this wine opened and we can watch some trashy TV?"
Caitlyn forced a smile and walked towards the living room, dragging her feet like dead weights.

Jamie felt sorry for poor Caitlyn, she had been with Peter all of her adult life and were teenage sweethearts, he hated seeing her like this. Simultaneously he couldn't get rid of Andrew from his mind. Every thought that entered Jamie's brain just seemed to be outrageously filled with him and he couldn't do anything about it.

After demolishing 1 bottle of white zinfandel and half a bottle of Gordon's Gin (only alcoholic thing left in the cupboard) mixed with diluting orange juice (only drinkable mixer left in the cupboard) Caitlyn and Jamie's faces were now lit up by smiles and Caitlyn was feeling in high spirits again. Jamie had managed to persuade her how much Peter still adored her and that it was only normal for us 'adults' to be focused on their careers, especially working more in order to gain a promotion. He also managed to convince her that

193

Peter was doing all of this extra work for her benefit, for them as a couple. She understood that he was most probably correct and admitted that Peter had been saying these same things all along.

The even better news was that she didn't now have to have a lonely week on her own while Peter busied away at work, and didn't need to lose out on her luxury lodge in the country as Jamie had suggested that they all could still go. "I bet you could add us on to the booking? Maybe we could invite Sexy Stuart too?"

Immediately Caitlyn was on the phone and she managed to salvage the holiday with the travel agent. And although she would've ideally preferred to be going away with Peter, she was ecstatic that she wasn't losing out completely and she managed to add Jamie, Jennifer and Stuart on to the booking. Jamie and Caitlyn were now busy discussing what they were going to pack and the activities they were going to undertake. The excitement of going on holiday was back!

"Shit, I've not been to the gym today!" Caitlyn exclaimed, now worried.

"And?"

"I always go, I need to look good in my bikini!"

"You look fantastic! In fact, you look a bit too skinny these days. You can skip the gym for one day for God's sake!"

Caitlyn thought otherwise but she mentally decided to do double the workout she had planned for tomorrow, she had the time anyway as they were on holiday she reassured herself.

"Plus," Jamie added, "we're not going to Spain or anything. You'll only be in your bikini for the briefest of moments when we're in the hot tub – it's just us, and we've seen it all before – and more!" Caitlyn giggled "I know!"

The first day of the holiday was now over and Caitlyn had successfully finished packing for their road trip and was sitting alone in the living room watching some old Sex and the City episode repeats on TV. She had now completely sobered up from earlier and had even managed to do a little of the marking she had planned for the first few days. Jamie had abandoned his car at hers as he had ended up having far more to drink than he anticipated but instead of crashing at hers, he got a taxi back to his own flat. This was a sensible decision as he knew now that he was going away for a few days he wouldn't have the same amount of time to do all of the school work he needed to get done before the return to school the following week.

Caitlyn had her laptop open and had attempted to do some development work for the new curriculum but found herself straying onto Facebook. She browsed Peter's page but there wasn't much activity and couldn't help be a little miffed that there didn't seem to be any photos of her at all on his page and his profile picture was one of him and a work colleague at a football game. In fact, she noticed that she wasn't even listed as his girlfriend on Facebook. How hadn't she noticed this before? Was he embarrassed of her?

She reminded herself that Peter was cautious about sharing information online and didn't use social networking sites as often as her and her friends but she still was more than disappointed at not even a mention. Whereas on her page he was at top of her friends list, she had requested him to add her as family or as his 'in a relationship' and even had an old holiday snap of them together as her profile picture. That photo always made her smile, reminded her of the happy holiday they had to Cyprus.

She quickly navigated on to Cameron's page, browsing his latest activities and posts that the privacy setting would allow since she wasn't a direct friend. There was no immature stupidity, it was just him keeping in contacts with friends and football buddies. There were a few new photos from nights out and football matches that she was able to view and she couldn't help but stare at the pictures in lust. He looked handsome, self-assured but not over confident. That dark hair slightly overgrown in an out-of-bed styled way with gorgeous piercing blue eyes. She noticed that a few of the photos he was in running gear and it looked to be taken outside of her gym.

She recognised a few of the others in the snaps. I wonder if he is in the gym's running club? She had heard that a club had started and the personal trainer at reception was always encouraging her to join but she always declined. She was tempted as it looked fun. Her perusal of photos was interrupted by a chat message from Jennifer.

Hi C, how r u?

Hey Jen, good, u?

Gr8! Thank u so much for this trip, we can't wait! Why couldn't Pete make it?

His stupid work, long story. Jamie will tell you.

Aw OK. What are you going to do now instead?

Huh?

Instead of the trip?

I'm still going – doh!

A few minutes of inactivity went by before Jennifer replied again.

But thot u were giving it to me n stu?

Shit sorry Jen, I was meaning either the 3 of us or 4 us could go, I still want to go if that's OK? I'd love to meet Stu and get to know him better.

Ohhhhhhh, right. No bother I'm sure Stu will be fine with that. We get enough sexytime anyway lol.

Haha, r u sure?

Yeh, course just miscommunication on my part. I'd love for yous to get to know him better. I'll talk 2 him now. BRB

Jennifer quickly called Stuart to excitedly ask him but disappointingly, Stuart didn't seem as keen as she'd hoped and made some excuses that it might not be possible for him through work and other commitments. Although she was delighted that after he went away and made a few phone calls he called back to say that he would be able to make it after all. Sometimes she had to remind herself that not everyone gets school holidays, and need to speak to their managers to get time off work. She was really pleased that Stuart happily agreed about joining the 3 friends, and wasn't too disappointed that they weren't going on their own. "As long as we have our own room and we get some alone time in the hot tub I'll be happy," he goaded.

Jennifer typed back quickly to Caitlyn to tell her the good news. They decided together that it would actually help them get to know Stuart better too and Caitlyn and Jamie were keen to give them some 'alone' time too. If Stuart was to become a permanent fixture in Jennifer's life then it was only about time to start to get to know his friends better, so this was an ideal situation to do just that.

Caitlyn had hoped that Peter would be a little annoyed and jealous to find out that she was still going on the trip and would say that he would miss her. But unfortunately and sadly for her all he could moan about was that she was still spending money on a holiday, he didn't seem at all bothered that he wouldn't see her for nearly a week. He actually seemed vaguely pleased for her to go away. "Don't worry," she reassured him, "the cost is now split between four. At least it will keep me busy since you're not rushing to take time off with me."

"I suppose," is all that Peter could muster. She couldn't help but sulk a little that night, maybe a little bit over the top in the hope that Peter would put his arm around her or try and seduce her but yet again, nothing. She stomped around the apartment, avoiding eye contact and giving one syllable answers to his questions, but he didn't even seem to pick up on her mood. Instead Peter looked disinterested and pottered about on his work laptop all night occasionally sighing loudly or speaking to himself. She eventually decided to head to bed early in the hope that Peter followed soon after but he never and she fell into a dreamless and discontented sleep and awoke again to an empty flat early the next morning.

Peter must have left for work already she groaned, he never even kissed her or said goodbye. She was getting fed up with this but she was determined to put it out her mind and get on with all the school work she had to do and plan for her holiday this week. The thought of the holiday put a smile back on her face and she quickly pulled on her gym gear without as much as a brush of her hair and headed to the gym grabbing a banana for energy on the way out the door.

Caitlyn felt completely de-stressed after the gym, she pushed herself hard, managing to run 6 miles in just under 45 minutes on the treadmill. Her clothes were now soaked with sweat and her face glowing red but the endorphins were pumping around her body and she felt ready to take on the world, all negative thoughts about Peter and their relationship had escaped her. As she walked to the exit, she could see a big crowd of people gathering in the foyer dressed in leggings and fluorescent clothing, the gym's new running club she surmised. She regretted not putting on her more stylish gym gear or at least sorting her hair this morning as she scanned the room quickly praying that Cameron wasn't there to witness her in this hot and clammy state.

"Caitlyn!" she heard as she tried to sneak out of the main door. "Caitlyn!" the voice shouted again grabbing her attention. She looked round and it was one of her spin buddies Emma and her personal trainer friend, Scott – and Cameron! He was in their company, oh no! "Oh hey," she said, "just heading home."

"Been on that treadmill again?" Scott asked smiling.

"How could you tell?" Caitlyn sarcastically jested back looking down at her wet clothing.

The group chuckled and Caitlyn tried not to acknowledge Cameron, acting as if she didn't recognise him.

"Why don't you join us with the new running group?" Emma piped in.

"And embrace the great Scottish weather?" Caitlyn asked with raised eyebrows but with a smile.

"Ha ha, yeah – it's great!" Emma said honestly, "at least the Glasgow weather keeps us cool!"

"And you're a great runner, I've seen you on that treadmill loads, you'd do brilliantly on the road," Scott said.

"Oh I doubt that, I do occasionally run outside, but prefer the consistent weather of the treadmill! I'd be rubbish and you lot would be flying ahead I'm sure!"

"Not at all!" Emma said encouragingly, "plus, it's much better and easier going as a group."

"I've seen you in the gym lots too," Cameron started to interject, "I bet you could outrun most of us in this group!"

She blushed as she turned her head to Cameron and made eye contact and tried to look as if she had just realised that it was him. "I don't think so, Cameron, but thanks! Maybe I'll give it a go next week."

"Yay!" Emma said, "It would be great to get some more girls. You could help me train for the Glasgow 10k!"

"Now hang on, you never said anything about doing a race, don't put me off just yet!"

"Have you never run a race?" Scott asked as Cameron stood beside, awaiting an answer.

"Nope," she admitted sheepishly.

"Oh you'd love it and I bet you'd do fantastic, I'm sure of it! Right, get your bum here next week and see what you think."

"Yes," Scott and Cameron both said in unison, "next week."

"Right OK then, next week. Anyway I better dash, got to get organised for my holiday to Kintyre."

"OK, I'll hold you to that missus, see you next week, 10am sharp."

"OK, see you then!"

Caitlyn couldn't keep the grin off her face as she walked home to her flat, in fact she was positively beaming and practically skipped to her front door. Caitlyn was also taken aback but really thrilled with the group's flattering comments and she was now really keen on joining their group. Nevertheless, she was quite nervous but it was exciting! Caitlyn had always thought about running in races and joining a running club but she never thought she was good enough but after their kind words she was really determined to join up with them. However, she also knew that it was an occasion for her to see Cameron more regularly and was looking forward to that more than anything.

Chapter 34

Jamie and Caitlyn arrived at the cottage earlier than Jennifer and Stuart. They settled in quickly, nosey-ing about the property, checking out the facilities and cramming the fridge with wine and food whilst turning on the surround sound with Jamie connecting his laptop filling the cabin with a chill-out Coldplay album.

"Looks like we're in here," Caitlyn shouted through to him from the bedroom. Jamie followed her through and saw the two twin beds.

"Yeah, I don't think Jen would be too happy if we bagged the big double."

"I'm fine with that, I don't want to share a bed with you anyway!"

"Why, thanks. You've just missed your opportunity for the holiday of a lifetime then!"

"I think I'll live with it. Now let's get some wine!"

They traipsed back into the large open plan modern kitchen and poured themselves some Prosecco, relaxing back on the large black corner couches. The open fire was already smouldering and Caitlyn lit the pillar candles that surrounded the living area just as Jennifer and Stuart entered.

Caitlyn hadn't really spoken to Stuart much at all before so was unsure how the four were going to get on, but she thought they were going to get on just fine when Stuart bundled bags of groceries onto the worktop and exclaimed, "Well hello, guys, who would like Stu's famous strawberry daiquiris?"

The next few days passed by ever so quickly with the days spent out walking the beautiful countryside, along the pristine beaches or cycling the hired mountain bikes on the demanding cross trails around the hills of Campbeltown. Instead of eating out every night the group decided to take turns with cooking meals. Afterwards they sat either on the veranda drinking wine looking out across the Atlantic watching the sun set, dipping into the hot tub, occasionally swapping it for the warmth of the living room when the cold descended for the evening. They had nipped into Campbeltown early in the morning to get supplies from the local bakery store on Main Street, picking up freshly made bread, rolls and cakes. Caitlyn bought the most delicious apple turnover Danish pastries which tasted just as good as she remembered them from her childhood trips to the area. The group couldn't get enough of the local goodies and couldn't resist popping back into the shop to stock up on pastries to take back to Glasgow.

The group were together most of the time but Jennifer and Stuart sometimes disappeared briefly on their own which was understandable as a new loved-up couple. They all got on marvellously, not even a tiny argument had arisen which amazed even them. Stuart fitted into the group of friends perfectly, he was funny, smart, outgoing but not over the top and seemed such a great match for Jennifer. He acted like a perfect gentleman helping her in with her luggage, preparing breakfast in bed for her and showering her with attention, kisses and cuddles when in their company. Jamie and Caitlyn agreed on this and talked in private of how they were tremendously pleased for her as it was obvious that she was extremely happy and comfortable with him, making it look effortless to be so in love.

Stuart also made a conscientious endeavour to get to know Jennifer's friends. He asked them questions and really listened to their answers, genuinely making new found friends which pleased Jennifer no end. Caitlyn couldn't hide her jealousy towards the affection between Jennifer and Stuart. Peter rarely showed her any attention anymore and never in public. She really wished he was here and they could go on romantic walks or share a kiss together in the hot tub under the stars with a bottle of champagne. Her friends picked up on her feelings but thought that she was just missing Peter and disappointed that he couldn't make the trip. In a way that was true but more and more often Caitlyn's thoughts moved to Cameron and the feelings that she had when he was around. She was enjoying every minute of her holiday but was looking forward to returning home and starting the new running club.

Caitlyn was unaware that Jamie was also longing for someone at home. There was someone, Andrew, that he couldn't get out of his head and he was desperate to chat about him to his friends but knew he couldn't broach the subject. After a few glasses of wine each night he would mention Andrew in conversation as with fellow teachers you couldn't help but talk a little bit of school. Although he was cautious not to bring him up too often in case his crush was discovered. As he lay in the single bed each evening he couldn't help wonder what Andrew was doing. Who was he with? Was he with his family? Was he thinking of him? He constantly checked Facebook on his phone for any updates that might involve him but nothing.

By the last day of the trip he got so angry with himself that he mentally decided that he had to get Andrew out of his mind. It was never going to happen, he was a married family man, his boss for God's sake! There was no future so there was no point in getting embarrassed or hurt over this. He knew this was true and needed to try to stop thinking about him but it was so hard to do. Everything he did seemed to remind him of him and every daydream always ended up about him, he just couldn't help it!

Chapter 35

Jennifer had returned from the holiday refreshed and relaxed. She had an amazing trip to beautiful Kintyre with her favourite people – her best friends and her boyfriend. Yes, she said it, her boyfriend. Her amazing, sexy, thoughtful, kind, gorgeous boyfriend. They had had such a romantic time and Stuart showered her with love and affection every minute he could. Their sex life was amazing and she was actually pretty tender after being with him non-stop for nearly a week, although she didn't want a rest from him! Jennifer was also ecstatic that he got on so well with her friends. She did worry at the beginning as Stuart didn't seem keen to go and thought he was a little stand-offish, but once he had made the decision to go and was organised he was more than enthusiastic.

They couldn't keep their hands off each other on the drive up to the cottage and couldn't contain their lust for more than a few hours. Stuart sneakily drove them to a quiet country road en-route for him to have his wicked way with her in the car while it was still daylight. Before she might've been embarrassed or tried to discourage other boyfriends from doing such daring things but she was just so attracted to Stuart she couldn't say no. Luckily they weren't caught in any compromising positions and they carried on their journey afterwards as if nothing happened although they couldn't help giggling about it for hours later as if they were teenagers in love. That's what she felt like they were – teenagers, falling in love for the first time. Just the thought of Stuart made her weak at the knees and she was certain her heart thumped harder at the thought of him. She couldn't remember the last time she felt so strongly about someone.

She now felt like she was ready to be faced with the challenges that her job threw at her. Jennifer was so pleased and was feeling more confident. She had worked hard on developing some new approaches and methodologies to deliver her lessons with her more demanding classes. She had implemented some more active learning and a more structured assertive discipline approach into her lesson plans. She had been giving out more verbal praise to her pupils and rewarding them with a new merit point system building up to prizes at the end of term and it was going really well so far. She had included some games in her lessons to make it more fun and engaging, but she was also trying to reinforce the school rules and remind them of the consequences of their actions.

She started back from holidays by going over the school rules with all her classes. In a way it felt like she was treating the pupils more like Primary school children than Secondary but in a way it was actually giving them more responsibility for their behaviour so it also treated them like the young adults that they were. And all of the classes, even in the senior school, were positively responding. The first few weeks back in term she had treated it like her project, reviewing every lesson and discussing it with her PT. The grades of her pupils were also improving as well as the attendance of her classes. It didn't happen overnight nor were the results dramatic in anyway but she was in high spirits that progress was being made.

She felt happier and her worst class (with the dreaded John and co) seemed much more settled. Even John was taking part much more and she didn't need to discipline him quite as often. Although she did find that the one period that she had the class after lunch on a Friday was particularly boisterous and she had resigned to the fact that the noise level was never going to be very low on such occasions. Pupils were always usually hyper after eating and drinking copious E numbers and fizzy juice at lunch and remarkably worse at the end of the week on a Friday period 6. Pupils weren't allowed to purchase such things like these anymore on the school premises but the kids always made a point of going to the nearby High Street especially on a Friday lunch.

On this particular day she had started the lesson in what the pupils thought of as quite a dull way with some questions from the previous lesson's work on the board. This was done intentionally to try and settle them as well as test them on their knowledge. She was hopeful that they could get some of their independent work completed for their portfolio as the deadline was looming and unfortunately you couldn't just do all the fun activities all the time like play learning games or interdisciplinary group tasks or they would never pass a single exam. With their new routine and rules now set in, the pupils quietly got on with their work after a few minutes of commotion of getting into the classroom. Even John had taken off his outdoor clothing and had even remembered his jotter which was a feat in itself. OK so 8 out of 30 of them still had to borrow a pencil but so what, they were here and they were working.

"Now it's only starter questions so I'm not expecting full sentences at the moment, short answers will suffice." She never really expected full sentences from this class at the best of times but this instruction was trying to encourage the poorer kids to at least attempt the questions. "Try your best and if you can't remember, just leave it blank and we'll go over the answers in just 3 minutes."

She was actually really proud. They all looked up at the interactive whiteboard and studiously scribbled into their jotters without a word. It was like a changed class. She stopped them after a few minutes and they swapped jotters to peer assess their work and they discussed the main features of the last lesson which progressed into the next topic for today and adding into their portfolios. With a little coaxing they all took out their folders from the filing cabinet and set about their work autonomously as Jennifer walked around the room answering a question here and there, supervising all of the work. But it was quiet. Quiet. She was contented and full of pride. She walked back to her desk and printed off a few more worksheets, glancing up every now and then to ensure they were still on task. Silence.

And just like that the silence was broken. Mayhem ensued. Laughter erupted from the class and cries of "look, look!" as some of the kids pointed at the door. She had purposely closed over the door so that they couldn't be interrupted from other classes walking by, but there was a little window pane where you could see out. There stood Mr Greig, pulling faces at the pupils, more than distracting them from their work but putting them off for the entire period. As the kids pointed, laughed and started joking, the noise level rose considerably and Jennifer knew she would never get them settled again. Obviously he aimed to do this, she thought. She was so angry she wanted to open the door and greet him with a punch in the nose! He was still pulling faces through the pane looking like a right idiot and it seemed that he was trying especially to get the attention of John, and he was biting. But instead of reacting, she laughed too, even though laughing was the last thing on her mind, trying to show the kids that this nonsense didn't get to her and that it hasn't spoiled the lesson.

"Just pull a face back at him," she joked to the class and they all did, seeing who could come up with the funnier face. Mr Greig smirked outside the door but she could tell that this was not the reaction he had hoped for, she thought he had probably hoped that she would march out and shout at him as well as get in a panic and shout at her 'uncontrollable class'. Although there was nothing more she wanted to do than march out to him demanding he stop immediately, she remained calm. He soon walked away and Jennifer tried to quieten the class to get back into their work. Unfortunately it did not go back to the conscientious effort that was 5 minutes ago but the majority of them were continuing with their work nonetheless.

After another 15 minutes of working and answering questions she decided to stop them and play a plenary bingo game using Geography terminology from the cloud formation topic with them which they thoroughly enjoyed. She couldn't help but smile after the kids all left her room at the end of the lesson. The pupils were really starting to respond to her. Even when some of her colleagues tried to knock her down she still managed to keep control.

Maybe she wasn't as bad a teacher as she first thought. Jennifer felt even more fantastic when she was leaving work for the day on her way to see her new, amazing and sexy boyfriend Stuart, waving goodbye to Mr Greig whilst smiling broadly and looking carefree. He grimaced noticeably at her positive reaction which just made her smile even more.

Chapter 36

Jamie had also thoroughly enjoyed his trip away with his friends and had tried to suppress his jealousy of Jennifer and Stuart's new relationship, but he yearned for what they had. He had had plenty of partners before but truthfully he had never felt as if he was even close to loving them, well loving them for longer than a few weeks that is. Whereas, the feelings he now had for Andrew just seemed more intense than he had ever had before, and he was certain it wasn't just lust. He wanted to be with him even just to chat about the most mundane things, just to be in his company, even to sit in silence he would be happy! His friends were oblivious to the fact that Jamie had these feelings and always thought on Jamie loving the life of a singleton, not realising that he wanted a 'proper' relationship too not just one night stands like before.

Jamie mused about how wonderful Andrew was – he admired his career progression and how he coped with such a stressful job at such a young age, not forgetting his effortless style and still managing to balance his family life. Yes, family life Jamie reminded himself. He was certain that Andrew had some feelings for him too. Didn't he? Or was he just imagining all of this chemistry?

Despite going into school every day and loitering about the senior management offices trying to look busy since their return back to Glasgow, he hadn't caught a glimpse of Andrew. It wasn't actually until the end of the first week back that he finally got to speak to him on his own when Jamie was back being busy with his full timetable and thriving on the challenge that teaching gave him.

The curriculum was going through a major restructuring so there was so much work to do on top of the already demanding job. Every class was different and every pupil unique. There had also been some new additions to his classes which was inevitable with families moving to the area and placement requests. This gave Jamie some extra work and it took time to get the pupils up-to-date with the classwork as well as become familiar to the rules and routine of his classes. It was only natural for the pupils to take a few weeks to adapt to their new surroundings and make friends.

It always amazed him that most kids found their feet in new schools dramatically quickly compared to how adults would fit into a new workplace. One of the new arrivals though, Dylan Morlie, was proving to be harder work than he anticipated. He came to the first lesson without any bag or pen and no information was provided by his last school which made it more difficult for him to gauge his progress and differentiate the work. Nevertheless, it only took 5 minutes for Jamie to realise that this young 12 year old boy had severe learning difficulties. His eyes couldn't focus and couldn't retain information or answer simple questions that he was asking. Dylan was scanning the room and would mimic animal noises as he pointed at pictures and photos in the room that caught his eye. And although he was still trying to teach the 30 other pupils in his class he quickly spotted that this was his normal demeanour and he was not 'play acting' or trying to be belligerent. Without trying to draw

213

attention or make it obvious to the rest of the pupils he managed to settle him with a wordsearch whilst he contacted the Learning Support department who assisted children with learning difficulties and behaviour problems. The staff there confided that they had received no information from his previous school, and he was a pupil who was in looked after accommodation so no data had been offered from parents or guardians either on his development.

Jamie had some experience in dealing with children with learning difficulties and included many within his classes, some classes having 6 or 7 pupils that had recorded needs such as autism, Aspergers and ADHD. All of them needed extra time with work and more preparation was always needed to prepare differentiated work, but he preferred to try and include them in mainstream lessons rather than exclude them to the Learning Support department if possible. Although this was not always appropriate as some couldn't cope with the social aspects of the class or with some of the activities set on their own. Some pupils were also entitled to a support assistant who helped them during classes and he suspected that Dylan would be one of these pupils.

However, the Learning Support department informed Jamie that their resources were really scarce today due to staff absences and asked if Jamie could keep him within his class until they could release an assistant to collect him nearer the end of the period. Jamie agreed and continued with his lesson but unfortunately had to change plans so that he could sit with Dylan for the rest of the period. It was obvious that he couldn't even cope independently with the basic

214

wordsearch and whilst Jamie was on the phone he had begun to sway from side to side in his chair whilst loudly barking like a dog. Some of the other pupils had begun to notice and were pointing and giggling.

Jamie had to admit that this bizarre behaviour was something he had never seen and wasn't really sure of how to address. He didn't want him to become singled out or bullied by his peers, so he tried to shield him from the others, glaring at them discreetly to focus on their work. They obeyed. He asked Dylan about where he was from and what school he used to attend, but he just stared blankly, repeatedly mumbling words and staring into space. Jamie wasn't sure whether to laugh or cry but knew he must try to keep nonchalant at least not to draw attention from the other pupils. He felt sorry for this new boy, how must he be feeling? Was he even aware of what he was doing or where he was? Jamie felt uncomfortable and awkward talking to him but continued to try and build a relationship. Dylan was doodling over the page of the wordsearch so Jamie gave him a fresh piece of paper and asked him to draw a picture which he seemed pleased with. This gave Jamie a bit of time to focus on some of his other pupils who had been trying to get his attention and to monitor their work.

Andrew had been in and out of classes looking for certain pupils to issue behaviour cards all week but had barely acknowledged Jamie much to his disappointment. However, this particular period he had stopped to chat to Jamie briefly but unfortunately it was all work related. Andrew sternly demanded that 2 pupils from Jamie's class were to report to the Depute Head's office. The students sheepishly followed the order. Others in the class looked round stifling their giggles but continued to work hard just in case they were spoken to next. As he was leaving his classroom, Andrew subtly apologised to Jamie for disrupting the class, and commended him for the control that he had with his class especially as the class was notorious around the school for being a handful. Jamie loved accepting the compliment modestly and tried to twist the conversation around to holidays or weekends but Andrew was obviously busy and didn't wait long. This was probably a blessing as Dylan had now got up out of his seat and had wandered over to the window and was staring aimlessly out at the dreary day outside.

He observed him as he stood, rocking back and forth muttering words underneath his breath, scratching his left forearm with his right hand furiously. Not long after, Dylan's guidance teacher arrived and escorted him to the Learning Support department where he said they were going to assess his needs and decide on an educational plan for him, much to the relief of Jamie. He didn't think it would be fair to Dylan, his classmates or for a teacher to let him remain for the time being.

It can be intricate enough dealing with pupils of varying ability levels in the class but having a pupil on that scale of challenging behaviour, albeit harmless, would prove almost unmanageable and to no benefit for him to remain in class.

Before Jamie could be too disheartened by Andrew's lack of communication, he received an email from him at the end of the

216

working day. This wasn't an unusual occurrence at work but he immediately noticed that there were no other recipients. He hastily double-clicked with his mouse trying to take in all of the text at once.

Hello Jamie

Sorry for the abruptness of my visit earlier but I had 8 pupils to catch before the next class, you wouldn't believe how many behaviour cards and exclusions I've had to administer since our return from holiday and it's not even a week yet!

Anyway, I've been meaning to try and catch up with you individually for a chat – could you possibly come to see me next week at some point? I've got a lot of meetings but ask Frances in the office and she will schedule a meeting in my diary.

Regards

AJ

Jamie read it again. And again. He wants to meet? What does he want to discuss? He DOES feel the same way? He has to! There's definitely chemistry between them, he knew that, maybe this meeting would be the start of something? But what about his wife? His family? Was it a heterosexual pretence? His imagination started spinning out of control and he hit the 'reply' button before he had time to stop himself. He battled with the wording of the email, writing sentences, paragraphs, re-reading and then deleting back to scratch. He then left his computer to mark some of the jotters piling up on his desk to buy some time, he didn't want to come across as desperate either. Then after just 2 jotters he gave up and returned to compose the email. He was the Head Teacher after all, he would maybe expect a prompt reply. After another 5 minutes of redrafting the email he eventually settled on his message.

Hello

No problem. You're a busy man, you weren't abrupt – no apology necessary! Have I done something wrong – am I getting put on a behaviour card?!

I'll see Frances later about an appointment.

Regards

Jamie

He wasn't sure if 'Hello' was too informal and he didn't know whether to address him with his first or second name and after much deliberation he decided not to mention his name. Jamie also wanted to inject a little humour and wanted to ensure that he asked a question within it to try and encourage a little dialogue. He re-read the email and spell-checked it at least 10 times before eventually sending it at the click of a button. He then waited another hour in school marking the remaining jotters on his desk and preparing the first 2 lessons of tomorrow, checking his inbox every few minutes to see if Andrew had replied. He knew he would still be in school until after 6 and he could see out of his window that his car was still parked. Eventually, around 6.30pm as Jamie was packing up his things for the evening he received an email. He excitedly refreshed the page and looked up expectantly. It was from him. His eyes lit up and he read the email feverishly with anticipation.

You would never be in trouble! Just something I've been meaning to discuss with you for a while.

Speak to Frances and I look forward to seeing you next week.

AJ

Jamie stared at the screen, re-reading and thinking about the wording and the construction of the message looking for some hidden meaning. He is looking forward to seeing me! I wonder what he wants to discuss? He squealed excitedly to himself trying to refrain from smiling too much. Does he want to profess his undying love for me and wants to run away with me ditching everything just to be my partner? Hmm probably not but he too was looking forward to the meeting nonetheless!

Chapter 37

Caitlyn's last few weeks back at work had been hectic since the trip to Kintyre. She had been helping out with the drama group's Christmas show preparations along with Jamie, and although they still had 10 weeks left to go the work to be done in advance was immense. Every interval, lunch and after school had her undertaking one job or another – helping with rehearsals, photocopying scripts and music sheets, booking gym halls for practices and organising costumes. Caitlyn didn't mind though and it kept her mind occupied, less time to think about her recent relationship troubles with Peter. She had also hoped that since the departure of Cameron from school that her little silly 'crush' would be 'crushed' but thoughts of him continued to fill her head from time to time. She tried to push them out by focusing on her work.

Unfortunately things hadn't become any better between her and Peter. They had barely been alone together since her holiday as he had been working away a lot, and when he was there although they hadn't been arguing Peter seemed to lack any interest with Caitlyn in the bedroom. She had tried to make advances on him but every time he always had an excuse– *too tired*, *have to work* or a *sore head*.

Caitlyn felt dejected and useless. Peter didn't even text or call her whilst she was away, she didn't think he missed her at all. He did seem happy when she got back but all he wanted to do was sit on the couch and watch TV if they had any spare time together. Caitlyn loved curling up on the sofa with him but sometimes there wasn't anything said between them from an entire evening and she felt lonely.

It was now Saturday morning and as promised she was going to attend her first running club training session. She had bought herself new stylish black and hot pink running leggings and matching t-shirt from a sports shop online as she hadn't had a chance to go to the shops, and it allowed her to keep the purchases quiet from Peter.

Although she never usually wore any makeup or thought much about her hair when going to the gym she took a bit of time to make an effort today, pulling her hair neatly back into a slick ponytail, wrapping her blonde hair around the bobble affixing a clasp to secure the style. She applied a little foundation, a touch of highlighting blusher along with some waterproof mascara and pale natural lip gloss. She stared at her reflection in the mirror feeling a little silly as she was only going to outside where it was probably pouring with rain and howling with wind ready to mess it all up as well as sweat all over her new clothes. She didn't care though, she was allowed to look good for a change, at least she looked the part she thought. She was really nervous as despite running most days she had never ran with anyone before, never mind a running club. She was starting to have second thoughts.

After some self-motivating speeches in her head Caitlyn finally set off for the gym. She tried not to look too eager and arrived with just a few minutes to spare. She spotted Cameron immediately. Looking relaxed and handsome he laughed and joked with some of the other runners at the registration desk. He was wearing black

221

shorts and an indigo blue vest top and expensive looking trainers. He looked in fantastic shape. He wasn't super slim like many runners, just lean and toned. She hung around the back of the group, hoping not to get noticed by him and she glanced around to see what everyone else was wearing. The majority of people were wearing similar clothing to hers, most of the women wearing leggings with a few wearing shorts and t-shirts despite the cold weather. No-one else looked new though, they looked liked seasoned pros all tapping their pricey looking watches and discussing races and she was beginning to panic when her friend Scott spotted her.

"You're here!" he exclaimed.

"Yip, I'm here!"

"Fantastic, welcome to the club, Caitlyn, you're going to do brilliantly I'm sure. We're only doing an easy run following the river Clyde and canal tow path today, so just take your time and go at your own pace." He smiled friendly and reassuringly at her.

"OK. Is there anyone I can run with – anyone quite slow that isn't going to leave me behind?"

"If you want to team up with Chantal over there, our Club secretary who deals with new members. She isn't slow, just like you aren't, but she will show you the ropes and if you want to go faster or slower just you decide. If you want to cut the run short just come back to the gym and we all meet up afterwards, if you want, for a breakfast in the gym café."

"OK. Thanks" she stuttered.

Within minutes the group of 20-odd runners headed out into the bright sunshine of Glasgow following the river Clyde, where they passed some of the city's famous landmarks such as the Finnieston Crane, SECC and the newly built Hydro arena. Chantal jogged alongside Caitlyn welcoming her to the club, asking her polite questions about her running experience and fitness goals. Caitlyn really enjoyed the friendly banter and got on brilliantly with Chantal. Caitlyn was really pleased that she managed to keep up with her somewhere in the middle of the group of runners continuing her discussion with her for just over an hour before both returning to the gym.

"Wow, brilliant effort Caitlyn, you did great on your first day! We ran 9 miles in 1 hour and 12 minutes." She stated matter-of-factly as she hit a button on her watch.

"Really? That's the most I think I've ever done!"

"Great pace, we were pretty fast today. I'm really pleased with that." She said wiping the sweat away from her brow.

"Me too. I loved that!" she exclaimed honestly. She too was sweating profusely but she felt great, an even better high than just her normal workouts in the gym.

"So will you be back next week then?"

"Yes, definitely!" she said without hesitation.

"Great. Some of us run midweek informally too and you're more than welcome to join us. We're training for a 10k and half marathon in a few months."

"OK thanks, I might just do that."

"Are you coming to the café for breakfast?"

Caitlyn looked around anxiously looking for the rest of the running group, most of which hadn't returned yet. She would love to go for breakfast with them but she felt guilty and wanted to get back home in time for Peter returning from work. He had promised he would finish early today and she wanted to spend some quality time with him like they used to at the weekends. Caitlyn was hoping that they could both go a nice long walk in the West End through the Botanical Gardens or Kelvingrove Park and stop off for a nice coffee and cake at one of their favourite delicatessens. They used to do this frequently every week but hadn't had time to visit in a long time. Her tummy grumbled at just the thought of carrot cake with cream cheese icing. They might even take a stroll down Ashton Lane for a few drinks. She loved leisurely Saturdays and spending them with Peter in the West End, it was one of her favourite places in the world.

"No sorry, not today, I've got to get back, got plans in the afternoon with my boyfriend. He's treating me – hopefully some nice lunch and wine."

"Lovely! Well no problem, maybe next time. Catch you next week then."

"OK, yeah see you next week. Oh and Chantal, where is the rest of the group?" she tried to add in casually, although she just really wanted to know where Cameron was.

"They're probably not finished yet, think most of them were doing 15 miles today so were going further."

"Wow, 15 miles?"

"Yip I know, most of them like doing more than 10 miles for their long slow run at the weekend."

"That was slow?"

"Ha, well don't worry, maybe not us today, we went pretty fast and should've probably taken it slower, maybe we could go slower next week and go further?"

"Yes OK, I'd really like that, actually I'd love to try and aim to get to 10 miles. Thanks very much! I'm buzzing!"

"Excellent! Yeah double figures is a milestone, pardon the pun! Ok Caitlyn, see you next week."

"Great, see you then!"

As she walked out the gym's automatic main doors she bumped straight into Cameron and one of his other running buddies.

"Sorry!" she exclaimed, "Oh so sorry, I didn't see you," looking up to meet Cameron's smiling gaze. Typical, she thought, annoyed that he would see her in a sweaty horrible state but she was pleased that she got to see him again even just for the briefest of moments.

"It's OK, no problem. You were fast today, just as I predicted!" Cameron continued as his friend walked on into the gym leaving them on their own standing outside the main entrance.

Caitlyn blushed, "Hardly, not compared to you lot!"

"Not at all, you are a really good runner and with more training you will be excellent, one of the club's best women runners I bet."

Caitlyn's cheeks reddened deeper and she laughed, waving her hand modestly dismissing the compliment.

"Fancy coming for some breakfast? Recovery food? Best part about the training!"

Yes! she screamed inside but she found herself declining the invitation. "Sorry, in a rush today but maybe next week." This time she noticed herself forgetting to mention her boyfriend.

"Great, that means you'll be back?"

She giggled flirtatiously playing with her hair, "Yeah I'll be back, really enjoyed it. I loved it actually."

"That's brilliant, erm... Miss? Sorry, not sure what to call you now out of school?" suddenly his confident demeanour looking slightly nervous.

"You can call me Caitlyn, you are out of school now."

He changed back to his poised self, a broad grin showing all of his perfect straight white teeth coming over his face. "Well ok, Caitlyn, I'm glad you came today, I'll see you next week then."

"Yes, see you next week, Cameron" she replied, smiling back making full eye contact.

They were both still standing there, it felt to Caitlyn as if they were getting even closer, she could smell him. It wasn't an unpleasant sweaty smell that some of the other gym-goers had, it was a masculine musky smell, faint of deodorant and the outdoors. Both of them didn't move, she didn't want to leave, she enjoyed the conversation for a chance but she knew she had to go.

"Right then," she eventually said, "have a good weekend and see you next week."

"You too Caitlyn, bye, see you next week."

And before anything else was said she turned on her heels and strode towards her house. She could feel his eyes on her as she walked away and was desperate to look over her shoulder but kept looking straight ahead, concentrating not to trip and look like an idiot in front of him but she just couldn't wipe the wide grin from her face. Caitlyn acknowledged everyone she passed with a friendly smile as she walked cheerily home. Is it possible that Cameron liked her? Did he find her attractive? She didn't even think her boyfriend found her attractive anymore, so how could a young gorgeous boy possibly find her appealing? She couldn't quite understand it but she knew it was possibly true and she couldn't help but feel more than pleased about the fact that she was 'fanciable'. It had been a while since she felt that appreciated or desired. She didn't want to admit it either but she started to think that the feelings between her and Cameron might be mutual.

When she arrived back at the empty flat, the mess that Peter had left behind didn't annoy her as much as usual and even his voicemail left on the answering machine declaring he would be 2 hours late wasn't enough to hamper her good mood. Caitlyn used the time productively to clean every room in the house, scrubbing the bathroom whilst singing along merrily to the radio. Three hours went by pretty slowly even though Caitlyn was kept busy and there was still no sign of Peter. She had enjoyed the time to bathe, preen and pluck and slipped on one of her favourite dresses that always made her feel good. Peter had always loved her in that dress too, he said it showed off her sexy curves. Guiltily she still thought about

227

Cameron a little but tried to push him from her mind. She posed and changed accessories a few times in front of her full length mirror until she was reasonably happy with her reflection. She sat bored on the couch, flicking channels with the remote and checking her mobile continuously every 5 minutes until Peter eventually walked in the door.

"I'm so sorry Caitlyn!" he shouted as he flung off his shoes to the side, dropping his suit jacket to the floor. "Things are just so hectic at work, it's non-stop at the moment, I just couldn't get away."

"Hey, it's fine, you're here now."

"Yes, I'm here now."

Caitlyn walked towards him to kiss him but he pulled away instantly.

"What's wrong? Don't you want to kiss me anymore either?" she asked, half joking but half serious.

"No, no, I just need to brush my teeth," he said as he covered his mouth, "coffee breath, not good!" Peter walked into the bathroom and Caitlyn heard the shower run.

"Why are you showering? You showered before work this morning."

"I'm just freshening up."

"You've only been working for a morning and we're late, I'm starving. Our wee coffee shop will be shutting soon."

"Have you not had lunch?"

"No, you said you were taking me out, I had no idea you would be so late."

228

"Are we still going out?"

Caitlyn hesitated, getting annoyed now "Well, yes I thought that is what we planned. Lunch and maybe a few drinks?"

"Oh sorry we grabbed something quick at work to eat, I thought we were maybe going to just get some coffee as I was hoping to see the football. But I'll come with you for lunch, just give me 10 minutes."

Caitlyn didn't reply, she was pretty angry now and more than a little disappointed. She walked back into the living room and switched on her laptop. She would continue with some of her lesson plans while she was waiting on Peter. She kept an eye on the time though and noticed that 30 minutes went by before Peter came back into the room but she stopped herself from moaning at him, she didn't want to get into another argument, she just wanted to enjoy their time together as they didn't get a chance to do that very often anymore.

"Shall we go?" Peter stood at the door entrance and she couldn't help but smile at him as he looked so handsome and he smelled good.

She walked up to him to kiss him and this time he obliged, pulling her close to his chest. The kiss was short but left Caitlyn wanting more, it had been a long time since they had been this close and intimate. "Maybe we should just eat indoors?" she suggested seductively, nuzzling her nose into the nape of his neck slowly stroking his back working her hands down to his hips.

"Well it would save us money... but no no no, not for you missy, I promised taking you out and that's what I'm going to do," Peter said taking her by the hand. "Plenty time for that too when we get home."

"Oh OK," Caitlyn said pretending to sulk, "as long as we go to bed straight away when we get home?"

"Straight to bed," Peter confirmed and saluted as if on soldier's orders.

They walked hand in hand to the café but they barely said a word to each other. Caitlyn couldn't help thinking that things just weren't 100% right between the two of them. Normally they couldn't stop talking to each other, filling each other in on what was happening at work or their plans for the future. To people looking on at the young couple they would've thought they were a close, romantic pair but as far as Caitlyn was concerned at the moment, nothing could be further from the truth. She felt agitated and not at ease like before. Peter spent most of the time in the coffee shop reading the weekend papers and engrossed in the football scores on his mobile phone, leaving Caitlyn to eat alone. She tried to get his attention and attempted to talk to him about her morning joining in with the running group, but he seemed disinterested so she eventually stopped talking altogether and just tried to enjoy her food although she had lost what appetite she had left.

"I thought you were hungry?" he eventually said, looking up over the sport pages.

"Nah, not as much as I thought," she replied shortly looking unhappy, hoping that Peter would pick up on her sadness and pay her more attention and see that she wasn't her usual self but he seemed oblivious.

"C'mon then, let's go home?"

Caitlyn's hopes picked up, maybe he just wanted to get her into bed? Well that was fine with her, she began to smile again. "OK then, let's go home."

By the time they got home and settled after Peter phoning his parents and having dinner it was almost 10 o'clock and his promise of an early bed didn't seem to be happening. She had retouched her makeup even although they had no plans to go back out, but she was determined to look as sexy as possible for Peter. She really was trying to make a concerted effort but he seemed oblivious to her advances. She sat down beside him, caressing his upper thigh and moving in close. She could see him smile out of the corner of his mouth and she took that as the green light, hitching up her dress straddling him starting to unbutton his shirt but instead of reciprocating he pushed her off.

"Caitlyn!" Peter shouted.

"What? We haven't had sex in ages! I thought you might want me, what's wrong?" she pleaded trying not to sound pathetic.

"I do! Sorry just not right this minute, can't we wait until we get to bed?"

"Sorry I was just trying to be spontaneous, I thought you used to like that?"

"I still do but c'mon Caitlyn, we've grown up. I've been working all the hours under the sun for us and I just wanted some time to watch the TV and catch up with the football."

"Football!"

"Yes, football. I've not seen any of the games this week as I've been working late and because I took you to lunch I never seen anything today either."

"Well sorrreee! And, lunch? Really, it was 3pm and you'd already eaten, hardly a romantic lunch for us! You spent more time on your phone checking out the scores anyway!"

"I never did, I've hardly had a chance to see any football, I've just been so busy!"

"What about me? You've hardly had time for me, surely your priority isn't work then football – do I not get a look-in?"

"God, Caitlyn, just give me an hour, please? You can sit with me and we can share a bottle of wine? And then I promise I'll make it up to you," his face started to soften and he held his hands out to her for a hug.

Caitlyn was still mad, she felt hurt and unwanted. Was she that repulsive? He'd rather look at men on the TV than her!

"Can't you just record Match of the Day and watch it tomorrow? We've got all day and I could do my marking. I just miss you."

"I miss you too, babe. It won't be like this forever, my work won't always be so busy."

"I know, you always say that. So can we just go to bed then with that bottle of wine and maybe a tub of ice-cream?"

He laughed as he pulled her close to him. "You are naughty as ever!"

"Just as you like me!"

"How about a compromise? We'll watch a little tonight with some wine, then we can get the ice-cream for dessert in half an hour?"

Caitlyn rolled her eyes but agreed petulantly, "OK, get watching it now, I'll get the wine."

She went through to the kitchen to get the bottle and could hear the football come on to the main TV. She decided to kill a little time by logging on to Facebook as the laptop was lying open on the kitchen worktop. Caitlyn was only on a few minutes as all the status updates on the news feed was already annoying her with people out having fun or having romantic nights with their other half. She couldn't help be jealous. She hadn't felt like this before, normally she felt somehow superior in a way. She had Peter, a sexy handsome respectful man that loved her to bits and her sex life had always made others green with envy but now she just felt unwanted and lonely. She ran to the bedroom quickly and changed into a sexy lace lingerie set, along with stockings and suspenders with 6 inch black stilettos. She placed the two wine glasses onto a tray and walked slowly and seductively into the living room, bending over in front of Peter to serve his drink. "White wine?"

Peter nodded, not even noticing her sexy outfit, eyes glued to the TV.

She picked up her glass and sat beside him, gulping it down nearly in one but not saying a word to Peter. She was waiting on him to turn around to see what he was missing. Did he see and didn't care? She got up slowly, walked to the kitchen to retrieve the bottle. "More drink, sir?"

"No thanks, babe."

Caitlyn poured another glass for her right up to the brim and sat perched at the edge of the seat drinking it quicker than she should. She finished the bottle of wine before Peter could even get half way through his glass.

"Ah fuck this," she said under her breath as she stood up, alcohol going to her head. "I'm going to bed" she said louder this time.

"OK honey, be there soon."

But he wasn't. Caitlyn kept her outfit on, expecting him to the bedroom within 15 minutes but after an hour he still hadn't appeared. She walked back into the hall, tiptoeing to the living room door, peering through the crack half expecting him to be watching porn or maybe asleep but no there he was, watching another game of football he had recorded earlier in the week. So much for a compromise! Caitlyn too was tired and she couldn't be bothered with an argument so decided to let it be for this evening.

Well fine, if he couldn't be bothered then neither could she, she wasn't going to make any more effort she thought. She was confident that he would feel guilty and come grovelling tomorrow. However, she had always thought that her and Peter were soul-mates, destined to be together forever but his behaviour over the last few months had made her seriously doubt this. In fact, she was starting to think that they weren't meant to be at all.

Chapter 38

Jennifer arrived at work on Monday morning with a spring in her step. She had another wonderful weekend with Stuart and she was remarkably happy with how their relationship was blossoming. He had spent practically the entire weekend with her at her flat and they barely left her bedroom apart from the occasional trip to the kitchen for food supplies and also to the bathroom for a lovely big bubble bath for two. However, she had felt a little guilty taking over the flat and leaving Jamie on his own but she figured that he was a big enough boy to keep himself entertained for a while. She wasn't his only friend and she just wanted to be with Stuart every second, he was all that she could think about. He was adorable and kind and ridiculously sexy. They were at that stage in the relationship where everything they did was exciting and new. They wanted to have sex every waking moment and when they were apart they were sending dirty text messages and now even email messages midweek.

Although unlike other relationships Jennifer had had, regardless of how brief, she had always enjoyed finding out more about them, adding them on Facebook, looking at their photos of previous encounters, holidays and experiences as well as their other friends. She had never been in a serious enough relationship to have linked it on Facebook so it was a bit annoying to her that Stuart didn't even have a Facebook account. However, it just made him all the more intriguing and mysterious! She had asked him as she found it quite strange as he was very IT literate so that fortunately wasn't the problem but he explained to her that he just didn't agree with it, he only wanted to share his information with his close family and friends. At first she felt a bit offended as if he was being condescending, but after getting to know him much better she learned that that was just part of his nature, he was a private person and his friends and family meant a lot to him and she respected him for that. She just wished she knew a bit more about his family and friends. Stuart had been introduced to her friends but she didn't even know who his friends were.

Jennifer had already received an email from Stuart this morning and considering that he had only left her 30 minutes earlier she was quite impressed. Jennifer was in an incredibly good mood for a dreich Monday morning. She decided not to reply immediately, not to seem overly eager, and waited until lunchtime when she had a few minutes to compose a short, witty and tempting response where she invited him to dinner tonight. She had been hoping to get invited to his house but this still hadn't happened yet and they always met out or went to hers. In fact they were barely ever out together, and if they did meet, they never stayed out for long. At the start Jennifer just presumed it was because of lust and they couldn't wait to get each other to bed but now he actually seemed quite cagey at the mention of his home or going out in public with her for more than an hour.

Jennifer knew she was being paranoid as she had asked him outright before about his past and why he was asking so mysterious and Stuart always had a sensible answer. He had a busy work-life and had to look after his family. Jennifer thought that he may have an ill parent as he sometimes dashed out quickly and if she asked him about it he would look sad. She didn't want to put pressure on him at this early stage of the relationship and loved all the attention she was getting from him especially in the bedroom! However, she really wanted to do other things with him like dine out in nice restaurants, or have some drinks in the pub or go to the cinema. They hadn't argued yet but it had came close when they were lying in bed on Sunday morning and Stuart had said he had to nip away for a few hours in the afternoon but mysteriously wouldn't say where he was going. This had annoyed Jennifer a little and had pressed it further but could see from his eyes that he didn't want to talk about it so she dropped it.

Sure enough he was back by 3pm leaving her enough time to dry her hair and re-apply some makeup that she hoped looked effortless. New boyfriends were hard work and she would need to get another appointment this week to get her legs and bikini line waxed, she didn't want him to see her looking hairy! She used to leave it until every 6 weeks if she could but now she had halved that time, not wanting to risk Stuart catching her off guard with a stray hair! Plus, she was now having to wear makeup every day and instead of leaving her hair to dry naturally a few days of the week she was curling it or straightening it into a new style. She even had time to squeeze in twenty minutes of lesson planning before Stuart's return for the forthcoming school day, so she couldn't complain.

Her great mood had got through a long and tiring day at work but she was ready to get home into a relaxing hot bath.

"Fucking whore! Ya fucking dirty wee trollop!" Jennifer heard squeals and a scuffle emerging from the corridor outside her classroom. It was the end of the school day and most of the kids were filtering down towards the main door but a few stragglers remained in the hall and two girls were now rolling about trying to grab at each other's faces and hair. There were only another few pupils in the corridor but they didn't try to help split it up like Jennifer hoped, they just made it worse by crowding round them and egging them on to fight more. "Fight! fight! fight!" the chants grew louder and some of the other kids rushed back to catch a glimpse of the girls scratching at each other venomously. Some of the spectating pupils looked on wide eyed and laughing, some were now recording the scene on their cameras desperate to share the debacle with their friends. She could see John was amongst them and she was surprised he wasn't encouraging it more, instead he hung at the back, peering over the other boys to get a look at the fight before disappearing down the corridor quietly.

"I'm gonna fucking rip your extensions oot, ya smelly bitch!" the smallest girl shouted as Jennifer pulled her off the other girl.

"Are you fuck, ya daft wee fanny, go and run back to yer wee boyfriend – he's hoaching anyway!" the taller blonde girl with very orange fake tan screamed back as she stood up, straightening up her tie and combing over her dodgy hair extensions. Jennifer recognised her as Tiffany, one of the girls from her troublesome third year class.

238

She must have only been around fourteen at the most and her boxing partner must be younger she assumed. She didn't teach her but thought she had known her from being on canteen duty – Courtney she thought she was called.

"What is going on?" Jennifer found herself roaring at the pair. Both of them started screaming at her trying to sound innocent and the younger one starting bubbling, black tears from mascara rolling down her cheeks. Some of the other girls in the corridor had now taken sides and were roaring abuse at each other.

"That is quite enough everyone!" Jennifer raised her voice again authoritatively. She scanned the small crowd, mentally noting who all was there before telling them all to scarper; there wasn't anything else to see, before escorting both girls down to Andrew Johnstone's office.

"She started it, Miss," Tiffany said huffily, "she shagged my boyfriend and Kelsey's boyfriend!"

Courtney screamed back instantly, "Fucking lying cunt!"

"Language!" Jennifer screamed at her. "Stop this abuse just this minute. I don't want to hear another word from either of you. I am extremely disappointed in the behaviour of both of you. Violence is never acceptable under any circumstance and I am appalled by the language you are both using, it is disgusting!"

Both of them hung their heads to the floor but continued walking and Jennifer lead them into Andrew's office and quietly explained to him what happened, whilst they waited in the waiting room, on separate sides of the room, refusing to make eye contact with each

239

other. "Thanks Jennifer, you seemed to handle this well. I think blood has been boiling with this pair for a while and I'm surprised this hasn't happened before now," Andrew whispered to Jennifer so the girls couldn't overhear. "And between you and me I'm actually glad it happened in school so we can now try and deal with the situation rather than it happen on the streets of Glasgow on a Saturday night where it could've turned more vicious. Are you OK?"

"It seemed pretty vicious to me but no real harm done and yes I'm OK, thanks." Jennifer realised she hadn't really thought about her own safety or harm until now. She could feel her arm hurting a little where Tiffany had pulled back on trying to get free, but she was sure it would only be a little bruise.

"Good. I'll speak to their Guidance teachers and will phone in the parents. Could you please fill in an incident report with Cathy from the office? Thanks."

And with that she left to get back to her classroom. Teaching really could be interesting, there was always something going on! Although she was so glad not to be Andrew right now. She would bet the parents were just as difficult if not more so than the stroppy teenagers.

Although she was a little flustered with dealing with the incident, by evening she was chuckling about it over dinner as she conveyed it to Stuart. She very rarely told details of her work to anyone outside school and always kept details confidential but she wanted to share today's story about the Neds fighting, thinking it would give him a laugh, and sometimes sharing helped her de-stress.

"Are you OK?" Stuart asked concerned.

"Yes, of course," she giggled, "I'm fine, the girls are fine too. Fighting over some silly boy I'm sure."

"What school is it you work in again?"

"Hillend High. Same as Caitlyn, Jamie and Caroline remember?"

Stuart looked somewhat annoyed and didn't say another word.

"It's quite a mixed school as you can tell. It has a large school roll. Lots of kids from lots of different backgrounds and areas of Glasgow. I've got some difficult classes this year," Jennifer continued but Stuart looked as if he had lost interest. "Oh God I'm sorry, didn't mean to bore you with the gory details of my work! I don't normally moan about it, in fact the majority of the kids are great but you do get the odd exception!"

"I can imagine."

"It's usually the teachers that are the hardest to work with, especially the old ones. There's this one teacher called Tommy that makes my working life a misery. Och sorry! Done it again, sorry I'm used to chirping away to Caitlyn or Jamie who will join in with the teacher chat, I forget it is tiresome to everyone else!"

"Don't be daft," Stuart smiled, "I love hearing you talk regardless of what the topic is... although I would rather you would keep the bickering children talk for others," he said as he leaned over to kiss her slowly on the lips, stroking her cheek softly with his hand.

"Deal," she replied between kisses, leading him by the hand towards her bedroom.

Chapter 39

Jamie was extremely nervous about the meeting with Andrew but he was excited too. He had wakened extra early but couldn't even eat his breakfast he was that anxious, although as soon as he took a seat in Andrew's room he felt more at ease. He now considered himself more like a friend than a boss but he still had butterflies like it was a first date. Not that he would know what that was like, it had been years since Jamie had a long term boyfriend and even then it was barely for over a month. He had never got close to anyone and found it hard to make a true connection with a man. To be honest, Jamie hadn't really yearned for a 'proper' relationship the way his heterosexual friends did. He had always preferred to be single life, hooking up with guys occasionally. Until now.

He spent all weekend daydreaming on what it would be like being married to Andrew. Sharing his life with him, shopping, watching TV, eating out and going to the cinema. And of course the sex life. He was so jealous of Jennifer and Stuart's new relationship and a little disappointed at being forgotten in favour of them two locking themselves into her bedroom all weekend leaving him all alone. Caitlyn was with Peter as per usual and his other single friends had now moved on to pastures new or had settled down with people and he felt rather lonely doing nothing on a Saturday evening.

"Thanks for coming, Jamie," Andrew said pleasantly, ushering him to take a coffee but he politely declined and started to twitch his hands, suddenly becoming more worried about why he had been asked here.

Jamie didn't need to wait long to find out.

"I've been meaning to chat with you for a while now," Andrew began and Jamie looked up at him, making eye contact.

"That sounds ominous," Jamie said smiling trying to relax the mood.

"No, not at all," replied Andrew, reciprocating the smile.

"I've been watching you over the last year, Jamie, and I'm really pleased with the work you do in the school."

Jamie could feel his cheeks burn up and looked away from Andrew, modestly not looking at him direct.

Andrew continued, "Your Faculty Head speaks extremely highly of you, you are well respected by your peers and importantly you are also commended by your students."

Jamie sat speechless. He was overwhelmed by the flattering words of praise from Andrew but was now uncertain of where this was leading.

"The reason why I asked you here is that I want you to be a permanent member of staff and I would like you to consider of taking on the role of a pupil mentor."

Jamie still sat there without words.

"I realise that you have been here for a few years now and I've been determined to get you a permanent contract but in addition I would like to help progress your career for you. I think you would be ideal to take on a role as a mentor, a first line guidance teacher to the pupils. Not only for you but I am very keen to keep you here within Hillend. I'm sure other schools will be aiming to get you on board and as a career driven young man, I'm sure you've thought about your future," he added.

Jamie nodded quietly, trying to force a smile on his face.

"Are you thinking of going down the line of department head, Jamie? Or possibly a Guidance role?"

Jamie didn't want to admit that he hadn't really thought about career progression right at this moment, he enjoyed his job and although wasn't the best paid in the world was quite happy in the position he was in. Plus, he loved teaching, he knew that if he was to become a department head then he would spend less time in the classroom. "Erm, I had thought about it a little but I'm happy just building up my teaching experience, that is what I enjoy."

Andrew smiled widely, "Yes, yes I totally agree, I thought you would say that and I would hate to lose you as a classroom teacher. That is why the mentoring could be the ideal advancement for you and gives you the opportunity to develop on the Guidance side too if that's what you would like. It won't eat into your beloved teaching time and will require extra responsibility but I think you could step up to the plate no problem." He looked directly at Jamie hopeful for an enthusiastic response.

Jamie continued with the meeting, making all the right noises, agreeing to become a mentor for the school and sorting out a permanent contract for him that would not only give him more security but some extra experience for his CV too. Unfortunately, the school couldn't offer much of a pay rise for the mentoring job and Jamie didn't have much extra time in his timetable but with Andrew's persuasion he was keen to give it a go.

Jamie left the meeting after around an hour more than a little deflated. He should be overjoyed, it's not every day someone's boss praises their work openly and head hunts them for a possible promotion. But he wanted more. He expected some sort of flirtation. He had hoped that Andrew had made the meeting under false pretences, hoping to strike up a relationship with Jamie, making all of his daydreams come true. But that wasn't the case, it was obvious now that Jamie's feelings for Andrew were not shared by him and any feelings were professional with admiration and respect.

The regular observations and discussions between them had become more often only because Andrew was grooming him for a promoted post. And the friendly banter in the staff room and in the nightclub really was only friendly words from a colleague, a heterosexual married colleague at that! Jamie felt like such a fool!

How could he have ever thought that there was something more? He walked back to his class trying to suppress his tears. He realised though that the tears weren't through being upset but were tears of rejection and embarrassment. Thank God he hadn't made a move on Andrew or said anything hugely humiliating, it could have led to complete disaster – career destroying moment avoided, phew! He was eternally thankful that he hadn't shared any of his shameful delusions with any of his friends. He normally couldn't keep a secret for more than 5 minutes so it was gratifying that he never disclosed any of his disgracing thoughts of his boss, his fantasies sounded like such a cliché!

Jamie went through the rest of the school day on complete auto pilot, doing all tasks that he was meant to complete but with no flair or passion like his usual self. He wasn't really thinking about anything in particular apart from the bottle of wine in his fridge.

Nevertheless, Jamie was a real believer in what is for you won't go past you and as he walked home feeling alone and forlorn he had a self-realisation moment as he came across a young couple kissing on a bench. As he glanced over at the young couple in love he realised that he wasn't really upset about Andrew, he was upset about being desolate and alone. Deep down he knew that nothing was ever going to happen between him and Andrew and although he found him extremely attractive, he recognised that it was the steady relationship that he desired, someone to be with long term and share life experiences. He had plenty of short term relationships with men and had plenty of fun, but now he yearned for something more, something more meaningful.

"Oh my God," Jamie said out loud breaking up the two young pupils snogging, "I think I've grown up." The couple looked at Jamie after his bizarre outburst and then continued to kiss as if oblivious to the presence of one of their teachers. Jamie picked up his pace, now looking forward to getting home and sharing his revelation to Jennifer. He no longer felt disappointed, why should he be, this was a new chapter in his life, one to look forward to. He was gaining a permanent contract and a promotion at work – something that is hard to come by nowadays. He knew that this was all part and parcel of growing up and something to look forward to. He will find the man of his dreams in due time and he was still happy with taking time to find that person, now he just knew what he was looking for.

Chapter 40

"Do you have to get a license to keep a monkey in this country Miss?" one of Caitlyn's delightful second year pupils asked her in all seriousness in the middle of a lesson on algebra. Some of the other pupils looked up and Caitlyn stared back at the boy in disbelief.

"Pardon, Fraser?"

"Do you have to get a license to keep a monkey in this country?" he repeated as a few of the girls next to him giggled.

"Why do you ask?" she asked curiously, careful not to be too dismissive in case in some weird way that it could somehow be related to the topic, however, she was almost 100% confident that he was just trying to be disruptive and look for attention amongst his peers.

"I don't know," he said loudly, looking around at his classmates for encouragement, confirming to Caitlyn he was just attention seeking and aiming to distract others.

"Well, why don't you wait in at break time and we can do some research to find out."

"Urgh, no it's OK, I'm not that bothered."

"No, no that's fine, Fraser. I'm interested now too but let's keep it until after we've finished our school work. Please do not share any other silly comments with the class unless it is relevant."

Some of the pupils laughed quietly, this time at him, not with him.

He nodded solemnly, picking his pen back up.

Caitlyn wandered round the class checking on each pupil's work and ensured she looked over Fraser's work as sometimes she found that when pupils acted out in class it was because they didn't understand the work or didn't know what to do. However, she was surprised that he had actually completed the task first. She had known he was a capable pupil but his work showed a strong ability for Maths and she realised that the task set was not testing enough for him. She praised him quietly and set him another, more complex formulae to challenge him a bit more. She often had to give out differentiated work within her classes as each pupil had different needs, but this was time consuming and was difficult to mark. Some lower ability children didn't like being given different work also as it highlighted their ability level to the rest of the class and could leave them prone to bullying, so she tried to do it as discreetly as possible but sometimes this was just not feasible.

At the end of the class Caitlyn carried out a summary of the main points of the lesson and asked the pupils to use her interactive whiteboard to fill in the answers. She let the pupils volunteer themselves to come out to the front of the class. Sometimes she would ask certain pupils to come out but today she let them choose. It was the usual suspects that came out, the self-assured pupils who were able and confident in front of the others. She could see that Fraser looked disinterested yet again and he was trying get the attention of the girl sitting in front of him without much luck. The class filtered out of the room after the bell rang and Caitlyn quietly asked him to wait behind. He burled his eyes but he remained in class.

"Is everything OK, Fraser?"

"Yes."

"You produced some good work today, Fraser. You seem to have a talent for numbers, particularly the equations we are doing at present."

He looked back at her expressionless.

"However, your behaviour needs to improve in order for you to fulfil your full potential. Is there a reason for the disruption today?"

Silence.

"Please tell me you're not really interested in buying a monkey?" Caitlyn asked smiling trying to be light-hearted.

He laughed out loud, "No."

"OK then. Well, let's have no more chat of it and focus on your work. I'm going to move you there," she said pointing at a seat at the front of the class, "so that you can't be distracted or distract others. I know you can do well in this subject and I want your behaviour to improve and for you to try your best, OK?"

"OK."

"Good, OK, see you next lesson, no monkey business!"

"OK," he said now smiling and walked out her door just as the bell rang again to signal period 3. No time for a quick cup of coffee then either as she looked out her lesson plan for this class.

Chapter 41

The rest of Jennifer's week after the 'fight' had been relatively uneventful. Her classes were going OK and she had a tonne of paper work and reports to complete but her new teaching techniques were working pretty well. She had been covering a few classes in her non-contact time as there were a lot of staff absences this week and had even noticed that the two girls that she had pulled apart were now back to being best buddies. She had later found out from one of the Guidance staff that her poorly behaved student, John, was one of the 'boyfriends' that was accused of having sex with the other girl. The fight caused a bit of stir around the school and even the teachers in the staff room had a good gossip about it, nothing new there. But then Jennifer was handed a note from one of the office ladies as she entered the school the following Monday morning.

The note said *Please report to me asap, A Johnstone*. I wonder what that is about? she pondered, but didn't wait long to find out as she walked down to his office just before 8am and knocked lightly on the door.

"Come in, Miss Hill," Andrew said loudly and she entered his room tentatively. He sounded formal and she began to feel nervous. "Morning, Mr Johnstone, you asked to see me?" Jennifer asked timidly.

"As you may have heard after the girls fight last week there has been lots of rumours going about regarding the girls involved, in particular their sexual relationships with other pupils. Now I know this is nothing new, we know that pupils get up to these things outside of school, but the welfare of our pupils is paramount and we must not brush cases like this under the carpet, especially as one of the girls involved is only 13 years of age."

"Yes, I totally understand. I have spoken to their Guidance teachers and completed an incident report as well as a Child Protection disclosure as in our school policy like you requested."

"Thank you, Jennifer, I appreciate that, and it is because of that the fight has been escalated to powers above including possibly getting the Social Work department involved."

"Really? OK, I can see how that might happen. Although I should highlight that that might not be necessary now as I've seen the girls have resolved their differences," Jennifer said trying to lighten the tone of the meeting and she knew these incidents happen all of the time.

"Yes, I have heard that. However, I'm not finished. The fight between the girls you may recall was also filmed by a few students."

"The joy of modern technology," Jennifer said sarcastically, rolling her eyes.

"Indeed. Well, because these videos have been taken into evidence in this specific case, it also features you."

Jennifer racked her brain quickly, mentally trying to ensure that she hadn't done or said anything wrong and she was certain that everything was fine. "Yes unfortunately I was aware of that, not my best of TV appearances I can imagine."

"The video clearly shows you pulling Tamara away from Courtney."

"Yes I'm sure it does, that is what I did," she looked back at Andrew, now confused and a little worried.

"That is my point, Jennifer. As teachers, responsible adults, we are not supposed to get involved with fights, Jennifer. Not physically, anyway, you shouldn't have touched either girl."

Jennifer couldn't believe what she was hearing. "But I stopped the fight, what was I supposed to do? Let them gauge out their eyes and pull out their hair?" she said now raising her voice.

"I know it seems silly but that is the policy of the school, the rule of the authority, and it shows on the video that you clearly violated that rule, albeit it's clear to anyone that you did it on good intentions. The parents could have claimed, and have done in the past, that the teachers were part of the fight or on someone's side. The rule was made in accordance to new legislation there to protect children and to protect teachers."

"I only stopped the fight to protect the children, they could've seriously harmed each other, they were lucky!" Jennifer was now close to shouting and close to tears.

"I know, I know that, but it has been pointed out externally that this incident has taken place. I personally am not taking it further as I know you did it with the children's wellbeing at heart, but I want you to take that as a serious warning and to remember not to do that again."

"I was only trying to help!" she pleaded.

"I repeat again, I DO know that, Jennifer and this will not be held against you but the guidance teachers might have another word about

254

the incident with you. They have discussed it with the girls and their parents, and we are lucky that they all know that it was the girls that were out of line and have no plan on taking the matter further. But just try not to act completely on instinct if a situation like this arises again in the future. Is that understood?"

"Yes," Jennifer replied solemnly.

"I needed to bring this to your attention, Jennifer but don't let it get to you. The world is just a bit too politically correct and health and safety mad these days, and we can't do anything anymore without someone on our backs. Just be careful, this warning is about protecting you too. These things are going to happen more and more often and we just need to deal with them professionally as ever, OK? Hopefully this matter won't be taken any further but I cannot guarantee that."

"Yes," she replied again.

"OK, I'll let you get back to prepare for your classes," as he stood up to indicate the end of the meeting. She stood up quickly and backed out towards the door, "OK, thanks."

Jennifer marched along the corridor towards the staff toilet, barging into the nearest cubicle and broke down in tears. It felt as if it she was a pupil getting reprimanded by the Head Teacher unjustly. She hadn't done anything wrong! Or she hadn't thought she had. Sometimes this job just seemed unfair, all she was doing was trying to do best by the students, she meant no harm – couldn't everyone see that? Jennifer couldn't wait for the end of the day and the week already.

Chapter 42

November and December were always exceptionally busy months in school but fortunately for the pupils and teachers they always passed by really quickly and Christmas time would soon be upon them. Caitlyn, along with her colleagues, was extremely busy with assessments and development work for the new curriculum and she was continuing to be stressed with her personal life too, as things hadn't really improved with Peter either. They hadn't had any major arguments but were bickering at each other for the slightest of things even although they didn't see each other that much. Most conversations were over what they were having for dinner or paying bills, definitely nothing romantic or sexy. Her suspicions continued to grow about him having an affair but she was too scared to bring it up with him. She realised that she was actually petrified of it being true as she had no idea what she would do. She had been with Peter for years and had always imagined that they would be together forever and never thought of an alternative life.

Further strain had been added with the addition of the school play organisation to her workload. Jamie was supposed to be leading the production but since starting his mentoring role, he had fallen a bit behind and Caitlyn had been trying to pick up the slack. She had also been 'volunteered' by her department to help create the preliminary exams, which would look good on her CV they reminded her, so she had spent many nights looking over past papers and extracting questions that could be used. Normally she would have protested but with Peter working long hours and her friends busy also, she accepted and got stuck right into the job. After the exams were over it was then time to get them all marked and double checked which was incredibly time consuming. Caitlyn took it very seriously, after all, the pupils grades are what helps them progress in the future. One wrong mark could be the difference between a pass or a fail and pupils may be relying on these grades to get into colleges or University, she wanted to do it right. All she seemed to be doing was working, going to the gym and now, her new passion, running.

She had continued running with the group every weekend and had now began running midweek with a few of the regulars. Joining the running club had introduced her to a new set of friends that weren't teachers and she looked forward to meeting them after a tense day at work. Running round the streets and parks of the city let her forget about all the papers needing marking, the screaming teenagers, school politics and of course her troubles with Peter.

And although Cameron only attended the club at the weekends, she enjoyed his company and his attention to her. Not that she even admitted that to herself out loud, let alone anyone else. There had never been more than mild flirtation between them both, but she loved it and it made her happy when she felt like she was being ignored by Peter. Peter was another thing to worry about, the affair suspicion was mounting. Alarm bells should have rang in her ears long ago with the sudden change of habit and the increase of him working late, strange lifts home and telephone calls, but he was always so loving and faithful, he just didn't seem like the type. But they were barely sleeping together at nights and she had now found a text message on his phone from someone 'unknown'. Caitlyn had never snooped in his phone before but her suspicions had made her curious. She didn't want to seem untrusting but she couldn't help herself. She scanned the texts briefly, around 10 in total, all from the last few days and strangely with very little content, more one or two syllables a message but one in particular caught her eye.

Unknown: I think C might know, we need 2 b more careful
Peter's reply: - Really? Don't worry x

Caitlyn was fuming, what else could that message mean other than him having an affair? And that whoever the bitch was thought that C might know? Her? How could he? How dare he! No wonder he didn't want sex anymore, he was getting it with someone else! She felt like such a fool! Why didn't he just say to her? She should have known! She never understood the point of people having affairs, why couldn't they just be honest and split up with their partner if they wanted to start a new relationship with someone else?

Rather than wake Peter up and start an argument, which she really wanted to do, she decided to find more evidence before accusing him. She didn't want to make more of a scene than need be. Maybe there would be a perfectly logical explanation, she hoped. One thing for sure is that she would find out. And she would confront him.

Chapter 43

By the end of term Jamie had practically forgotten all about his 'crush' on Mr Johnstone and was thoroughly enjoying his new role as a pupil mentor. He had to go through the recruitment and selection process for it within the school even though Mr Johnstone had already head-hunted him for the job, but was now fulfilling his duties as a mentor with great delight. It did mean a lot more work on top of his already existing big workload, but he was enjoying the challenge incredibly. He was involved in preparing and delivering Personal, Social and Health Education lessons as well as English lessons which were very different to what he was used to.

He had to become much more involved in the family life of the children which was very hard work and involved a lot of red tape and admin but it also added a lot of interest and spontaneity to his job. It was very time consuming especially dealing with behaviour, late-coming and truanting issues, and with continued hard work from Jamie, some of these issues were being resolved. However, some just felt impossible! Many of the children under his remit were well known around the school for behaviour problems – some refusing to do any work, fighting, alcohol and drug abuse, shouting or even hitting teachers. It was appalling some of the things that pupils had done.

Jamie also became more aware of the backgrounds of a lot of the children in the school and it really opened his eyes. He didn't realise that quite so many pupils that attended his school came from really deprived backgrounds. In fact, he never knew that such poverty still existed in Glasgow. Some pupils that he knew of that were unruly in some classes or always getting into bother now seemed like achievers. Some pupils were carers for their parents due to ill-health or disability, some pupils were looking after themselves as their parents were alcoholics or drug addicts, and had done so since Primary school. Some children were adopted or fostered for a variety of reasons and had been re-homed and most were dealing with varying levels of personal problems. A few of the other support staff had disclosed that they have visited some of the homes and that they were in an appalling state with dampness, rot and disgusting odours and couldn't believe that they were fit for purpose. Some kids' roles at 12 or 13 year olds were looking after their siblings, cooking and cleaning and acting like a parent. Many of the pupils came from homes that had parents living with them but were in abusive homes and the Social Work Department were heavily involved.

In addition, quite a high proportion of pupils came from homes where the parents were unemployed and on benefits. He was also horrified to find out that some pupils' parents were in prison for various charges – mostly for petty crimes or drugs but one stood out to him – a mother had been jailed for attempted murder - on the father! This was really shocking to Jamie. Most of the time normal class teachers aren't privy to this information and may just see the poor behaviour of the child and not realise the background to it. This was of course in addition to what could maybe be called trivial

260

matters such as sibling rivalry, family problems of divorce and separations as well as more hard hitting things that affected the pupils in school such as bullying, sexual awareness and personal safety.

As a mentor he was now privy to a lot of the confidential files which helped him understand some of the pupils backgrounds and behaviours to help him deal with some of the issues faced with guidance, and it also assisted him plan his lessons and made him deal with some pupil confrontations a little differently or more leniently than before. He had spent many evenings and weekends doing the extra work for the new role but this didn't bother him at all. Mr Johnstone and other colleagues were full of praise for his work so far and the pupils were very responsive. He also had to admit that the extra money, albeit quite small, in his pay packet was also welcome.

He was still trying to work on the school play that was now more like pantomime and was pleased he had good friends like Caitlyn who had helped out amazingly along with some of the other teachers, but it was hard trying to fit it all in to the working day. Jamie hadn't had time to catch up with his friends or been out socialising in a while, but he had been persuaded by Caitlyn and Jennifer as well as his department to go the Christmas work night out. As the event drew closer, Jamie started to dread it as didn't see where he could find the time to fit it in and he could see it far enough but he was now really looking forward to it as well as the 10 days holiday over the festivities. He always liked the last few days in school before the end of term as everyone was in good spirits and the kids were so excited for Christmas. He liked to wind down his classes, and pupils started to drift off and absence monitoring was a little less strict. It gave him some time to do some fun activities with his classes like creating Christmas cards or novelty calendars as well as partaking in some of the shows, presentations and of course the Christmas service at the church.

He had worn his new shirt today for the staff night out and couldn't wait for the bell to go at lunchtime to signal the celebrations to begin. It was traditional that after the church services and the children were dismissed, most of the staff would join together in the canteen for a Christmas lunch and some wine. He couldn't wait!

Chapter 44

Jennifer was feeling a little lightheaded from the home made mulled wine that was served at the morning interval, Jean Docherty, the Art teacher's traditional gift to staff each year, and she was glad she didn't have any more classes to teach. Even the smell of the concoction was likely to make people feel giddy! The school staff normally joined together for an extended interval on the last day of term for mince pies and homemade mulled wine and it always set up the holidays on a positive note. Andrew Johnstone always said some nice farewell words to anyone leaving and wished everyone happy holidays and by the time it got to the staff lunch, the school became very informal and just a little fun, allowing some of the staff to get together. For a school with over 1,000 on the school roll, on this last day of term they would be lucky to even get 100 attending.

Many of the staff left immediately after lunch as they had to rush away to get home to organise kids or were driving off further afield, but there were usually around 30 colleagues that remained to continue to have some wine before the school shut down for 2 weeks. It was a nice atmosphere in the school over the past few days and it was obvious that all the children and the teachers were looking forward to their holidays. Jennifer was certainly looking forward to hers, it had been a tough month at school not just with the usual heavy school work at this time of the year, but she was also still continuously stressed with her challenging classes even although there had been a noticeable improvement since the beginning of term. Her meeting with Andrew had also played in her mind over the last few weeks too. However, although she remained positive about Andrew as a Head Teacher, she had been left with a sour taste in her mouth about the whole experience with the girl's fight and had been extra vigilant and careful about the way she carried out school business from then on. She thought it was all political correctness taken far too far. When she was at school it would be expected by teachers to break up a fight – surely parents would want that rather than their kids being battered and bruised even more?

She certainly didn't condone violence and wanted to ensure her pupils knew this, but now there were so many rules for teachers to follow. You weren't allowed to console a pupil by putting your arm round them if they were scared or sad, or even pat them on the back if they do something brilliant even in PE. You were instructed never to be alone with any pupil regardless of the situation and never leave your door shut. And now you were also not allowed to split up a fight even if they were knocking lumps out of each other.

As Jennifer had predicted, it turned out that it was Mr Greig who had played a part in it being brought to Andrew's attention about her involvement in the argument, and she had since had words with him. Ruining lessons was one thing but potentially ruining her career was a different matter, one that she wasn't prepared to take lying down. She was so mad she felt she had to say something to him, it was none of his business and everyone knew she did nothing wrong. Even the 'You Tube' evidence proved that although she might've 'slightly' touched the girls to separate them she was doing more good than harm.

He seemed genuinely surprised at Jennifer when she approached him about it. She thought very carefully about her wording and walked into his classroom after school quickly before he had time to leave for the evening and she confronted him. She didn't ask any questions, or get angry or wait for him to retaliate, she just stood her ground said how disappointed she was to be 'ratted on' by an experienced teacher and that she expected more from her colleagues. She also told him that if he ever had a problem with her or her teaching methods that he should come and say to her face and not speak behind her back.

She felt exhilarated and relieved as she walked away from him afterwards, so much so that she was nearly sick! Ever since this point he actually seemed to have a new found respect for her and didn't seem to annoy her as much. In fact, now he would acknowledge and smile in her direction if he walked passed. Nevertheless, the incident hadn't improved his enthusiasm for the job or the kids. He continued to shout and dictate lessons to the pupils regardless of their ability and refused to change his teaching style for anyone if he could be bothered to teach them anything that day. More and more pupils continued to be referred by him to senior staff and be given detentions or sent out of class. It looked to other colleagues like he couldn't control his classes and didn't seem to want to. The older classes that he had didn't have as many behaviour problems and he seemed to genuinely get on well with

265

them, but any time that Jennifer was in his class with them they seemed to be talking more about football and school gossip than on the topic of work.

She had to cover his classes a few times when he was off ill (which seemed to be very regular) and although his class were supposedly more able than hers, they were a lot further behind with their portfolios and projects than they should be especially for December. She didn't think this was very fair on the pupils and privately she questioned Tommy's ability as a teacher. To the students' dismay Jennifer took the time to develop resources for his class and issued them with catch up material and revision notes in his absence.

She didn't dare say anything to Tommy himself as she didn't want to cause further conflict, especially as he seemed to be keeping out of her way at the moment and that was just the way she liked it. She just wished that one of her superiors would speak to Tommy on his behaviour and his teaching. She had heard rumours that some pupils and parents had complained about inappropriate remarks that he had made about them and the standard of teaching received, but nothing seemed to ever be spoken about and she certainly didn't want to be the one to bring it up. She had discussed it privately with Caitlyn and Jamie before and they both had heard the speculation of complaints about Tommy and they all had a moan about the situation but agreed that that seemed to be the case with some of the older generation in the teaching profession unfortunately.

266

"Are you coming?" Jessica one of her colleagues from her department asked from Jennifer's classroom doorway, breaking her daydream. It was time for the Christmas staff lunch and Jennifer had put on her new red dress especially for today. She was looking forward to going into town afterwards and soaking up the atmosphere of end of term and meeting up with Stuart at the end of the night. She had an extra special surprise for him underneath her lovely new dress too, black lace hold-ups with matching lace thongs and bra! She had never dared wear something so revealing before but Stuart made her feel so confident and self-assured. She felt so sexy in them and couldn't resist taking a quick photo of herself in the morning with her camera phone which she immediately texted Stuart with to let him know what he could look forward to.

His reply didn't disappoint and he seemed as eager to meet her too, to unravel his special Christmas gift early. They were spending the next few days together and were planning on having a Christmas meal together in Jennifer's flat. Unfortunately Stuart had said he had already made plans for Christmas day with his family so they wouldn't see each other, so they were going to try and make up for it beforehand. Jennifer had never spent Christmas day with a boyfriend before and hadn't ever been in a serious enough relationship to want to do so but she had hoped that he would've maybe invited her to go with his family but sadly not the case.

She didn't want to sound pushy and suggest it, so she accepted the invitation with her own Mum and Dad to go back down South to visit them for a few days. She was looking forward to this immensely as her siblings would be there too, but she knew she would miss Stuart terribly – they had barely been apart more than 24 hours in the past few months. She did casually mention to Stuart about coming to meet her parents for the holiday period and she was desperate for him to come but didn't want to come across as needy. Stuart had said it would be better that he met them on another occasion before descending on them over Christmas which she understood but she couldn't help feel dejected. She knew her parents and her brothers and sisters would love him and she was desperate for them all to meet. Even her Dad seemed to approve from what he had heard so far. Maybe this time next year? she thought. Maybe they would consider moving in together in a year's time? She hadn't felt this strongly about someone in such a long time and was surprised about how relaxed she was about taking their relationship to the next level.

"Come on Jen, our wine will get warm and our turkey cold ..." Jessica joked as she walked along to the next classroom to round up the rest of the department. Jennifer nodded her head back at where Jessica once stood, "Yip, just coming, wait on me!" she replied as she shut down her computer for the last time that year and switched off all of her lights including her little Christmas tree she brought in for her registration class to decorate. Teaching wasn't that bad, she thought, she'll miss this room and her kids over Christmas. She locked her classroom and followed Jessica down to the dinner hall where all of the teachers had already convened to celebrate the last day of school together. The dinner ladies had done a wonderful job for the staff lunch. The canteen had been transformed into a dining area decorated brightly with Christmas colours while the CD player played quietly in the background a mix of festive tunes. The lights had been dimmed, candles lit and the lights were glowing on the large Christmas tree in the corner and despite the tiny kid sized plastic tables and chairs everyone seemed to be enjoying themselves.

The staff had devoured a 3 course meal with all the trimmings and were now finishing off the wine on the tables and getting merrier by the minute. Nevertheless, they were still drinking out of cheap plastic cups and taking their turns to wash the remaining dishes to help out the canteen ladies but that didn't spoil anyone's fun. As the numbers started to dwindle, plans turned to taking taxis into the city centre to have a few more drinks and meet up with some other colleagues from other nearby schools, and it became apparent from the cleaner's stares that they best get a shift on before they were asked to leave! Around 25 teachers hovered around the main doors of the school waiting on taxis and lifts from other colleagues, anxiously covering their heads with coats and umbrellas to barricade themselves from the sleety horizontal rain they were faced with.

Caitlyn could see some of the other teachers rushing to their vehicles, bundling piles of jotters, exam papers and folders into their car boots for over the Christmas holidays and she was thankful that she took all of her stuff away the previous evening. She hadn't actually taken too many papers as she knew she could do a lot of her lesson preparation and development work on her laptop. She was

269

hoping to fit in lots of fun activities too, surely the holidays were one of the perks of being a teacher!

Chapter 45

Caitlyn was normally excited for Christmas like a little girl. But she just couldn't rally up much enthusiasm this year. She loved the build-up and enjoyed carefully planning and preparing for the big day.

Caitlyn collected all of her family and friends addresses in a neat address book and she updated her Christmas present and card list every year around October so she could begin purchasing gifts. Caitlyn enjoyed being organised and getting all of her friends and family the best of presents, she loved making them happy. Caitlyn never stuck to a budget at Christmas and it didn't bother her at all that she was using all her money on spending it on presents for others. She also adored the Scottish cold winters, sitting indoors cosy by the fire watching her favourite films, particularly in December watching festive movies as well as shopping under the Christmas lights in busy Sauchiehall Street or Buchanan Galleries, taking a break to ice skate at George Square or enjoy a hot chocolate with mini marshmallows. She usually did this with Peter and he was normally just as excited for Christmas to arrive but it just didn't seem the same this year. He was continuing to work late (*or so he said*) and he also informed her that he couldn't get a date free to take her to the Pantomime this year. Taking her to one of Glasgow's pantomimes had been tradition for Peter since him and Caitlyn had begun seeing each other so she felt a bit deflated that he was pushing it aside for 'work' this year. She resisted the urge to fight him on it as their arguments had been ever increasing and it was really getting her down. She still had a nagging feeling that he was seeing someone else but he was still affectionate towards her occasionally and when arguing he always insisted that he loved her and didn't want to fight. Surely if he was cheating he would just end it with her? She really didn't want to finish with him and although she had been appreciative of Cameron's attention and couldn't help notice that he was attractive, she knew that she wasn't in love with him and that she couldn't imagine being with anyone else other than Peter. She just missed the way they used to be and wish they could spend more time together again.

Caitlyn was continuing to run with the running club and she loved it. With some encouragement from her new friends she was even hoping to do some races in the new year. She had tried to discuss it with Peter, even invite him along but he just laughed her off. "Running isn't a real sport," he said.

Caitlyn was hoping that Christmas would rekindle their romance especially as Peter had a whole week off work over the holiday period so Caitlyn had hoped some quality time would help fix whatever had become broken in their relationship. She and Peter used to swap texts and emails frequently throughout the day but they had become more irregular over the last 6 months, in particular since Peter had started doing a lot more overtime at work as he said he didn't have the time to reply at work. She had tried sending a sexy text to him the other weekend only to get no reply. Afterwards, once back at the apartment he apologised profusely saying that he didn't get it until he was home. He was getting more useless at looking at his personal phone by the minute.

She did get excited yesterday when he texted her from work but it was only to remind her to pick up a parcel from the post office and to ask what she was making for dinner – not very exciting! She really wanted to make an effort and put the sparkle back into their relationship, especially in bed. They still were making love but it was very infrequent, not at all what it was like before. Peter didn't seem half as enthusiastic or motivated, he just seemed tired and disinterested most of the time. Today, however, being a little bit tipsy from the fizzy wine she was determined to give it another shot and try to get that spark back. She had been speaking to Jennifer on the phone last night and was utterly jealous of her new and exciting relationship with Stuart, in particular their fantastic sex life. Of course Caitlyn understood that they were just going through the 'honeymoon phase' like every beginning of a relationship, but she also knew that her's and Peter's relationship had really dipped recently and she desperately wanted to get it back on track.

Nevertheless, she never admitted these feelings but Jennifer gave her inspiration when she told Caitlyn of her plans to dress up in a saucy outfit tomorrow and tease him with a photograph. Caitlyn decided to do the same thing. That would surely get Peter's attention she thought. She dressed up in her red satin corset which used to always drive him wild with desire. She was going to send the photograph to him in the morning but she lost her nerve but now feeling more confident with the help of some wine, she sent it to

273

Peter as she stood outside waiting on a cab. She decided to leave the message blank, the photograph could do all the talking. Caitlyn felt a rush of adrenaline and excitement and she hit the send button and she zipped her phone away into her bag and vowed to herself not to check it for a while or she would make herself crazy, she wanted just to enjoy some time with her friends. Hopefully Peter would get the hint and there would be no waiting late in the office tonight.

Chapter 46

Jamie couldn't believe that Andrew would be one of the staff members left at the pub at the end of term gathering. It's customary for most of the Senior Management Team not to come to social gatherings, usually so they don't get any hassle and leave it for the staff to let their hair down without their bosses being in their company. There had been a few occasions in the past, so Jamie had heard, that some of the depute heads were given abuse and got into some arguments with staff after a teacher consumed a large quantity of pints of lager at the end of term celebration causing a bit of friction back in the school afterwards. The management team had been cautious of social get-togethers ever since.

However, Andrew was different. Although he was an effective Head Teacher and had the respect of his staff and pupils, he was still fun and liked to socialise with his staff. In fact, he always made a point of being at the majority of the events on the social calendar and it didn't cause a negative impact on the turnout of staff. The Head Teacher attending in fact probably helped boost morale of his workforce and he didn't come across like he thought he was superior to them in anyway, in actual fact he seemed like one of them which was quite a strange concept in some educational establishments.

Nevertheless, he definitely didn't get legless drunk like the majority of the staff! Although he looked to have fun, he remained composed throughout. He did have a few drinks though and took his time to speak to everyone, making time for each and every member of staff which Jamie really admired and he appreciated when he came over for a chat. With hindsight Jamie realised how silly he had been to think of Andrew otherwise but he was worth a daydream he thought. Jamie was especially embarrassed but extremely grateful he didn't let on to his friends and not least Andrew about his silly fantasy.

The night had gone well so far and Jamie, Caitlyn and Jennifer along with a handful of other teachers were still in the same bar 2 hours later. It was still only 7pm but it had been a long day and many of their other colleagues had disappeared home. Jamie hadn't tried to make conversation with Andrew like he would've tried desperately to earlier on in the year, but he was still pleased when Andrew came over to him for a chat when the girls went to the bathroom.

"How have you been Jamie?" Andrew asked him kindly, looking directly into Jamie's eyes, genuinely interested in his answer.

"Good thanks, you?"

"Very well, I'm enjoying being out tonight, we've got a good staff, always up for a laugh."

"Ha, yes, we certainly have good nights out anyway!"

"And I've been keeping tabs on you," Andrew continued, standing a little closer to Jamie, Budweiser bottle in hand.

"Have you?" Jamie's eyebrows rose curiously. God he was attractive, he thought. The wine wasn't helping his feelings, they were just rekindling his old attraction and Jamie was conscious of trying to distance himself from him.

"I've been hearing you are doing exceptionally well in your mentoring role. Well done. I knew you would be fantastic. You have a great rapport with the kids."

"Thank you, Mr Johnstone, I appreciate that. Not that it's true but I'm working hard at it. Its challenging work but enjoyable. Thank you for giving me the opportunity," Jamie gushed modestly.

"Jamie, how many times – please call me Andrew. We are friends," Andrew said softly and leaned over to touch Jamie's arm.

Jamie flinched a little at his touch, "Sorry, Andrew, I mean."

Andrew smiled broadly, "So what are your plans for Christmas, Jamie?"

Jamie sighed unenthusiastically, "Nothing exciting really. Going home to see the folks and hopefully catching up on some sleep. And of course I've got some school work to get on with too," he quickly added.

Andrew laughed again. "I'm sure you do. Make sure you make time for yourself to rest too, that's important. Some people in our line of work can run themselves into the ground. It's a stressful job especially nowadays. That's nice that you are spending Christmas with family."

"I know, I do have work to do but I've planned in a good break too and am looking forward to it. It will be good to catch up with my parents and my brother."

"Not spending it with a partner then?"

Jamie looked at him trying to gauge his expression. "Erm no, not at the moment."

As if reading his mind Andrew replied, "I thought a nice young man like you would have a boyfriend on your arm?"

Jamie flushed red instantly, "Nah, nothing serious at the moment unfortunately."

"Unfortunately, huh? Fortunately for some I bet," Andrew replied edging slightly closer to Jamie, eyes smiling. "So you're on the lookout then?"

"Well, if the right person comes along…"

"I'm sure he will, Jamie. I thought a charming attractive man like yourself would be fighting them off?" Andrew jibed as he jokily elbowed Jamie in the ribs.

Was Jamie imaging this? Was the alcohol making him think Andrew was being more flirtatious than he really was?

"One day hopefully" Jamie replied sheepishly.

"I might just know the perfect person you would like for a date," Andrew continued.

"Really?" Jamie asked, searching his face again for answers. Was he meaning *him*? He couldn't tell. Was Jamie's now drunk imagination getting the better of him?

"I think so, well I think you would get on with him great, same sense of humour, similar ages etc. Do you want me to set up a date?"

Jamie hesitated, not sure what to say. Surely if it was a friend of Andrew's he would just say their name rather than a blind date.

"Not that I'm saying you need me to find you a date or anything, sorry, I just have someone in mind I know VERY well, who I am

SURE you would like. Sorry, say no if you want!" Andrew started to ramble uncharacteristically.

"It's fine," Jamie replied uncertainly.

"Do you trust me?" Andrew continued, "One date?"

Jamie now felt compelled to laugh.

"Is that a yes then?" Andrew probed, his eyes smiling back at Jamie "One date?"

"Yes, yes OK," Jamie agreed, smiling back.

"Excellent! I know you two will be well-matched, I just have a feeling. Oh and don't tell anyone about this just yet, OK?"

Is it because it is *you*? Jamie wanted desperately to ask, but just nodded back, "Sure."

"Are you on Facebook? I'll find you and we can arrange?" Andrew asked quickly as he could see the girls coming back from the toilets.

"Erm, yes, OK," Jamie replied, trying to sound confident and assured when he was really feeling more than confused at that present moment.

Caitlyn and Jennifer arrived back at the table, clearly drunk but on seeing Andrew they tried to impersonate their sober selves with not much luck.

"Hello girls," Andrew warmly greeted them.

"Hi Mr Johnstone," they both giggled in unison like teenagers, both trying to compose themselves with their 'serious' faces but Andrew just laughed with them.

"Andrew, please. I'm glad to see that you're enjoying yourselves. It's been a long, hard term."

"Yes, it definitely has," Jennifer replied to him, a more serious tone to her voice but he didn't seem to pick up on her infliction.

"Well, I better get going and leave you young things to party on!" Andrew spoke as he stood up, his hand still lingering on Jamie's arm slightly.

"I hope you all have a wonderful Christmas and enjoy your holiday."

"Thanks Andrew." Jamie replied.

"Yes, thanks, you too," the girls chorused.

When he was out of earshot the girls turned round to stare at Jamie in the face, eyes agog "Weellll?" they looked at him expectantly.

"Well what?" Jamie asked, half smiling.

"What was that about?" Jennifer shouted.

"Are you Mr Johnstone's, sorry *Andrew's*, new best buddy then?" Caitlyn added.

"What? No, what are you talking about?" Jamie tried to ask innocently.

"We could see you from over there, all intense conversation and smiley flirty smiles," Jennifer accused.

"And every time he talked to us, he only looked at you."

Instead of disagreeing, Jamie couldn't help but ask "did he?"

"Jamie and Andrew, awww, BFF's" Caitlyn taunted as Jennifer laughed.

"Stop it! Don't be daft," Jamie argued but inwardly hoped that it was true. However, he didn't want to tell the girls about the blind date. It was going to be his secret.

"I hope you bought your BFF a Christmas present now, Jamie?" Jennifer joined in in the playful jibing.

"Maybe a nice arran woollen jumper?" Caitlyn joked.

Jennifer laughed, "Maybe more like some woolly handcuffs!"

Jamie remained silent, arms crossed.

"Ach don't be so precious, Jamie, we're only winding you up!" Caitlyn said, delicately messing his floppy hair.

"I know, it's just a wee joke. But I tell you, from afar if we didn't know you pair you could've sworn that you were lovers!"

"Ach weisht you pair, I'm getting fed up with your rubbish banter! Plus, poor Andrew was only trying to be nice, he is only in his early thirties remember!"

"Yeah I know, and he's hot!" Caitlyn added, "If we didn't know that he was married, I would've put a bet on tonight that he was gay and would've had you back at his by the end of the night!"

"Definitely!" Jennifer agreed, "Shame!"

"Well he's not, so it looks like I'm going to need to find another handsome stranger!" Jamie argued defensively, but couldn't help the fantasies swirling through his brain. Is Andrew secretly gay? Maybe I wasn't misreading the signs all along. Maybe I wasn't so silly to think that he liked me.

The girls had already started scanning the room for potential guys for Jamie once again. Pointing and giggling at various men in the bar, as they commented on whether they thought they were gay or not. He pretended he was doing the same but it really didn't interest him in the slightest anymore. He had thought he was over his crush with Andrew but it was starting to reappear, especially after their little flirtatious chat. He definitely did feel a spark between them. Some sort of connection. Maybe it was just a good friend thing. But now a date? Was he setting me up with a friend? It all sounded so mysterious. Was it really him and that's why he wanted it kept quiet? Maybe he wasn't imagining the attraction all along.

Chapter 47

Jennifer had left Caitlyn and Jamie just before 9pm to meet up with Stuart. She could barely contain her excitement and from his saucy text messages throughout the day it sounded like he couldn't wait to meet up with her either.

Can we go to yours tonight? she asked in the last message before re-straightening her hair in the ladies bathrooms and re-applying her makeup. She also had a quick wash and sprayed some deodorant and her favourite Chanel Chance perfume to freshen up. Jennifer couldn't wait to see Stuart's reaction at the sexy underwear! She would prefer to go to his for a change as she wanted some peace from Jamie and she was still a little bit annoyed that she had never been taken to his house yet.

Sorry babe, I'm already on my way to yours. She instantly forgot her disappointment and jumped in the nearest taxi straight to her house. Hopefully Jamie wouldn't return home for at least another few hours yet. The night was still young!

As she walked into her close of the tenement flat she could see the silhouette of Stuart in the darkness. He walked towards her and without saying a word he pressed his wet mouth hard against hers into an intimate kiss. Normally Jennifer would be embarrassed and usher him upstairs to her flat immediately but she was slightly drunk and was caught in the heat of the moment, enjoying every second kissing him back. His strong arms picked her up and started to make their way slowly and clumsily up the flight of stairs without pausing for air. She couldn't wait to rip his clothes off and couldn't concentrate to open the locks of the doors that normally took her 2 seconds. Stuart's wandering hands added on at least 5 minutes that felt like an eternity to her, she was so turned on for Stuart she could barely contain herself. They fell into her flat and grabbed at each other's clothes, having rough passionate sex on the hall floor, clothing scattered around them. Jennifer was so excited that she came practically instantly when they changed position, straddling him moving on top and Stuart climaxed quickly after. They remained motionless in silence for a few moments before they lay down on the wooden floor in each other's arms, satisfied and still only half naked.

"What the fuck?" they heard Jamie scream about 30 minutes later, they must've fallen asleep. Jamie stood in front of them but had his hands clasped around his eyes so that he couldn't see them.

"Argh!" Jennifer squealed as she reached out to pick up her clothes, "Sorry, sorry, shit, shit, shit - so sorry, Jamie!"

Jennifer and Stuart giggled like little school children as they tried to cover up their private areas and dash into Jennifer's room.

"Sorry, mate," Stuart said as he ran into the bedroom.

"You do have a room you know, Jennifer!" Jamie shouted after them, standing still in the corridor with his eyes covered. He wasn't really angry and the couple could tell that but he was still quite surprised to discover them in the hall of all the places especially with the main door still ajar. "What if wee Mrs McGarrie from Flat C had to see this nonsense? She'd never take our bins out again!"

Jennifer and Stuart jumped into the big double bed still sniggering at being caught. "Told you we should've went to your place," Jennifer said as she cuddled up to Stuart's now naked body.

"Hmmm, yeah maybe you are right, maybe the next time," Stuart said as he pulled her closer into his chest.

Jennifer smiled happily. "OK," she replied softly, enjoying being so close to the man that she loves, she felt so happy in that moment.

Chapter 48

Caitlyn and Jamie shared a taxi home at around 10pm. She was a lot drunker than she had planned to be and was starting to slur her words. She had been checking her phone every two minutes since Jennifer left but there was still no reply from Peter. She was getting angrier and angrier by the minute and her mind was starting to wander off and think about him being with another woman. But then she tried to justify his behaviour so it wouldn't cause an argument, especially at Christmas... maybe he never got her sexy text? Maybe he didn't have signal? She had vowed to herself that she wouldn't call him but when she was in the taxi she automatically reached for her phone to call Peter. To her surprise he answered nearly immediately. "Hi, babe," he said.

"Oh you're there, wasn't expecting you to answer."

"I'm here, I'm home. How you doing? You ready for coming home yet?"

"Yeah, um, I'm on my way now."

"Good, I've made you some tea."

She softened a little, "Have you?"

"Yip, I've made you beef stew and dumplings."

"Really? Wow, I could do with that now!" she said, her mood changing.

"You got the munchies?" he laughed, "Yeah I thought you might need food."

"Thanks, babe. Did you get my text?"

"You mean the one with the photo?"

He got it!

She giggled, unsure of his response. "Yes! Of course that one! Why didn't you reply?"

"I didn't think you wanted a reply, there wasn't any message in it." he laughed, "but I'm looking forward to seeing you in the flesh."

Caitlyn hesitated before replying, "Really?"

"Yes, really, really, really, REALLY. You know I love those undies on you."

"Did you not want to reply saying that?" she replied, still a little miffed at his lack of response.

He laughed, "Of course I did! I'm sure you know I love that by now. Although I wasn't going to sit about at my desk with your half naked photo on my phone to compose a reply, you are for my eyes only!"

She seemed more satisfied with his reply now, "I certainly am!"

"Are you in the taxi now?"

"Yip, will be just a few minutes."

"OK great, see you soon."

Two minutes later, as promised, she was climbing the stairs up to her flat, slower than usual due to her wine consumption but she was feeling happy with anticipation of seeing Peter. He greeted her at the door and she sloppily kissed him on the doorstep. Peter pulled back after a second or two, "Whoa kitty, how many have you had?"

"Just a few," she lied as she tried to lean on his chest.

"Well come on in and I'll heat up your dinner."

"No!" Caitlyn protested, "I want some nookie first!"

"Don't you worry," Peter said as he pulled her close and planted a kiss on the top of her forehead. "There will be plenty of 'that' to follow. But you need to eat first and I want you to enjoy the lovely dinner I prepared for you."

Caitlyn didn't argue, her body craved food and she loved Peter's homemade stew, perfect for a winter's night although she had her suspicions from Peter's lack of sex drive lately whether this was just a ruse to deter Caitlyn for a while. She was extremely pleased to find out that Peter wasn't lying and after devouring a large plate of stew, potatoes and dumplings, Peter allowed Caitlyn to lead him to the bedroom. She had sobered a little but still felt confident on stripping sexily and slowly in front of Peter as he lingered on her every curve. "I just want to go for a quick shower," Peter paused.

"What? Now?" Caitlyn demanded.

"Yes, sorry, I've been in these clothes all day and I want to be clean!"

"Maybe I'll join you?" Caitlyn offered, seductively slipping off a shoulder strap of her silky bra.

"No it's fine, I'll be 1 minute!" Peter interjected.

Caitlyn pouted "Oh. Don't you want me all naked and wet in the shower?"

But he was already in the bathroom, she could hear the water pouring down onto the wet room floor. "1 minute!" she heard him shout from within.

Fine, she thought. She would use the time to set the mood with some candles. A minute passed and she could still hear the shower so she pushed the clothes off the bed to make room. As she did a large folded glossy card fell out of Peter's jacket. Peter's pockets were normally filled with train tickets, receipts and coppers but this caught her attention. Her curiosity got the better of her and she scooped it up from the floor. She quickly realised from the branding on the front that it was for an expensive jewellery shop.

Oh damn, she thought instantly she's ruined her Christmas surprise! She loved being surprised by gifts and Peter usually always gave her a great surprise for her birthday or Christmas. She started to carefully put it back into his pocket but she could hear the water still pouring down from the shower and she couldn't help but look inside to see how much he spent or if it gave any clues. She opened the card tentatively and gasped, nearly shouting out loud in shock – he spent £500! £500, she couldn't believe it! It didn't give a description only the price.

Peter did usually go all out for Christmas and liked to spoil Caitlyn each year. She reckoned sometimes he spent around £300 on her which was far more than she did on him, but he always swore that he had to spoil her and that's what made him happy, even though they were strapped for cash most of the time. She always told him that she didn't want him to do this but secretly she loved being lavished with gifts! Although this year they had made a pact to only spend £50 as they were so skint and although it didn't seem romantic to her she had hesitantly agreed. Nevertheless, she knew

289

she would never just spend £50 on him. She loved to indulge him and seeing his expression as he opened all of the individually wrapped parcels that she gave him. This year she had managed to buy him T in the Park tickets (the biggest open air concert in Scotland held every summer). This was no mean feat as it was always sold out within minutes and Peter had longed to go for years but never managed to get hold of the lucrative tickets. This time Caitlyn had worked hard to use contacts and track down a 'friend of a friend of a friend' that managed to get them for her and she couldn't wait for Peter to get them!

Now she also felt elated that Peter had gone to the trouble of getting her an expensive gift, she wasn't the only one breaking the £50 per gift rule! And he had even picked her some jewellery on his own. Could it even be an engagement ring? She didn't want to get too excited! She felt so gratified but also completely ashamed and guilty that she had ever suspected him of being unfaithful. He had been working all this extra time and he was spending some of his hard earned cash on her, giving her lavish gifts. She carefully placed the receipt back into his pocket as she heard the shower being turned off. She jumped on to the bed and lay provocatively as Peter walked into the bedroom in only a towel, still wet from the shower.

God he looked sexy! It had been such a long time that they had spent time together like this to appreciate each other. He joined her on top of the bed without saying a word and kissed her hard on the lips, his hands groping at her body, removing her underwear in swift movements as he kissed the nape of her neck greedily. She reciprocated hungrily grasping at his body, pulling off the towel and pulling him close to enter deep inside her. They continued to make love for what seemed like hours before collapsing beside each other hot, sweaty and out of breath.

Satisfied and sleepy, Caitlyn rolled over to Peter to stroke his face and looked into his eyes. "Where did that come from, Petey?"

"Was that OK?"

"Are you being sarcastic? That was more than OK. Well overdue... but more than OK!"

"Yeah well I know we've not done it as much as usual, I'm sorry, I've been so tired with work and really stressed. We should maybe do it more though as that certainly relieved any stress!"

"I second that!"

"I mean it Caitlyn, I am sorry, I know I've been a rubbish boyfriend of late, it will change though. After this overtime job is up, I won't need to work such long hours."

"It's fine Petey, honest. I just want us back to normal. I miss you. I've been lonely," she said honestly and sadly. "I certainly want our sex life back to normal – I've missed that!"

"I have too, Cait, I have too. We'll not leave it as long the next time, I promise!" he said staring into her eyes, stroking her hair.

"I'll hold you to that," Caitlyn replied jokingly and pulled in close to him. They both lay there naked, spooning each other in the dark.

"Are you still awake, Peter?" Caitlyn eventually said, breaking the silence.

"Yip, what is it?"

"I love you."

"I love you too. More than anything. More than everything in the world."

Caitlyn smiled contentedly as she cuddled in closer to Peter. She felt happier than ever in that moment. This was all she wanted, she thought. Caitlyn was thoroughly looking forward to Christmas with Peter and her family now.

Chapter 49

Jamie woke up groggily the next day around 11am to Jennifer jumping on top of him.

"It's Christmas Eve!" she shouted in his face, "Wakey wakey!" now bouncing on the bed.

"You are too happy, why aren't you hungover?" Jamie groaned huskily, pushing her off.

"I am surprisingly feeling just fine!" she said brightly, now opening up the curtains letting in the mid-morning sunshine.

"Jennifer! Argh, let it be dark! Stop being annoying, I need to wallow in my own misery and I normally have you to do this with, I don't need happy excited and in love Jenny penny right now!" Jamie mumbled pulling the duvet over his head to get away from the light.

"Why thank you dear friend, I am glad you want me to be as miserable as you and that you are thoroughly ecstatic that I am in love and no longer on my lonesome," she said sarcastically.

"I AM happy for you Jen, you know that, but I am just extremely jealous of you – jealous of you getting raunchy sex in the hall, jealous of you just generally being in love and your happy smirky face and jealous that you don't have a bloody hangover and I do after last night!" Jennifer heard him rant from beneath his covers.

"Oh Jamie," she laughed as she lay down beside him on the bed and hugged him from over the covers. "I am really happy, I really really REALLY like him. Do you think he is nice?"

Jamie peeked over the sheets. "Of course I do, I wouldn't let my best friend go out with anyone, you know. I am pleased for you Jen, I am, I think he could maybe be the one for you. Honestly."

"Really?" she squealed, unable to keep the grin off her face.

"Really. He seems decent. Although he won't be round for long if you do this to him too. This is a form of torture, let me sleep!"

She kicked her feet at the end of the bed excitedly before jumping up. "No! Come on Jamie, it's Christmas Eve. Get up so we can meet Caitlyn for lunch before we all head home for Christmas, I'm going to miss you lot!"

"I'm not going to miss your shenanigans, I'm looking forward to some peace and quiet!" Jamie rolled over.

"You liar, you love me really. OK since I am in a good mood I will go and make you a nice coffee in bed to wake you up, but then you have to get up as I need to get away sharp after lunch to ensure I'm up home before Santa!"

"Urgh," Jamie jokingly groaned again. "OK then hen, that's a deal, three sugars for me today."

As Jennifer pottered away in the kitchen singing along to her Christmas playlist of old favourite festive tunes, Jamie reached for his phone and checked his messages. Only a few messages from some work friends wishing him a good Christmas and one from his brother arranging to share a car back home later this evening. He checked his Facebook messages. One new message. His phone seemed to take ages to load as he tried to access it. It was from Andrew! Jamie couldn't quite believe it, he double tapped the message quickly to open it up, Andrew's face staring back at him from his phone. Jamie could feel his heart beat double quick in anticipation.

Hi Jamie,

Hope you and your friends enjoyed last night, I had fun socialising with all the staff, we have a good bunch! Anyway, as I mentioned and if you are still keen I'd like to set you up on this blind date (hush hush)? I promise you he's a good guy and I just know you two will hit it off. I know you said you were away for Christmas Day but will you be back before Hogmanay? If so, could you make Boxing Day or thereabouts? 7pm, Ivy Bar on Argyle Street?

Have a nice Christmas,

AJ

Jamie re-read it 3 or 4 more times, trying to decipher any hidden meaning. Could it really be him, or was he just innocently setting up a friend? Jamie was uncertain but he was excited too, he was definitely going to go for it, what was there to lose? Although unlike his other dates and escapades he was keeping this under wraps, not even uttering a word of this conversation to his best friends. He wanted to be sure of the situation or run the risk of getting his feelings hurt and he also didn't want to break Andrew's trust. And although he wanted to reply instantly he defied the urge and decided he would do it after lunch. He didn't want to come across desperate in any shape or form!

Jamie had already organised to come back to Glasgow for New Year's Eve celebrations with his closest friends Jennifer and Caitlyn along with their partners at Oran Mor. It was an exquisite reformed church at the head of Byres Road at the corner of Great Western Road in the West of the city. It was a highly elegant venue where they could have a traditional Hogmanay celebration with a 4 course dinner with haggis, champagne and a wee dram of whisky at midnight to toast the bells not forgetting a Ceilidh until the early hours. They had gone the year before and loved every minute and although it was expensive they had snapped up tickets at the start of the year in preparation. Jamie had even booked to hire a kilt for the occasion. He hadn't planned on coming back to Glasgow so soon after Christmas, nevertheless, he would quite happily do so as he was sure he would have had more than enough of his parents by then anyway and had some work to do back in the city. A Boxing Day blind date could be something to look forward to!

Chapter 50

Caitlyn, Jennifer and Jamie gossiped and re-counted last night's antics merrily for over an hour whilst munching into their favourite hangover cure of burger, chips and a milkshake in the American style diner 'Ketchup' in the West End of Glasgow. It was freezing outside and the cobbles on Ashton Lane had frosted over and the other bars had trees and twinkling lights decorating their entrances and the group were getting into the Christmas spirit even although they weren't partaking in their usual alcoholic beverages. Although it was only midday, it was already quite dark outside and the restaurant and other bars were heaving with patrons. It was the perfect time for the friends to relax and exchange the Christmas gifts they had bought each other which perked them up no end trying to shake and feel them trying to guess the contents. "Don't peek!" Jennifer shouted at them, "You have to wait until Christmas morning!"

Although the friends were really close, they all still had their secrets. Caitlyn was afraid to admit to them that she thought her long-term boyfriend no longer found her attractive and possibly suspected him of having an affair. She was embarrassed and upset by it all and really didn't want to share it. She didn't think they would understand. However, the last few days with Peter had been so much better between them, she was relieved. Jennifer was extremely happy with Stuart but she still felt something missing and didn't want to discuss with her friends that she hadn't been invited to his flat yet, she knew they would find that suspicious. As far as they were aware she had stayed at his on a regular basis. Jamie also didn't let on to the girls about his chat with Andrew and certainly didn't tell them about his Facebook message about a date. What would they think? He didn't even know what to think!

"Well, I'm glad my hangover has subsided!" Jamie exclaimed, patting his belly. "Thanks, burger" Jennifer said as she let out a small burp as the others giggled at her.

"Hmmm, very ladylike!" Jamie exclaimed.

"Yes, phew! A burger and chips always sorts me out," Caitlyn added.

"I don't know where you put it," Jennifer said to her. "You demolished that meal and I'm sure you had your usual hangover roll and sausage and Irn Bru too this morning?"

"Ha ha, well yes that is my normal hangover cure but I went to the gym instead. Peter was working early and I was awake, so I sweated the drink out me on the treadmill!"

"That's how she can eat so much," Jamie said looking at Jennifer, "as she works out every day!"

"I wish I had your motivation, you look sooo fantastic! I just hate the gym!" Jennifer gushed.

"Aye right," Caitlyn blushed, "I do not."

"You do! No wonder all the pupils fancy you!" Jennifer continued.

"Shut up! No they don't. Plus, you both look great too and you don't do half as much hard work at the gym as me, I'm well jealous! If I didn't work out, I'd be the size of a house!"

298

"No you wouldn't! In fact, you are getting a bit too skinny – don't you be losing any more weight and disappearing on us now," Jamie said wagging his finger in front of Caitlyn's eyes as if scolding a child.

"I definitely am not! Look at me, I'm hardly Posh Spice, am I?"

"No, you aren't, you look great but just don't go overboard. Nobody likes a skinny girl with no womanly curves about her. Ach I'm just jealous! I bet Peter can't keep his hands off of you!"

"Enough!" Caitlyn declared, trying to quickly change the subject, deflecting away from a sex chat. "Actually, I have noticed I've lost a few pounds," she continued modestly, "but one of the most significant benefit of losing a little weight was not just being able to get into size 8 jeans without any muffin top, which I can by the way" she said jokingly high fiving them both alternatively, "but the best thing is that I've joined a running club."

"What? Since when? You never said," Jennifer quizzed.

"Just in the last few months. I always said I wouldn't, I'm not actually sure why. But my friend at the gym suggested it as I'm always on the treadmill, but I'm loving it. I'm getting faster and I ran 12 miles last week! I didn't think I'd manage that!"

"Wow, that's impressive!" Jennifer exclaimed.

"Yeah, well done honey, Jamie concurred. "You should do the Glasgow half marathon!"

"You should! Catriona in the PE department does it each year and she loves it. We would come and support you!"

"By support, we mean we would wait at the finish line with wine," Jamie giggled.

"But seriously Caitlyn, don't lose any more weight," Jennifer piped in. "It's not good for you to be too thin."

Caitlyn shrugged it off in disagreement. "Thanks, Jen. I know I'm not trying to lose weight, it just came off as I was exercising a little more. As you can see, it's certainly not my diet! But you don't need any motivation - you don't need to lose a single pound!" Caitlyn scolded, "And that's only with sex with Stuart as an exercise, now I'm jealous!"

"Yeah like you and Peter aren't!"

Caitlyn changed the subject quickly "Right, let's have one last coffee together before we all need to shoot off to our *wonderful* families?"

The others nodded in agreement and Jamie called over the waitress to order three lattes for the group. The three of them talked excitedly for another 45 minutes solidly, gabbing away about what they are doing over the holidays along with just a token amount of school work. They sat in silence for the last few moments, lingering over the dregs of coffee in the tall glasses. They were enjoying being in each other's company, not particularly wanting to leave as they all had long journeys ahead of them. Eventually they got round to packing up all their stuff and hugging and kissing to say goodbye.

They were all going their separate ways over Christmas but they would speak to each other regularly on the phone or online no doubt. Sometimes they would visit each other at their family's homes but this year they were leaving it until New Year's Eve where they were going to get back together along with some other friends to take in the bells together.

"See you in a week!" Jennifer shouted back to them as she climbed into her car, "Have a great Christmas!"

"Have fun and be good!" Jamie shouted to them both out of his car window as he honked his horn and drove away into the busy bustling streets, packed with people last minute Christmas shopping panic buying and trying desperately to get home.

"You too, I hope Santa is good to you!" Caitlyn replied back as she walked down the cobbled lane to Byres Road, pulling up her hood to guard herself from the sleety rain.

Chapter 51

Jennifer's Christmas had been amazing so far, back at home in Dumfries. There were no family feuds, just a lovely relaxed day with her Mum, Dad, brothers and sisters, and she received some thoughtful gifts. She had awoken leisurely, very unlike her younger days where she would get up before 7am, wakening up her siblings and racing each other down to the sitting room to see what Santa had brought them with mayhem ensuing, the living room a large mess of barbies, bikes and noise making toys. The family shared a nice breakfast around 10am with some Bucks Fizz and opened their presents together round the open fire. There certainly weren't as many presents like when she was young girl and the room was packed with gifts, but that didn't bother her in the slightest.

There was only one more present to open and that was from Stuart. She had kept it until last and was quite disappointed to be opening it on her own without him. She had wanted to be with him whilst she did it and she would love to see his reaction as she opened his presents from her. The look of dismay must have been written all over her face as her father kept asking her, "What's wrong, honey? Are you missing your boyfriend?"

"I'm not going to open this, I'll leave it until later," she decided. Her siblings teased her and her mother hugged her. "Why isn't Stuart coming? You should invite him again, it'll only take him 2 hours to get here, it's a fine winter's day, no snow lying at the moment and the roads will be deserted."

She perked up a little. "Do you think I should?"

"He is always welcome. I feel as if we know him already with all the good things you've said about him," her mum replied smiling.

"Thanks! I'll ask him later. If he doesn't, he doesn't. We can always open our presents when I see him next."

"Sounds like a plan, sweetheart," her Dad said, patting her on the head. "Who else has presents to open?" he said, now addressing everyone.

"I think that's them all open," her mother replied scanning the room, now filled with open boxes and wrapping paper.

"I think there is one left under the tree," her Dad said again and they all giggled. Their Dad always got their mother an extra surprise gift that she wasn't aware of, an old romantic they used to tease him. Their mother always fussed and told him not to bother but they knew she loved it. She picked up the small wrapped box and opened it tenderly, carefully ensuring none of the wrapping was ripped. Her eyes gleamed "Oh Dave, it's beautiful!"

"Only the best for my wife."

Jennifer peeked over to see in the box to see a lovely white gold necklace with a small pearl pendant. "Well in, Dad, it is lovely!"

Her mother went over and kissed her father and they hugged.

"Aww, Jennifer said, feeling soppy and missing Stuart more than ever, she would love to be together with him on Christmas Day.

"Oh boke!" Jennifer's younger brother Neil shouted. "You are too old for that mush! Where's my extra surprise present?"

303

"Sorry Neil, we won't do it again!" Jennifer's parents laughed, "Now who would like some more buck's fizz?"

Jennifer missed Stuart more and more as the day went on. She texted him and tried to phone him, but received no reply. She ended up having Christmas dinner with her family, without Stuart, which was nice, as always, but all she could think about was Stuart. She loved him and wanted to spend more time with him, especially today. As she was looking so unhappy, her mother suggested that she should go and surprise him and they could at least open their presents together. Her mother even had bought a small gift for him too.

"Do you really think I should drive back down to see him?" Jennifer asked her Mum.

"Well the day is over now, we've had fun but we'll probably now just fall asleep on the couch! You know us."

"And you're only going to sit there miserable and think about him so you might as well," her Dad added.

"She can't help it, she always looks miserable" her older sister jibed and she threw a cushion at her.

She had made up her mind, her parents were right. It had been a lovely Christmas day so far but this would make it perfect. It only took her 15 minutes to get ready and she was in the car and on the road. She blasted Christmas music out of the car stereo and it seemed like the shortest journey ever from her home town to Glasgow and actually an enjoyable one at that. She had never seen the roads so quiet. She couldn't keep the grin off her face thinking about seeing Stuart again and watching his shocked but pleased, she hoped, reaction. She was excited to see his home and to get to know him better, this was the perfect opportunity.

Jennifer knew exactly where he lived and it didn't take her long to find his street using her new SATNAV that her father gave her for Christmas (he loved giving her practical gifts that ensured her safety in the 'big bad city' as he called it).

She arrived outside his house around 7pm, still early, she thought and for some reason she started to feel nervous. The house was in a small cul-de-sac on the outskirts of Glasgow, semi-detached with a small garden and paved driveway out front. The lights were on both upstairs and downstairs and there were a few Christmas decorations outside as well as some pretty twinkling clear lights around the windows. Quite nice decorating for a male, she mused.

His car, a blue Ford Focus, was parked alongside a red Renault Clio, and there was a large Volkswagen Estate behind. She was now extremely nervous! She knew he was having friends over for Christmas dinner and didn't think that this would bother her, but it had dawned on her that although he had met most of her friends, and got quite close, she hadn't been introduced to any of his friends and he didn't really talk about them either. And, she thought, they were a bit older so they might be married and may even have kids! What if they had nothing to talk about or it was awkward? What if they didn't like her? She wished that they had had dinner earlier and he was on his own. She had imagined the romantic scene in her head over and over. She started to regret her decision to surprise him and tried to call him again on her mobile phone. It rang out once again. At least he would answer the door and maybe they could have a few minutes alone together before he introduced them.

She tried his phone again. It rang out once more. He must've left it upstairs or something, she thought. She tried to phone Caitlyn quickly for advice but it too rang out. "Well, I never drove all the way down here on Christmas Day for nothing!" she said out loud, forcing herself to get out the car, clutching on to the present that he had bought for her, still unopened.

She walked up to the front door slowly, sorting her hair and straightening her clothes as she approached the step. She tried to peer in the door pane but it was glazed over so she could only see shadows but could hear people laughing and joking inside. It can't be that bad then she thought, they sounded as if they were enjoying themselves, they can't be monsters! She rapped lightly on the glass of the door. Nothing.

She knew Stuart would want her just to come in without knocking but she felt like an intruder on Christmas Day and didn't want to just walk in uninvited in the middle of their meal. More confidently she knocked again and rang the doorbell. She could hear moving and she knew she'd been heard. She swallowed hard and looked at her feet anxiously as she heard the sound of feet walking up to the door. It swung open and she looked up, smiling nervously at Stuart who looked completely stunned at her arrival. Her eyes lit up and she felt her heart lurch at the sight of him, she was so glad she did this, who cared about his friends as long as they were together, that is all that mattered! Stuart stayed rooted to the spot in shock.

"Hi!" Jennifer eventually, "Merry Christmas!"

Stuart's expression remained stunned, "Hi."

"Who is it?" she heard a young voice from within shout out.

Jennifer looked behind Stuart and she could see they were at their Christmas dinner.

"Oh sorry to interrupt, I just wanted…"

But before she could say anymore, Stuart put his hand up as if to ask her to be quiet.

She looked again through the door to the dining room to see his guests. This time she started to take in what she was witnessing. There was an empty space at the head of the table where Stuart was obviously sitting but at the other end opposite Stuart's chair sat a 30-something pretty blonde woman. His wife? At either side sat 2 boys. She looked again at them, she couldn't believe it - one of the boys was John, the troublesome pupil from her class! To the other side sat an elderly couple, presumably his or *her* parents. She couldn't believe this. She thought she was going to faint, her legs felt weak. She stared without saying a word.

"Who is it, Stuart?" the woman shouted to him as they peered at the doorway to catch a glimpse of Jennifer.

"Just someone looking for directions," he replied to them and he came out on to the step in front of Jennifer and shut the door behind him.

She felt like such a fool. She was speechless.

"Listen," Stuart began, "I'm sorry I should've said…"

But she wasn't listening, she felt like she was floating above her body watching this happen from above like a scene of a movie.

She tried to walk back to her car but her feet weren't working properly and she stumbled towards the gravel as if she was drunk. Stuart lunged after her and tried to steady her to her feet. "Jennifer," he said quietly. "Jennifer, please listen," he said pleading with her, trying to gently pull her round to face him. She snapped into life and hit away his hands aggressively and forcefully. "Do not touch me," she said furiously. She did not care who heard. "Do not touch me again!"

She strode up to her car swinging the door open and jumping in, fumbling with the keys quickly trying to get the engine started. Tears were rolling down her cheeks and she couldn't bear to turn around to meet his gaze while he stood beside the passenger door. The engine kicked to life and she pulled away from the kerb with a jolt, pushing the car up to 30 mph before she'd even got out of his street. Her face was red with rage and she was now driving faster and faster, following the road without knowing where she was going, zipping dangerously through red lights. Before she knew it she found herself in an industrial estate, lined with business units and warehouses, all completely empty without a person or car to be seen. She came to abrupt halt and shut off the engine. Silence.

She couldn't even begin to comprehend the scene that she had just unearthed. She burst into tears, crying uncontrollably that seemed to go on forever. She was so upset. So confused. So angry!

She hit the steering wheel hard irately as she shouted and screamed out loud for anyone to hear. The horn on her car beeped wildly but she didn't care and continued to cry until she felt she couldn't produce anymore tears and rested her head between her hands on top of the steering wheel as she silently sobbed. Her mobile phone began to ring from her handbag. She let it ring out. How dare he? What was he phoning for – to apologise? To inform her of his happy family? To admonish her for ruining his perfect family Christmas? She rustled about her bag to grab her phone and looked at the missed call. It was Caitlyn. Damn! It wasn't even him! He wasn't even sorry, he didn't even care!

What was I? she thought. Just his little bit of sex on the side? Was he just using me for sex and I was just playing on his game? I thought he really liked me! I thought I was falling in love with him! *How could she not have known he was married?!* She just drove all the way down here on Christmas Day just to see him for a few hours.

What a fool! Devastated didn't even come close to how she felt. It actually felt like a physical pain, she could feel it deep inside her stomach and her head pounded like she had concussion. Was he just using me to help out with his son? Was he looking for information? Was he just keeping an eye on John? 1000 thoughts raced through her head at what felt like 100 miles per hour and she couldn't rationalise or stop them. Here she was on Christmas Day on her own in an abandoned car park of an industrial estate somewhere on the outskirts of Glasgow. She had left her loving family behind at home to go and see the man she thought she loved and wanted to be with her, but instead he was just a lying piece of scum and she had ignorantly fallen for his charms. And there he was, sitting at his Christmas meal with his wife and children! Wife and children! His family. She tried to recall in her memory the image of them, it stayed there ingrained like a permanent photo. Was his wife pretty? Young? She closed her eyes mentally torturing herself with thinking about how perfect it all looked. The boys sat there, toys and games all around, smiling and joking with their parents and grandparents like most families on Christmas Day. And to top it all off, one of his kids was John. John who had been the bane of her teaching existence in previous months and that she had lengthy confidential discussions with Stuart about him to help ease her tension and talk about strategies to overcome some of the difficulties in class. No wonder he had suggestions on how to deal with him and knew how to talk to teenage kids – he had two of his own! All these thoughts had worked her back up into an angry rage again and a wave of nausea came over her and she had to open the car door quickly as she retched on to the pavement. The tears started all over again. She caught a glimpse of her reflection in the rear-view mirror as she sat back inside the car. She looked horrendous, her face red and blotchy and tear stained, her eyes red and snot trickled down from under her nose onto her lips. This made her cry even harder.

There was no way she could go home now she decided. She wouldn't be fit for the journey especially as it was now extremely dark and it was turning really frosty. She definitely couldn't face explaining to her parents what had just happened. She didn't want to call Caitlyn back either, not just yet. She couldn't admit to anyone what had just happened, she couldn't tell them what a sucker she had been, not just yet, not on Christmas. What could she do? She didn't even know where she was! After a little time of just sitting in silence she decided just to go back to her Glasgow flat for the night, she needed some time alone to think and get her mind straight before she could face anyone. Her flat may be cold and lonely but tonight she could take some solace in an empty flat. She turned on the SATNAV and it instantly picked up her location and gave her directions back to her flat. "Thanks, Dad, at least I can rely on you, the only man I'll EVER trust!" Jennifer exclaimed as she started the short drive back to the West End.

Chapter 52

Jamie's Christmas on the other hand had been quiet and boring. So boring that by 1pm on Christmas Day he had already decided to drive back to Glasgow early. He had hoped for some time with his family over Christmas but his parents had invited his extended family over to the house for the festivities. This consisted of his mother's sister Jenna and her husband Ryan, his mother's brother Dougie and second wife Ailsa along with their two young children Lorne and Robert. Jamie genuinely loved his aunts and uncles and his little cousins, but after a drunken evening on Christmas Eve with them and being forced to spend Christmas morning with them when they awoke excitedly at 8am it was more than Jamie could handle.

He always thought his parents and brother acted differently around him when others were there. They seemed to bring out their aggressive side. Too much beer and wine with them and out came the sexist, racist, sectarian and homophobic jokes. It was nothing direct and they always did it flippantly as if they didn't really mean it, but it always made Jamie cringe, especially when they would overtly laugh about one of their gay friends and always tried to get Jamie to join in. Jamie's brother, David, who Jamie was very close to, could sense that it made him uncomfortable and was normally so sensitive when he was sober, but acted just like them when he was drunk and it infuriated him like nothing else. Jamie ended up going to bed early on Christmas Eve, just as his Uncle Ryan and Uncle Dougie were getting into an argument about who the best Rangers player was at the moment. When they were opening their presents in a matter of a few hours later the same argument had reared its head again. Jamie couldn't help roll his eyes at his Aunties, unfortunately a little too obviously. "What's wrong Jimmy? You not like football?" Dougie asked as all of the family turned to look at him. "Don't tell me you support *Celtic?*" his little cousin Lorne asked innocently. Jamie shrugged his shoulders, "Nah, I'm not really into football that much."

"So you ARE a Celtic supporter then," his Uncle Ryan joked and playfully punched Jamie in the shoulder. The jibes and taunts continued all morning, and even the boys' hyperactivity on Santa Claus delivering them shiny new red scooters didn't help the mood.

There was only so much of his family he could take and by late afternoon the family had already argued their way through Christmas lunch and Jamie couldn't wait to get back to the peace and quiet of his flat. His parents tried to discourage him from leaving but they didn't push too hard, they knew he was close to boiling point with his aunts and uncles. As he turned the key in his ignition to start the drive on his own, he finally managed to smile a genuine smile for Christmas Day. Plus, he had a date to look forward to tomorrow.

Chapter 53

Caitlyn's Christmas Day had started out brilliantly. With her busy lifestyle, it had been so long since she had seen her family and she had barely even had a chance to catch up with her Mum in ages. She used to always make a point of phoning her at least once per day, they were such a tight knit family, but in the last few years with her busy job her contact had lapsed. It had been even worse over the last few months. Caitlyn didn't want to admit it but she knew it was because her and Peter were going through a 'bad patch' as she knew that her mother would pick up on her unhappiness immediately and she didn't want to talk about it, not with anyone. She didn't even want to say it out loud as she felt as if she did that it would make it more true and somehow 'taint' her relationship with Pete.

Caitlyn had always had bother with sharing her insecurities with those that were close to her and tended to keep her feelings bottled up. She certainly didn't want to share with anyone that she suspected her boyfriend didn't love her anymore and potentially was seeing someone else! Nevertheless, she had felt much happier over the past few days and things had been going well again with Peter.

Just like every other year, Peter stayed with his Mum and his sisters on Christmas Eve and Caitlyn stayed at her family home where they drank copious amounts of fizzy wine all night and caught up with each other. They would always be reunited for Christmas lunch and to exchange gifts. It had been a lazy morning for Caitlyn, casually swapping gifts with her family but a little fuzzy from last night's alcohol and she was extremely excited to see Peter and to get her wonderful presents of course. She had spent so much time exquisitely wrapping each of Peter's gifts and had placed them under the large tree in the corner of the room. She felt like a little kid again as she kept peering out of the window to see if Peter's car had pulled up. Eventually, a little after 1pm, Peter walked in, arms full of presents and was warmly greeted by Caitlyn's parents. Her Mum and Dad had grown to love Peter and treat him like one of the family.

"What about my gift?" Caitlyn eventually said coyly into Peter's ear after her parents had opened their presents and had now left them in private.

"Ha ha, you'll get that later... but for now here is your present from me" he said as he handed over a shiny large red bag.

"Oooh, thank you!" Caitlyn giggled as she picked it up, her eyes prying in to see what other things he had bought her, "But first you need to open yours!" She pointed at the mound of presents awaiting him beside the tree.

"Are they all for me?"

"Yip, every single one!"

"All from you?"

"Yip! There are a few more presents for you from my auntie and my Gran but they are in the kitchen."

"Jeez, I'm a spoiled boy!"

"You certainly are Petey, so get opening!"

"OK, how about we do 1 present each?"

315

"Sounds good to me."

They both started opening and unwrapping the gifts, exchanging thanks and kisses after each one. Peter seemed delighted with his. Caitlyn was too – he had given her the box set of the Sopranos, some bath bubbles along with a head massager, but she was more excited to see what jewellery he had picked out as she looked at the small box that remained unwrapped at the bottom of the gift bag. She had tried to put it to the back of her mind and not get her hopes but possibly could it actually be an engagement ring? Surely not, she dismissed the thought. Plus although £500 was a lot of money, was that enough for a diamond ring? Maybe. She couldn't help but think about it. They had discussed getting married before and he had mentioned that he would like to spend at least a month's salary on her ring if the occasion was to arise, but it hadn't been talked about since.

"I've only got one present left," Caitlyn said, pretending to be sad. "Aw, you've saved the best until last I promise," Peter replied. "Caitlyn, I can't believe I'm not even half way through my presents, you have more than spoiled me again!"

"Ach you're worth it!"

He continued to open present after present, relishing each one.

"What happened to spending a maximum of £50?"

"Ha ha, yeah right as if we were ever going to stick at that!"

"Yeah well going slightly over budget is one thing but you've got me loads. I can't believe you managed to get us T in the Park tickets, awesome! I feel bad!"

"Don't be daft, you've done the same with me!"

Peter continued to open his presents and although he seemed thrilled with them, he looked a little crestfallen as he opened up one of his presents to find a stainless steel watch. It wasn't an expensive one but it was really smart and she knew that he would love it.

"What is up, don't you like it? I know you've got a watch already but I knew you wanted a dressy one and when I saw that I just thought of you."

"Aw Caitlyn, you shouldn't have, I love it!" he exclaimed as he walked towards her to kiss her on the forehead. "I really love it. But honestly, you really shouldn't have. We don't have the money for all of this. We're trying to save, remember?"

"Ach don't be silly, it's Christmas, when else can we spend money on each other?"

"I know, you're right. But now I feel bad, I thought we'd agreed that we weren't going to spend much on each other? I was trying to be sensible."

Caitlyn just smiled.

"And aren't you going to open your last present?" He said as he picked the small box up and handed it to her.

Her eyes danced and she held the box in her hands. She took a deep breath and unravelled the sparkly red gift-wrap paper. She slowly opened the box and she stared at the black stones before her.

"Aren't they great?"

"Yes, fantastic, thank you!" she stuttered, completely disenchanted and a bit bemused to what they were.

"I know it's not as much as you've got me, I feel bad. I knew you loved hot stones though."

"No, don't be silly, I love my gifts!" she said, unconvincingly even to herself. *What happened to her jewellery? Is he waiting until later as a surprise?*

"We did say we were limiting how much we were spending and I actually did go over budget. I hope you like what I got you?"

"I do. Thank you! I can't wait to start watching the Sopranos again – my favourite show, thanks!"

"And we can give each other massages with the head massager and the hot stones. My boss has them and she swears that they are amazing."

"Great."

"I know you loved the massages we got when we went to that spa last year and we've been working so hard recently we haven't given ourselves a treat like a spa in ages so thought we could bring the spa to us!"

Peter seemed genuinely enthusiastic about his presents and he did seem thoughtful, but Caitlyn couldn't help feel disappointed. "Brilliant idea, baby, we could maybe give each other massages later today?"

"Yes, that would be great! We could even go for a nice big bubble bath together first?"

"Sounds good, it would be good to get a bath instead of a shower at our flat..." It was a ritual for them to bath together when they were at Caitlyn's family home as they had a big Jacuzzi bath that

318

was big enough to fit about 10 people. They both loved it as they could lock the door and cosy up for ages without interruption. It always led to a sensual sex session followed by a power shower together afterwards.

Caitlyn felt a bit disheartened after opening her presents but she tried not to let it get to her as she ran the bath. Maybe the jewellery it was a present for his mother between him and his sisters or something? Maybe she had misread it, she was quite drunk at the time. She mentally told herself off, "You shouldn't have been snooping in the first place!" It had just built up her hopes!

Normally a lovely big bubble bath and a massage with Peter would make her feel so warm and happy but today everything Peter seemed to do just irritated her. He continued to talk about work, football, moan about the presents he had received from his parents, complain about the weather and just didn't seem interested in her and it was getting annoying. She tried to talk to him about her new hobby of running but he dismissed it instantly. He played off her advances for sex too and would rather play about with her new head massager that he had bought her. *Bought for himself*, she thought miserably. She felt as if she would rather be with her family without him or be with her friends. When they were having their big Christmas dinner, he continued to agitate her by winding her up and making jokes about her running and her job and Caitlyn got the impression that he was belittling her a little much to the amusement of her brother. "Yeah while I work 60 hour weeks Caitlyn gets days off for a little snow and even when she is in work she is finished by

319

3pm, that's like a half day to me!" he continued as him and her father drank pints of lager while her mum ran round after their every whim.

"Don't forget who you are talking too, Peter. I can tell you that work definitely doesn't just stop at 3.30pm. Unfortunately I know that from experience," Caitlyn's Dad joked with him. Caitlyn felt thwarted and forgotten and she busied herself by browsing on Facebook on her phone and drinking more wine, National Lampoon's Christmas Vacation on the TV in the background. Her thoughts drifted to Cameron as she started to feel tipsy and she wondered how he was and how he spent his Christmas Day. She wondered if he ever thought about her. I bet he would appreciate her, she thought. Cameron always found an opportunity when they were at running club or at the gym to speak to her and was always charming as ever. She had wondered if he had slight feelings for her too but she disregarded them and tried to put him out of her mind.

As she browsed Facebook, she could see that Cameron was online and she yearned to chat to him but forced herself not to make contact. He messaged her on the chat facility to say hi and she fought herself hard not to reply. "Are you coming to the running club night out tomorrow in Glasgow? I hope you are! You need to dance with me to keep scary Janine away from me!" he messaged.

She laughed out loud at his banter. No, she couldn't she thought, but it did seem tempting. She held back, she didn't want to start a conversation with him as she was unsure that she could trust herself at the moment. She had never ever cheated on Peter and wouldn't dream of it. She would hate herself even for contemplating it. Chantal and a few of the other running club members had been trying to persuade her to go to the Boxing Day party with them and it did sound fun. She would have revelled in going even just to be in the same vicinity as Cameron, some harmless flirting would be enjoyable too she thought as she had the feeling that he had a little attraction to her too. That was maybe too dangerous, she thought.

She had made some really good friends there, they were a good bunch and had really motivated and inspired her to run. She started to feel great about herself when she was there and realise that she actually had quite a talent for it. She hadn't really had a chance to tell Peter about her progress at it, he never really seemed interested but always so busy. Nonetheless, she wanted to wait with Peter and her family over the holidays, it wasn't often that she saw them anymore and it was the only time Peter had away from his work.

By around 11pm Caitlyn's parents headed upstairs to their beds and her brother left to meet up with his old friends at the local pub. Finally some time alone with Peter she thought. Unfortunately within what felt like seconds he fell asleep on the couch.

Caitlyn tried to wake him but he was in a drunken stupor and didn't stir. She huffed and puffed loudly, nudging Peter dramatically but he remained with his head on his chest, drooling on to his new shirt. "Peter!" she screamed. "Peter," she said quieter whilst leaning over him stroking his legs in an unsuccessful bid to wake him up. She gave up on trying to move him, she was a bit drunk and tired herself so took this as a sign to go to bed. She put away all the dishes into the kitchen and tidied up quickly before turning out all the lights. "Peter," she whispered in his ear, "are you wanting to come to bed? I've got the electric blanket on."

"Just coming, babe," he mumbled. She hung about for a few minutes and poured them glasses of water to take upstairs with them, she knew they would want them in the morning. "Are you coming then?" She left him in the living room in darkness as she went up to her cosy bed on her own. Peter must've joined her in the middle of the night as when she awoke in the morning he was beside her, still fully dressed and she couldn't help laugh at him although she was still a little annoyed at him. He just didn't seem to want to be with her, not like before anyway. His phone beeped from the side table.

"Morning, Peter" she said to him as she rolled over to kiss his unshaven face. He just groaned.

"A little rough are we, after all that beer and wine?"

Another groan.

"I've got you some water."

"Thanks," he croaked.

"Are you wanting to go a walk on the cycle path next to the Loch today?" she asked hopeful that the Scottish winter weather would hold out for them. They always used to try and take advantage of the gorgeous walkways and forest trails near her family Perthshire home, absolutely stunning regardless of the season. Of course there had been occasions where the romance and deserted areas have lead to the pair getting more than frisky in a secluded grassy dune but she wouldn't dare intimate that on a freezing cold day like today!

His phone beeped again.

"Peter, look at your messages, your phone is beeping again."

He kept his eyes shut and didn't acknowledge her. She was grateful that she didn't consume as much alcohol as him last night, she hated being hungover in the holidays, what a waste of free time. She might as well try and get a little more sleep though, it's not often she got a long lie anymore.

His phone beeped again after a few minutes.

"Peter! Please get your phone!"

After the fourth beep, she grabbed the phone herself to turn it to silent. The message received on the front screen stopped her in her tracks.

It was from a girl named "Grace". Intrigued and annoyed she read the text.

Thank you so much for the present, it is absolutely perfect! Looking forward to seeing you back at work tomorrow G xxx

Caitlyn's face grew red with anger and she threw the phone down on top of Peter. He didn't even flinch. She grabbed it back and re-read it. "What the fuck? Is it her you've fucking given some expensive jewellery to? Is it her you've been spending all this time in the office with? What happened to spending all of our holidays together and not working? But you're rushing back to Glasgow to your office to see *Grace*." Caitlyn shouted as she stomped about her parent's living room. Despite Caitlyn's rant, Peter remained motionless and blissfully unaware of Caitlyn's discovery. "And you don't even care do you?" she continued to scream "I'm fucking

323

completely naked! I've had a Hollywood bikini wax, a full spray tan AND I've lost 10 pounds in the last few fucking months and you haven't even fucking noticed!" She stared at him as he rolled over on to his side, starting to snore. "Well, I tell you, Peter, while you've not noticed me other people have. While you've been busy getting cosy with some fucking office junior slut other people have been noticing ME and I am enjoying the attention."

Peter started to stir, "Whoa, what's up babe? What are you angry at?" He obviously hadn't heard anything that Caitlyn had said but he was awake now.

"What is up? I've just told you but you don't want to listen. You NEVER want to listen to me anymore. In fact, I wasn't going to go back to Glasgow for the running club night out but do you know what, I am going to. Yes, I've joined a running club and I'm actually fucking good in case you are interested, thanks for asking!" she continued to rant as she marched around her bedroom picking up mini suitcase that hadn't been unpacked yet. "I am going back to Glasgow, on my OWN!"

She couldn't speak with anger and she didn't want to face her family, she just slipped out of the house without a word. Peter had tried to explain and tried to stop her but she was too fast. She was in the car within a minute. She knew she might be over reacting but her gut told her that Peter was hiding something and this was the perfect fit - he was obviously sleeping with this Grace girl at work.

Caitlyn knew that she probably shouldn't be driving as the roads would be icy, it was still dark and she was too angry and impatient to fully de-ice the windscreens. The mist was low and she couldn't see very well, but this didn't stop her from driving fast down the windy roads to meet the motorway. She was crying hard now, finding it hard to catch her breath. The slip road diverted her to a back road. "Argh!" she screamed. "Just my fucking luck! The fucking bloody fucking stupid motorway is fucking shut!" It would now take her an extra 25 minutes to get to Glasgow on the single track road. She drove hastily and rapidly, taking the bends with too much speed but she refused to slow down. Thoughts of Peter and his seedy mistress filled her head and she sobbed silently, snot and tears pouring down her face. Her mind was starting to fill in the missing blanks of Peter's affair and all of his working late, mysterious texts, lifts home and not wanting sex with her anymore was now all making sense.

As her wrath built up so did her speed and it wasn't before long she had racked up to over 90 miles per hour. This was completely unlike her, as she was normally such a cautious, careful and sensible person, but at this moment in time she felt as if it wasn't her, she was running on autopilot and that this wasn't real life. She felt like she didn't care that she was being erratic, driving faster and faster with rage on the winding icy roads. Her phone began to ring and she rummaged about her bag with her left hand to pick it up. She wanted to ignore Peter but she was intent on confronting him too. "Is that you phoning to finally apologise that you've been found out, you cheating bastard?!" she screamed while still feeling around for her mobile as it rang and rang. She was getting more and more frustrated trying to find the phone without looking that she gave in

325

and looked down at her bag for what felt like a split second but it was just enough time for her car to veer on to the other side of the road without her knowing.

She grabbed her phone and looked up just in time to see glaring headlights directly in front of her. Caitlyn screamed and tugged wildly at the steering wheel and put her foot on the brakes instinctively in an unsuccessful attempt to take control of the vehicle again and direct the car back away from danger. She tried in vain to manoeuvre her car away from the right hand side but it over compensated and the ice made the car skid off into the grassy ditch. It now felt like slow motion to Caitlyn, the car was tumbling over upside down and she couldn't do anything to stop it. Thoughts of her life with family, friends and Peter flashed through her head as the car battered her and creaked with noise until there was utter darkness.

Chapter 54

Jennifer didn't care that her neighbours were staring at her when she drudged up the tenement stairs lugging her bags up slowly behind her, tears still rolling down her cheeks. She couldn't care less that they were whispering about her and she couldn't care less how bad she looked. Jennifer thought that they had maybe tried to talk to her but she wasn't taking anything in and she definitely wasn't in the mood for divulging in any festive chit chat. She had gone beyond caring being thought of as ignorant by the neighbours. All she could see in front of her was *him*. Stuart. Stuart and his *family*. What a joke.

Her mobile phone continued to ring and ring from her bag. It was him. She stared at the screen displaying his name. She turned it off, she couldn't bear to even see his name appear on the handset. She let herself into the flat and sat down on the couch without turning on any lights. The house landline phone started to ring but she chose to ignore it. It would only be *him* again. She took it off the hook to ensure she wasn't disturbed again. She wasn't ready to hear from him right now. She lay down in the foetal position and closed her eyes, she just wanted to sleep and never awaken from this horrible nightmare.

Chapter 55

Jamie bounded up the stairs to his flat cheerily waving and wishing his neighbours a Merry Christmas. They didn't seem as friendly as usual or how he expected them to be on Christmas Day, he mused. He had been trying to phone Caitlyn and Jennifer to moan and joke about his terrible family Christmas so far and see if theirs had faired any better but had been unable to get hold of either of them. He was looking forward to getting the TV all to himself for the first Christmas ever. Jamie normally was forced to watch back to back soaps all day, along with the Queen's speech and other programmes he would never dream of watching on Christmas Day. This time, he could relax in the comfort of his own flat and watch whatever he wanted. It would also give himself some time to prepare himself for his big date that Andrew had set up. He couldn't help but smile in the hope and anticipation that it might actually be with Andrew himself!

When Jamie arrived at his front door the smile soon was wiped from his face. It was open! Someone was in his flat! He raced through into the hall but it was in darkness, silence. "Hello?" he called out. Nothing. Nothing looked missing or different and out of the corner of his eye he could see a shadow in the living-room. Someone was there. Without thinking he barged in, brandishing the nearest thing to him as a weapon which happened to be his new Christmas present of a bottle of Raspberry vodka. "What are you doing here?" he screamed at the shadow.

"Argh!" Jennifer screamed at the top of her voice, jumping up to her feet, shocked after being wakened up from a deep sleep.

"Jamie!" she shouted.

"Jennifer!" Jamie shouted back surprised. "You? What the hell are you doing here? It's Christmas!"

"Oh Jamie!" Jennifer started crying again. She couldn't bring herself to answer Jamie right now, she just wanted him to hold her. She collapsed into his arms and Jamie just held her. "Here, here honey," Jamie consoled her and stroked her hair, "everything will be OK." They held each other for at least another 15 minutes without asking any other questions.

"Now are you going to open that for us?" Jennifer eventually asked, signalling to the vodka bottle.

"Definitely. Time for vodka and sharing."

"OK."

Two vodka and fizzy waters later after improvising with mixers due to impromptu return and pathetically bare cupboards, Jennifer had filled Jamie in on her situation with Stuart. Jamie sat stunned and listened as she relayed all the details, only pausing for dramatic effect and taking big gulps of her vodka. She awaited Jamie's reaction and she poured them a third house measure glass. "Well?" she asked impatiently.

"Well," Jamie uttered eventually "I. Never."

Jennifer swallowed her drink in 3 gulps and began pouring another. "I mean, I never actually got a clue at all. He seemed soooo into me. When we start seeing each other I did ask about

329

marriage as he was older. I'm sure I did. I'm positive that he said he wasn't married. I'm sure I asked him that the first night we were together. I thought we had a 'connection', you know?"

"I don't know what to say, Jen. I'm totally flabbergasted!"

"You are? Fuck. I'm totally and fucking utterly fucking fucked, I was totally fucked over! I just can't believe it. What a fucking shitty married fucking lying cunt of a fucking bastard! Argh!" she screamed as she slammed her glass on to the worktop. "I know I'm silly but I really thought that he might be the 'one', you know?"

Jamie nodded, not knowing what to say, letting her do all the talking. "Fucking bastard," he echoed.

"I mean, I knew he was older but not that old. I thought he was in to me, he told me he loved me for fuck sake! What a fucking prick! Do you think he's done this with other girls?"

"No! I doubt it," Jamie eventually said. "Actually, I really don't know. I'm as shocked as you."

"I bet he has the sleazy dirty cunt, I hope his cock rots off!"

"Karma will out."

"Do you think he was still shagging his wife every night when he got home?"

"Doubt it. Maybe. Did she look hot?" Jamie wasn't sure now he was being helpful and was instantly regretting asking anything.

"Actually she looked alright for a thirty-something. She looked quite nice really. In fact, his poor fucking wife! She maybe thought he was out at work but instead he was off having an affair with an unsuspecting girl. I should fucking tell her so I should. I've got off

330

easy compared to her, I suppose! You know, I could've barged right in that fucking house and told them all what had being going and completely ruined their fucking Christmas, ruined their life just like he did when he shat on me, but I never! HE ordered me out like a fucking wee lassie to speak to in the street. What a dick!"

"What a dick."

"Oh Jamie, I can't believe I was fooled! I feel like such an idiot!"

"You're not an idiot, love. You are beautiful and clever and funny and sexy and he has lost out BIG time. It obviously just wasn't meant to be, there will be someone much better for you out there. Thank God you found out he was a piece of shit now rather than later. The only mistake you made was to trust a man and believe me, we all do it, it happens to the best of us," Jamie said smiling, pulling her close reassuringly as Jennifer started to sniffle again.

Although Jamie had silenced his phone earlier they could both see that his phone was lighting up constantly during their conversation like Blackpool illuminations but had chosen to ignore it. "Should we answer?" Jamie asked her.

"No! Well, not if it's *him.*"

"What about Caitlyn?"

"Yeah well off course, answer to Caitlyn. I need her in a time like this, she always makes me feel better. Although, that being said, she's only going to make me feel worse that she'll be sitting there with her perfect fucking boyfriend enjoying their perfect fucking family Christmas together."

"Yeah, well she does have it lucky in that respect. Wish she was here though as she is always good at prank calling or finding a way to annoy horrible exes and making us feel better."

"Yeah, she does, that's true, do you mind that time she made a voodoo doll of my old boyfriend Tim who cheated on me with that tart Emma in the 2nd term of our post-grad?"

Jamie roared with laughter, "Oh my god, I forgot about that! Yes! She made it do unspeakable things, ha ha!"

"Before finally launching it off the Erskine Bridge when we were driving to Balloch for the day, do you remember?"

"Ha ha, yeah good riddance, Timmy boy!"

"Is that her phoning?"

"Probably, I've not heard from her today, I normally hear from her on Christmas Day by now."

"We shouldn't have bothered going home for Christmas."

"I wish I stayed at home!" Jennifer slurred as took another sip of her drink. "Sorry, Jamie, oh crikey – sorry! I've not even listened to you at all. Why the hell are you here?"

"No biggy."

"No really, why aren't you home enjoying some family time?"

"Nah, no reason. People have too many high expectations at Christmas, including me. It was fun but believe me, 24 hours in my family's company is more than enough," Jamie joked as he poured them another large vodka.

"Aw Jamie, really? Was it that bad?"

"Ach no, not really, but my family is bad enough but Christmas brings it to a whole new level. In our household it means way too much alcohol and even a few hours with them after one too many fizzy wines is absolutely unbearable."

"Ha! Families, eh? Who'd have them?"

"Plus…" Jamie added, feeling that Jennifer might appreciate a change in topic, "I might have a date."

"A date? With who? When?" Jennifer excitedly exclaimed.

"I'm glad you're smiling again."

"Stop stalling and spill!"

"Nothing really to spill. It's a blind date actually…"

"What? With who?"

"Well, that's the point of a blind date dummy, I don't know who!"

Jennifer playfully hit him on the shoulder, "Duh, just tell me, how did it get set up then? Please tell me it's not a dodgy online thing?"

"No! I met him in a gay chatroom…"

"Shut up! Are you fucking for real, do you know the dangers of that? He's probably some 50 year old creep!"

Jamie laughed out loud, "Hold your horses, *Mum*! Don't be daft, I'm only kidding, it's not online. And I'm not telling you who is setting me up. I'm leaving that to your wicked imagination."

"Och, Jamie! Tell me, tell me, tell me, tell me, please please please!"

"Sorry, no can do. I don't even know if I'm going on it anyway"

"What? Yes you are – you have to go! Tell me! When is it?"

"Day after tomorrow I think."

"You think? As if you don't know! Well get yourself suited up and get on it, Mr! Tell me who is setting it up? Is Caitlyn in on this?"

"OK, OK. And no, she doesn't know either so do not tell her. I wasn't going to tell either of you until it had happened. Once I've been on it, I'll let you know who set it up OK?"

"Aw boo! But OK, fair enough."

"Right OK, my phone is going to lose its battery if I ignore it any more. We are popular I tell you that!"

"Right, answer the bleeding thing but only if it's Caitlyn."

"It is Caitlyn," Jamie giggled looking at the receiver, "she's back in the sticks, phoning from her Mum's, she must not have a reception on her phone."

"Or she's wasting her Mum's phone-bill instead of her own, that's what I do when I'm home, ha ha."

"Well hellooo and Merry Christmas sexy muthafucka!" Jamie jokingly answered the phone.

"Uh-huh. Oh my God, really? What? Where? Yes. No. Yes. OK."

Jennifer watched confused as Jamie's expression changed instantly to sombre and serious as he stuttered monosyllabic reactions into the phone as he jumped up to his feet.

"What is it, Jamie? What is she saying? Is everything OK?"
He held up his hand as if to quiet Jennifer until he was off the phone.
"Get your coat, Jennifer, we've got to go. We've got to go NOW!"
"What? Why? Where to?"

"The hospital. Southern General. It's Caitlyn. She's been in a car accident."

"Oh my God, what happened? Is she OK?"

"Just get your coat and your car keys, we've got to go!"

"Is she OK? Was that her Mum?" Jennifer had now got to her feet and was rummaging about her bag for her own mobile phone and as she turned it back on she discovered not only countless unanswered messages from Stuart, but from Caitlyn and her parent's home. "Shit, she tried to phone me earlier. Jamie, we've just demolished nearly all of that vodka, there is no way we can drive, we'll flag over a taxi on the street. Come on, let's go! Now Jamie, tell me, is she OK?"

Jamie turned round to face her, tears filling up his eyes, "I don't know Jen, I really don't know."

Jennifer was so grateful to Jamie who took control of the surreal situation and managed to get a cab almost instantly. Jennifer was still in a state of shock. She was never good at dealing with difficult and painful situations. All of what happened earlier with Stuart now paled into insignificance. She didn't utter a word to Jamie during the journey not even to reply to his questions. She sat quietly looking out the back window pane as they zoomed through the Clyde Tunnel, whilst Jamie was phoning various people including Caitlyn's parents again and Peter.

"We might be the first ones here, Jennifer, are you ready for this?" Jamie asked her. "She's in Intensive Care and she's unconscious but the Doctors say she needs people around her. I'm not sure how she is, but this is serious, Jen."

Jennifer just sat there, solemnly, looking out of the window. She prayed to God that this was some mistake, this can't happen, not to her best friend, not to Caitlyn.

"Peter and her parents are on their way, they shouldn't be long now." Jennifer managed to nod acknowledgement.

Jennifer and Jamie arrived at the Accident and Emergency room at the Southern General Hospital in the Southside of Glasgow in under 10 minutes. The friendly Glaswegian taxi driver had made every effort to get there as soon as possible and didn't even charge them the fare when they arrived. Jamie took the initiative once again to speak to the nurses at the front desk and Jennifer followed as they were directed to a small waiting room down a long grey clinical corridor on the 3rd floor where Jamie continued to talk to a Doctor.

"Jennifer, we need to wait a few minutes before we see her OK?" She managed to nod once again and Jamie took a seat on one of the uncomfortable chairs.

"Where is she?" Jennifer finally asked, "Is she going to be OK?" "She's in the next room to us, we'll see her in a minute. I don't know Jen, I think it's quite serious. I'm not sure if she's going to be OK."

Jennifer felt as if she was dreaming, trapped in some farcical nightmare.

"Don't worry Jen, it's Caitlyn – she's as strong as an Ox!" Jamie uttered, now changing to a more positive outlook.

The waiting room door creaked open and they both turned expectantly but were surprised to see Stuart standing there.

Jennifer soon sprung to life, "What the hell are you doing here?" she shouted as she lunged forward, eyes bulging with anger.

"Stuart, this is not the time or the place," Jamie added more calmly.

"Why are you here?" Jennifer screamed again, "You are not welcome!"

"I'm sorry," Stuart uttered, looking sheepish, "I really am."

Stuart looked over at Jennifer and then at Jamie, "I'm sorry. Peter phoned me, he was trying to get hold of both of you but it was just ringing out. He had my number and Caitlyn's Mum spoke to your Mum, Jen, and thought you were with me so, oh it's a long complicated story! But the main thing is that I'm here, I wanted to make sure you both were here and that you were OK and that Caitlyn was OK. Jen, I especially wanted to make sure that you are OK after earlier. I was worried. I wanted to explain. How are you?"

Jennifer just stared back at him at disbelief unable to speak a word.

"What do you think, you fucking dick?" Jamie started to shout at him, "She has just fucking found out on Christmas Day, Christmas fucking Day no less, that her boyfriend has a fucking Blue Peter ready made family that he failed to tell her about and now she's at the hospital to see her best friend who..." He cut his sentence short as Jennifer and Stuart looked back at him without an answer. Jennifer had never seen Jamie like this before.

Stuart moved towards Jennifer and tried to take her hand but she turned away. "Jennifer please, I can completely understand why you, why you both, are so mad. But you've got to believe me that you have got it all wrong. What you saw... what you saw wasn't..."

"Wasn't what, Stuart?" Jennifer asked, "Wasn't a nice family Christmas dinner I walked in on? Was it all just a figment of my imagination?"

"No, but let me explain..."

"Wouldn't it have been better to tell me a few months ago that you were married?"

"I'm sorry, I really am Jennifer. But everything else, everything else we had was real. Just listen to my side of the story. Let me explain."

Jennifer looked away in disgust. "Go away Stuart! Beat it! Really, just go, I can't deal with this right now!"

"I think you better leave," Jamie said to him, looking him directly in the eyes.

"I just want to let you know the real story, I want to be here for you Jen, I know you. I know you need me right now."

"I can't fucking believe you are here and saying all of this shit! You don't know me at all and I certainly CERTAINLY don't need you right now. I don't need you at all!"

"Right Stuart, I think you have upset her enough for one day, it's time to go. We have much bigger things to deal with today."

"I will, I will if Jennifer wants me to go." He turned to look at her with pleading eyes.

"I think that's fucking clear don't you think?" Jamie said stepping in in front of him.

"Jennifer, you've got to listen. Jamie, listen too. I want to be open and honest with you. Please let me explain."

"I don't think you are listening, pal, we don't need this today, do your shitty lying excuse of an apology another time," Jamie said now getting quite aggressive, squaring up to Stuart.

"I'm not a liar. I'm sorry Jen, please just listen. I can tell you all about it later but please let me be here for you now. I love you." Jennifer and Jamie stood in silence.

"I just didn't know how to tell you and there was never a right time. I love you so much. I do, I really love you. My marriage has been over for so long. Years in fact. We went through an incredibly messy divorce over a year ago now and I didn't want to get you involved. We're trying to keep things civil at the moment, especially for the kids, hence, the Christmas meal you witnessed. It is amicable but it's hard to see the boys. This has been so difficult for them. I love my kids, my boys, so much Jennifer, I didn't want to hurt you or them. Such a hard time for everyone involved. I wanted to tell you, I did. I'm embarrassed."

Jennifer looked at him, "Are you for real?"

"God, Jennifer, yes! I want to be with you! I'm so much older than you. I have so much history. I didn't think we were anything serious at the beginning so I didn't want to tell you about all my...

my baggage. I got married so young because my girlfriend of 16 fell pregnant and I thought I was doing the right thing but I never felt for her the way I feel about you. I didn't want to spoil what we had. I didn't mean to deceive you. But I was falling for you, deeper and deeper and then there was just never a right time. I was planning on telling you but I just didn't think Christmas was it."

"Is this the truth?" Jamie stepped in to ask.

"Yes! Cross my heart and hope to die. If you had waited Jennifer I would've invited you in. I have told my ex-wife about you. I've told her already I'm in love with you. But I've just not told the kids yet. I probably would have but then I found out that you taught one of them and that just seemed to confuse matters even more!"

Jennifer just started at him.

"And not only that but you found him a total pain in the ass, which I do too believe me, but the separation has been so hard on him, on both of them. The first proper Christmas apart was really hard so this year we tried to all meet together for the sake of them. And then you turned up…"

"Do they know now?"

"Yes. Well, kind of. I didn't want to say too much to them as I wasn't sure of 'us' after your reaction earlier. I wouldn't introduce you into their lives until I had spoke to you first and explained. God, Jennifer, I don't even know how you feel about it all. I thought you'd be put off by my baggage and I didn't want to lose you. I'm begging for forgiveness here, Jen, please give me a chance? Let me be here for you? I want to help you and support you today. I can't believe this has happened to Caitlyn."

"Caitlyn McDonald's family?" A small Indian man in a long white coat asked into the room, interrupting their conversation.

"Yes. Well no, close friends, her family are on their way, they won't be long now," Jamie said looking at his watch.

"Well, I'd like to wait until her family is here before I give you an update on her progress."

"But I thought we could see her?" Jamie asked.

"How is she?" Jennifer asked.

"You can go in the room if you wish but she is unresponsive at the minute. We are hoping she will come round in the next few hours. Hearing your voices might help. I'll tell you more when her parents are here."

Stuart stood close to Jen and whispered to her quietly, "I'm here for you, Jen. I'm not expecting you to forgive me instantly. You can make your mind up and shout at me later and we can discuss our stuff another time. But I'm here for you now if you need me."

She couldn't bring herself to talk to Stuart but she didn't think she could cope seeing Caitlyn without him. Stuart grazed his hand next to Jen's. She clasped it gently.

"You both go in to see her. I will wait here on her parents. I'll be here if you need anything," Stuart said to them both.

Jennifer and Jamie walked into the small room next door to the waiting room. Jennifer clung on to Jamie, pinching tighter and tighter as Caitlyn became visible.

"Caitlyn?" Jennifer exclaimed "Oh Caitlyn! Is that you? What happened?" Jennifer sobbed as she ran towards her best friend.

Jamie stood at the other side and just looked down at Caitlyn's motionless body, hooked up to monitors, needles in her arms with cuts and bruises over her battered pale face.

"Caitlyn? Can you hear us?" Jamie asked. He glanced over and caught Jennifer's gaze. She looked back looking just as scared as him.

"Oh Caitlyn! We love you. Please get better!" Jennifer whispered.

"That's Caitlyn's family here," the same Doctor announced "Can I speak to you all in the corridor?"

They all filed out into the waiting room, once more, this time embracing sadly with Caitlyn's parents and Peter, to discover how Caitlyn was recovering.

Chapter 56

The Doctor wanted to address Peter and Caitlyn's parents privately and Jamie was positive that they left out most of the gory details when they recanted her condition to them. He understood most of it but he knew that she was in a dangerous condition. However, it sounded as if the experts were very confident and positive that she could make a full recovery and that she was extremely lucky to be alive. She was going to need her friends and family around her to help her get back to her normal self. There was a possibility that she may never recover fully. God knows how she would feel mentally. It must've been torturous, Jamie thought. She may also be in a lot of pain and was on strong painkillers at the moment. Jamie couldn't believe it, he couldn't believe that his best friend Caitlyn was involved in such a serious accident. She was such a careful driver too, it wasn't like her. It just shows you that life is too short, that these freaks of nature can happen to anyone at any time.

Jamie started to feel emotional and sentimental. Wishing partly that he had been nicer to his family despite their annoyances. And wishing that he had someone to be with. Jamie wanted to share his life with a partner now, he didn't want to be alone anymore and although he wouldn't be going on any blind date now because of Caitlyn, he was going to seize the day and make the most of it from now on.

Chapter 57

A bright light shone into Caitlyn's weary eyes. It was sore and awkward for her but she forced herself to open her eyes ever so slightly, squinting to try and look around but she couldn't see anything but light. Where was she? She couldn't remember a single thing. What had happened? All she could see was light and then it all went black again. Darkness again. Blackness.

Some time later, unaware of dates or time, noise was all around her. She couldn't pin point what the noise was or where she was. This time she felt awake, she felt alive, as if she was fighting for life, she felt like adrenaline was pumping through her veins and it dawned on her what had just happened. Caitlyn knew she had been in an accident and she thought she could hear someone calling her name. She fought hard to open her eyes, "open, OPEN!" she screamed inwardly to herself but her eyes weren't responding. Again she could hear people, unfamiliar people now, males and females, saying her name. She wanted to call out and speak to them but her body continued to be responsive and lay still. "Can you hear us, Caitlyn?" "Are you there?" "Can you hear us?"

She was alive! She wanted to shout at them. She could hear them! She was fine! What was wrong with her? She couldn't feel any pain but she couldn't move. She felt alive so she must be OK? Her body remained stiff as a board and she used all of her energy and determination to try and wiggle her toes or move her fingers but nothing happened.

"Caitlyn? Can you hear me?" Peter. Peter, she recognised Peter's voice. He was here! Knowing that he was there and she couldn't speak to him or hold him made her want to cry. All she wanted to do was wake up and be with him and be reassured by one of his big hugs.

She could hear other people now, all around her, scurrying about. Was she still in the car?

Peter held on to her hand. She knew his touch, it felt warm and clammy. He squeezed it tight and stroked the back of her hand. She wanted so desperately to reciprocate and with every might she tried and tried to squeeze his hand back to let him know that she could hear him, but nothing happened.

Is this it? Am I dying? Am I slipping away? Or am I already dead?

Jennifer, Jamie, Peter and Caitlyn's family waited in the hospital for the rest of the evening. It was now after 3am and they were each taking turns at going in in pairs to visit her. The doctor reassured them all that she was improving with every hour and he was hopeful that it wouldn't be long before she was awake.

"Guys, you go home, you've been brilliant being here but you need your rest, it's Christmas," Peter said to Jennifer and Jamie.

"No! Don't be daft, we want to be here," Jamie replied.

"We'd just be at home worrying," Jennifer added. Stuart had left to collect some things for them but had promised to return. Jennifer didn't object.

"We really appreciate you all being here," Caitlyn's Dad said, "you all are good friends to her, we always knew she was fine back in Glasgow with you and Pete."

This was the most the group had talked in a while, they mostly just sat around looking at each other or the walls until it was their turn to see her. Caitlyn's Dad was the only one either pretending it was all fine or trying to keep everyone's spirits up. Either way it kept him sane and passed the time a little. They were all shattered but had no intentions of leaving the hospital.

It was around 5am that Caitlyn's Peter ran out of her room into the waiting room shouting, "She's awake, she's awake!"

They all jumped up collectively and her mother ran towards the door followed by her Dad and Peter. "The Doctor and nurses have been in," Caitlyn's brother continued, "they said that she looked good."

Jennifer and Jamie remained hesitant and allowed her family to see her first. "Come in!" Peter shouted to them after a few minutes and they walked in uncertainly.

Caitlyn lay there, Peter at one side and her parents and brother on the other. It was so emotional. They joined Peter and looked at her. "Hey Caitlyn, oh Caitlyn!" Jennifer blubbed.

"You could've put on some make up for us for goodness sake Caitlyn," Jamie joked.

"It'll take her a wee while to come round properly, but she seems to have full cognition. She'll be back to herself hopefully in no time at all. But you'll need to spoil her, she has been through quite an ordeal and will be in a great deal of pain although she is very lucky, there are no serious injuries to her. We'll assess her more tomorrow. Once you all have had some time together, we'll let her rest, she'll need some time for sleep," the Doctor said to them all. "I'll get another word with her and with Peter again in a few minutes, don't tire her out."

"OK, Doctor, thank you!" Caitlyn's Dad exclaimed, "Thank you".

"Thank you, thank you, Doctor!" Caitlyn's Mum repeated with gratitude.

Chapter 58

Caitlyn fought to open her eyes once more. This time she could see, she could comprehend. Peter, her family, along with Jennifer and Jamie, were beside her. She was overjoyed to be alive! Was she going to be OK? Her head ached like the worst hangover of her life. She couldn't move and she tried to speak but it hurt too much. Her mouth was so dry and she couldn't even gulp down fresh air. She felt as if she was pinned to the bed with wires. Doctors and nurses were visible to her and were speaking to her, saying her name, asking her questions but she hadn't the energy or the will to answer them no matter how hard she tried. Her parents and Peter were answering questions. What was her age? What day was it? What year was it? "We need her to answer some of these," the nurse instructed to her mother.

Caitlyn panicked and tried to wiggle her toes and move her limbs to ensure that she could still move. She used all of her energy to try and move but nothing really happened although she could still feel them, and after trying and trying she eventually managed to move her legs slightly to the side and wiggle her fingers.

"Don't worry Caitlyn, you are going to be just fine, you are doing so well," one of the nurses whispered to her. She felt so dizzy and disorientated, she wanted to hug Peter so badly, to feel him, to let him reassure her that everything was going to work out. She closed her eyes a little and allowed a tear to fall as she remembered their fight. Was he really unfaithful? Did he want to end it with her?

Could they work it out? All she wanted was to be with Peter. This felt like a life or death moment for her and her immediate thought was Peter, he had always been her true love and she just wanted him to hold her but she knew she had to deal with his possible infidelity, life was too short.

She felt startled all of a sudden as nausea took over and she started to vomit. The nurse ran to her aid and propped her head to the side as she was sick into a bed pan. Black-red liquid filled the basin. A little relief. She gasped for air and the nurse tried to get her to drink a little water from the side and she knew she must to feel better. She forced herself to sip as the nurse took the cup to her lips. It tasted disgusting, like poison! She kept sipping but it looked like the volume of the cup didn't reduce. She looked at her legs, her arms – was she OK? Had she broken any bones? It didn't look as if she had. She tried again to speak, "Am I OK?"

"What was that dear?" her mum asked.

"She's trying to talk!" Peter exclaimed. "You're going to be absolutely fine, babe, we're all here for you, I love you so much!"

I love you too, she tried to say but the words just weren't getting to her mouth.

A sudden pain rushed through her body and she tried to sit up to fight it. Her body started shaking and convulsing and she tried painfully to keep still. She cried inwardly at the embarrassment and the not knowing what was happening. The Doctor spoke softly and calmly to her friends and family who left the room. She tried to hold on to Peter's hand to insinuate that she wanted him to remain with

349

her. He looked back at her with sad eyes and she felt guilty for wanting him with her. He shouldn't be subjected to seeing her like this, she felt guiltily, but what if this was the last time they were together? What if this is was her way out of life? She wanted to be with him for just a little longer.

"It's OK, seizures are common, Caitlyn, at this stage, nothing to worry about. It'll all be over in a few seconds," the nurse repeated to her as she stared back at her helplessly. The nurse tried to rest her down back on to the bed as she lashed out for what felt like minutes but was only a matter of seconds before the fit was over but then she was sick again, this time more violently, more black liquid. The nurse held up a basin and another was holding her head. "It's OK, honey, get it up, you'll feel better for it."

The vomit spilled all over her and the bed sheets, as well as quickly filling the basin. She was mortified and she just wanted to feel normal again.

She tried again to speak but her voice became just a squeak.

"You're making excellent progress, Caitlyn," one of the nurses said to her smiling, patting the top of her shoulder softly. "How are you? Do you have a headache?"

Caitlyn squeaked again and managed to force herself to nod her head. She was determined to speak, all of her family were there, they looked worried and anxious and she wanted to reassure them all that she was fine. She was not going to be beaten. She has had a bad accident but she was alive, she was extremely lucky, and she knew it.

"I'm sorry," she finally managed to get out in a tiny barely audible voice, "I'm so sorry." She was, she felt so bad that she had driven in those conditions, whilst angry, and not been as careful as she would normally. She didn't intend to cause any grief for her family and friends, especially at Christmas.

"There's nothing to be sorry about sweetheart," her Mum said as she reappeared and perched at the end of her bed, "you are going to be OK and that's all that matters."

"Was anyone else injured? Please say it was just me?" So many thoughts were now filling her head and now her voice had come back, she wanted to ask so many questions. "Is the car a write off? God, I am so sorry everyone. I've ruined everyone's Christmas! Sorry!"

"You don't need to be sorry, Caitlyn! I was so worried! I'm the one that needs to apologise. I didn't hear you this morning and I think you got your wires mixed up..." Peter started to explain.

"That doesn't matter now," Caitlyn's Mum added, "we were just so concerned about you rushing away, we wanted you with us at Christmas. We are just glad that you are. You are so important to us, Caitlyn."

Caitlyn began to sob more heavily now as her Mum started to blub and the realisation of what had happened hit her, how could she have been so stupid? "Was there anyone else involved in the accident?" she asked again, anxiously.

"Don't you worry pet. It was just you, the driving conditions were horrendous today and you went off the road. You crashed into

351

the side and no-one else was involved. It was very serious, but you are one very lucky girl. You just concentrate on getting your strength back and recover," the young Nurse said to her as she hovered over her, placing a cold towel on her head to lower her temperature.

"Hi, Caitlyn, my name is Dr Rashid. How are you feeling?" the Doctor asked her.

"Like I've just been in a car crash," she retorted wryly trying to smile.

The Doctor laughed, "It sounds as if you are already making a good recovery. Surprisingly, you've not even broken any bones at all, maybe a pulled muscle here or there and some whiplash. You've got concussion so we need to keep you here for a day or two to keep an eye on you and let you rest, but like Nurse McLean said, you are one very lucky girl."

"Thank you. Thank you. I'm so sorry. I can't believe this has happened."

"We see it all the time, this is our job, no need to apologise. We are just glad that you are here and going to get better. You are going to rest and work at getting better, Caitlyn?"

She felt so weak and tired but nodded her head in agreement, she wanted to do everything in her power to get back to normal if that was possible.

And the first thing she wanted to sort out was her relationship with Peter. This accident had given her a huge shock. Life was too short.

"Mum?"

"Yes, dear, what is it?"

"Could you all leave me and Peter for a few minutes?"

Liz looked tentatively round the room but it was Caitlyn's Dad that answered, "Of course, sweetheart, let's give you two some privacy," and the three filtered out in silence.

"Oh, Caitlyn," Peter exclaimed as he came closer tightening his grip on her hand, "I was so scared of losing you. I couldn't imagine life without you... our future family together."

"Family?" Caitlyn questioned.

"Yes, family. Well I don't mean right at this present moment but maybe in a few years, it would be nice to have a little one around – don't you think?"

"What about your bit on the side?"

"What?"

"I know about her."

"You know what about who?" Peter had now raised his voice and was standing.

"Oh, don't come it, Pete. Grace! You haven't been interested in me in months. I would actually be flabbergasted if I ever became pregnant, given the lack of sexual contact we now have!"

"Caitlyn!"

"Well, you've been at 'work' all the time. It always comes first. Not me. I saw you getting a lift home one night with someone. And then I found your text today from her. Grace. I've been suspicious for a while but the text just proved it, you must be having an affair with her."

"Stop right there, Caitlyn," he was now smiling at her, laughing even.

"What? Do you think this is funny?"

"Caitlyn. No. I bought her a bottle of wine as I was her secret Santa for God's sake! You have got it all mixed up!" They stared at each other for a few seconds in silence before he continued, "Listen this isn't how I was going to do this. But I need to tell you the truth."

Here it comes, Caitlyn closed her eyes and waited for the confession to come. Could this day get any worse?

"Caitlyn, I love you. I love you so much. I apologise for my behaviour over the last few months."

Caitlyn couldn't help but start to cry silently again.

"Don't cry baby, please don't cry. I know I've maybe taken you for granted and spent far too much time at work, but it was all for a good reason. I only did it because we needed the money. I needed the money. Not just overtime and bonus money but a promotion. I've been offered an amazing opportunity to progress my career, I just needed to graft a little more, show I was committed. Along with that promotion I am going to gain a lot more money for a lot less hours, and I just knew that I needed to take a hit at the beginning to make it work."

Caitlyn looked on sceptically without saying a word.

"By January I'll have the promotion in the bag and there will be no overtime needed at all. Monday to Friday 9 to 5 from then on, I promise!"

"Why didn't you just say? You said you weren't getting any overtime money for the work you did anyway?"

"I know, but it was for an important reason. I've saved up the money in another account."

Oh my God, he's leaving me. He's been saving up to leave me!

"Caitlyn, I've been planning this for months. I'm sorry."

Caitlyn couldn't bring herself to look at him in the face.

"What are you saying, Peter?" She didn't have the energy to argue. If he was to finish with her, she wanted it over and done with and she can move on. This seemed like an ideal time for a fresh start.

"Caitlyn, what I'm saying is that I have been thinking about our future a lot. About my future and your future and what we both wanted." Caitlyn's stomach lurched, she felt sick again and she looked away.

"Please look at me, Caitlyn, I didn't want to do it this way. This was not how I planned it. I've been thinking about this moment for months and planning it in my head. I thought you might have had an inkling and I tried to hide it."

"Hide what, Peter?" Caitlyn couldn't help but get angry now, "Just spit it out! Have you been cheating on me?"

Peter looked genuinely surprised, "No! Of course not!" Peter picked up both of Caitlyn's hands, "Why would you think that?"

Caitlyn couldn't reply, she didn't know what to say.

"Never mind. Caitlyn, I need you to listen. I love you so much, you are the best thing to happen to me, ever. I'm sorry I've not been myself the last few months, but I've been trying so hard to save up this money and get the promotion for us and it's left me so stressed. For our future." Peter lowered down beside the bed and she could barely see him.

"What are you doing?"

He produced something from his pocket but Caitlyn couldn't see what it was.

"Caitlyn, I'll tell you exactly what I'm doing. I am proposing."

"You are what?" she sat up in her bed in disbelief.

Peter was on bended knee with a small black jewellery box open to reveal a sparkling diamond ring.

This time Caitlyn was completely and utterly speechless. This was entirely unexpected.

"Caitlyn, you are the most beautiful girl in the world and I have loved you from the minute I first met you. I want to make you my wife, I want to start a family with you some day and I want to eventually grow old and grey with you. I could not think of a more perfect person to spend the rest of my life with. Caitlyn McDonald, will you marry me?"

Caitlyn couldn't believe her ears or her eyes. She couldn't speak.

"I'm sorry, honey, this is not the way I planned it. I had planned for a really romantic setting at Hogmanay, I'm sorry for the setting but this moment just seems right. When you left today I was so confused and I tried to call you and call you. Then when we heard that you were in a car accident, I panicked. I've never felt so bad. I couldn't stop thinking, what if I never got to see you again? What if I didn't get the chance to tell you how I feel? To ask you to be my wife."

"Oh, Peter," Caitlyn felt overwhelmed. So much had happened in the past 24 hours and she couldn't believe this, she felt extremely silly and embarrassed now.

"I've been working so hard to save up not only for this ring but for our wedding and possible honeymoon. I've been really stressed with all the extra work and actually really stressed just thinking about this proposal. I was freaked out about asking you in case you said no. I was so nervous and anxious about trying to pick you out the right ring. And I was ridiculously scared about asking your father for your hand in marriage, but I did it. And, hopefully, with my new job we might even have enough money to put down a deposit for a bigger house. That is if you wanted?"

Caitlyn let herself smile.

"Does that smile mean yes? My knee is aching here!" he joked.

"Yes! Yes, definitely yes, I mean yes!"

"Yes, you'll marry me?"

"Yes!"

Peter jumped up, smile beaming, "You have just made me the happiest man on earth." He leaned over and kissed her on the lips.

"Oh don't!" Caitlyn protested, "I've not brushed my teeth, I'm disgusting!"

357

"You could never be disgusting, even if you tried. Now would you like to try on your new ring?"

Caitlyn nodded excitedly as she put out her hand for Peter to slip on the beautiful one carat platinum diamond ring onto her wedding finger.

"It's perfect! I can't believe you picked this yourself?"

"Well I had a little help."

"Ha ha, well that does explain a lot actually. And you really asked my Dad for permission to ask me to marry you?"

"Yes, God I was stressed out for weeks about that part. I wanted to do it right and I knew he'd appreciate the traditional approach."

"But when?"

"Just earlier today actually, well yesterday, Christmas. I had always planned on proposing to you around Christmas time or during winter down in Kintyre. You know, you've always said that the beaches there, Machrihanish or Westport were so special to you and you had the best of childhood memories from there. That's why I kind of got annoyed about the trip away in October, it really killed that plan. But then I thought I'd leave it until either Christmas Day or midnight on New Year's Eve, at Oran Mor. I heard you mention how romantic that would be, so I kinda put that plan into motion. And I knew I'd be seeing your folks over Christmas so I thought I would ask your Dad then."

"And what did he say? No?"

"He said yes of course, you cheeky monkey!" Peter nuzzled into her neck. "He said he would be delighted for me to become part of the family. Although he did force me to drink too many beers to celebrate and make me swear that I would look after you forever. He's a bit protective, your Dad!"

"Ha ha. Yeah, he is."

"Your friends are too."

"Did they know?"

"Well I've been hinting at it for a while with Jennifer and Jamie and I was going to ask their help to buy the ring, but I thought they might let it slip, so I kept it a secret."

"Good call."

"I was really panicking about the ring. I knew the type you liked and I do know your style but I wanted reassurance, so I asked Grace from my work to ensure I was on the right lines. Initially I asked Caroline from your work and she met up with me once as I knew you gushed over her ring. So I thought I would get something similar but she just pissed me off actually and constantly talked about herself, so I ditched her and tried myself. Eventually, with weeks of searching in shops and online, I decided on this one but don't worry, I kept the receipt. I just put a deposit down with the jewellers and they said if you didn't like it they could exchange it. I've got the money to pay the rest now but it's your ring and I want you to have it and love it forever, so if you don't like it I can take it back. I won't be offended, honestly!"

"Peter, it's perfect. I would have picked that exact ring myself, I love it!"

"Really?"

"Really! I can't wait to show it off!"

Peter sighed with relief, "You're not just saying that?"

"No! I love it, love it, love it! I wouldn't change it for the world." Caitlyn beamed as she kissed the large solitaire diamond on the shiny platinum band.

"Phew! I was hoping you would say that. And I wouldn't change you for the world. What an emotional day."

"It certainly has been," the elation of the surprise engagement now fading a little for the memory of her accident to sneak in. Peter was obviously thinking the same thing, as he asked her if she was OK.

"I'm fine."

"Are you sore?"

"Yes. I suppose. But you have made me feel better."

"I'm so sorry Peter!" Caitlyn started to cry, everything that had happened seemed to sink in.

"Oh honey, there's nothing to be sorry about, this wasn't your fault. You heard what the Doctor said, Caitlyn, my future wife, you will recover from this and I just know that we will have a wonderful family together. It's all I want."

"Really?"

"Yes, I love you so much, Caitlyn, and I can't wait for you to be my wife."

"I can't wait either. I love you too, Peter!"

He leaned over to embrace her and she closed her eyes as Peter softly kissed her on the mouth.

"Cut that out, can we come in yet?!" they heard Jamie squeal from outside.

"Stop noseying," Caitlyn warned.

"We were getting impatient out there," Jennifer joked as she appeared beside him, "Are you feeling OK, pet?"

"Yes, I'm sore but I'm feeling great in fact. Come in. All of you." Peter stood up beside her but continued to hold her hand, unable to keep the Cheshire cat grin off of his face.

"Why are you smiling so much?" Caitlyn's brother asked.

"Do you notice anything different about me?" Caitlyn asked them, once everyone had came into the room.

"You have a cut on your forehead," her brother said.

"You're wearing a lovely hospital gown?" Jennifer asked.

"You have no makeup on? This is not a good game for you right now, darling," Jamie said smiling.

Caitlyn and Peter laughed heartily, "What about her hands, do you notice anything about her hands?"

Caitlyn showed off her hands, wiggling her fingers proudly to try to emphasize her new engagement ring.

"Oh my goodness!" her mother exclaimed jumping up and down, "Let me see! Congratulations!"

"Argh!" Jennifer and Jamie screamed and rushed towards her, showering her with congratulatory hugs and kisses.

"What's going on?" Caitlyn's brother asked.

"I asked Caitlyn to marry me," Peter said proudly, "and luckily for me – she said yes!"

"On yersel, big man! Well done, congratulations, little sis!"

Caitlyn's mother now was in floods of tears. "Here, here," her Dad consoled her, "you've been crying all day, Liz."

"I know, but this time it's happy tears."

"Did you not know, Mum?"

"No! Why would I know? Did you know, John?"

"Well, you could say I had an inkling..."

"And you didn't tell me?"

"I didn't want to spoil the surprise!"

"I'm so happy for you both!" Jennifer squealed.

"I apologise for the non-romance of it all in a hospital, I had other plans, honest, Mrs McDonald."

"Don't apologise to me, I couldn't think of a more romantic gesture, Peter, after the emotional rollercoaster we've had today, Christmas Day, than topping it all off with something this special."

"Well," said Liz, "Welcome to the family, Peter."

"Thank you." Peter squeezed Caitlyn's hand again and kissed her again.

"Oh it's so exciting!" Jamie said.

"We've got a wedding to get planning!" Jennifer added excitedly.

"And a stag night," Caitlyn's brother added, winking at Peter.

"And a hen weekend!" Caitlyn added, smiling at Jennifer.

"I hope I'm coming?" Jamie asked, screwing up his face dramatically.

"Of course you are, you'll be a bridesmaid. Well an usher or something at least!" Caitlyn laughed. "And will you be my chief bridesmaid, Jen?"

"Oh, of course! I'd love to!" Jennifer said, hugging her.

Caitlyn pulled back a little, she was starting to feel a little sore. "Right, all this excitement must come to an end for the day. Let's let you rest, pet, the Doc said we shouldn't tire you out."

"Yes, we'll go and let you sleep, come back tomorrow."

Caitlyn didn't want to see them go, especially not Peter, but she knew she was exhausted and her body craved sleep. "OK. That's probably best. Do you think I'll get out tomorrow?"

"That's wishful thinking but the Doctor did say that you were doing great and they will monitor you over the next 24 hours. You never know. Best to get some rest and we can evaluate in the morning?"

"OK."

Everyone said their goodbyes, taking turns to hug and kiss as they left Caitlyn's room one by one, eventually leaving Caitlyn and Peter alone once more.

"How are you feeling, honey?"

"I'm elated, I've never been so happy. However, I'm also feeling really tired and weak and I feel as if all my muscles ache!"

"Aw baby, I wish I could take the pain away from you. At least you are still here, alive and well. I don't what I would do if I lost you. I'd be heartbroken. Devastated."

"You're not going to lose me." Caitlyn could feel her eyelids starting to droop, she was that tired.

"You've made me so happy by agreeing to be my wife. Our wedding is going to be the best day of our lives, a day we will always remember."

"Forever and ever."

"Forever and ever and ever."

Caitlyn closed her eyes and nearly instantly fell into a deep sleep. Peter waited a few moments until she drifted off, before kissing her softly and leaving the room, barely containing his happiness.

Chapter 59

After the turn of events over the past few days, Jamie was really unsure about going on the blind date now, but after much persuasion from Jennifer he turned up at the bar wearing a new casual suit he had got from his parents at Christmas, along with a good helping of the new aftershave Caitlyn had bought him that he loved. He had spent ages on his appearance and had shared the remainder of the bottle of Raspberry vodka with Jennifer for some Dutch courage before going fashionably late. He peered into the bar tentatively as he approached the door. He scanned the room of the unfamiliar pub and saw that the place was very quiet. Andrew had said that his date would be wearing red and be at the bar. Jamie could see a tall figure sitting on the bar stool with his back facing the door. He was wearing a deep red shirt. Jamie thought it looked like Andrew from the back. Jamie's heart was palpitating, his palms were sweating and he could feel his cheeks flush red. He stood still, unsure whether to approach him or not.

"Can I help you?" a waiter asked Jamie, putting him on the spot.
"I'm meeting someone thanks," and he walked forward to the man at the bar.

Jamie closed his eyes briefly and took a deep breath trying to calm his nerves, "Hi."
"Hello, Jamie?"
"Yes," Jamie choked back.

"Pleased to meet you," the man said from across the bar, standing up to shake Jamie's hand.

It wasn't Andrew! Jamie realised. Although it looked remarkably like Andrew, Jamie thought bemused.

"Hi, I'm Matt, Andrew's brother." It all seemed to make sense! Andrew hadn't been asking me questions about his love-life for his own sake, it was for his brother Matt! Jamie felt like a royal chump as the realisation kicked in.

"Pleased to meet you too, Matt. I'm Jamie. Ahhh, you are Andrew's brother," Jamie confirmed.

Matt laughed heartily, "Yes, I am indeed, the younger and better looking brother," he said charmingly holding Jamie's gaze as Jamie laughed along with him. "I don't know why he didn't say to you, he's always wanted to try and set me up on a blind date with someone from work. I've eventually given in to him. Only because he said many good things about you, of course!"

"All good, I hope?" Jamie replied smiling, taking the seat that Matt was holding out for him. Jamie was surprised to feel quite at ease, despite the shock of who the date was with, he felt quite relaxed.

"Would you like a glass of wine?" Matt offered out another glass.

"Yes, please"

"I thought I'd just order the bottle so it would at least look like I was with someone if you stood me up!"

"You thought I wouldn't come?"

"You never know! I'm glad you did though."

"Me too."

"Cheers."

"Cheers!"

They clinked classes and shared a smile. I hope I live up to the expectations now, he thought. I'm smitten already, he is gorgeous!

Jamie shouldn't have worried, after an hour of excited conversation, swapping stories and discussions about each other, before they knew it the Merlot bottle was empty and they hadn't ran out of conversation once, no awkward silences so far.

"Can I get you another drink?" Matt asked as he tilted the wine to see if there was a dribble left.

Jamie hadn't planned on waiting for so long but he hadn't counted on the date going so well. Why not, he thought. "Yes please, I think I'll have a Jack Daniels and coke this time, please."

"Coming right up. Good choice, Jamie, I think I'll have the same," said Matt, smiling as he stood up and went to the bar.

Jamie admired him from afar and couldn't help get quite excited, maybe this could be the start of something special, this could be the best date that he had ever had.

Chapter 60

Since Stuart's grovelling apology in the hospital to Jennifer, he hadn't tried to mention it again in front of anyone but had been begging her to listen in private. Stuart had run many errands for Jennifer, Jamie and for Caitlyn's family during her stay in hospital as well as just being there for support, and Jennifer couldn't help feel grateful but she didn't want to tell him that. Not yet anyway. Jennifer finally agreed to meet with Stuart again to let him explain in full. She nervously told her parents what had happened between them and she was shocked that even her Mum told her to give him a chance and listen to what he had to say. Jennifer always found it quite uncomfortable talking to her parents about relationships, but she wanted to get their approval, especially with her situation.

"I've never seen you so happy, Jennifer, and as you get older it's very hard to find someone without any past experience whether it be wives, children or exes of some sort! Go for it, go and see what he says and make him work for forgiveness!"

"Really? You think I should meet him?"

"Of course! He is obviously sorry from the number of phone calls, texts and the way he was there for you and your friends after Caitlyn's accident. I would say that he deserves a second chance. He never meant for this to happen I'm sure. I can understand where he was coming from not telling you immediately."

"I know, so can I. I just feel as if he's broken my trust or something."

"Listen, Jennifer, we don't choose who we fall in love with," Jennifer's Mum said, trying to be sensitive and fair. "Life is too short, you don't want to not take the chance and then always regret it. You know, your father was married before me."

"What?" she had never heard of this before!

"Yes. He was married and divorced all before he was 25. No kids mind you, but I met him shortly after and we fell in love. If I had been put off by his 'baggage' then this wonderful life and family we created might've never have happened."

Jennifer sat in silence, she was still shocked at her Dad's divorce revelations. "But I'm so young, I can't act like a step-mum?"

"No-one is asking you to. Not just yet anyway. Go and meet him, one step at a time."

Jennifer nodded her head, "OK. Thanks Mum." She always valued her Mum's advice and she took it by phoning Stuart immediately. The thought of breaking up with Stuart made her feel sad and she was desperate to see him again alone. However, she had to admit she was a little bit apprehensive about him having an ex-wife and kids. She had never been in that situation before but she knew if she wanted them to have a future, which she did, then she would need to deal with it.

Stuart had booked a table for them at Gambas, an intimate seafood restaurant that Jennifer had always wanted to go to. She arrived later than Stuart asked, which was quite unlike her, but she wanted to make him sweat.

He stood when she saw her approach. "Jennifer, thank you for coming. You look beautiful." He pulled her chair out for her and she took a seat without saying a word.

"Jennifer. I'm sorry… I'm sorry for everything. I'm sorry for trying to explain at the hospital but I was just so scared of losing you. You are the best thing that has happened to me in such a long time. I mean it when I say I love you. I want to be with you forever."

Jennifer just looked back at him, stunned, unsure what to say.

Stuart continued, "I don't want to scare you away with all my baggage and I know we've not been together long, but I really think there is a future for us. I didn't want to spoil it at first and tell you about my crazy ex-wife and my kids. I love my kids, dearly I do. But I've been getting such a hard time with her and well, the kids, John especially, have been taking this separation really hard, and you know fine well how he's been acting out. God, when I found out you taught him too, that just made it even harder to tell you!"

Stuart continued to ramble on and on and on to Jennifer until she finally interrupted him, "Stop! Stop!" she cried out to him.

"Stop?"

"Please stop," Jennifer said smiling back at him. "It's OK. I think I understand. Although if you really do love me like you say you do, you should've been able to tell me. I feel hurt. I feel as if you have broken my trust."

"Oh, Jennifer, I'm so sorry. Christmas Day was not the way I had hoped to tell you. I wanted to tell you so often but as time went on it just got harder and harder. I really am sorry. Please forgive me. Say you will forgive me?" Stuart pleaded with her.

"I need to know that you are going to be honest with me if we are going to make this work."

"Of course. Jennifer, this was all just a misunderstanding. Let me make it up to you. Please?"

"OK," she eventually agreed with a little smile.

Jennifer and Stuart ended up spending the next few days of the holiday together, not just in her flat but at his house too. Although she protested at first, Stuart even persuaded her to be introduced as his girlfriend to his sons. He was determined to show her that he was serious and wanted her to be part of his life. She was mortified and excruciatingly nervous at meeting John but was so shocked that he and his younger brother Joe took it surprisingly well and didn't seem too bothered! They both seemed like they were on their best behaviour, rather charming actually. In fact, once they had been formally introduced, they went on as normal, barely noticing that Jennifer was there and carried on watching the football and playing their computer games. Even Stuart was quite taken aback by their nonchalant resilient behaviour.

"You were great!" Stuart complimented her after the meeting.

"I never did anything!"

"You did. You were calm, kind and pleasant, that's all I could ask of you. I'm not asking you for anything more, I just want to be open and honest with you." He put his arm around her lower back.

"Thank you. It wasn't as bad as I thought! I thought they'd hate me."

"How could anyone hate you?"

"Ha! You'd be surprised, just ask all of the teenagers in my classes, they can't stand me!"

"Not at all. John actually says very good things about you, one of the best teachers in the whole school he says."

"No he doesn't!"

"He does, honest."

"Well, they definitely don't act like they think that in class!"

"No child ever does, do they?"

"I suppose not."

"Anyway, let's get back to us. Are we OK?"

Jennifer smiled cheekily, "Yeah, we're OK. Better than OK, we're good. Just no more secrets. Ever."

Stuart smiled broadly and pretended to salute, "Yes, boss, no more secrets, agreed. Fantastic, I'm so glad we're good. I thought I had lost you. Does this mean you will still accompany me for dinner and dancing on Hogmanay?"

"What about the boys?"

"They are at their aunties, they'll be in great order waiting up late with their cousins."

"Oh, OK. Well in that case then, most definitely, I can't wait to see you in your kilt!"

"You mean you just want to know if I'm a true Scotsman," he whispered into her ear and playfully squeezing her bum.

She glanced over at the boys to ensure they couldn't see them. "And are you?" she whispered back.

"You'll just need to find out on Hogmanay."

"I'll look forward to it!"

Chapter 61

As predicted by the medical staff of the Southern General Hospital, Caitlyn did recover quickly. Due to her determination, along with a little bit of consistent nagging to the nurses, she managed to get released from the ward two days later. Caitlyn was excited to announce her news to the rest of her family and friends and wanted to celebrate, but she still had very little energy and had completely lost her appetite.

For the time being, she was pleased just to be in Peter's company. Peter had insisted that she stayed in bed and he was doing his utmost to make her feel better and well rested, practically waiting on her hand and foot. He prepared her favourite foods even though she could barely eat anything, and persuaded her to take on liquids and reminded her of her medication. He recorded her favourite shows for her and cuddled up to her as they watched her favourite films. She felt quite guilty for ever suspecting Peter of wrong doing as it was now obvious to her how much he loved her and cared for her.

She loved every minute of spending quality time together in the comfort of their own home as if they had just fallen in love all over again. She couldn't wipe the grin off of her face, especially when she cast her eye over her new favourite item of jewellery on her wedding finger. She was the happiest she had been in months, you wouldn't think she was just recovering from a nasty car accident. Caitlyn was amazed at how many cards, flowers and get well wishes she received from friends, family and colleagues.

The running club had sent a lovely fruit basket and even Cameron had taken the time to send her a Facebook message. However, the thought of him now made her recoil in embarrassment that she once considered him romantically. She really appreciated his message and his friendship that had developed since him leaving school, but she now knew her feelings for him were never real. It obviously had been a little insignificant 'crush' that her mind had developed due to the lack of attention she was getting from Peter at the time.

However, she now realised it wasn't worth another thought. It definitely was not worth risking her relationship with Peter or her career over. She was glad she never made her feelings open to anyone else but herself as that could've been disastrous, she just wished that she had overcome and suppressed those feelings a long time ago. All Caitlyn ever really wanted was to be appreciated and feel loved, by Peter, and Cameron was just there at the wrong time to fill the void when Peter wasn't giving her as much love as she required.

Her parents had waited in Glasgow to try and look after her and be with her but there wasn't really anything they could do and Peter assured them that they didn't need to stay, she was in safe hands. Her parents were uncertain but the couple promised to visit them in the New Year once she was feeling better and they could all celebrate their engagement together. Everyone seemed relatively happy with this decision and her parents left for home again after countless hugs and embraces. Caitlyn couldn't wait for this year to end and a new year with new beginnings to start. And of course, a wedding to plan!

Just a few days later, Caitlyn and Peter, Jennifer and Stuart and new budding romance Jamie and Matt, stood smiling with glasses of champagne in hand counting down the bells for Hogmanay underneath the dramatic ceiling mural in the impressive auditorium of Oran Mor. The lights were dimmed and the ceilidh band played. They had enjoyed a sumptuous 3 course meal including traditional haggis, neeps and tatties accompanied by an array of wines and whiskies. All the hard work in school and recent troubles that had happened had been quietly forgotten to take in the moment and enjoy each other's company to celebrate the turn of the year. The girls were dressed in their best formal gowns and all looked stunning. They had even got their favourite hairdresser Mairi to style their hair for the occasion and it made them feel like celebrities for the evening. The men had hired tartan kilts in various tartans and looked incredibly smart, and handsome.

The group of friends were reminiscing, discussing resolutions and were happily chatting amongst each other. Even though Matt and Stuart were relatively new to the group of friends, they fitted in brilliantly and it felt as if they had been friends for years. The group joined in with the big crowd of party-goers in the hall counting down the last 10 seconds of the year before screaming, "Happy New Year!" and embracing each other. The group all welcomed in the New Year, a fresh start, by raising their glasses and dancing to the traditional Auld Lang Syne.

"Here's to friendship and love," Peter announced, raising a champagne flute.

"Aw you big softy!" Caitlyn chided as she cuddled up to his side.

"Here, here, friendship and love," everyone else mimicked, giddy on the fizzy wine, raising and chinking their glasses before taking a large gulp.

"Happy New Year everyone - I hope it brings everything you wish for!"

The End.

A Subtle Sadness by **Sandy Jamieson** is a rigorous exploration of Scottish Identity and the impact on it of the key Scottish obsessions of politics, football, religion, sex and alcohol. It deserves to be read by everyone seeking to understand the Scottish character.

A Subtle Sadness focuses on the family and personal history of Frank Hunter, a sad Scotsman with a self-destruct streak enormous even by normal West of Scotland male standards. Frank Hunter is a product of Scotland's unique contribution to mixed marriage, with a Protestant father and Catholic mother. A man of considerable talents, in both football and politics, he brings a peculiarly Scottish approach to the application of those talents.

A Subtle Sadness is the story of a 100 year fight for Scottish Home Rule, from 1890 to 1990,

A Subtle Sadness is also the story of the emotional and political impact of Scotland's quest for the World Cup, with 5 consecutive qualifications in the crucial years from 1973 to 1989 covered by the book.

A Subtle Sadness covers a century of Scottish social, political and football highlights, with disasters and triumphs aplenty, culminating in Glasgow's emergence in 1990 as European City of Culture.

A Subtle Sadness is also a reflection on sadness, depression and mental health as affected by that Scottish identity and those key obsessions. And a searing scrutiny of the Scottish male capacity for self-destruction. Illustrating that capacity to the full, Frank Hunter's story is a memorable and haunting one.

A Subtle Sadness can be purchased in any of the following ways.

From the Ringwood website   www.ringwoodpublishing.com for £9.99 excluding p&p, or ordered by post or e-mail for the same price. All copies signed by the author.

From www.amazon.co.uk either from Ringwood(a signed copy) or from Amazon (unsigned copy).From any good bookstore or online bookseller

The e-book version is available for £7.20 from the Kindle Book Store or Amazon.co.uk

Calling Cards by **Gordon Johnston** is a fresh and exciting addition to the ranks of Tartan Noir. It is a novel exploration of the impact of stress and trauma on individuals, encompassing their resort to addiction, recovery, and denial. It highlights the influence of the equally corrupting desires for success or revenge. Linking the small Scottish worlds of journalism and politics, it has been favourably compared to State of Play in its creation of an intricate network of linked strands, as it builds to a compelling climax that leaves many people changed forever.

"An anonymous email leads West End Journalist Frank Gallen on a quest to unravel the links between a campaign against a housing development proposal in Kelvingrove Park; personal and political corruption at the highest level in Glasgow City Council; and the increasingly frenzied activities of a Glasgow serial killer.

Gallen and DI Adam Ralston engage in a desperate chase to identify the serial killer from the clues he is sending them, in time to stop him from implementing the climax of his campaign of killing."

"Calling Cards is a fascinating examination of people under stress. Extremely well-written in a fluid style very easy to read, it is both the story of an increasingly desperate hunt for a Glasgow serial killer, and an examination of how people cope under intense pressure. It marks the arrival of a new and very welcome addition, Gordon Johnston, to the ranks of distinguished Scottish crime writers."

"Calling Cards is a psychological thriller worthy of a place in the top rank. It is well-written, and easy to read with a fast flowing style."

Calling Cards can be purchased in any of the following ways.

From the Ringwood website   www.ringwoodpublishing.com for £9.99 excluding p&p, or ordered by post or e-mail for the same price. All copies signed by the author.

From www.amazon.co.uk either from Ringwood(a signed copy) or from Amazon (unsigned copy).From any good bookstore or online bookseller

The e-book version is available for £7.20 from the Kindle Book Store or Amazon.co.uk

Torn Edges by Brian McHugh is a riveting mystery story linking modern day Glasgow with 1920's Ireland.

When a gold coin very similar to a family heirloom is found at the scene of a Glasgow murder, a search is begun that takes the McKenna family, assisted by their Librarian friend Liam, through their own family history right back to the tumultuous days of the Irish Civil War. The search is greatly helped by the discovery of an old family photograph of their Great-Uncle Pat in a soldier's uniform.

The McKennas quickly realise that despite their pride in their Irish origins they know remarkably little about this particular period of recent Irish history. With Liam's expert help, they soon learn that many more Irishman were killed, murdered, assassinated or hung during the very short Civil War than in the much longer and better known War of Independence. And they learn that gruesome atrocities were committed by both sides, atrocities in which the evidence begins to suggest their own relatives might have been involved.

Parallel to this unravelling of the family involvement of this period, Torn Edges author Brian McHugh has interwoven the remarkable story of the actual participation of two of the McKenna family, Charlie and Pat, across both sides of the conflict in the desperate days of 1922 Ireland.

"Torn Edges is both entertaining and well-written, and will be of considerable interest to all in both Scottish and Irish communities, many of whom will realise that their knowledge and understanding of events in Ireland in 1922 has been woefully incomplete. Torn Edges will also appeal more widely to all who appreciate a good story well told."

TORN EDGES can be purchased on www.ringwoodpublishing.com for £9.99 excluding p&p or ordered by post or e-mail. It is also available online from Amazon.co.uk and from all good booksellers.

The e-book version is available for £4.99 from the Kindle Book Store or Amazon.co.uk.

Paradise Road by **Stephen O'Donnell** is the story of Kevin McGarry a young man from the West of Scotland, who as a youngster was one of the most talented footballers of his generation in Scotland. Through a combination of injury and disillusionment, Kevin is forced to abandon any thoughts of playing the game he loves, professionally. Instead he settles for following his favourite team, Glasgow Celtic, as a spectator, while at the same time resignedly and with a characteristically wry Scottish sense of humour, trying to eke out a living as a joiner.

It is a story of hopes and dreams, idealism and disillusionment, of growth in the face of adversity and disappointment. Paradise Road examines some of the major themes affecting football today, such as the power and role of the media, standards in the Scottish game and the sectarianism which pervades not only football in Glasgow but also the wider community. More than simply a novel about football or football fandom, the book offers a portrait of the character and experiences of a section of the Irish Catholic community of the West of Scotland, and considers the role of young working-class men in our modern, post-industrial society.

The road Kevin travels towards self discovery, fulfilment and maturity leads him to Prague, enabling a more detached view of the Scotland that formed him and the Europe that beckons him.

"Written in a thoughtful, provocative yet engaging style, Paradise Road is a book that will enthral, challenge and reward in equal measure. It will be a powerful addition to the growing debate on some of the key issues facing contemporary Scotland"

Paradise Road can be purchased on www.ringwoodpublishing.com for £9.99 excluding p&p, or ordered by post or e-mail for the same price. It is also available online from Amazon.co.uk and from all good booksellers.

The e-book version is available for £4.99 from the Kindle Book Store or Amazon.co.uk